THE WOLF HUNTER

MARK GILES

Noir
West

Every book has a hero. Mine is between the
pages, invisible but there:
Cdr. Claude F. Giles

Thanks—I love you, Dad.

to contact the author:
giles5440@gmail.com

or visit:
noirwest.com

The bullet is the hunter's method of communicating his intentions to the animal.

Barrett's Bullet Talk: The Ethical Hunter

MONTANA: WINTER

High on the Absaroka Range, above the borders of Yellowstone Park, it was a hunter's moon. Two wolves were far ahead of the pack they led, all senses alert, keenly aware of the night. The snow had a crystalline glint; it crunched as they cavorted through the drifts. They were playing, jumping up on their hind legs, feinting towards each other like any two domestic dogs. One had known the presence of humans, as evidenced by her radio collar and a name, Brindle, given to her while in captivity.

A three-year old, she had been reintroduced into the wilds in the hope that she would breed. Her mate, the pack's Alpha Male, was as large and wild as a wolf could get, his size an indicator that he had migrated south from the far northern wastes of Canada or possibly Alaska. No one knew for sure. He had won the leadership in the usual manner, by attack, by slaying his predecessor. The snow-white Alpha and his new followers had eaten the corpse, leaving only the head and spinal cord. They did not waste meat.

Brindle was pregnant now, and her pups would be raised communally, hopefully then to become the progenitors of a long and successful line. The future of the wolf pack, designated Absaroka 1, was entirely in her womb, as no other pair would breed this season. There was not enough of a margin in the pack's energy budget to allow extra mouths to feed. The principles that guided them towards the future were clear, even elegant. But how wolves had evolved their system was unknown. This was why Absaroka 1 was being studied.

In their play, the two let their guard down for a moment. The snare was made out of nylon—it did not have the odor or heat signature of metal. Modeled after the Native American design of a birchbark noose, the plastic wrapped around her leg. Brindle tumbled, was jerked back with a painful yelp. She bit at it, but there was no give to the material. Her mate joined her, sniffing cautiously. The more she pulled back, the greater the pain. Finally she settled in the snow. He lay down next to her to provide some body heat. They waited.

In time, their ears pivoted towards a distant sound: a snowmobile. The White Wolf got to his feet, nuzzled his mate. She too stood as best she could, but there was no escape from the plastic. He gently took her foreleg in his jaw, set himself, breaking her leg with one snap of his jaw. She tried to bite him, snarled, fell back in the snow, yipping in shock and fear. He quickly severed her tendons and muscles. In one spasm she leapt away, her paw left in the snow. It was not as painful as it might have been—her extremities had begun to freeze.

She was free, but the furious engine rasp was upon them. Then the noise stopped, and they heard human voices. She tried to limp away from the sound. The Alpha Male, in her defense, was bounding through the snow towards the men when a bullet tore into his flank. He flipped end over end, fell into a depression at the base of a juniper stand. He could only lie there as he heard the rifle crack again.

CHAPTER ONE

Annie Mann waited for her cappuccino, idly looking down the length of the narrow building. The whole block had been built in the 1890s during one of the fits of prosperity that interspersed decades of Montana doldrums. Boom and bust had been part of the life cycle of Stanley ever since the days of the cowboy, an era still celebrated here in the Range Rider Café.

Annie was sensitive to style. It was, in fact, the root of her business and her fortune. Almost by instinct she studied how the owners had dolled it up in Cowboy Chic. The Old West was represented in the basic bones of the place, the exceptionally high ceiling covered in embossed tin, walls plastered over with stucco which had separated from the underlying brick here and there. They had left the old paint on the plaster, a sort of mustard yellow that was not unattractive. Very period.

Her coffee came, passed over a counter that introduced the modern design element of a thick slab of steel that had been chemically treated for a deep, almost chocolate patina. The same dark metal had been used for the lighting and fixtures, art deco representations of cowboy stuff: pistols for door handles, tiny copper cowboy hats over the halide lighting strung up on wires.

As she shifted her weight, the wide plank floors creaked. On the weekends, they were liberally coated with sawdust to soak up any chaw that missed the spittoons. Old wooden casks would be rolled out of the back, their tops piled high with peanuts to go with the beer. As confused as the rest of the town, the Range Rider spent its days as a sort of Starbucks in tooled leather, its nights serving draft beer to guys in Dickies workwear. But the place—and the town—kept the tourists, the city's new herd animal, happy enough.

At first glance, she could have been taken for one, a pale white outrider in a long, even dramatic coat, as black as her tailored jeans. Her boots had never been on a cowgirl; they were unabashedly Italian. And they did not smell of manure. She casually modeled a raw silk blouse contrasting an electric blue silk kerchief a good four feet long. Her hair was short and auburn—there was some serious coin in that unstudied look. She didn't pretend to be a local, even though it had been ten years since she had given up the West Coast. Annie had grown to love the open spaces, especially the ones in her own life. It was simpler here, and she valued that.

But still she was the outsider, especially notorious as the Wolf Lady. AKA The Wolf Bitch to the less genteel. And also known as the woman who took the

Walker property out of the big, always-reaching hands of Wilhelm Spatz.

She ambled out the door, returning to the street scene that she had helped create: Stanley Frontier Days. She had long thought of it, privately, as the kickoff to Spring Promote Stanley Days. It was meant to be the opening salvo of a series of vernal events. After six years, it had finally attained the critical mass that was making it one of the must-do weekend events in Montana. The winter season was winding down, and while there was still snow on the slopes of the nearby resorts, the downhillers needed to be enticed to stay.

Over the years she had fought, cajoled, co-opted, to get Stanley into something resembling the new millenium. In a small town where swinging dicks had been the rule, she brought a feminine toughness that made her case, along with a few enemies. She didn't care. The local power structure, largely based on aggie interests, coveted the money visitors brought. They just didn't like the out-of-towners. Didn't like them on general principles. The outsiders were godless lefties, trying to pry the land, the guns, the ethos, right out of the locals' cold, all-but-dead hands. It was, in other words, politics.

And that meant money. There was only so much in a valley that had been a mono-economy for almost a century. One based on the price of beef, and to a lesser extent, horseflesh. If there was one thing Annie understood, it was money. The Great Chairman once said all power came out of the barrel of a gun. Mao was yesterday's news: it now came out of a wallet. These riders of the purple sage had been sadly lacking their cowboy Hillary Clinton—someone to put up a better fight. Except maybe Spatz, the one rancher in the valley who had a few brains, if more gonads than was wise.

Annie had repeatedly rolled over the locals, had gotten much of what she wanted. Which had included this weekend event that combined cow-punchin' folkways with her passion, which was the Earth. Capital E. All of the events carefully designed, she hoped, to show a modicum of style. Not that the locals would know style if they stepped in it.

One glance down the street told the story: wannabe cowpokes ambled down the streets lined with Audi SUVs. The far ranges, Absaroka to the south and east, Galatin to the west, were holding back the last of the winter storms, the jagged peak-lines combing out the clouds. On a clear cool day like this, it truly was Big Sky Country. There was live fiddle music, the horse parade had just finished—the road apples were still steaming. There was both a kid's fun fair, and slightly more adult booths with handicrafts, food—including authentic pan-fried trail bread—a massage kiosk. Even a tattoo artist from Fargo, North Dakota, working out of an old Conestoga wagon.

And her booth, actually a marionette theatre, for Wolf Ranch. The ranch was her haven for wolves in a land where they had few supporters. She took a seat on the wooden walkway, her feet dangling over the edge. She saw the puppeteers walk behind the drawn curtain, the kids seated in front on benches that jutted out into the street. She hadn't bothered to ask for a variance. What were they going to do — pass up the money she brought to the table? The curtains swept open, and the kids screamed delightedly as the first puppet, a stylized wolf, popped up. He looked friendly, but not too cartoonish. Design was important.

Like puppet shows from time immemorial, the story was part pratfall and part message. She had first seen marionettes on the streets of London some two decades ago, a classic punchinello full of obscene jokes with a strong whiff of hell's brimstones. Morality plays had been just about that: morality. And this was how she viewed the reintroduction of wolves into Montana, indeed, into the whole wide world. She was for it.

The play went well. She had hired a troupe out of her native San Francisco, and from what she had seen, they were good enough to bring back next year. She let her mind wander for just a moment as a sunbreak lit up the street. She soaked up the warmth that took some of the chill off the air. It wasn't too bad a day. The clip-clop of shod horses had been part of the background, but now she heard a louder tattoo of hooves rapidly bearing down on the center of town. As in most small western municipalities, Main Street was also the main highway. The Sheriff and his meager crew were supposed to be stopping traffic from powering through. Then she saw who it was.

It was the all-too-familiar Kenton "Red" Richie, fulltime ramrod at the Rocking R Ranch. Red and his boss, Wilhelm Spatz, had been a thorn in her side for years. The animosity, in fact, went back to the date of her purchase of the ranchlands adjoining the Rocking R. Ever since, it had been like a bad episode of *Bonanza*, with fightin' 'n' feudin' over everything from fence-lines and water rights up to, and especially including, sex. Wow, *that* had lit the Spatz fuse. And her latest gig, the reintroduction of wolves, hadn't exactly brought peace to the valley.

Annie could almost see the wheels turning in Red's gourd as, lasso in hand, he scattered tourists ahead of his steed's foaming head. She noticed his face was livid from the cool air, or maybe his exertions. He twirled the lariat—he was actually pretty skilled—up high, rodeo style, caught a loop over a corner support. His pony, a gelded paint, obediently set its rear legs, horseshoes sparking as it came to a halt. The horse was almost as much a showboat as its rider. The kiddie audience squealed in delight as their parents pointed their cameras and cell phones at the action.

Red gave a somewhat anachronous rebel yell, put some tension on the rope as his pony crawfished in reverse. "I declare these here puppets endangered!" He splayed out his stirrups and pulled the whole tent down on the puppeteers, who rolled to safety out the sides. The audience clapped wildly. Red undid the rope from his pommel, let it fall as he jerked his horse's head around, narrowly missing the face of a tall, hard-bitten man who had appeared out of the crowd. Red roweled his spurs down the flanks of his mount, but the stranger had it by the bridle. "Get your hand off," Red snarled. A crosshatch of pinkish red scars played tic-tac-toe on one side of his face. It was how he had got his moniker.

"Don't cut his mouth and I will." They locked gazes as Annie came up next to the horse.

"Back off, Red," she said.

"Make me." Red sounded like a pissed-off ten-year-old. "And unhand my horse, shithead."

"Make *me*." The tall stranger gave a thin smile.

"You boys need to grow up." But Annie had to laugh. The stranger nodded, let loose of the bridle.

"You're right," he said. He had a quiet, husky voice that Annie liked.

Red released his pressure, and the horse settled down, losing some of the wild look that had come into its eye. Annie didn't need any crushed tots just now. She would deal with Red, and by extension Spatz, later. The stranger stepped back. Red started to bolt away, but instead reined in. "Fuck you, Slim."

They sized each other up in a way that Annie thought was as old as time. He didn't wait for an answer, but sped off down the street to more applause. The line between reality and theater could get pretty thin, she thought.

A little kid's voice piped up out of the cheering crowd: "And the horse you rode in on!" That got a round of applause.

She turned to see the man looking at the wreckage of the tent. "You should see the matinee," she said.

"Annie Mann." She held out her hand, and they shook. He was an outdoors man all the way, his hands chapped and red; the contrasts between their skins was almost laughably apparent. Coarse and fine, like sandpaper.

"Page. Page Deschamps."

"French name. Louisiana?"

He nodded. "I was looking for you." Annie looked surprised. "I've got a letter you sent."

He pulled it out and handed it to her. She recognized it immediately. "Let's go see the Sheriff."

Sheriff Ben Manyhorse was down the block doing crowd control. He gave Annie a quick smile, nodded to Page. The Sheriff was an imposing figure, a good three inches taller than the Cajun. Ben had the straight back, flat stomach and big shoulders of an NFL tight end, and why not: he had played for Boise State back in the day. He had the ageless look of a Native American, dark- skinned, with high cheekbones and slicked back hair under his broad-brimmed hat. He was wearing his usual uniform of a padded nylon flight jacket and bootcut twill slacks. His only departure from postcard perfection was a mouthful of crooked, yellow teeth — he looked like a pack-a-day man, yet didn't smoke. One of his front incisors was stainless steel; she sometimes thought he had gone for the metallic look just to make him look more dangerous when he smiled.

But right now he was the genial politician. The two men shook hands. "Ben Manyhorse." Page raised an eyebrow. "My granddad stole many horses."

"Sounds like one or two of my relations. Page

Deschamps. Page of the country, in Cajun. I'm a federal Marshall with the Wildlife Service. We got a letter from Ms. Mann . . ." He stumbled over their name, blushed slightly.

"Everybody does that—just plain Annie will do."

"About poaching in the area." He paused. "So here I am."

The Sheriff nodded. "I sent a letter from Annie on to you. With a cover letter to your supervisor from my office."

"I just got back in the Lower 48. I spent the winter up in Alaska, chasing a poacher named Johansen and his crew."

"Did you get him?"

Page had a distant look for a moment. "Yes."

Ben slapped him on the shoulder. "Let's go talk some law enforcement." He turned to Annie. "If you don't mind?"

She returned a meaningless smile. "Sure. I'll find out what you're up to, anyway.

CHAPTER TWO

The Sheriff's office was in the back part of the courthouse that anchored one side of the old-fashioned square at the center of town. The floors were well= polished linoleum, the walls in two shades of institutional green laid down back in the Nixon era. The Sheriff held open a swinging door that led behind the booking counter. Manyhorse had a corner office full of dusty enameled file cabinets and a metal desk right out of war surplus. It looked like the outer offices: utilitarian, publicly funded. And the taxpayers didn't seem to be spending too much on law enforcement. The Sheriff gestured to an old leather chair, went over to get some coffee from a cheap plastic coffeemaker. He held the pot up. Page shook his head.

"You have her letter on you?" He gave a tight smile, the kind made by men with bad teeth. Page thought he sounded more like a college guy than a cowboy. The Sheriff waited as Page got it out of his shirt pocket, handed it over. Manyhorse took a quick glance, tapped it against his stainless tooth as he thought about it. "I assume you'll be undercover?" He held his hand out. Page took out his wallet, folded back to show his medallion. Ben took it, sat down behind his desk, put his feet up. "What are you going to use for a cover story?" He tossed the wallet on the desktop.

"I thought you might fix me up."

Ben unfolded the letter, looked over its creases. "Looks like you got this wet."

"I went in a river on my way out." Ben looked sympathetic, made a shivering noise.

"It was cold. I'd like to keep my name; it's not known out here, and that way I won't slip up. I'm not usually undercover anyway," Page added.

Neither man seemed in any hurry to speak. The Sheriff finished his thinking. "I was hanging back during that little scene—I like that you didn't buzz him." He tapped the badge with a boot heel. "So, Page, let's play it this way for public consumption. Let people think I brought you to the office to have a friendly word about Red and the way you handled him." He paused. "And his horse."

"Did I hurt his feelings?"

"The horse? I think he'll live. Red's part of the problem, though." He thought some more, shrugged. "Actually, it's not a bad opening move—get Red mad at you."

"How much is he part of the problem?"

"Fair bit. Here's the basic outline—I didn't want to go into naming names in a letter. Too much politics around here." He made a general wave in the air, taking in all of Montana. "Red works as the foreman on the Rocking R Ranch. Owned by one Wilhelm, or Bill, Spatz. Comes from German stock. Stubborn, but a smart man. He's a major player in the local power structure, just rich enough to buy a few votes here and there. Like a lot of us, he sits on a few hunks of BLM land, which he treats as his own. But they're scattered around. It isn't one big spread. He's got some cattle, some horses, runs hunting parties up into the mountains. Fancies himself a crack shot, good in the saddle. A man's man, and not just in his own head." Sheriff Manyhorse tightened his lips.

"You're not real close."

"Off the record, he's kind of a prick."

Page smiled tightly. "I get your drift."

Ben shifted in his chair, eased his hip holster out to the side. "A century ago my people would have staked him out for the ants. His great granddad was a Factor. You know what that was?"

"Supplied goods to the, uh, Native Americans."

"Ripped off us Injuns—all the tribes. Flour full of weevils, blankets lousy with pox. Then the Spatz clan bought up all the prairie they could get, or got sweetheart leases on government land for a few dollars a year."

Ben took a deep breath. "I'm getting worked up." He stopped for a beat. "It's their sense of entitlement. Like they own every last bit of the land. That it is OK to deplete the wildlife until the animals are gone. They take, and they don't put anything back."

"Like strip mining, but whole species instead of coal or gold," Page responded.

Ben saw the hard look in Page's eye, and he liked

it. "So, we need—I need—federal help to bust up at least some of the poaching. And it's got to be behind the scenes, because nothing is up front in this valley."

"Spatz is doing the poaching?" Page asked.

"Not a doubt in the world. He practically advertises. If you ever get out there, check what's hanging in his living room."

"I might do that. Any suggestions how to get things going?"

"I'm thinking we build you an identity. Jack of all trades, intinerant. How did you arrive in town?"

"I rode the dog."

"Perfect. Get a low-level job, maybe for Annie Mann."

"She's no rancher, is she?"

"Actually, she owns more acres than Spatz. Took the Walker Ranch right out from under his nose. Land he wanted. It would have tied together some of his own holdings, not the BLM stuff. Forever."

"So she blew him out of the water. Annie packs some firepower."

"If he's so hooked up . . ." Page wondered.

"How'd she go to the front of the line on the Walker deal?" The Sheriff showed his terrible, metal grin. "Pillow talk." Page looked puzzled. "Her head was on the one next to his."

Deschamps whistled. "Ow. She hit him where it hurts."

"They were breaking up. She saw he wanted the Walker place, so she took it away from him."

"Then she gets going with the wolf thing: gasoline on an old flame. At one point they actually lived together out at his ranch. Something made it go sour."

Page nodded. "I think I might take a cup of that tarry crap you're drinkin'."

"It's your gut, Page. Then let's take it on down to the basement. I've got something to show you. You want me to hang on to your badge?"

Page thought about it, shook his head as he took back the wallet. "Not just yet. But soon."

The basement held cells down one corridor, but they took the opposite direction past a small firing range which bracketed the wire mesh cage of the evidence locker. At the end of the corridor the heating plant was noisily thrashing. Ben stopped at the firing gallery. "You got a piece?"

"I brought my rifle and my 9 mil service piece. They're over at the bus station with my backpack."

"That's good. We've got some bogus Idaho licenses, blank. We'll paper you up so you look like a drifter. Too bad you're, ah, older; we could make you a skinhead. Prison tats, all that good stuff."

Page put down his coffee, took one arm out of his jacket, rolled up his sleeve. His biceps were festooned with tattoos: naked chicks, daggers in hearts, some cabalistic signs. The Rat Fink on a Harley was his favorite.

"Damn. You didn't get those for this job did you?"

"I've had 'em a whiles."

The Sheriff's smile was more open now. "We'll

make a crook out of you yet." They came to a wire cage as Page put his coat back on.

"Here we go." The sheriff spun a padlock open, entered the mesh gate. "This is some of the stuff we've confiscated. Mostly when we pull someone over, or go to a trailer on a domestic beef. Some of our local tweakers keep stuff like this out behind the meth lab."

It was a charnel house, the bits and pieces of animals stacked on shelves, in boxes, hanging out of cabinets. Fur, freeze-dried heads, bones, feathers, antlers. Internal organs, dried, pickled. A baby bear embryo. Necklaces made of eagle's claws.

Sheriff Ben Manyhorse abruptly turned, exited the cage. "I hate this shit."

They were both quiet as they went upstairs. They stopped in the lobby. "Sometimes I'm not all that professional."

"I think I need to look for that job."

"Annie Mann? Wolf Ranch? "

Page gave a tight smile. "Actually, two jobs."

"How's that?"

"Work for both sides."

"Outstanding." Ben showed his teeth in a wolfish grin.

CHAPTER THREE

Page went to the outskirts of town, a five-minute walk. He entered the bus station, an Art Deco relic from the 1920s, got his gear out of baggage claims. His rifle, zipped up in a ripstop nylon bag, didn't earn a glance. This was gun country, where a rifle was just another tool.

He headed back downtown, looking for a diner; he was hungry from the last leg of the ride down from Canada. As he passed a hardware store, Annie came out, hefting a canvas shopping bag over her shoulder. "Hold up a minute."

He looked her over more carefully as she came down the steps: she was maybe late thirties, in good shape. Hard to tell—he was never any good at guessing ages. Her only hint of the sun was a spray of freckles. Annie wore no makeup as far as he could tell. She looked expensive—although he wasn't sure how he knew that, either. He waited as she came up. "Annie. Not Mann."

"I know."

"You might have forgotten." She didn't look too worried about the possibility. She radiated self-confidence. He wasn't sure, but that might make her irritating. "Where you headed?" She asked.

"Lunch. I'm hungry."

"You a meat-eater?"

"There's something else?"

"Come on. I know a good place." She set off at a quick pace towards the backside of the town. They took a cross street to a more open area behind the main drag. They rounded a modest, spired church, cut through to its parking lot. He saw a helicopter parked there, hidden by the batten board structure. The chopper was done in polished aluminum with a large, crimson wolf's head painted on its side. The helicopter looked like what the Army called a Loach; he had no idea where the name came from, but he'd seen a few in his military days.

"Some people have Range Rovers. I've got one of these."

"So you park wherever you want?" Page asked.

"Pretty much." The front compartment's door was open. He could see a pair of feet on the other side of the hull. He followed her around, saw a short, wiry guy in a puffy down vest and ball cap closing up an access panel. "Ready to lift?" Annie asked. The man had a nicely trimmed beard and the obligatory sunglasses. Page thought he looked vaguely European. She turned to Deschamps. "My pilot, Josef." She pronounced it "Yo-sef." "Meet Page Deschamps."

Josef came over and shook Page's hand. "French?" he asked. "Myself, I'm Israeli." He put an extra syllable into the word.

"Louisiana."

"Ah, Cajun. 'Walk on gilded splinters.' "

"Huh?"

"You know—Dr. John, Alain Toussaint. Gris gris man!"

"Sure, right. This a Hughes?"

"500C. Hot rod of the skies. Where to, Annie?"

"Home. And step on it; Page might be hungry."

Josef opened the rear baggage hatch, pointed out a lumpy sack, bloodstained at the edges. "Meat we've got."

He took Page's backpack and stowed it, gave the rifle an extra heft before sliding it in without comment. Annie got into the back, showed him the seatbelts and headgear. She plugged their sound-canceling headsets into the chopper's radio/intercom. In front, Josef went through his checklist; there was a clacking as the igniters lit off the turbine, which began to spool up. She nudged him in the ribs. "Admit it, this is pretty cool." Her voice was amplified, surprisingly clear over the rotor sounds as the little ship began to vibrate.

The last time he'd been in a chopper, he'd been aiming over the skids at a wolf fighting to get through the deep Alaskan drifts. For now he'd let her think he was a yokel off on his first flight. He definitely was not going to tell her about his wolf-killing days. Just thinking about it, and all he had learned up north, made him detest his past. He would, at least here in this valley, be Page Deschamps, and not just in name. In deed.

Ten minutes took them out into the wilderness, then across some fenced-in grazing lands. When Page sighted the buildings ahead, he was impressed. As Josef flared out, he saw their destination was a concrete helipad, with a painted bullseye and four rather oversized landing beacons at the corners. The pad was behind a large building, a classic old barn. Near the helipad was a grassy open space dotted with half a dozen teepees. He could see kids playing soccer out on the grass.

A gravel road made a hard right, the top pointing almost due north. There were other much more modern buildings on both the west and north, done in a sort of adirondack style. A bronze statue was dead center in a circular turnaround. He was pretty sure it was going to be a wolf. Tour buses were parked parallel to the northernmost building. "Visitors Center," she pointed out. "The wolves are in the pens. Most of it's off-limits to visitors." To the east were high metal fences which were, in places, overhung by a screen of leafless trees. Page caught a glimpse of several wolves in the fenced-in compound just before they landed.

As they got out, something in the cockpit caught Page's eye: a smallish rifle, clipped to the inside of the center frame between the doors. It had a folding stock made out of fluorescent orange plastic. Josef came over, dragging the sack of meat for the wolves. Page nodded at the gun. "SAR rifle." Josef said. "Ruger."

"30-06?" Page asked.

"Yes, it is. The Canucks use them for their search

and rescue teams. What's in your gun tote?"

"Nosler M48."

"You shit me."

"I shit you not."

"Well, a tinker's only as good as his tools. And that is some tool."

"The hot rod of guns." They both laughed.

Annie came around the bubble front of the Hughes, listening to someone on her iPhone. "Talking shop?" She gave them an all-knowing look. "Josef, haul your meat, then bring me your maintenance logs in, oh, an hour. We have to get the bird serviced this week. We'll be eating out on the patio." She gestured for Page to follow. "Leave your stuff—someone will pick it up."

He ignored her, got out his gear and followed. The building on the west side of the drive was a house, and it was big, with a full-length covered porch. The upstairs, judging from the number of dormers, had a lot of rooms. To the left, as they faced the house, a screen of cedars separated the driveway from a patio set between the end of the house and a much smaller place, a cabin really. He thought it might be a guest cabin.

They stepped into a dark entry, almost a lobby. She pointed to a wall of hanging coats. He dropped his gear against the baseboard, hung up his coat and stained gimme hat. She noticed his hair was silvery all the way up. He looked like he had slept on it—it stuck up in several places. She noticed other things as well: he was probably as old as he looked, the other side of forty-five. She wondered what held his pants up—like a lot of thin, tall guys, Page hardly had any ass. Again, the sandpaper analogy came to mind, but maybe more at the emery paper end of the scale: tougher, with the high, hard shine of metal, or diamond. Annie thought he would be tough in a fight.

Page couldn't help but stare as they passed through a baronial dining room, far bigger than any family could ever use. The kitchen beyond was on a similar scale. To him it looked completely over the top, someone's fantasy of what a kitchen should be. A slim young Hispanic woman was at the big gas range, frying up strips of steak; his stomach gave a lurch. "Check out the stove," Annie said.

He did, nodded. "Big."

"No," she said with just a trace of impatience. "The brand."

He looked at the back of the range, saw a stylized wolf's head. "Wolves make stoves?"

She laughed, a light superficial one. "Wolf is a company. I'm sorry; branding is my business."

"Branding cattle?" He seemed genuinely puzzled.

This time her smile was more genuine. "You *are* the outdoor guy. Let's go out on the patio and we'll clue each other in. Unless you're the bashful, tongue-tied cowboy type."

"Why shur, lady."

The Hispanic woman looked around and smiled. He went over to her, offered his hand. "I'm Page Deschamps."

"Yolanda." She put down the onion she had been peeling and shook his proffered hand.

Annie came over and took him by the arm. As she led him away, she leaned in and whispered, "I think your steak will be just right."

*****

They were sitting outdoors on a patio formed between the main house and the smaller guest cottage, which was still bigger than anything Page had ever lived in. A covered walkway connected the two buildings, forming a backdrop, as well as sheltering them from a modest breeze. The cedar hedge completed the encirclement, blocking them from the driveway. Page wasn't sure why, but his lower body felt warm; there was heat coming up through his feet. He took a quick glance down. "It's heated," Annie said. He looked surprised. "Hot water coils under the pavers. I come out here a lot—and I don't mind a little warmth."

He shook his head in disbelief. "A week ago I was in a one-room cabin with an old wood burning stove."

"Eating chunks of venison and shitting over a hole?" She noticed his grimace. "Not ladylike? Don't get mad. I'm trying to figure you out."

"Why bother."

"Meaning we're from two different planets?" She gestured around her. "Yeah, I've got the big estate, the helicopter. Staff, like Josef. I have two PhDs working for me. I am, in fact, a corporation. So what. All I really occupy is some airspace just outside my skin. The rest of this is just a series of illusions: eyes for sight, nose for smells. The world is all input."

"Lady, you have totally lost me."

Yolanda came out with a wheeled serving cart, made a show of putting a steak smothered in picante sauce in front of him. There was a small silver insulated box with ice and bottles of San Miguel, both dark and light. She added a coffee serving set that seemed to be genuine silver. His last coffee pot had been in enameled blue spackle.

"Thank you." He gave her a little smile. After she left he waited for Annie to begin; she pushed her food around on her plate, which was made out of some colorful, thick porcelain. It probably cost a small fortune, too.

"Go ahead. I'll take a bite in a minute." She let her gaze wander above the cedar breaks, taking in the stands of aspen on the hills that formed the horizon line. "How about this. Something we both understand: love of the land. You must feel that."

He nodded. "The planet. Earth."

"You make it sound like a hippie slogan."

"It is." He thought as he chewed. "It does."

"Fair enough. That's pretty nebulous. OK, how about this: something in here." She touched her heart. "More than a concept. A feeling. Like patriotism, but a love for everything, not just a country. Bigger than that."

He stopped, looked at her. "Keep eating," Annie

said. "Is your steak OK?" She put a small forkful of salad up to her lips.

"Best meal I've had in three months. I think it was boiled weasel."

She rolled her eyes, patted her mouth with a cloth napkin. "I may never make my point. Try the Jamaican Mountain Blue." He looked puzzled. "The coffee."

He did try, and it made him smile. "Damn that's good coffee."

She caught the sarcasm. "Folgers crystals. Christ, I haven't thought of those in years. I give up." They both laughed. Annie leaned back; her meal was apparently done. Page, who abhorred waste, figured her plate would get scraped into the garbage. "Moving on . . . you're a hunter." It was a statement, not a question. "So, what do you hunt?"

He took another sip, diluted it with some cream. "I hunt men." It pleased him that he was able to surprise Ms. Annie Mann.

"With your big rifle? Bang bang?" She looked incredulous.

He twisted on one hip so he could get his wallet out. He showed her his badge. "Just to make sure you know I'm for real. And I poach poachers. Bang bang and bang."

She bent forward, studied it for a moment. For the first time her smile was big, radiant. It lit up her face, and he realized that under the slightly glossy exterior of the super-successful woman, there was something, or someone, else. "How does that work?"

He seemed to hunt for his words, like a laconic man looking for his next sentence. "I was just in Alaska. After a Swedish ex-pat named Johansen. He poached all around the Katmai Peninsula, in and out of the park. Bears, mink, eagles in season. He didn't care. Trying to make a buck." Page took a sip of beer. "I wanted to turn him, get him paroled. Set him out to catch another poacher, and so on until we have them all on our side. Or in jail."

"Mission accomplished?"

He looked pained. "No."

"Got away?"

"I had to kill him."

"Oh. I'm sorry."

He shrugged. "You can't win them all." He looked straight at her. "He sure didn't."

"I want our poachers caught. But I'm not into revenge."

"I understand. Every poacher I ever met was from a poor background. I call it an economic crime."

"You might find it different here. One of our state's most beloved traits is a rampant hatred of Big Government. Skinhead Aryans to Big Aggie, they want the jackbooted Feds off their backs."

" 'Live Free or Die.' "

"I've been feeling pretty alone. When I talk about poaching out here, they act like I'm a communist."

"They probably figure all the animals are theirs."

"That's the attitude, all right. Are you going to work undercover?"

"Haven't decided. I need to get the lay of the land. Scout things out."

"Well, I know who it is—"

He held up a hand to interrupt her. "We'll get to that. But first, tell me about yourself."

"To help you with the case?"

He smiled, thin-lipped. She could almost see the cables stretch in his weathered face. He probably didn't do it much. "Maybe."

And so she told him some of her basic facts: the ski weekends that exposed her to the place, her increasing need for the solitude of empty spaces. She had a pretty good idea what Ben and Page had talked about, and she wanted to be open right from the start. This seemed like an honest man, so Annie didn't skip over the details of her affair with Spatz, how she had found him exciting and different from the city guys she'd known. He was outdoors, but well read. Sometimes crude, always profane, a man's man. He had vigor. And he knew local politics like a horseback Machiavelli. She'd even admired his ruthlessness. For a time.

Page clearly found it a little hard to understand what she did for a living; she didn't think this was quite the moment to give him the gory details about semiotics, the use and abuse of symbols, wordsmithing, internet memes, all the things that went under the rubric of "branding." He probably didn't know what a rubric was, and that was all right with her. She simply told him she developed identities for products, corporations, even individuals, when they could afford her. From his evident ignorance of the Wolf gas range logo, he appeared to be less than enthused about the subject of brand management.

As they talked back and forth, he seemed moderately impressed that she used her filthy lucre to do some good in the world. But it was clear: money meant nothing to him. He didn't get money, he didn't *want* to get it. She did try to tell him how little she cared, herself. It was a means to an end, a tool to buy the tools to help preserve a corner of the world that had come to be her home. She wasn't sure if he bought that. After all, she was the woman who heated her freaking outdoor patio.

When she told him of her growing love for the place, she lost her words for a minute; sometimes she got so tired of her own babble. She didn't want to sound like a first date, for some reason.

After a few moments of silence, Annie realized she had said enough. Clearly, as they sat soaking up the weak sun, looking around them at the sky and the roll of the hills, they seemed somehow to be com-municating. She hadn't experienced that in a long, long time. It felt good. It even felt right. Which also felt good.

CHAPTER FOUR

The April air was crisp and cold, and storms could still blow off the Arctic Shield for several more months, but change was in the air. As the snows receded to the higher peaks, the surviving herbivores were able to forage more successfully. With nutrition came the intense and very pragmatic urge to mate. The big predators, too, shook off their lassitude and set forth to hunt game. It was another turn on the wheel of life: procreation begat new animals, which in turn fed the higher orders. Grass became flesh as flesh ate grass. Or each other.

For the humans, the change reopened some areas that had been snowbound. At the end of Highway 278, an unpaved road led further into the Absaroka Range. The spine ran north toward Livingston and Bozeman, and south over the Wyoming border into Yellowstone. At the very end—and the reason the road was there—was a private tract of land that was owned by a very private West Coast family. It had been deeded in perpetuity to the couple's alma mater. Stanford had set the land aside, chartered as the Stanford High Altitude Biologic Research Area.

Lee Chun waited in the car until Lisa opened the gate. He pulled ahead, heard the welded-pipe crossbar clang shut behind his Saab. They had rebuilt the gate last year; their wooden one, so totally appropriate to the landscape, had been smashed open by some Yahoo's 4x4. The steel could take a much bigger hit. A small metal flag, taken right off a mailbox, was somewhat hidden behind the support post. The protocol was to swing the arm up vertically to signal that an authorized visitor was on site. They would drop it back down when they left. The snow was unmarked ahead of them. If there had been fresh ruts, but the flag was down, they were supposed to immediately turn around and leave. This was too isolated a place to have a confrontation with the locals—especially when they were likely to be carrying guns. She put the arm up.

Lisa Betz slipped into the Saab, making sure the seat heater was maxed out. She was a California girl and loved her warmth. He looked at her, waited. "What?" she asked.

"Put your seatbelt on," Lee chided her.

She waved her hand, taking in the narrow lane wending away through a high alpine meadow. "It's not like we're going to be in a head-on." She punched him in the ribs, having fun with him. "Live a little."

Lee took them up towards the ridgeline at a snail's pace, which was appropriate. They were hot on the slimy trail of *oreohelix pygmaea.* The tiny mollusk, or more correctly, its study, was the reason that two attractive, highly intelligent young people were way up in the back of beyond. This whole project was, in fact, Lisa's first experience of the wilds—she had always been a city girl.

Oreohelix, or the pygmy mountainsnail, was listed as a G1, a species of concern. Physically small, under 15mm, they were thought to be highly vulnerable to extirpation. In layman's terms, a die-out. Lee was up here to prove that they were in fact surviving by moving to higher altitudes. Which meant a climb was ahead of them.

She looked at her paper map. "Over on the left. There should be a trail up to the top."

"You could look it up on the GPS. Try my Garmin."

"It's in the back. Besides, we're practically there."

He parked, carefully let the turbo spool down before he shut it off. It had been his first new car and it was going to last him forever. They got out, stretched. The direct sun felt good, the air was sharp and clear, and there was little wind. He popped the tailgate of the wagon and they got their gear out: small pre-labeled containers for the shells they were going to collect. Gore-Tex outerwear, back-packs, an Olympus OM-D DSLR camera that geo-recorded the locations of each shot. Its eye-fi SDHC card was also slaved to their Android, which in turn was loaded with USGS large-scale contour maps. Even their canteens were relatively hi-tech, with built-in purification.

"Let's go and do a little science, hon." Lee said. They were a couple who seemed made for each other. Lisa came from a contentious Jewish household, where every dish passed at the dinner table seemed to trigger some argument. Lee's family, mainland Chinese, ate dinner to slurping noodle sounds and a few grunts that indicated which bowl to pass. Both children, then, had found something delightfully different in the other, not only in their cultures but in their outlooks on life. Lee, in particular, seemed to lift her up, with his joy in music, movies, pop culture.

She had once asked him why he was so outgoing. He had smiled and told her anything outside his parent's house was so full of energy that it made him feel alive. She found him to be as far from the studious Chinese guy stereotype as it was possible to be. That he loved her, the worry wart, was another great mystery. One she was never going to try to unravel, thank God.

The couple headed up the trail. Lee pressed the key fob, heard the Saab chirp as it locked itself. He wondered why he bothered; there was nobody up here.

*****

They worked their way up a slope of loose shale, then down into a swale that stretched a mile or so in a north/south direction. Lisa followed a few steps behind, aware that she was mimicking Lee's mother's ways—which was to say the old Chinese way—of a few steps back. She was aware that Lee took the lead in most things—she was just a quieter person. And he was always pleased with the things she showed him, like music and movies, things his family had frankly never valued. He was, academically, just a little sharper than she was, and it was book learning that got him ahead. At least in the school world. She wasn't sure how he would have done in the real one, and she figured she would never know. They were destined for academia.

"Check this out." He had stopped, looking down at the ground.

She looked around. "We're kind of low for *oreohelix*."

"No, these tracks." He knelt, pointed to some depressions in the gravel. "Hooves."

She took a look at a nearby drift of snow. "I think it might be a moose."

Lee laughed. "No way that's a moose print. Besides, these aren't cloven. We need a trusty Indian scout."

She looked around. "Are there wild horses up here?"

"That might be it. Let's follow them for a bit."

"Lee . . ."

"I don't think these are new. Besides, nobody is up here. Just you, me, maybe a few marmots." He signaled for her to follow as he headed for a stand of mature aspens and birch.

Under the trees the trail became clearer, as if it had been used more than once. The snow under the shade was hard, the crust punctured by considerably more hoof-prints, which seemed to be going in all directions. The majority led into a V-shaped gully, about forty feet wide at its mouth. The snow was roiled, mixed in with the humus of the forest floor. At the joining of the walls of the gully, there was a curiously flat, vertical surface. As they approached, they saw it was clearly man-made: a wall of logs and a hump backed roof that bridged the two angles of the gully. It was, apparently, a home made cabin. From ten feet away the whole structure blended in completely with the terrain.

"Nobody mentioned this to us."

He found there was a door, made of old saw-cut lumber, as aged and dark as the rest of the structure. It was held closed by a simple hasp. "Knock knock," Lee joked. Lisa held back; the place was giving her a bad vibe.

Lee pulled on the crude latch, dragging against the leafy debris at the base of the door. He could smell earth and rot as he cautiously stuck his head in.

"Lee . . ." Lisa warned. He ignored her, got out his flashlight, shone it inside. "Jesus H. Christ!"

"What is it?"

"A bunch of dead things. Hanging from the ceiling. Wait outside." He slowly stepped in. The space was narrow, and he had to duck to get his head under what seemed to be a fox hanging from its tail. He lit it up with his flashlight. The animal had been gutted. Other creatures were suspended from the crossbeams, which were small logs furry with bark and moss. There were low pallets on either side of the central aisle that went to the back wall. Rolled up sleeping bags were shoved in a corner. Some blackened skillets and pots hung from pegs driven into the back wall. There were empty chili cans under foot. "Home sweet home," he muttered.

He felt something brush his shoulder, jumped nearly out of his skin. "Lee, it's like a gallery—an awful gallery." Amy's hand was squeezing his shoulder.

He handed her the flashlight, got his camera out. "Get the flashlight on this."

"I'm totally spooked." She played the flash around the space. "Some of these are from endangered species. Eagle feathers. Those pelts are martins, and that's the head of a Dall's Sheep. This is terrible."

"Just a few more pix. I should have brought the flash.

We'll take this as evidence down the mountain; the law will want to see this."

"Will they care?"

"Poaching? Hell yeah." He took more shots, turned for a different angle. The room, already dark, went into total eclipse as something blocked the light coming in the door. Lisa gasped, dropped the flashlight. Reflexively, he raised the camera and fired off a final shot.

CHAPTER FIVE

The Alpha Wolf held Page with dark eyes: a fixed gaze, deep as a hunter's night.

"What happened to his haunch?" Page asked. The White Wolf, some fifteen yards beyond the cyclone fence, had been shaved down on most of his upper rear leg. From the growth of the fur, it had happened some time ago.

"Bullet wound," Annie said. "Midwinter. It nearly killed him."

"Big guy."

"The biggest we've ever measured: he goes a full meter at the shoulder."

"Must be a metric wolf." He gave the tightest of smiles.

"So, OK—he's 40" at the shoulder, over 140 lbs."

"That's Alaskan-sized, maybe from up on the Arctic northern Canada. A long, long ways from here." Page spent a moment taking in the animal. "Something made him come all this way . . . "

"You ought to know the answer to that."

"Huh?"

"The urge to mate. Don't you listen to country music?"

"You make it sound so romantic."

"Romance is dead, soldier. Come on over to the barn; I want to show you something."

He hesitated a moment. "I hope you're not like cowboy coffee."

"Bitter?"

"Damn."

"Hey, words are my thing. When it comes to action, not so good."

Sure, he thought, but he kept it to himself. He gave the wolf one last look. Page was not an introspective man, and he had no real empathy in his soul. But this wolf, so still and yet so full of purpose, had moved him. It was not in any way vermin, or a pest, or an economic nuisance. It was a big, powerful, maybe even beautiful, animal.

*****

They were standing at the eastern edge of the driveway, facing the bus turnaround. The Visitors Center blocked the view to the north. Annie's big house took up the western quadrant of the circular drive.

Directly across—to the east— were the fenced-in runs he had seen from the air. Annie had explained the wolves had about four acres inside the fence. It was high enough to keep out climbers—human ones. There was a viewing pen reaching to the Visitor Center that had an internal gate. Only a few wolves, those who would never go back to the wild, were allowed into that area. The majority of the wolf pen, or habitat as Annie called it, was screened by a mix of cedar breaks, overhanging trees, and a matrix of rock escarpments and caves at the far end. The breeding pairs were kept away from most human contact. It was important that they imprint their pups with as much training as was possible in a basically artificial environment.

The primary mission of Annie's Wolf Ranch was the raising and release of wolves. Her goal was to bring the wild populations up to a sustainable level. To this end, Wolf Ranch's staff used a variety of techniques, including tracking collars, to monitor the packs in their wild state. They also conducted numerous field studies, including DNA sampling, blood analysis, and habitat studies.

This was the science side. There were also programs to educate the general populace that blood-crazed lupines were in reality bullshit myth. Certainly, in North America there had only been one claimed human fatality from wolf attack. And that was controversial.

From puppet shows to formal meetings, it was Annie's particular mission to swing opinion around to the concept that a healthy environment, wolf-friendly, was good for the economic landscape. Tourism was at the top of her list. Folks with cameras, not guns, were starting to find their way here. Eco-tourism. Since the reintroduction of wolves into Yellowstone National Park, the government estimated that yearly park income directly attributed to wolf watchers was at least $35 million per year. In ten years, close to $300 million. In the same ten-year period, the various agencies, some private, had reimbursed ranchers in four states a total of $360,000, for livestock killed by wolves. Even elk hunters had found that the herds they hunted had increased in population since the wolves resumed culling the herds of the weak and old. Yet this was, she knew, a perceptual battle, to be fought in the minds of the general population. Hence, her mission.

Unfortunately, other people like Spatz made a good living guiding hunting parties into the wilderness to bag a trophy elk. Or, it was hinted, bigger game, like protected bear and mountain cat, even Big Horns and some of the rarer antelope. If it had horns or fangs, it seemed to attract a certain breed: moneyed, unscrupulous, often from overseas.

Annie had long maintained an intelligence network, particularly at the regional airport, to chart the comings and goings of these "dickless jerks," as she put it. And she had met more than a few out at Spatz's ranch, back in the day.

Locally, despite some of the old timers' prejudices, Annie, which was to say Wolf Ranch, had made some progress. It helped that her organization paid out cash for any documented livestock predations. She had made it a personal policy that *any* mauled animal would be covered. She wasn't about to wrangle over what made what type of bite-marks for a few dollars. She had plenty.

They started back across the driveway towards the barn that abutted the helipad. "Stick your head in here for a minute, Page." She slid the big sliding door open, the low sun illuminating a packed earth floor darkened by oil and countless decades of animal waste. He walked in, stopped dead.

"Man, a Power Wagon." His awed tone was approximately that of an art lover stepping into the Sistine Chapel. He walked around the behemoth, stepping in and out of sunbeams glowing with airborne motes of barn dust. It smelled like every barn he'd ever been in, with an extra hit of alfalfa and old crankcase oil. "She's a '48 or '49."

"Are all trucks female?" she laughed.

"Just the good ones. Look at those fenders." The truck's swells and curves still wore the original dark green livery, with contrasting black fenders. It stood tall on immense U.S. Army-style treads. He peered inside, took in the heavy brown vinyl on the seat, white bakelite knobs, the original molded rubber floor covering. It had minimal instrumentation, a manual transfer case, with a Hi-Lo gear split.

"It only has about twenty thousand miles—it never really left the ranch."

"This is like finding gold." He nodded at a logo painted on the cab door. "Walker Ranch. Or did you brand this too?"

"Give me a break. The Walkers sold it to me. They threw in a few thousand acres with the truck."

"The big land deal that got Spatz all twisted?"

She looked at him. "So *that's* what the Sheriff talked to you about." Page just gave her a distant smile, his eyes still on the Dodge. "Everything you see around here, everything that is new, was done in the last two years. I kept their barn, because I like barns. We did put some rooms in upstairs; I lived here while we built up the rest of the property. Josef has a room up there when he's on call."

"So the wolves are new, too?"

"Yes. I bought the whole project from a woman on Vashon Island in Washington State. The whole project was undercapitalized, to say the least."

"Instant wolf."

"And instant wolf lady. You like the truck?"

"It's pretty fair."

"You get it running, you get to use it. We *are* going to be working together, right?"

"We haven't really talked about it."

"Oh yes we have. I've just about completed your interview."

"Doing what? Mucking out stalls?"

"No." She pointed to some stairs that zigzagged up the far wall. "Come on upstairs. I'll show you where you can stay. I think we'll call you a field assistant. You can track?"

"If it walks, I can trail it." There was a hint of pride in his voice. She was pretty sure he was not the kind to brag.

She stopped part way up the stairs. She considered him with a direct look that almost made him flinch. He had never cared much for others opinions, especially about himself. His self-analysis had always been simple in the extreme. He had certain goals, and a few—very few—strong beliefs. And yet, here in this strange place, a ranch for predators, he suddenly wanted to get a passing grade. He returned her gaze, and something passed between them.

After a tour of the upstairs, a collection of comfortable, basic rooms, they went back down to the other half of the lower floor. It had all the warmth and charm of a veterinarian clinic, which it was.

The place was big, well lit, utterly lacking the barn ambience of the rest of the structure. It was empty at the moment, but Annie was able to locate the items she wanted. She laid them out on a stainless steel examination table: a radio collar, its leather strap still riveted together, a hunting knife, and a plastic container with a bullet in it. He examined the collar first. "Somebody sure made a statement."

"Yeah. 'Fuck you.' They stuck the collar to a tree with the knife after they decapitated her."

He nodded, held the collar up; she noticed he had to squint a little to see it. She figured him not to have reading glasses in his shirt pocket. "How did it go down?" he asked.

"They snared her, then they closed in."

"How did they know where to look?"

"We found snowmobile tracks after we homed in on her collar. When they stop moving like that, it's usually bad news. We're pretty damned sure they can track the collars, too. She'd gnawed off her forepaw, but she never got very far. They shot her—shot them both—did the head thing, skinned her out."

He sensed the tension in her voice. "We're not doing a murder here," he pointed out.

"I try not to get all New Age; these are tough animals for a tough environment. But still, Brindle—"

"You name the wolves?"

"We keep records on everything—it's easier to remember a name than a file number. She had the most unique coat . . ."

He put down the collar, hefted the knife. "That's mildly interesting."

"Her name?"

"No, the knife. It's called a Ka-Bar. Standard issue with the Marines. But they made a million. No big deal." He put it back down, looked in the container.

He found some tweezers, used them to lift out the bullet; he looked at it critically. "Do you have a magnifying glass?" She walked over to a laminated countertop that ran the length of one wall. It had a workstation with a magnifying glass on a long swinging arm. She clicked on its ring light. He looked at the enlarged image of the projectile for few moments. "I'd have to say it was a Nosler Partition. It's their claim to fame. That's why I use their rifle."

"So the shooter used a Nosler?"

"I don't know. Their ammunition can fit just about anything." He found a set of tools standing up in an old 49ers mug, selected a small pick. "We could get a lab to analyze the propellant—might be a custom load. Some guys like to build their own."

He held it out to her. "See how it mushroomed out? It has a thin wall between two alloys—kind of fillers. They flare out real even; ups the killing power." He had the enthusiast's look, like a car guy talking about V8s.

"Could we do any of that TV detective stuff?" she asked. "You know, lands and grooves, ballistics tests?"

"Why bother. It's not a crime scene." He put the bullet back in the container. "Oh, I get it: make fun of Mr. Fed."

He paused a beat. "One question I do have . . . "

"What?"

He looked at her, shrugged. "How come this bullet didn't kill old Whitey out there? He must be one tough hombre."

CHAPTER SIX

It was the part of the day she loved best—the lucent half-light of what Zane Grey liked to call the gloaming. When the wind died, as it had today, there was a heavy feel to the air, with just the slightest grass-laced odor of spring. The house was quiet and the kitchen cleared away. There was no staff in the house for the next few hours. She had been able to wrap up her business day without incident. She was not particularly gifted at clearing her mind of the day's concerns. But she had found that putting on some loose clothes, making herself a drink, and generally futzing around upstairs were little tricks that could help calm the Brownian motion of her mind.

Annie had once tried to learn to meditate. She had told her trainer she had a tough time getting her mind to stop for more than a few moments. He had congratulated her on getting that far. It had taken another year to finally learn that slowing the mind was *the* most monumental of tasks, not just for the Western mind, but for all of humanity. Her conclusion, after some study, was that the talking mind was connected with the getting of things. The things being connected, in turn, to a person's hopes, dreams, plans.

All built around the central tenet, the absolute premise, of the all-important self. So often she wanted to escape that inner being and couldn't. Not just because she had a western mind, or that she had any great calling, or was important to the universe. She simply could not quite convince herself to stop believing that some things were worthy and some were not. A scale of values she mistrusted, because she had seen what values and beliefs did to the world. Yet, she could not escape them or their consequences.

And so she was far from her natural, urban habitat, in a wilderness of her own choosing, somehow linked to a wild creature that had been devalued by mankind. She knew she was being a contrarian, assuming the role of speaker for the wolf. It was, she suspected, a role her life instructors would quietly question. But it was turning out to be the only center she had.

The upstairs of the main house was the one part of the property that was off-limits, no maids, no uninvited guests. When the place was built—designed—she had specified no upstairs phones. Computers were also banned. It was an indirect lighting kind of space, candles more than candlepower.

There was a central hall divided into two sections, the north and south wings, by a walk-through stone arch. The stone was part of a two-story structure that formed the center of the house. It allowed her to have a fireplace upstairs. The south wing included her bedroom with an adjoining sauna and bath. She could pad down the hall after a soak, to read or space out in the living room, which took up half of the north wing, its soaring picture windows facing to the west.

Across the open hallway was a full boat library straight out of an old timey *Masterpiece Theatre*. The library overlooked the driveway. The dormered windows, complete with cushions for reading nooks, gave her a view over and beyond the wolf pens. She often came here in winter to catch the morning sunrise above the ranges to the east.

The living room was in reality a sunken space, its borders defined by built-in couches done in a wine-dark leather. Wide steps led down to the tiled floor that had radiant heat built in. She was not a fan of wall-to-wall carpet. The upstairs had small indirect lights built into the step's risers or running along the baseboards, allowing her movement without the harsh glare of overhead lights. She liked it dim; she liked moving past dark wooden panels that rasped under her fingers as she passed. And she could stand in front of her windows and know she wasn't even a silhouette. These simple rooms echoed a need for privacy that was part of her being.

The sunken pit was faced on the south wall by a floor-to-ceiling fireplace. There were two niches in the fieldstone built in for her speakers. A wall of glass faced west. The panes had a special coating that blocked reflections. It was like looking right into the outside world. The view-shed was all hers out to the horizon.

Her only concessions to the modern world were some strategically placed reading lamps, a few pieces of art on the remaining wall to the north. And her big-ass stereo. Her Dad's actually. There were just the two speakers, giant old Klipschhorns the size of a sumo wrestler, and nearly as heavy. She'd re-oiled them herself, leaving untouched the crayon marks she had made on them when she was five years old. One of the few times she'd ever seen her father, a very sweet man, go completely ballistic.

Her father and mother had been partners in a company that repped hi-fi gear throughout the western states. The 1970s had been a time of tremendous energy in the home electronics business, a time of great innovation. McIntosh, Marantz, a new player named Sony, Thorens, Teac had all been in the line-up. As the companies prospered, her parents had found themselves part of the whole Bay Area music scene, from Bill Graham Productions to Wally Heider Sound over on Hyde, across from the Blackhawk Jazz Club. From their home in Mill Valley, David Crosby and Grace Slick were only blocks away. As a young girl she had helped her mom and dad wine and dine Baez and Bennett, had a memorable dinner with an up-and-coming comic named George Carlin. Always interested in words and language, he had been the first person to mention Marshall McCluhan to her. That had been her introduction to what would become her study of semiotics—and the basis for her career.

A special favorite of the family was a warm, exotic woman in her early sixties, an Incan princess (and she really was) with a prodigious four-octave voice: Yma

Sumac. She had been indirectly responsible for the death of her parents.

Annie's amp was a classic Marantz tube set-up built into a side table. There was no remote, so she wanted the knobs fairly close. She was lazing next to the amp and turntable on her one chair—a firm old Backsaver recliner—looking at the tubes glowing in the dimness. It was a warm, inviting light, much like the sound. The tone of the old equipment was soft, even dulcet, a long way from the harder-edged digital age.

She allowed herself one brandy, a de Montal from the Armagnac. The turntable was spinning real vinyl, her old DGG copy of a piece by Thomas Purcell: "A New Ground," an elegant, minimalist piece for harpsichord. She'd picked up a passion for Purcell when she had been in England dealing with the inquest. She'd learned that student performances were free most afternoons at the London Conservatory. She'd had a lot of time on her hands during the hearings into the death of her parents and forty five other souls. Not that they had found anything in the end. Literally nothing, not even wreckage. The Vickers Viscount had been a British charter that disappeared off the coast of Peru; her parents had gone down with it. With no cause to be found, there had been no one to blame. Just lost forever in the Pacific blue. Gone.

She still had a record of Yma Sumac over in the rack: "The Voice of the Xtabay." Mom had liked it so much that they decided on a trip to the Andes. Yma had arranged a whole intinerary of people to meet, musical acts to check out. Annie had been fifteen years old when that flight went down. By the time she heard Purcell for the first time, she'd felt like she was a hundred. It was not a feeling that ever quite went away.

Purcell finished and she lifted the arm of the Thorens. It was a pure, minimal machine, just the way her father had liked it. It helped her pay attention to the music, the little rituals of cleaning the record, dropping the needle gently, putting the record back in its sleeve when she finished.

The death of her parents had been the start of adulthood. Their money had educated Annie, given her a footing in the business world. From tragedy to success via higher education. How would she ever explain to her new found lawman just how empty that education had left her?

She was restless. She tightened up her robe and went into the library to see if there was something she wanted to read. The room sensed her presence and put the lights on dim; she could just see out the window towards the wolves. Not that she could pick them out in the dark. When they had put in the trees that screened the wolf run from the driveway, she had made sure that she could still look down on the creatures who were becoming the focus of her life. Why was she doing it? Was she playing at caring, or did she genuinely care? For wolves, for people, for anything?

The classic wooden sliding door was open on the old barn, light slanting out onto the drive, bright enough to highlight the gravel's textures. She'd shown

Page the battered roll-out tool chests that had come with the barn. Beat up Craftsman stuff from Sears, basic tools for keeping a smallish ranch running. That old truck sure had made his eyes gleam. If she was buying him off—and the word was not yet in—he went for cheap. And why would she even try. He was here on a job of his own; he probably had a life. She hadn't even asked. She had Range Rovers, new Tundras, a Kubota tractor. All the toys. She flew a Citation II, for Christ's sake. But she wondered if anything else she had—or even did—would impress him. Did she care? Wow, she thought. Round One to Winston Churchill's Black Dog of depression.

CHAPTER SEVEN

For Page Deschamps, the next week passed quickly. He spent his days learning how Wolf Ranch was run. It was clearly the brainchild of its founder, although Annie seemed to keep behind the scenes. It was a smoothly oiled machine: the tour buses brought in the visitors, who dropped their dollars and left feeling good about themselves. The research staff was not yet in evidence, as the wolves themselves were just coming out of their winter dens. Page knew this from the tracking team, which monitored the location of the pack's more important members. Now at the top of the roster were the former Beta pair. Apparently the information from the tracking collars allowed them to determine that the Betas had successfully mated; in some unknown way the pack had sensed the loss of the Alpha bitch and her unborn pups and made an adjustment to leadership within the pack. How they knew this was way beyond the present bounds of science. The scientists, who were scheduled to arrive in the next few weeks, would give it a try, but barring some miracle breakthrough, they would spend yet another season collecting data.

The tracking team had an air arm, which was Josef and the Hughes 500. Page went up on several test flights as they burned in some new electronics, including a

Yagi-style antenna mounted between the skids. Since they were both staying upstairs in the barn, they tended to hang out together in the evenings. When Page wasn't learning the ropes, he spent time working on the old Dodge. It was a brutally simple device, stone age in its simplicity. Which suited Deschamps just fine.

A high-pressure ridge had brought in some unseasonably warm days. The evenings were also mild; Page would often work with the doors open. The wolves were pretty quiet at night. When he heard howls, they were usually from coyotes back up in the hills. One evening, a black bear tried to rummage through the garbage cans, but everything was squared away. The wolves in the pens had reacted to that, but otherwise they were generally calm. Page had never lived even remotely this close to wolves. Just across from the barn, they gave the property an air of expectancy, but their animal wildness never seemed to break through. Like prisoners everywhere, they were in cages, and the cages had crushed their spirits. So it seemed to Page. He could relate to that.

Page was not a meditative man, and using his hands kept his mind still. Which was fine, as he didn't like to think about things. That was the great gift of the wild: it occupied the senses and left the soul quiet. The rhythm of the work on the Dodge was almost as soothing, but it required a tangible object for his focus. To him, this was perilously close to the human world of acquisition, one he had always tried to avoid. Still, he was glad for the distraction, as it helped pass the time until he had fully adopted his "legend" as a small potatoes drifter.

*****

It was the next Friday before Page felt ready to go out in that new identity, to go to work. The Range Rider Café was all lit up as he nosed the old Dodge into one of the angled slots in front of the bar. He let it idle for a moment, the untreated exhaust, rich with hydrocarbons, coming in his open window. There was still more tappet noise than he liked. His mechanic's skills had gotten pretty rusty.

Time to get the show on the road, he told himself. Since the quiet wastes of Alaska, he'd been far away from any sort of crowd. But he didn't anticipate any trouble and wasn't going to carry. It didn't go with the image he wanted to promote: not-too-bright ranch hand. However, he had taken the precaution of slipping his 9mm Glock into the battery box under the floorboards. His badge was in there as well. Just in case. He saw that this was the Happy Trails Hour; there was a fair amount of Friday night hoopla leaking out into the street.

He stood outside the door until a couple pushed in. He had a thing about stepping through doors—that one moment without a good sight picture always gave him pause. It was a moment of vulnerability, and he didn't do vulnerability.

It was not a smoky warren, nor was Merle jerkin' out his heartstrings. But there was the obligatory band, with a rigged-out young cowgirl doing some old Ian & Sylvia piece about trucks and wheat fields. Not bad, actually. The band looked, to his unpracticed eye, like they had day jobs at Microsoft. The lighting was pleasant and low. He didn't hear any too-drunk voices raised in argument, or the whiney self loathing he'd seen all too many times in bars far and wide. There was a soccer game on the TV, for Christ's sake. He noticed there was an open archway into another room — he could hear pool balls clacking in there.

Page sidled up to the bar, signaled for a beer, was bemused to find he had to make a choice. He went for something called "Custer's Last Stout." It cost a staggering $8.00. After a few sips he let his gaze go to the man he had followed to the bar, his old asshole buddy Red. He caught the ramrod's eye, gave him a neutral nod. Red was with a couple of other cowpuncher types, all of whom looked remarkably authentic, right down to a runty tribal dude. They looked a little out of place, like they might have been recruited by management to give the place a more "real" ambience. Red made a "c'mere" gesture that didn't seem particularly unfriendly.

"Hey, Slick," Red said. "Boys, meet . . ."

Page went over to introduce himself. "Page."

"That's a girl's name," one of the guys, a thin galoot, observed. But they all nodded, polite enough for bar etiquette.

"I met Page here at the Spring Wing Ding. He saved me from a runaway horse." Red said to his buds. Actually, Page thought, they looked more like Red's crew, waiting around to do evil deeds, if only in their own minds. It was hard to take them seriously.

"Old Thunder?" one of them asked. This started a general discussion of which horse it was, how horses were God's dumbest animals, and general cowboy talk. One of them asked where Page worked. Red butted in on that one: "He's ram roddin' Miss Annie. You boys remember *her*."

Page didn't get what the insinuation was about for a moment. Then he remembered the Sheriff's soap opera summation of the tempestuous relationship between Annie and Spatz. "I wouldn't call it that," Page said.

"You will—give the bitch time."

Again Page refused to rise to the bait, if that was what it was.

"I'm wrangling wolves, if you can believe it." Page took a hit of the beer. He screwed up his face; it tasted weird. They gave him looks of sympathy; no man should ever have to stoop so low in the beer universe. "It's a job. I was on my uppers."

"You could work at the Rockin' R. We need warm bodies, right, Red?" Slim asked. Red shrugged. He was looking into the next room, taking in the pool tables. The band knocked off for their break.

"I'm not really a cowboy—don't have the skills."

"So what are you good at?" Red asked pointedly. His attention had definitely shifted elsewhere.

Page looked him in the eye. "I hunt. I track."

"Hey, Red, we could use—"

Red cut the cowboy off with a cutting motion, palm

flat. "I don't think so. Page here made his bed." He smirked. "He can lay in it. Let's go." He looked at Page. "Put your gay beer on my tab. You get the next one." Page held the other man's gaze. It was clear they were going to take this to another level, but tonight wasn't the night. Each had decided: *asshole*.

There was a man waiting for the whole crew down at the far end of the bar. He had just stepped in from the poolroom, putting on a heavy plaid mackinaw. Three Asian men, probably in their forties, followed him, lined up like ducklings. They were dressed in poofy down jackets and blue jeans. One was wearing a crimson Elmer Fudd hunting cap. The big man had to be Spatz. Red was practically tripping under his master's feet.

Spatz ushered the Asians towards the door, almost shooing them along with a straw Stetson hat. He had a head of curly, iron-gray hair, a full beard, well trimmed. He was a pretty big man, pushing sixty, but very fit. He looked an outdoor type. He also looked totally and completely a boss. As they trooped past Page, the rancher wasted a moment to give him a glance, one of quick appraisal. Then an equally prompt dismissal.

Which was just the way Page wanted it. He was just a little grain of sand in the oyster's craw, but that little grain could grow into a hard knot. That might be fun.

CHAPTER EIGHT

The next day, Saturday, turned out to be sunny and warm. Annie slept in late, then had some basic breakfast things brought up. Before she ate, she slipped out of her nightshirt and looked at herself in the bathroom's full-length mirror. She had always thought of herself as bony and a bit flat, but she noticed that as she aged she had acquired a very light layer of softness just under her skin. Her hips no longer poked through; there was a little curve there. She decided, on the daily basis of her mirror moment, whether or not she was overeating or getting enough exercise. But she was doing OK. So, two soft eggs, dry toast, cooled British style on a little rack she'd brought back from London. Coffee, no cream or sugar. She remembered some old Ian Fleming book where 007 ordered figs and coffee, black. He'd wanted to keep his figure, too. Not that she was some sort of Jane Bond.

She lounged around for an hour with a book, then went to make some calls from downstairs. Annie maintained her office here, with all the latest aids, including a microprocessor-controlled "follow me" electronics set-up. This part of the house was the exact oppositei of the upstairs. She could access any of her

songs—tens of thousands—from a wall-mounted
keypad, or simply by speaking. Her tunes or, this
morning, the news would then follow her from room to
room using each locale's hidden speakers. It was also
slaved into her answering and online services. She could
even dictate directly to her computer, logging ideas as
they came to her. As she entered the office, a
disembodied voice gave her a list of messages. Two were
particularly interesting. One was a report from a lab in
Mountain View that was working on some new angles in
radio collars. She would get to that later. The other was
more prescient: a heads-up from one of her informants
at the airfield. She was already going to meet Josef and
the Hughes at the airport's service center where the
chopper would get its 2000-hour service. A perfect way
to casually check in with her sources, find out what was
up with Spatz and his merry band.

She put on her hiking boots in the foyer, touched
up her hair with her fingers, added the merest touch of
lip-gloss. She grabbed a man-bag from a hook in the
hall and went to find her new hire. Annie was going to
show off the property to Page. He was going to show off
the truck.

Annie went up the barn stairs to his living quarters.
She gave a knock on his door, which was slightly ajar.
She stuck her head in, noted the empty room. She
lingered a moment, taking in the fact that the place
looked almost completely unlived in. The only sign of
his occupancy was the quilt and pillow on the floor. It
appeared that that was where he slept. His rifle, in its

rifle case, was leaning in a corner. There was a bottle of water on the dresser, but no other sign of a rich personal life. He seemed like a man who would keep his cards close to his chest, not a New Age guy at all.

She thought he might be down with his one emotional connection—the Power Wagon—but he wasn't there, either. As she headed over to the wolf run, she heard the Hughes revving up with a distinctive whop-whop as it lifted up and away. The miracle of flight, she thought. A miracle that made her uneasy. It touched her with a fear she didn't let anyone see, just as she never talked to anyone about the images she had of her parents deaths: the sickening plunge, the screams in the cabin. The terror more than the death, which must have been instant. Or had it been? Did they belly in to the warm Pacific, did the plane float? Were they in a raft, dying by inches . . . She closed her mind to the images that lay just beneath her surface.

Page was in the pen, but not with any of the staff. This was a no-no, not that a wolf would attack a human. They never did. That was part of the strange bond that many people, including herself, felt for the species. Almost as though they were one short evolutionary step away from the family canine. In fact, Annie had been more frightened by the occasional bad dog than by any wolf she had ever met. The rule was more for the protection of animals that might have to go into the wild. Over familiarity with humans had been fatal to many a wolf.

Page had his back against the fence, squatting down

on his haunches. Some forty feet away, the White Wolf was standing in the "alert" position, trying to figure out the dynamics of the scene. Annie lowered herself just behind Page, speaking through the wire mesh. "Wolves don't like us down at their eye level. They think you're challenging them."

He looked back over his shoulder for a second. "No, he thinks I'm visiting."

"You do this often?"

"It's how we've been starting the day. He never comes any closer than this—he's a smart one." Page slowly got to his feet, turned to smile at her. "Good morning."

She looked around, agreeing with him. "Nice day."

"Just a minute. I'll let myself out." He joined her in the drive. "I never really thought about wolves before. Especially as, uh, individuals. You think they have personalities?"

"I don't know, Page. I get the feeling they have souls. Or maybe a collective soul. When you hear them calling in the night, man, that's a real mystery there."

"Up in Alaska, when they have the big kill-offs, they stack the wolves up like logs. Frozen stiff. Like it's a war, and they're the enemy."

"That's the kind of raw emotions that are just under the surface here, too. I worry some crazy thing, maybe not even all that important, will touch the match and the whole place goes up in flames."

"Like I said—war."

"Have you been in one? Iraq?"

He shrugged. "Not worth talking about. Speaking of something else, where'd the chopper head off to?"

"Josef will meet us at the county airport. The Hughes needs its service. We use the same mechanics as the state does, and we may need some lead time." She guided him towards the open barn door. "I had Yolanda make up a picnic basket. I thought we could take the truck into town. On the way, I'll show you around the ranch. Sound good?"

He said that it did.

CHAPTER NINE

Sheriff Manyhorse had come in just before noon—he was about to throw a grenade among the troops. All but two of them were waiting in the small, all-purpose conference room. He'd even brought in the off-duty staff, although he had let them stay in their civvies. Normally he liked to start the week off with an action summary, touch bases with the men—and three women—of the force. He'd learned all about inclusion, all-voices-heard, no-idea-too-small, from some college courses on management. He wanted to look good; he had an election coming up. And morale had been rotten ever since an Indian had gotten a special appointment after the last chief had died in harness. It didn't help that he, the Redskin, was smarter than anyone in this crew. Book smart, college smart. He didn't know if that was good or bad in this business.

The atmosphere wasn't much better out on the streets. He had angry parents—there had been a toilet paper spree after the Stanley Owls had been humiliated in the countywide basketball tourney. A meth lab had blown up in a double wide, and the landlord was angry with the fuzz for not busting the tweakers *before* the fact. There was a "prowler" knocking over garbage cans; in all likelihood it was a rogue raccoon. If so, why hadn't it been caught, lined up against a wall, and shot?

He got a coffee, went in to see his staff. After some chair scraping and a few coughs, he got right down to cases. A particular case. "First, the Chun/Betz situation. They've been missing for close to a month now. The snows have cleared. No sign of them. Until now. Brenda will fill us in."

He nodded to a woman officer, a slim, slightly plain-faced brunette in her thirties. She looked like a school-teacher, amiable enough, not too assertive. But she had one of the better minds on the force. This was going to be her moment to sink or swim.

"Ah, right, chief." She had a laptop on one of the old pine tables, a cable running to a projector. She clicked an image on the screen hung on the far wall. "This is the gate to the Stanford research property. And this . . ." She changed to a close-up. "This is a small metal flag they use as a signal that they are on site. If the gate is unlocked or open, and the flag is down, they back off. There might be trespassers. The locals don't know about this," she added.

"Some good old boys wrecked that gate last year. We know how this county is overheating on the whole issue of land conservation," Manyhorse pointed out.

"You might have mentioned it," one of the men said. There were a few laughs.

Brenda continued, "The flag was up when we went out there to look for them. That probably means they felt it was all clear. More importantly, it indicates they *were* there at some point. Stanford hasn't had anyone else going through the gate. They had us check it out ten days into their disappearance. The officer we sent up noted the flag's position at that time. We have, therefore, been pretty sure this is where they disappeared."

"Unless they drove out and forgot the flag," someone pointed out.

"It's a bit thin. But it's what we had. Until now." Manyhorse took a sip of coffee, played it for a little drama. He wanted them excited instead of bored, which was where they had been on this case. It was time to rock their world.

"These are scientists. Their Stanford advisors gave us a full profile. They were sharp, not pointy-headed nerds. So we have a couple, a loving couple I might add, soon to be married. Solid folks. The flag is still up, and I don't think they forgot. I believe they're up there." He had their attention now. Maybe, like him, their minds were focusing in on the cold high mountains.

Ben produced a folded sheet from an inside pocket. "As we all know, there are many ways to track stolen vehicles. OnStar is one of the best. The missing vehicle is a 2010 Saab 9-3 wagon. We thought it had OnStar, but that was the year GM dumped the Swedes. Some had it, some didn't.

"We checked. This one didn't. No Lojack, either."

"So we're still boned?" someone said.

The Sheriff gave them a quiet smile, let them focus on his menacing teeth for a moment.

"Have we found the car?" Brenda asked.

"We have."

The room seemed to come alive; the group looked like it wanted to roll out the door and hit the highway. It was a shame to bring them down a notch. "Unfortunately, it's in another state. In long-term parking at the Boise Airport. They got our bulletin and looked over the lot. Not that many Saabs in the world, so eventually it was spotted."

Brenda asked if the FBI was going to come in.

"This is now an interstate investigation, so yes, that means the Feds." They all groaned. "We are keeping the crime scene—if there is a crime—right here on our turf. Brenda, you are to liaise with . . ." He got a card out of his pocket. "Agent Colby White. He will spearhead the investigation of the Saab as a crime scene. I understand Agent White is flying in as we speak. They are bringing in a Lear with a forensics crew. We will extend to him and his people every courtesy.

"One final point. I am asking for the State Patrol to prepare the cadaver dogs." The buzz in the room died down. "I know. Not a pleasant thought. But I think it's time."

He let them soak up the seriousness of the situation. "I will work out more assignments this afternoon. This is going to break, and it is going to break our way. If you are off duty, go home. Get some rest. Brenda, be sure to ask the FBI to cc the crime report for the Saab. I'm going out to Wolf Ranch."

"Gettin' a trackin' wolf, Chief?" one trooper asked.

He gave him a hard look. There was a right way to call him "Chief," and a wrong way. "No. Their chopper."

"It's at the airfield right now," Brenda said. "It flew in about two hours ago."

He gave her a little smile. "Good catch. You come with me." Brenda hopped to it. She seemed to have found her game, which made him feel a little more confidence in his team. He hoped mightily the others weren't in over their heads.

CHAPTER TEN

Annie's plan was to drive in with Page in the truck, then supervise the helicopter's service. In reality, she was not strictly needed, since Josef could handle the details. And it was also not strictly necessary that they took the Power Wagon; she had plenty of rides. Any one of which would not be, at this moment, compressing her spine. But she thought of it as Deschamp's vehicle, because it seemed to be like him: basic, raw-boned, timeless and yet old-fashioned. He looked the perfect match as they pounded along a rutted back road on the way down to the river.

A large mogul launched them both airborne, her head just hitting the tin roof. "Oops!" he grinned. He graunched it down a gear, the engine's fan roaring as he used it to slow down a tiny bit.

She pointed to a fork to the right. "About a mile." They soon found a cow trail dropping down into a narrow defile, the ruts going right into the slowly moving water of a modestly wide river. Page looked at her; she nodded yes. He put the hand brake on, got out to lock up the front axles. He got back in, engaged compound low, and let the engine idle them down to the edge. The Power Wagon jerked and bucked a bit as it found some underwater tracks, then splashed across in about three feet of slowly moving water. "It won't be that easy in another month," he remarked.

She smiled, let him work it up the other side. "On that rise is a good spot." He found a clearing, parked under a stand of cottonwoods, shut down the engine. He sat for a moment taking it all in. "Nice view." There was scattered snow in the shade, but the trees were starting to leaf out. The major snowpacks up on the peaks were pure white, the still air a cornflower blue. Spring was in the air.

"I come here now and then. This was once open range."

"Cattle came down this trail. Not so long ago. Good place to ford. You own this now?"

"I do. No more cows for this girl—I'm letting it all revert."

"So all this could start a range war?"

"Like, sheep versus cows?"

"I was thinking water rights."

"Don't forget the crusty sidekick, the lost mine, ghost riders, and so on. Did you go to cowboy movies a lot?" Annie got the old picnic basket, a classic wicker weave, out of the bed of the truck.

"It was the only thing I could sit through. I liked Roy Rogers a lot."

"Next time we'll come here on a horse. Maybe two. Come on, let's eat." Annie said.

He flipped out the tailgate, and they spread things out. He dug right into the sandwich. She opened two bottles of beer, handed him one. He took a swig. "This designer stuff is starting to taste better." He looked at the label. "Fat Tire Amber. What's that mean?"

She laughed. "Marketing. I'll interpret for you."

"It's right there in plain English."

"No, no. There are all kinds of messages here. There's even a science around this stuff. Semiotics." Page rolled his eyes. "No, really! Look at the shape of the bottle, the color of the glass—that's to give it an old-time feel in your hand. Nostalgia." She turned the label around to him. "See the bike? The fat tire is to remind you of your old Schwinn bike. Red is an 'up' color. Here, it reminds us of times that were good."

"I wasn't drinking beer when I had a bicycle."

"Doesn't have to make sense. Just sensations. Pleasant associations that leave a tiny hook in the back of your brain."

"Saying: buy me."

"You got it. And that is the core of my business. In general, marketing. More specifically for me, branding. I create an aura, a feeling about a product, or even a person. Politicians do this big time."

He groaned. "I still don't get the bicycle."

She thought for a moment. "I think the brewer toured across Europe on a bike. Maybe it had fat tires, maybe not. But Skinny Tire Amber doesn't have the right sound."

"Isn't 'fat' kind of a negative word?"

"Good point. But this is an indulgence. Words like 'rich' or 'creamy'? They sell."

"I like the word 'beer.' Period. Anybody do that?"

"Well, they were selling things with just bar codes in the last recession. Didn't turn anyone on. You can buy a white car, but it will never, and I mean never, be called white."

"Snow white?"

"Ick. Too Disney. Try Dover White. White Cliffs of Dover. Maybe a Jag, the whole heritage thing."

"You have all this shit in your head?"

"Most people's heads are jammed with this crap. Semiotics is the mind's shorthand: symbols and the meaning behind the meaning." She stopped, a little embarrassed. "I get carried away. Somehow I don't think I'm going to impress you with a lecture on designer handbags!"

He thought for a moment. "Back at the house, in your kitchen, the stove had a wolf on it. What's cooking got to do with wolves?"

She laughed again. He thought it sounded good. "Not a thing. That's just the family name of the founders. Al and Hyman Wolf."

He gave her a really genuine laugh in return. "Hyman? I give up!"

"Yeah, Hyman's not a real forceful word choice. You want strong? You're driving it."

He thought. "Power. I can live with *that.*"

After they finished their lunch, they packed up and headed towards town, taking the slow route. Sometimes they stayed on cow trails or jeep tracks, sometimes following old fence lines, with the bare posts still standing sentinel—Annie had had the barbed wire taken off years ago. Her holdings were extensive, some 14,000 acres, roughly twenty square miles. And it *was* relatively square, as the borders were the old north-south, east-west metes and bounds laid out in the 1890s. As she pointed out various features, she talked about her vision of how the land could be used. It clearly was a radical departure from the past; she seemed to be proud of that fact. Page detected a note of radicalism in her tone, a take-no-prisoners sense of conviction.

Her wolf program was similar to those the Feds had developed in Yellowstone. There, entire wolf clans, such as the Druid Peak Pack, had become virtual superstars, with visitors—and their dollars—coming in from around the world. And just to observe, to experience from a distance. Human intervention, including culling, had been curtailed. It was not an interactive, living diorama—in the park the wolves had primacy over visitors. Other than to researchers, the wolves were off-limits.

The Druids, in particular, had flourished. The pack, located primarily in the Lamar Valley, had peaked at thirty-seven wolves in 2001—the largest wolf pack ever recorded. They had succeeded because their primary food, elk, had also thrived without predators. In their own culling program, these primal hunters had first taken the easy prey, the so-called "grandmas" of the elk population. In just a few years, the actual ecology of the valley began to change: lazy elk, the old and the weak, had browsed for seven decades on aspen and willow shoots, denuding much of the park of its premier timber. Every animal, from beaver to Bison, had been affected. But by the new millennium the vegetation had responded to fewer elk, and beaver habitat, with new trees available, had expanded. In time their water ponds would fill with silt to become new meadows that would feed those ruminants that had survived the wolves.

The elk population, after the first wolf kills, had come back stronger and more aggressive. An elk that stood around soon became a dead elk. In time, the culls made the herds stronger, and now more wolves died under hooves than by gunshot. At this point in time, in many states the wolves were either already delisted from the Endangered Species Act, or were up for review. About 1,700 wolves were thought to be in the United States. Another 12,000 or so were over the border in the Canadian Rockies, a few migrating south like Annie's White Wolf.

Page listened and pretty much kept quiet, just enjoying the day, the company. He knew the circle-of-life line of reasoning well. It was what had brought him here. He did not question the argument; he felt he was not enough of a thinker to do so. The concept of life as a battle between animals, or groups of animals, seemed to be an ancient, immutable law.

In that battle, he saw the gun as an extension of a man's hand, his reach. Just as a knife was modeled on a tooth or claw, a fish hook a thorn made large, the bullet was the ultimate pointed stick. And nothing more than that—just an extension of his hand. The killing hand.

As far as he thought about these things, he felt the automobile had done plenty of murder in its time. But San Francisco liberals weren't out burning Toyotas in effigy. Leastways, not that he'd heard.

"Cat got your tongue?" She poked him in the ribs. "I get carried away sometimes."

"I don't mind. It's a nice day."

"So you're having a little fun? I sometimes think of you as one of my team—I forget you're here to catch poachers."

"Poaching poachers." He smiled.

"Mmmm . . . a nice analogy. Strong sense of word play; makes me think of eggs cooking . . ."

"*No mas!*"

"Deal. Let's go to the big city. I'll buy you another beer. You can pick the label."

CHAPTER ELEVEN

They never made it to the Range Rider. Annie got a call on her iPhone as soon as they got in range of a cell tower. The small regional airport was abuzz with activity. There was a plain Learjet on the tarmac behind Annie's colorful Wolf's Head chopper. Some of the Hughes' inspection hatches were open. Josef was sticking his head in while talking to a mechanic in blue pinstriped coveralls. Both turned as the Dodge pulled up. The aviation mech looked it over with the appraising eye of a man who worked on machines. He gave them a nod, held his gaze on Annie for a beat too long before he went back to checking items off on a clipboard that balanced on an internal stringer.

Next to the Lear was a small crowd, including the Sheriff. Two of the local police Tahoes were idling in front of the wing. "Big doings," Page observed.

"Something's up."

"You said you get some reports out of here—from that mechanic guy?"

She snorted derisively. "The opposite. He's probably in the other camp. I'm the Rich Bitch."

"But he works on the chopper? Is that safe?"

"He's not the only mechanic here. But he goes on

all the check flights. It's his ass, too. For really complete teardowns, we fly it to a bigger place in Boise."

The Sheriff came over, said hello. "What's up, Ben?" Annie asked.

"We've got a lead on those missing kids." He explained about the Saab.

"So is that the Feebs in the jet?"

"Yup. But we want to get to the Stanford site for a looky-loo. We'd sure appreciate it if you could fly us up. The county will pay for the gas. Or is it down for service?" He nodded towards the mechanic.

"Just some routine maintenance. We were going to do some observing before dark. There's supposed to be the remnants of a pack migrating over the border. Isn't that right, Page?" He had no idea; this was all news to him. But he nodded.

"Well, how about you drop me off? The Tahoes will be there in a couple of hours. They can haul me back. Page, you could maybe take in the scene?"

"Wasn't it weeks ago they disappeared? Not sure what I could find," he shrugged.

Manyhorse nodded, started to say something, saw a man coming out of the doorway of the jet. Page saw he was a black man, late forties, very slim; he was wearing a blue FBI windbreaker.

"Excuse me a moment," Manyhorse said. As the Sheriff went over to the jet, Josef joined Annie and Page. "We've got the chopper in for service on Monday. We can leave it here at the end of today." He nodded towards the jet. "The Feds are excited. Like ants when you stir them up."

"You heard what's going on?"

"I was talking to their pilot in maybe two minutes." Josef laughed. "We gossip, then compare benefits. Annie, *he* gets a pension!"

Annie looked at him fondly. "And you get home cooking every night. Where's that guy going to be sleeping? A cot in a hanger? Anyway, Manyhorse wants a ride up to where those kids disappeared. We tanked up?"

He nodded, glanced quickly at Page. "What about that other thing?"

"Did you double-check it?"

"The usual sources. I've even got the waypoints set in the nav. Can't guarantee the exact spot . . ."

"Am I missing something?" Even as Page spoke, his eyes were elsewhere. The FBI dude was looking over at Annie's little group. He felt a small tingle of apprehension down his neck, like the world was turning on a pivot, going to a new place. It got worse when the Sheriff pointed at Page. The FBI man took a long look before glancing away, speaking a few more words.

Page casually leaned on the hood of the Dodge, watching the Sheriff and the Fed out of the corner of his eye. After another short conversation, the agent went back up into the plane. By the time Sheriff Manyhorse was back, the biz jet was already starting to spool up. "So, can I get a ride?" he asked.

"Ah, sure. We'll drop you off, do our thing, then come back for you around sunset." Annie nodded to

Josef, who went to help button up the Hughes. Page and the Sheriff stood for a moment, both lost in thought. "Oh yeah," Ben said. "Agent White said hello."

"White?"

Manyhorse laughed. "Names are weird, aren't they. I got my family name because my grandfather stole horses — many horses — from the Utes. Agent White is, let's be honest, a very dark man. And when I said do you know Page over there — you both being Feds — he just looked blank. But when I said Deschamps, he kind of mulled it over, then said, 'Yeah, I know a Deschamps.'"

Page nodded, the icy tentacles spreading. "I'm surprised he didn't come over."

"They have to get over to the airport where they found the Saab. But he said he'd talk to you later. There was something he wanted to ask you."

*****

The 500C seemed to struggle as they clawed for altitude, something familiar to Page as the rotors bit into thinner and thinner air, the washed-out blue of the sky stretching to infinity. The turbine, too, would have less oxygen to burn as it went higher up the mountain range. It gave him some time to take in the rapidly approaching snowline, the sharply etched line of peaks. There wasn't a cloud in the sky; it looked cold and empty out there. But gorgeous. This truly was God's country.

He wondered where the two bodies were. The abandoned car gave him a bad feeling. He was, in general, a pessimist when it came to mankind and its faults. "How long was the Saab at the airport?" he asked Manyhorse, keying his mic.

"We don't know yet. They'll do a full-court press on the forensics."

"Does the airport parking lot have cameras?"

"Cameras are everywhere, my friend."

Page snorted derisively. "In the name of terrorism."

"The feebs will check it all out," Ben said without enthusiasm.

They rode the rest of the way in peaceable silence. Page came out of his reverie as they flared in for a landing. Annie turned around in the front seat, spoke through her set. "Sheriff, do you mind if we lift right out of here?"

Ben started to answer, but Page cut him off. "I'd like to look around for just a second."

"I have to keep the turbine spinning; this altitude makes a restart harder," Josef told them. Page thought the Israeli sounded impatient, almost rude. The Sheriff and Deschamps got out of the back. They were on the only level ground around, right at the gate that guarded the entrance to the Stanford Biological Research Area. As the Hughes whistled in the background, the two lawmen went over to inspect the gate. "This is the flag?" Page asked. It was still up.

"They drop it back down when they leave."

"So, the flag up—that indicates they never left?"

"That's my guess."

"So they're still up here?"

"I'm pretty damn sure of that."

"But you searched?"

"We had up to twenty people on scene at one time. Forest service, local cops, off-duty firefighters, civilians on horseback. Everyone but the Girl Scouts."

"Big country."

"Goes for miles."

"You searched when there was more snow on the ground, I guess." Page indicated the drifts of snow that were starting to melt after the days of sunshine.

"It snowed twice, so we don't know if we missed anything. Since we never saw any tire tracks from their car, we probably missed some sign. That's what we are going to do now. Look for tracks in the soil. Could use your help."

"You got it." Page looked towards the chopper. "But not right now. Apparently, I have someplace to go. Later."

"Yeah, later." Manyhorse produced a key, unlocked the gate. As the chopper lifted away, Page saw him trudging uphill. The ground looked completely unmarked by tires. "Josef, can we go up the trail a ways?" There was no reply, but they followed the twin ruts at a low hover, no more than ten feet above the ground. He was a very smooth pilot, Page realized, as he studied the terrain.

But he didn't see anything. Not then.

CHAPTER TWELVE

Red had the Japs wrangled by 6 a.m. Or were they dinks? At this point in his career he didn't care who the fuck they were; the foreman had had them up to his eyeballs. They wanted everything "just so," as if hunting were some sort of a science. The food they ate—Christ on a crutch. And they dressed up like little kids playing Big Game Hunter. Like any fifty-year-old Asian was going to look good in woodland camo.

But he made nice anyway, listened to their gripes about how tall the horses were, like the round-eyes had picked them to make every slope look smaller. Hell, they *were* smaller. Maybe next year Spatz would get in some Shetland ponies for the next big elk hunt.

Red had started out in life on a ranch; it was the one thing he knew inside out. Well, that and maybe doin' time, first in Juvie, later up at State. Spatz had found him there, working as a trustee at the Montana State correctional facility, which trained some of the less violent types in animal husbandry or ranchland management. It had been better—way better—than rotting in a cell with the spics and the niggers. Not to mention the fact that his basically bad temper had, more than once, gotten him shanked. Or how he got his scar and his nickname: his face pushed into a hot waffle iron.

He had never been a joiner, but when you were whiter than white, you either went with the Brotherhood or bent over for some older, bigger, nastier guy. So, for a while he was part of The Race, won his Iron Cross, wore swastika inks on his biceps.

The hothouse atmosphere of the pen, along with his winning personality, would have seen him dead at twenty-five, but he had some skill with horses, and some liberal fairy got him a spot on the nearby Montana State Penal Ranch. He was a natural with animals—they didn't lip back, and without a soul brother around every corner, he was able to relax enough to seem human when the review boards came to the ranch. And while he was never going to be college material, he knew which side was buttered, and could talk the talk just enough to avoid taking the gray bus back to the slammer. Then Spatz showed up.

He had been a quiet dude, a physically big man even ten years ago, with a barrel of a body, thick hands. Like a Viking with that beard—darker then—and those hooded eyes. Spatz must have seen that Red was a marginal bet—he seemed to read right between the con's eyes, boring into his brain. But Spatz played the game, said the right words to the parole board, even posted a bond. The whole shooting match. Three weeks later they were driving out the gates, everything he had in the world thrown in the back of a big Ford F-350. Red still remembered that it had had tooled leather inside. The upholstery smelled like money after the stink of the joint.

They'd pulled over in the middle of North Bumfuck, Montana, and Spatz had taken off his jacket, tossed his cowboy hat on the hood, and given a very short indoctrination speech. He'd said he knew Red's story inside out. The drunk dad, the drunker mom, the petty crimes, the bigger crime. "And I just want you to know, Red, that I don't care about any of that. You're a product of your environment."

"That's right, Mr. Spatz. But I can change—"

Spatz had held a hand up. "I don't want you to change."

Red had shrugged. "OK. I can also do that."

Spatz had held his hand out, reaching for a handshake. Red had gripped the hand, and found himself down in the dust, with his elbow doing a 180. Spatz then used it to lever Red's face down into the prairie. "No, Red. Don't change. Except for one thing. There is only one top dog in any pack. I think, way down deep, you know that. Horses, dogs, wolves. Elk, ducks, men. Even chickens have a pecking order. Am I right?"

It had been hard to talk, facedown next to a cow pie, but Red had finally nodded. When Spatz let him up, he had said the one thing Red still remembered to this day. "Red, even you don't know how dangerous you are. I will never touch you again. I will never humiliate you in front of anyone. Never. We will complement each other." He had let go, even helped Red to his feet. The pain had brought tears to Red's eyes; he'd thought about sucker punching back, just to make the point. But Spatz had slapped him on the shoulder. "We all have to bend to someone, or some thing."

"Who was that? For you, I mean."

"Haven't met him yet. Maybe God." Then Spatz really blew Red's mind when he gave him a longish kiss on the lips. "Just like Judas and Jesus," Spatz had said, holding Red's face in both hands.

Red knew a gay kiss when he met it; he'd been in lock-up with guys who were never going to get near a woman again. So he knew gay, and this wasn't it. He finally broke free and managed to say, "Which one are you?" Spatz had laughed and broke the tension, that day long ago. "I'll keep you guessing, Red."

Ever since then, it had worked out. Although on mornings like this, he had to wonder. Red had a crew that he ruled, the way Spatz ruled him. They weren't the brightest tools in his saddlebags, but at least they looked the part. Slim—which meant he was skinny enough—and Brister the guy with bad teeth, stained by chaw. Brister was kind of a nothing, and didn't really hang with Red and his crew. Which included Chester, a high-cheek boned Indian with bandy legs, the result of a one-night stand between some cowboy and an Oglalla Sioux. He was quiet, was their tracker. Considering he never washed, it was amazing how he could sense game. Red had tried calling him Moe, but his three stooges didn't get the reference.

Spatz let them play their parts, to the obvious

delight of the corporate types they dragged around: big spenders from Asia, a few Europeans, the rest Americanos. They were supposed to be colorful but polite, like movie cowboys. There were other guys on the ranch, but Slim and Chester, along with Red, were the A-team. The hunters.

Spatz wasn't one to loosen up, but one night, playing cards with a few beers in him, he had told his crew that they were in the fantasy business. The Marlboro Man wasn't available, so they would have to do. If they seemed a little cartoony, like fake cowpunchers, that was OK. More than OK—it was expected. After all, he had pointed out, they could drive out in a bunch of Jeeps and nail the elk or the bighorn with a Dragonov sniper rifle at a thousand yards. But their clients came for an experience, which meant they expected certain things, like a silent half-breed, a guy with a wad of chaw in his cheek, a ramrod with a lethally ugly face splattered with that reddish grid. It was all good. It was why he had picked them.

And once they got out in the wilderness, they had to deliver, bag that mountain lion, or even better a bear. Yeah, a grizz for the office back home. If the bear was protected, then it was just too fuckin' bad. True, they would run out of bears after a while, but at thirty grand a pop, the money was real, real good.

But first, they had to get to the animals. This morning had been the usual cluster fuck, but finally they hit the trail. It was an all-Asian party, with the Mr. Big of the company riding next to Spatz. The second stringers talked among themselves in some idiotic language as they adjusted to the saddles. Red knew from experience that by the end of the day, their butts would be pure volcano. He also noticed that they had brought some guy, a videographer, to record the epic adventure. Jesus.

They jingle-jangled along for a few hours, getting up into the BLM lands that went all the way up the far range. Spatz had a valley picked out that would give them some clear sightlines down into the grazing areas of the meadows. The elk were heading up from the lowlands, seeking their ancestral mating grounds in the ridges. Spatz knew this, but so did the predators. At the bottom of the killing pyramid would be the varmints, like coyotes and beaver. Worth a plinking shot or two. Target practice. Next up, any wolves that wandered by. An easy kill. Basically, they were too dumb to avoid humans; it was like they had some dog in them.

Much more of a challenge would be the big cats, and the bears also were pretty damned cautious. Elk were wary but pretty easy to locate, especially since they were now bugling their gonads off. Dalls Sheep, now there was the cream of the crop: wily, sure-footed, way the hell up in the mountains, hanging off ridges no man could ever hope to climb, especially packing a rifle. That was a premium trophy. Yeah, it was a regular supermarket of wildlife up these slopes, and they were there to bag their limit. And their limit was all they could kill.

Chester sat up in his saddle, where he had looked

like he was asleep. He twisted around, looked behind them. It was a full half-minute before Red could pick it up, a distant buzz, like an angry bee coming up behind them. He just had time to rein his horse around before the buzz went up in volume, the sun glinting off the curved Perspex of a helicopter. Even as it came at them, even before he saw who was in the cockpit, he knew it was the Wolf Bitch and her Jewboy pilot. The Hughes, at well over a hundred knots, literally blew their hats off as it passed less than ten feet over their heads. The Asians bailed as their horses reared; Slim nearly lost an arm as the pack mule he was leading took off in a bucking gallop. The chopper arced up, did the helicopter equivalent of a wingover, and made a second pass. Annie was clearly visible in the copilot's seat. She had a big grin on her face as she flipped them off.

Red tried to get his gun out of its scabbard, but the chopper swooped around, burning off speed for altitude as it headed up the slopes to chase away any game. They were clearly going to try to ruin the whole day for the party.

Cursing, Red dismounted to help the gook CEO off his ass; he hadn't realized a Chink's face could turn red. Spatz, a pretty good horseman, had kept his seat. He rode over to Red and leaned down. He looked ready to explode.

"Boss, we need to do something about those crazies." Red pointed at the distant chopper.

Spatz gave Red a steady look. "I've been on it, asshole. That day is coming. Comprende?" Red slowly nodded that he did. But he didn't. It showed on his face. Spatz gritted out every word, "When you want to trap a wolf bitch, what's the easiest way to do it?"

"Set a trap. Maybe poison—cyanide cartridge."

"That takes patience. A trap, not an assassination." I want her dangling on a hook. It takes longer than dying, Red." Spatz looked Red in the eye, that hooded look again, the one that said he was dead serious. Red wondered if he was talking about something harder, more permanent. Like, between the lines. Red kind of hoped he was. It would make some things in Red's recent past a little easier, for sure.

"So what makes a trap work?" Spatz asked.

"Bait. You bait the trap." Spatz waited for more. "It's gotta be bait she wants. But . . . what would make her put her neck in the noose?"

"Just look around you, knucklehead." The foreman took in the horses and mules bucking, saddles and packs in disarray. Brister and Slim dusting off the dude hunters. Chester sitting stone-faced, like some dime-store Indian. "All I see is us."

"Exactly." Spatz grinned, tight-lipped, full of a repressed rage that Red could only guess came from Spatz's past. Hatred for Annie, for sure. "Maybe we'll be the bait."

"But how do we get to her, Boss? She never comes within gun range. She's got that fuckin' chopper. We couldn't do it on her ranch."

"No shit." Spatz's tone was withering.

"There can't be no witnesses."

"I'm aware of that. There are wheels within wheels, Red." Spatz whipped his horse around and went to placate the clients. Red stood for a moment, contemplating his boss. The guy was no pussy, for damned sure. Red would have to tell him the whole story some day, let the boss know he was no pussy either when it came to violence. But not today.

CHAPTER THIRTEEN

Special Agent Colby White was not used to the cold that had come in with the setting sun. D.C. at this time of year would be well into cherry blossom season. Here in Boise, specifically the long-term parking lot for the airport, it was just above freezing. The forensics team he had brought in on the jet had the area cordoned off and had set up lights for the rest of the night's work. The surrounding pavement had been eyeballed, although the odds of finding something after this much time was close to zero. Those were the kind of odds White had played and won, once or twice in his career. As northwest regional director he was not, perhaps, the ultimate FBI success story—but he was not an ultimate careerist, either. He likened his life to that of a foot soldier who had won a few battlefield promotions. Maybe an NCO-type who made it to the middle officer ranks.

Man, it was getting cold out here. He stamped his feet, pulled his jacket up around his neck. The scene he was looking at was familiar: an empty car in a quiet parking lot. Unlocking the wagon had been a doddle. Most of the interior had been gone over, hundreds of glassine bags carefully filled with fibers, dirt, hair, skin particles, food crumbs. If someone had sneezed on the steering wheel, they would find the sputum. That something would pan out seemed unlikely. But then again, the odds were not infinitely against a CSI moment.

Some cop show kind of a breakthrough would be welcome. The missing grads case had peaked well up the media charts as recently as ten days ago, with its great mystery of a couple who were young, smart, and in love—and missing.

All along, the conundrum had been that these kids were not flakes. Certainly not the kind to neglect calling home. The girl had been from a sheltered home. And the guy seemed capable enough. Not the types to be fifteen minutes late for dinner with the parents, let alone disappear for so long. Why would they? No motive that he could see.

Whoever had parked the Saab at the Boise airport, the nearest one with a good choice of airlines, had probably been watching too much CBS themselves. In fact it struck him as a real possibilty that the someone in question wanted to put down a false trail. One meant to hide the true facts. To White, this particular setup was borderline amateur, virtually a statement that crime had been done. And that crime, in his book, would be murder. For reasons as yet unknown. He couldn't see any motive for crime in the context of what the grad students had been doing. Researching snails up on an empty ridge just didn't sound like a reason for someone to waste them. But then, a lot of creeps didn't need a reason.

He really didn't have that much to do here at the moment. Stuffing glassine envelopes with smutz from under a car seat wasn't his thing. Any breakthroughs that came from this scene would come out of the lab work the FBI did so well. Left with little to do, he tried to look on-the-ball as he sipped a coffee, leaning on the warm hood of an idling Boise squad car. He was the big honcho, dark and menacing. He'd polished his managerial arts under some master's level hard-asses. But he found himself identifying with the grunts wielding the midget vacuum cleaners, adjusting klieg lights, filling up the plastic sample cases. He even had one kid making a map of any objects found within a ten-foot radius of the Saab. By hand! White felt a little like an off-color Simon Legree. The shoe was truly on the other foot when the black guy was cracking the whip.

Ah, what the hell. He went around the side of the police cruiser, signaled the cop inside to zip down his window. Agent White bent low, felt the warm air gust out of the cabin. "Can I get some food out here for the troops?"

*****

Colby got back to Stanley in the very early morning hours. He ferried his crew over to the Sunset Motel in the Tahoes the Sheriff had provided, saw that two FBI vans, neither with 4WD, had been delivered. He was too tired to horse around with them, although the keys had been left with the night clerk. He had a list of rooms they had been assigned. He was glad to see they had put him on the end as he had requested, with an empty room next to him. He had sleep apnea, and the snoring would wake the dead. And it wasn't exactly dignified.

He got the room the way he liked it, the wall unit running to give him some background noise. One dim light over the desk. Out of habit he flipped on CNN while he got out of his shoulder rig, kicked off his shoes. Soledad O'Brian, looking as foxy Hispanic as ever, was running down some political developments as a huge impact launched him face-first into the side wall. In a fraction of a second, someone fairly tall— probably a man—had his arm up and back as he put the grind on Agent White's face. The son of a bitch had been lurking in the bathroom. Maybe it was a thief. Colby used the standard moves to break the hold, tried to rake the guy in the shins with his heel, but he didn't have his goddamned shoes on.

The guy returned the favor by stomping White's toes, then twisted him onto the bed facedown, jamming a bony knee in the small of White's back. The FBI agent went slack, hoping to loosen the hold for a second, before reversing direction and arching up. He thought his spine would explode in crunchy white fragments, the pain was so bad. And he couldn't get any air into his lungs; the first impact had knocked most of it out. The chokehold around his neck didn't help, either. Man, he was boned.

White relaxed, tacitly giving in for the moment. His

assailant got the message, allowed some air to expand the FBI man's rib cage. Every muscle in his back was on fire. Whoever the hell this was, he knew how to take somebody down.

"I hear you wanted to see me."

Special Agent White did not recognize the voice. What worried him more was that he felt his handcuffs slide out of his belt holster, felt them click around one wrist, then the other. Royally boned.

The guy flipped him over, reached behind to the desk, palmed White's service piece. White groaned. "You're not even carrying. I feel like a dick."

His tormentor sat on the desk after taking off the safety. It was the guy calling himself Page Deschamps. "Who am I?" he asked White.

"Fuck if I know."

"Not Page Deschamps?"

White sat up on the bed, slid over towards the pillow end, propped himself up. "You know what an octoroon is?"

"A cookie? White in the middle?"

Agent White couldn't tell if the guy was kidding. "In New Orleans, everybody humped everybody. White on black, black on white. Very French, back in the day—like the 1800s. They devised a system of castes, according to your racial mix. A quadroon was one-quarter black, or was it white?"

"Is there a joke here, Mister White?"

"Yeah, my name. What can I say? Anyway, an octoroon is one-eighth dark. Page Deschamps was a semi-black man. You're a sorry-assed redneck."

"I always thought he looked like a Hawaiian—frizzy hair, always tanned."

"Was?"

"Well, I'm sure not Deschamps. How did you know him?"

"I run into most of the Federal types who work the northwest—met him at a law enforcement seminar in Seattle. They called him The Preacher, I think. He gave the keynote address."

"I think I've heard it."

"Where—the State Pen?"

"That's not nice."

"I'm not feeling nice. Where is he?"

"Dead."

"You do him?"

"Is that the sort of thing you ask a guy with a gun?"

"What have I got to lose?"

"Some sleep." Page let the Glock droop down a few inches. "I'll tell you the story."

"Undo the cuffs first."

"Story first." Page was no spellbinder. His narrative came out flat, with little intonation, at least at the start. He talked about his past in about two sentences: a wild young man with one skill, shooting. Thrown out of the Marines as a discipline problem. How a weekend poacher in the Michigan U. P. became a full-time killer of wildlife. Some of it even legal. Bagging wolves for bounty had gotten him the tag line of the Wolf Hunter. But there was more money in illegal game, and definitely more of a thrill.

"Stickin' it to the man." White drily observed. The Wolf Hunter ignored the jibe; his eyes were far away as his voice finally got some emotion. "I was on the wrong track, like a wild animal that kills when it doesn't need to. Page tracked me down in Alaska, where I was working for a dude named Johansen. Page took me like *I* was big game. I was looking at time in the joint. But he was so . . . I don't know. Kind. Like he knew where I came from. Understood my past."

He stopped for a moment, letting images go through his mind. "He made me see the light. I don't know how. I was a hard case."

"No shit. So how did he die?"

"I was working with Page by then. He'd turned me around, sitting up there all those winter nights. He sent me on ahead to set up Johansen. The Swede got on to me, and we had it out in the snow. One of those him-or-me deals. I had to drop him. Page showed up later. We were snowed in for almost two weeks; we talked about everything. About what was going on in this valley. I offered to help here in Montana."

"That was never going to happen."

"Yeah, I blew that when I killed Johansen. Anyway, we left when the weather broke. I was going to turn myself in. Then Deschamps went in the river, breaking trail over the ice."

"Where?"

"The Moose River. He slid under the edge." There was a long beat. "I couldn't get him out; his pack came off in my hands. I could see him down there, like looking down through a sheet of glass." Page stared off into the distance, eyes far outside the room, seeing something he didn't like. Maybe himself, White hoped.

White also thought there was a ring of truth to the story. Not that anyone would ever find much evidence. Might never even find a body. "Let's say your story is true. Why didn't you just head back to the Lower 48 and get back to doing what you apparently do so well?"

The Wolf Hunter gave a little snort of derision. "He was a *really* good preacher. I bought into the whole thing. I had his pack. And I had his badge, his gun, some letters that had been sent to Fish and Game by Annie Mann. AKA the Wolf Lady."

"Wolf Lady?"

"Yeah. You saw her at the airport next to me and the Sheriff. She wrote to the Feds about big-time poaching in Stanley Valley. Even got a follow-up letter out of Sheriff Manyhorse. "

"So what was the plan—impersonate a federal officer, be the big hero? Are you a lawman wannabee? A groupie? That's insane."

"I . . . " He thought about it. "I wanted to make up for my past in some small way. Go undercover or something. Carry on the work that Page was doing. Set a poacher to catch a poacher was Page's motto. Who knows the criminal mind better that the criminal?"

"Unless he's out of his own mind."

"Yeah." He sounded wistful. "Then *you* show up. The F-B-I. I could see you somehow had me made."

"So you assault a federal officer."

"You going to hold that little thing against me?"

"Undo my bracelet and find out."

"Fair enough." The Wolf Hunter went over to the agent, got the keys out of the holster, undid his hands. But he kept the gun in his hand.

"So what do I call you?" White asked with a sneer.

"Let's stick with Page for now."

"I'll not bring dishonor on a good man's name."

"Just while I'm undercover."

"That won't be long, then."

The Wolf Hunter's reply surprised him. "Good."

"What do you mean, good?"

"Blow my cover for me—that's why I came here."

"Are you shitting me—after all that touchy-feely about changing your ways?"

"I have. But Spatz doesn't have to know that."

"Spatz. Who is he?"

"He's the guy this is all about. Here's the letters Page got." He pulled a sheaf of folded papers out of his down vest's inside pocket. White scanned them for a minute.

"He sounds like a bad actor."

"Page wanted to get someone into his operation."

"I'm confused. You're in his avowed enemy's camp—this Annie person."

"I'll tell Spatz that—"

White held up a hand. "I am beyond tired. And you've got my head whirling with your Junior G-Man crap. Let me sleep on this. We're done."

Page nodded, put the Glock on the table by the door, and left. White started for the door, grabbing his piece, but something held him back. Maybe it was just fatigue.

White went to the bathroom, pleased he didn't urinate blood. He took three ibuprofen, ate half of a Clif bar, shucked out of his clothes, and rolled under the sheets. He lay for a moment, felt the fatigue wash over him as his back unknotted from its recent beating.

This guy was something else. The crook with the social conscience. Wait until he told the guys back at the office. Or was the man doing business as Page Deschamps just another head case? In White's experience, few if any full-grown criminals suddenly developed a moral compass. At least he could check up on him.

He groaned. If he had bothered to get the jerk's true name. But big deal: his prints were now all over White's firearm. He might as well have dropped off his CV. Maybe the detective was slipping, but only a little, he thought. Then he was asleep.

CHAPTER FOURTEEN

In the next few days a high-pressure ridge brought in some unseasonably warm weather. The sun acquired real strength, slanting under a canopy of quaking aspens up on a high ridgeline. The rays of light seemed to glint off the pure white snow that covered the round slope at the foot of the stand of trees.

As the snow melted, a shape emerged from under the hard icy crust. Trickles of water flowed from the snowpack, running down to moisten the thick mulch that had been exposed the previous day.

Set into the mulch, and of much the same color, was a smooth mahogany curve, a woman's calf poking out of the soil and snow. It curved down to a foot, still encased in a hiking boot. The skin was dark, the flesh crystalized from freezing. Above the curve of the calf, the thigh swelled into the half exposed buttock. Taut, ice-hard, disappearing into the drift of soil, the brown curve hinted at some shape yet to be revealed.

*****

Annie's day started out with some ambiguity. She was puzzled because Page had not come "home." But then, she asked herself, what *was* his home? She didn't even know if he had one. Maybe a tarpaper shack down in Louisiana, with some pretty mama waiting for him. Funny how she had never asked. It was a mystery she wasn't going to solve until she saw him again. He was a big boy, he didn't have to say where he went. It would have been nice, though . . .

Work kept her busy throughout the day. She had a teleconference with an actor who had hit forty and wanted to retool his image. She thought about telling him to do what DiCaprio had done, but this guy was a *star;* it was too late to become an actor. They both agreed on that—at least he knew his limits. She told him some things they might discuss, arranged for a face-to-face later in the week. She'd have to fly to SoCal for that one. She made a note to have Josef get the Citation ready.

The afternoon passed with yet another call, this time a teleconference with an East Coast start-up. Their worries, not all that different from an actor on the cusp, was about the image they wanted to project on the roll-up to their IPO. As the CEO put it, "We're low-hanging fruit, we want to be plucked." They wanted new branding and a full-court media blitz. Action words. The fruit thing was inelegant but apt; she saw clumps of bananas, a passing gorilla wearing a Google t-shirt. She shot them a fees schedule, and they didn't flinch. So that would entail yet another flight. She would have to give herself enough time to come up with some better word pictures.

The late afternoon weather was deliciously sunny,

almost balmy, by Montana standards. She felt like saddling up one of the horses and going for a ride up the far side of the ranch. But she didn't like riding by herself. She wandered out to the barn, spent a few minutes messing with riding tack, giving her mare a rubdown. She finally tossed the curry comb aside, went upstairs, tapped on Josef's door. He answered with a flying magazine in his hand. "Hey, Annie," he smiled.

"We need to go to LA later this week."

"LAX?"

She thought for a moment. "Burbank would be better. ETA about 1630."

"I'll file a flight plan. Wheels up around noon?"

"I'll firm up that time tomorrow. Seen Page this morning?"

"Not yet. You need him?"

"Um, not really. I was looking for someone to go riding with me." She gave him a look.

"Not this boychik. I hate horses. They hate me."

"You're just afraid of heights. Well. If Page shows up . . ."

"I heard him kicking around this morning. He drove out in the Dodge right about sunrise."

"Could you, um, check his room? I'm kind of puzzled as to where he went." He looked at her with a wry smile, led her down to Page's door. He went in for a moment, came back out. "It's safe," he chuckled.

"He still sleeps on the floor?" she asked after she looked in.

"I guess he's the rugged type."

Annie went to check out the closet, which was empty except for a few pillows on the upper shelf. "He keeps his rifle in here, doesn't he?"

Josef shrugged his shoulders. "Maybe he sleeps with it," he laughed.

Annie went back out in the hall, latched the door shut. "Why would he take his gun? It's not hunting season. And he doesn't have a license, anyway."

"Come on, Annie. You think that would stop him?"

*****

Later that afternoon, her puzzlement turned to real concern. She was back in her office when a new hire—Lori, she thought—knocked on the doorjamb. She stuck her head through, as though peering into the lion's den. "Hi, Annie." She cleared her throat. "This is weird, but when we went to feed the wolves, well . . . one was missing."

Annie put down her work; it could be serious if one of them got out among the human visitors. Especially with so many kids visiting each day. "You searched back in the dens?"

"Uh huh. We got most of the staff to do a sweep. He's not inside the fence. And the fence is intact."

"Which wolf?"

"The white one."

Annie thought. "He never goes in the caves. Just stares out through the fence. You checked with the vets?"

"They aren't even examining him anymore—he's just about ready for release. And they didn't send him to the vet in town, either." She paused for a moment. "One of the portable cages is gone, though."

Annie's stomach did a little back-flip. Page was gone, off with the Power Wagon. His rifle, his only real possession, was also gone. And so was the cage and the White Wolf. It was a strange mix of coincidences. "OK. Thanks, uh, Lori. I'll look into it."

After the young woman left, Annie sat back, trying to look at this from Page's point of view. This was something she was supposed to be good at, decoding the other guy's POV, to find the key word, the image, the angle. Page had the Power Wagon, and there was, she was pretty damned sure, a cage in back. And in that cage there most likely was a wolf, a feral one. Page, as far as she knew, didn't even know how to get old lobo out of the wolf run. Wolf and cage would weigh in around 300 pounds. He was a wiry cuss, but that seemed like a lot of weight to heft up onto the tall Dodge's tailgate.

You could bet he was operating on his own; it just fit in with her image of him. But then, that image could be in error. An error of the heart.

*****

Page dropped an elk, a three year old, around dusk. The Power Wagon, with the White Wolf in back, was just on the other side of a nearby rise. This was good wolf country, up above the ranchlands down in the valley. It was crisscrossed with elk runs, dotted with clumps of cover, some standing water and vast grazing areas for the wolves' prey.

He cut off a haunch, about all he could carry. The Dodge was out of sight—it would have spooked even a young elk. He also didn't want the White Wolf to hear the rifle at close range. There was no need to traumatize him with the same sound that had killed his mate. Page (the name now seemed his own) had not made the wolf's day when he had used one of the wire-looped poles to wrestle the big male into the cage.

He schlepped the meat back to the Dodge, threw it in the back. The wolf looked at it with no particular interest. "You hungry, boy?" he asked the wolf, then realized he was talking to it like he would a dog. It lay in the cage, a pose Page called the "resting alert" position. Like he was waiting to see how things worked out.

Page got in the cab, started the Power Wagon. He went down into a little hollow, the hard old tires slipping in the dew that was settling in. He set up a quick camp, got a fire going. He cut a few slices off the haunch, set them on sticks to grill. He let the quiet night sounds settle in, mostly the soughing of the wind through the trees and grasslands. The wind had carried away the stink of his exhaust, and the world was the way it had been for eons.

Satisfied that the wolf had had a chance to smell the kill over the rise, he opened the wire bales of the cage's gate. The wolf did not hesitate—he bolted out, leapt off the back of the truck, hit the ground running. The wolf went out about twenty yards, then turned to look at the man. They held each other's gaze for a long moment. Page wondered what the big dude was thinking; it looked like it was sizing him up. Or reassessing.

Then it was gone, loping towards a tree-fall and on out of sight. But he could still sense it out there. It felt good, more than he had expected, to release an animal from that deadliest, most killing of all prisons: boredom. The wolf would die out here, and maybe soon. But it would die free.

Maybe he, the Wolf Hunter, had paid one small installment on the debt he owed the planet. One he could never fulfill. But he would try.

He felt a little freer himself as he returned to camp, built up the cook fire. He had a few items liberated from the barn, including a speckled enamel coffeepot he put right in the coals. Yolanda had given him some bacon from the kitchen, a few eggs, a small bag of coffee. That would be his breakfast. He pulled the wolf cage out of the truck, folded it up. He spread out some horse-smelling blankets on the old oak bed of the Power Wagon.

After dinner, just as he wrapped himself in his blankets, he heard a wolf howl. The Alpha Male had returned to the elk carcass. The call said, "Here's food." It was a call to the old pack and to the old ways.

CHAPTER FIFTEEN

Sheriff Manyhorse arrived in town early the next morning, full of determination. Determined that his people would look good. Or as good as they could, considering the personnel he had to work with. He had called them in for an early walk-through before the FBI showed up. And he had gotten up even earlier to get in the office and collect his own thoughts.

He parked his county Impala in the rear of the courthouse, got his briefcase out of the back seat, along with his Smokey the Bear hat. He cast an eye over the sky, which was just going from the golden tones of sunrise into what promised to be a clear, blue day. Winter, barring some crazy snowstorm, was finally DOA. He thought about how nice it would be to get the studded snow tires off his ride. Ben was thoroughly sick of the vibration and noise from those carbide tips. He used his big hoop of keys to let himself in the back of the building, breathed in the usual odors of linoleum and wax, with a not so subtle overlay of stewed coffee. The smell of sweat and failure that came up from the cells below greeted him further down the hall as he neared the stairwell.

A good looking young guy, tapping away at a laptop,

was sitting on a wooden bench outside the twin glass doors to the station proper. He stood up as the Sheriff came up, jiggling his key ring. Tallish, not great posture, with a frizzy head of blonde hair that looked a little like early Art Garfunkel. Like Art, the guy was painfully white, maybe in his late twenties. Ben immediately suspected that he was a reporter. "Sheriff Manyhorse?"

"Guilty." Ben let a touch of coolness into his voice. He had a million things to do, and this wasn't one of them.

The man seemed ill at ease. "John Gruder. Palo Alto Police Department." He stood, folding up his laptop. He held out a hand.

The Sheriff took it, showed his scary teeth for a nanosecond. "Sorry. You looked like a reporter."

"Don't worry—although there's already a shitload out front. Uh, pardon my French." The Sheriff just shrugged. "That's why I had the janitor let me in the back. I showed my badge—no need to come down on him, by the way. I'm not here to step on any toes."

Manyhorse swung the doors back on their latches. He signaled for Gruder to go towards the back. "My office is in the rear." He led the Californian through, tossed his briefcase on a corner of his desk, shucked out of his nylon bomber jacket and hat. He gestured towards the Mr. Coffee. "Fire that up." He turned on some lights, opened the venetian blinds, checked the radiator. He'd been trying to get the super to turn the steam furnace down, but the janitors cranked it up at night. He hated a closed-in room. To dissipate the heat, he switched on the ceiling fan.

He dropped into his chair behind the desk, waved the younger man into a chair. "You are what . . . a Detective?"

Gruder nodded, started to make himself comfortable, but decided to first get out of his coat. "Forensics. Stuffy in here." He collected his thoughts for a moment. "The P.AP.D. is offering my services, but only if you want or need them. As a departmental courtesy."

"Unofficial?"

"It could be that way, if you like." Gruder smiled nervously. Manyhorse noticed he had perfect white teeth. He wondered if Palo Alto had a dental plan. "That is to say, I would stay on *our* books. So there would be no charge to your shop. And as an advisor, I am, or would be, totally under your authority. We just want to see this case resolved. Period."

Manyhorse gave him a stony face. "You're sayin' we can't afford your high falutin' California expertise?"

Gruder looked shocked. "Not at all! I was just, well, these days all our budgets are, I'm sure – "

Ben laughed. "I'm pulling your chain."

Gruder thought about it. "Um . . ."

"Kind of an icebreaker. You know, the Red Man/White Man bonding thing."

Gruder finally relaxed. "I admit, I am a little nervous. I'm just a city slicker."

"So that'll be it for Redskin humor. I don't see how we need a forensics person at this point. No bodies.

Which reminds me—just a moment." The Sheriff took out a pad of post-its, wrote a note, which he stuck on the edge of his desk. "I need to put a call in for the cadaver dogs from the boys at State."

"Actually, it's computer forensics. Electronic media."

"There aren't any computers involved. Are there?"

"Well, the Saab has some computing power, as you and the FBI know."

"We only found out about *that* last night. From them."

"Yeah. Um, sorry about that. We got the message about the Saab from the family, sent it on to the Feebs. We may have failed to cc you. If so, I apologize. It seemed more like a federal thing, since it was in a different state."

"They let us know. It wasn't too embarrassing."

"Again, I apologize. Anyway, we have had access since almost Day One to the missing couples' home computers, as well as the work stations they used on campus. We have gotten permission from both families to hack their passwords. That got us a lot of material out of their laptops, as well as information dumps from their social media sites. Facebook, tweets, some clubs they belonged to. They even had some blogs going. Quite a bit of this product, as well as the bulk of their Stanford work, went into the cloud."

Sheriff Manyhorse digested this for a moment. Like a lot of Native Americans, he liked to think before he spoke; he wasn't worried about a little bit of dead air.

There had been plenty of that around the kitchen table when he had been growing up. It didn't seem to bother Gruder, either. The young man got up to check on the coffee, poured two cups, held up the sugar. Ben shook his head. Gruder also took it straight. He put the bigger mug in front of the lawman, then sat back down.

"We may look a little backwoods, but we've heard about your kind of work. We do an occasional embezzlement case, or a drug bust where some tweaker keeps his records on his iPhone, if you can believe it." Gruder nodded that he could. "But I don't see how that is going to fit in with the investigation."

Doors banged out in the office, several pairs of feet making the old spruce floors creak. Brenda stuck her head in.

"Chief, we're . . . oops, I'm sorry. You've got someone . . ."

Her boss gestured her in. "Brenda, Detective Gruder. Palo Alto P.D. He's a forensics guy. Electronics, computers. Brenda might be a good person to bring you up to speed."

"No problem, Chief." She seemed happy to have a new face on the case. "We've got the desk space. You need a computer, Detective?"

He showed her his laptop. "I'm good. And call me John." He stood. "Anything else, uh, Sheriff Manyhorse?"

"The FBI will be here in a few minutes. Sit in on that. One request." John looked attentive. "I hate leaks. The FBI hates leaks. I'm betting you do too."

"They destroy the very backbone, the fabric, of the law enforcement community."

"Well . . . "

"Just kiddin,' Chief."

The big Indian snorted. "OK, fair's fair. But wait until you meet Special Agent White."

"Ah, surely he will appreciate the white man's humor?"

"Give it a shot." Manyhorse showed his teeth, smiling at some private joke.

After they left the office, Brenda stopped for a moment in the hall. "One thing, detective. When you call him 'Chief,' you'd better mean it."

He looked at her in all seriousness. "I put a capital 'C' on it." He gave her a little wink as they went out into the bullpen, where she gave him a desk. As she went into the conference room to set things up for the morning session with the FBI, she glanced back at their newest member of their crack team. He sure had a cute smile.

*****

Page woke up stiff and a little cold; he smelled a bit like horse. He tossed back the blankets he'd scored the night before from the barn, looked around the bed of the Power Wagon. Yolanda had packed up some basics for him, including a high-end, name-brand frying pan. Lined with some no-stickum stuff. He slipped on his boots, kicked the coals back to life, went to gather some firewood.

He put some oil in the pan, even though it didn't need it, fried up some eggs and slices of bacon off the big slab she had given him. Page tried to toast some bread over the flames, but it was some sort of health-freak nut loaf; it just crumbled and fell into the coals. He put the eggshells in the tin coffee pot, put some water in from a big insulated jug, let it come up to temp. He added some ground coffee, noting the bag said "shade-grown." He didn't know what that meant.

He sipped the brew, catching a few particles between his teeth, just like a real cowboy. It was a beautiful day, full of promise. It felt good to be outdoors, despites the aches and pains he always got in the first hour. He walked around his little campsite, didn't see any wolf tracks. The big whitey was back in *his* world, and would have to make it on his own. Hopefully he hadn't gotten too soft.

Page was not much of a thinker, but he tried it as he packed up the Dodge. Which took about five minutes. He had a nearly full tank of gas, the day was young, and he could be in another state by tonight. That he had about ten bucks didn't bother him. He had his rifle, and he had a strong back. Something would come up. He cranked up the flathead six, settled into the seat. It wasn't really a thought, more an image, that made him sit for a moment: Annie's face.

He hadn't thought about her much when she was in front of him. Sure, he liked the way she looked, especially her eyes. The way they went right into him, he felt like he was really in the room with her. Let's face it, he found himself thinking: she's pretty high-end for you, boy. Way smarter, too. He couldn't understand 50% of what she was up to, especially whatever the hell it was that made her so much money. That was something else that made him uncomfortable, now that he was trying to think things out. There was no way he could ever fit into her scene. And he didn't want to. Well, maybe a little.

He did sort of get the whole wolf thing. Pretty clearly that was an obsession, somehow tied in with Spatz and his crew. Or maybe just Spatz. Page knew hatred when he saw it.

So he could head on down the road, park the pickup at a bus station somewhere, let her know where it was. Take a Greyhound out somewhere new, ditch Page Deschamps forever. He thought about it, realized how the old ranger had hooked him in. He wanted to be Page, the Good Guy. It made up for the Bad Guy he had been. Unbidden, a face flashed in front of his eyes. A big man in a heavy jacket, a rifle falling from his hand. Johansen, surprised as all hell at the blood welling out of a clean throat shot.

And then Deschamps, that honest old coot, holding out his hand from under the ice. Reaching for something? Or handing something off to the ex-con who had become his friend?

"Page" decided that he was going to act like the real one until something made him stop. Deschamps had often talked about a sense of mission, how it gave meaning to life. He would keep that mission going. He seemed to remember that Spatz's ranch was to the southeast. He pointed the nose of the Power Wagon in that direction. Anything that came between him and the enemy's camp, well, he'd drive right over it. He'd keep the mission simple that way. He could do simple.

CHAPTER SIXTEEN

Ben's meeting went well enough. Agent White and his Feds had shown up to give a concise report on what they had found at the Boise airport. Forensics had a couple of things that had been sent back east to the national lab: gravel from the grooves in the tires, fiber samples from both the upholstery and the Saab's cabin air filter. Someone had sneezed on the windshield, so that was being checked for DNA matches in the national databank. A shred of tobacco had been found while swabbing off the dash; it should yield some saliva.

White explained that while this data would prove useful in a prosecution, it wasn't getting them any closer to finding the bodies, let alone any perps that might be involved. The old conference room, which also served for meetings of the city elders, was packed with both local cops and FBI types. Ben had noticed, somewhat sadly, that the two groups didn't seem to mix. Gruder sat off to one side, although Brenda was within whispering range.

White looked over at the Sheriff, turning the meeting over to him. Manyhorse did a quick recap of the search efforts so far. He said that they would continue focusing on the Stanford property, since they had no other leads at this time. With the snowmelt creeping up to higher altitudes, it might be time to sweep the area again. He said that State's dogs were now on call, but cautioned them that the canines were of limited use — they covered ground at a painfully slow rate. The handlers needed some breakthrough to allow them to zero in on a workable location. That would be the task of people on the ground. Which meant they were going to have to search the area yet again. He could sense there was little enthusiasm for this. The FBI crew just looked bored. To pep things up, Ben asked Gruder to speak.

Gruder looked surprised, but he was quick enough to launch right into what he was doing. There was literally an avalanche of electronic data available. Manyhorse noticed that the Feds seemed to perk up as John described a long list of information webs, pipelines, and caches that were available. The guy obviously dug his work.

So far, he said, the search of the two grad students' electronic world hadn't revealed any last-moment calls for help. Whatever had happened, in his opinion, had been sudden. Noticing the stir in the room, he immediately added that this was just his opinion.

"How strong is that opinion?" White asked.

Gruder thought for a moment. "Intuitively?"

White grunted. "If that's all you've got."

"OK. There's no cell phone service up there. If someone did them harm, took their car, they would, in all likelihood, take the batteries out, or destroy them."

"So what about the car? I did some checking and

GM owns—owned—Saab. It would have had OnStar, which GM can track. Right?" Brenda asked.

"Unfortunately, the owners didn't subscribe to the OnStar system. So it effectively disappeared."

"When did they make their last call?" the Sheriff asked.

"About 1400 hours on the 19th. They were about sixty miles from the gate to the Stanford property at that point." He looked at a small flip notebook. "They called off his phone. Just a 'hello mom' call back home to let the folks know they would be out of cell range until that evening. They were lining up a birthday party for her father." The room was silent for a moment. They were all thinking the same thing, Ben sensed. A pretty important event to miss.

"Anything else?" Manyhorse asked.

The room started to rustle as people gathered up their papers and notes. "Well, one thing." Gruder looked lost in thought.

"And that is?" Special Agent White asked. Ben had thought the agent seemed grumpy this morning, and he kept holding his ribs. Like they hurt.

"Well, the camera."

"We don't have any camera," White groused.

"The kids took a lot of gear up there—I checked with Stanford." Gruder pointed out.

"And again, we don't got. Nada."

"Still . . . Lee was a certified camera nut; he posted his work all over the place. Snapfish, Picasa, Photobucket. But I was particularly interested in his

Flickr account. He had over 200 photos. And they were good."

"Gee, that's great." The agent was getting downright rude, steadily rubbing his side.

"And they were geo tagged."

Ben looked puzzled. "What does that mean?"

John explained: "When most cameras takes a photo, data is stored in the picture's file. Embedded. Like the camera model: he had an Olympus OM-D. And the lens used, like an $f85/1.8$. Settings for white balance, color temp, exposure. And the location of the photo, expressed as a GPS coordinate. You click a little tag on the Flickr site and a map—in his case Google Earth— pops up showing where the picture was taken. It allows—"

White cut him off. "I'm sure it's one super camera, detective. But so fucking what. How on God's green earth does this help us?"

"Well, actually it isn't the camera. It's an SD data card called Eye-Fi that slips into the SD slot." Gruder saw White roll his eyes, and hastened on. "You know, the digital memory card. Eye-Fi has a tiny transmitter built in. Uses GPS to locate itself. And it sends the picture up to the cloud. Or to his computer. Maybe even Costco." Someone raised a hand. "We checked them." Gruder added. The hand went down.

"How does it get to the Web?" someone else asked from the County Mountie side of the room.

"It is automatic whenever it gets near a hotspot.

"I'm not following you," the Sheriff said.

"It transmits a signal, but it's not anywhere near strong enough to, in effect, make the equivalent of a phone call. So it piggybacks off something with more strength. Like a cell phone—the user's own cell phone, maybe. But these cards can also interface with the net wherever there is Wi-Fi. Maybe at an internet café."

"So the camera hasn't, what, called home? Yet?"

Gruder thought for a moment. "I would have to look at his photo files again. Also, check with Stanford—the camera may be tied into their web servers."

"So we might get some photos, with GPS info embedded. Right?" Manyhorse looked at Gruder with a brief ray of hope.

"Well, not always." Both lawmen glared at him. "The camera has to be near a hotspot. There are huge areas of this state that have no cell-phone coverage, let alone wireless internet."

"And no downloads have been made? By this super camera?" White's scowl became a more speculative look. He started to ask something, but Gruder held up a finger.

"Just one other thing, Agent White." They both waited for Gruder to drop the other shoe. "The camera has to be turned on when it enters a hotspot." White groaned. Manyhorse went back to looking grim.

"Who would be stupid enough to do that?" White said through gritted teeth.

"Someone not too technical?" Gruder didn't sound very hopeful.

CHAPTER SEVENTEEN

Whenever the mighty Power Wagon came to a stream, it easily forded across. It cut through stands of aspen, green leaves quaking in the light breezes. If Page couldn't go through, he went around, following the contours of the Montana high country. When he saw cattle, he stopped to look at their brands; when he saw a few Rocking R cattle, he figured he had arrived.

There were cattle licks—fresh blocks of salt near watering holes—and windmills pumping into large concrete troughs. It was prime cattle country, just settled enough to make a go of it, the steers and heifers molding the land with their hooves and their appetite for grass.

It was monoculture, where the beef pressed down on the land, made it something living. But also artificial, the hills browsed down, manicured like a park.

When he came to a fence, he drove right through it, a small gesture for Annie and her hippy-dippy earth-hugging friends. No wonder there had been range wars, the farmers and the cattlemen fighting for the right to reshape the land to their own ends.

Page knew where he stood, after a winter with the real Deschamps. He was now on the side of the wolf. Let the predators shape the place, bring back the big wild game onto the wheel of life.

He spotted a ranch down in a sheltered valley, a fairly big outfit: barn, stables, tidy looking corrals. As he went down the hill in compound low, gears snarling under the floorboard, he tried to come up with a story. He was all too aware that he was winging it, taking the headfirst dive where thought followed action. Followed well behind. He had led a life based on rashness, the big gamble, with the inevitable unforeseen consequences. He'd had his share of spills, many a crash and burn as he tried to outfox the law, the community, the damned government. It was time to call up some of his old self— it wasn't that long ago that he had been a bad man. He had the scars to prove it. And the tattoos.

He wheeled up to some cowboys hanging around what looked like their bunkhouse. At first glance, it looked rugged, of a piece with the main house. But he also noticed that the sides, dressed and split logs, were plumbed and level. The windows were vinyl-glazed and double-paned. There were several late-model SUVs parked around, including a Toyota Land Cruiser that Page knew was worth at least $70K.

It struck him as a movie set, but the cowhands were seedy enough. Every one of them had some stigma that was easily read: one looked as dumb as an ox, another probably an alkie. The Indian guy looked pretty threadbare, but maybe slightly sharper than the others.

And Red, as large as life, full of venom just below the surface. He sauntered over, paused to hawk up a wad of phlegm and chaw. "We've got a road right over there,

Slick."

"I was lookin' over the land—might buy me a spread."

"Sure."

"The Boss Man in?"

"I'm the boss around here." Red leaned on the door, about to stick his head in the cabin. Page pushed the door open, rocking Red back on his heels. As he was getting out, he heard barking. A huge dog, well over 100 pounds, came bounding towards the truck. Page stayed in the cab with the door open. Red let it snarl for a few moments before he grabbed it by the collar. "Don't let Friskie fool you—he's a sweetheart," the foreman said.

"Yeah, right." Page got out, keeping one eye on the giant dog as he headed for the house, admiring the fine millwork. It was a quality place, way above any normal rancher's pay grade. Annie's was twice the spread, but this wasn't bad. Maybe Spatz had inherited some bucks. Or maybe something else was in play. He went up the steps, knocked once on a big, green-painted door, let himself in. He thought he might as well brazen it out. He also wanted the dog on the other side of the door.

It was a big central living room, with more large rooms radiating out from the center. It was a little like Annie's hacienda at first glance—apparently rich people's ideas about the rustic life were from the same catalog. But this place was absolutely festooned with the dead. Animal heads up to the rafters, two bearskin rugs, a mounted Big Horn Sheep—very rare—over in one corner. Over the fireplace, big enough for a roast ox, was a wolf pelt. Brindled. He went over to look at it. He heard a gravelly voice behind him. "My bitch wolf."

Deschamps turned around, nodded. Spatz was just coming in the room, a book in his hand. "You make it sound personal." Page said.

"How?" Spatz sounded fairly interested in what Page was saying; he didn't seem to care that some almost total stranger was standing in his living room.

"A wolf is just an animal. No more. You put a lot of hate into those two words."

"Bitch. Wolf. I don't know, they just seem to go together. But, no, what you heard was pride. That bullet went right through the wolf into . . ." Spatz went over to a circle of big, wood framed leather chairs. He sat down, opened a humidor. "Finish my sentence, and I'll give the man a cee-gar."

"I don't smoke."

Spatz didn't bother to look up. "Right into the heart of a real bitch. Red. Drinks. The rye." He lit his cigar with all due ritual. "Bring a glass for yourself," he added to his second-in-command.

Page took a chair, took off his ball cap. Spatz was in blue jeans and a big red down vest, some kind of Eddie Bauer thing. He had reading glasses hanging from a neck cord. The gentleman rancher, Page thought. Red put down a bottle of OK but not great whiskey and three glasses. "I'm not a damned waiter," Red grumbled.

Spatz looked at Page. "Red's my XO. Every organization needs one. Pour for the gentleman."

"Fuck you." Red made a drink for Spatz then

slopped some of the rye into his own glass. Spatz moved slow, uncoiling like a big strong bull of a man, poured a half glass for Page. He lifted his own. "Absent friends."

Page raised his glass, returned the salute, took a sip. "Pretty good."

"I save the best stuff for just a few people. Not for the likes of a Page Deschamps."

"Wouldn't have it any other way."

"Is that irony I detect?"

"I wouldn't know irony if it hit me in the face."

"Damn! I believe it is." He took another puff. He had all the time in the world. "Now and then, some news comes across my desk." Spatz took another sip, mixed it in his mouth with his cigar smoke. "Today's newsflash: Page Deschamps is dead. Any comments?"

Page twisted on one hip, prised out his wallet. He pulled out the badge, tossed it on the table. "I took it off his body." Red picked it up, turned it over, handed it to his boss.

Spatz looked at it for a moment. "Then you are . . ."

Page had kept the wallet open; he tossed an old Illinois driver's license Spatz's way. He read it, curled a lip in disbelief. "Marion?"

"That's how I learned to fight."

Red looked confused. "You a Marshall or not?"

"Deschamps was a ranger—federal wildlife service," Spatz pointed out. Page wondered how he knew that. Inside source?

"So how'd you get his badge?"

"I took it off his corpse, up in the Yukon."

"You put him on ice?" Spatz asked with a slight smile.

"Ha ha." Page took another sip; he had no idea where this was going. He decided to steer it along. He told a short story, one where he had been cornered by Deschamps, killed him out on a frozen river, dropped his corpse through the ice. The rest was true enough: the letter, the tie-in with Annie while he scoped out the scene. He painted himself as a guy trying to make a buck as a hired gun, an expert poacher and tracker. A man with some inside dope to sell. Page got a certain satisfaction from Red's brooding—he thought someone was challenging him for a job. Page wasn't good at reading people, but he sensed some sort of weird connection between Red and his boss. There was subservience, but also a sense that the XO and the CO had some bond he didn't understand.

"So . . . now you're in my house telling me you're a bad old boy named Marion Hargrove, from North Asswipe."

Page tried to keep a poker face. "That FBI guy, White? He knew Page from some conference way back when. I figured my little scam was up, so I high tailed it out of Dodge."

"What a load of crap."

"Here's the letter from Annie to Deschamps." Page pulled the weather-beaten paper out of his shirt pocket, reached it over to Spatz. He read it carefully, handed it on to Red. "Can he read?" Page asked.

"So you're a bad guy out to make a buck—exactly

how?"

"Annie, the Wolf *Lady*, is loaded. Need I say more?"

"Boss, this is total bullshit—he's trying to, what's the word—trap you!"

"The word is entrap. He'd have to be wearing a wire for that to work. And *that* would take a warrant. Which would require probable cause, that you and I, oh my God, are trapping and killing poor helpless critters. And I would have heard about that long, long ago."

"But the FBI is here—"

"For those missing kids. The FBI doesn't give a rat's ass about poaching. So our guy here—well hell, let's stick with Page—he's gone to Plan B. Annie toss you out of the sack, soldier?"

Page was fair at reading animals, not so good with humans. But even a rock head like himself could tell this was a loaded question. There was fire in Spatz's eyes.

"She's cold as ice."

"Not hardly. Oh, no, not hardly." The big man had a faraway look, somewhere back in time, with some image in front of those hard eyes. Some wonderful image that turned to sawdust as he tried to hold onto it.

Page's own love life had been hit or miss, random comings together, most frankly carnal, never very satisfying. But he knew what that look meant: regret. He kept his mouth shut.

"Can you do her some damage? I'll pay for that."

"I thought I might help you in your, uh, hunting business. Which looks like it's going pretty good." Page gestured around at the big house.

"I'd like to kill every one of her damned wolves."

Page looked at him. "That name on the license doesn't mean anything to you."

"It don't mean shit, Sparky." Red swept it off the table. "I can buy one for twenty bucks."

"Well, they used to call me the Wolf Hunter, up north. So yeah, I could help you out."

Spatz looked sharply at him. "I've heard of *that* guy. What kind of rifle you swing with?"

"Nosler. 30 ought 6, double-chambered rounds. I hand roll my own loads. I shoot, I trap, I use gas. I kill them from helicopters, in blinds, with deadfalls, run them down with snowmobiles. Everything but my bare hands."

"You hate wolves?"

"I got bounty money, first for pelts, then heads, now its ears. Ears are smaller, easier to carry. I got a lot of money from Alaska—check it out. Use the girlie-name license."

"You probably shot every sled dog in the state," Red grunted.

"Don't be jealous, Red. So, a guy called The Wolf Hunter. You just might come in handy. I want to hurt Annie any way I can—but don't go trying to read my motives. There's a bigger game here than you pea-brains can ever know. So show me your rifle. I could use some intelligent gun talk."

They got up. Spatz gestured for Page to lead the way. He took one step, saw an eye signal from Spatz to Red. Before he could react a pile driver hit him in the kidney. He felt his short ribs bow in, tried to turn and lash out, fell over one of the chairs. Red landed a flurry of punches on his spine and sides. Page rolled up in a ball, his eyes tearing in pain. "Get his shirt off," Spatz ordered. Red obliged by ripping it open. "Now check the pants—they wear wires everywhere."

Red did a rough but thorough job frisking him. "Clean, Boss." He laughed, the first spiral before he lost control. "I could get a corn cob, do him right."

Spatz went to the door, called out into the yard for some of the boys to come in. They clomped through the room, expertly dragged Page out and down the steps, tossed him in the dust.

Spatz took Red aside. "Red, you have to learn how to use humiliation to your advantage. You cornhole this guy, you create a rage. That rage can come back to haunt you. If the guy is a Fed—which I doubt—you'd really get the government down my neck. Your neck."

Spatz thought for a moment. "And they already are looking at us. You know the Sheriff has a hard-on for me, right? Now he's asked for federal help."

"Well, yeah."

"So that's valuable information. You see that don't you?" Spatz put a hand on the other man's shoulder. "I've been trying to get you to think, Red. You've got that fire in your belly, the fighter's reflex. I like that in you. I really do. You add a little brainwork, well, hell . . . then you're the total package. Be all you can be!" Spatz slapped him lightly on the scarred cheek.

"Gotcha." He looked like he was trying to take it all

in.

"One more thing while I'm in my lecture mode. Is it OK to talk to you this way? I'm not making you feel small?"

"I'm good. I'm good."

"You know when you break a wild bronc, you make him yours. You possess him. You get off on this, I know you do. But it takes so much more than violence. The real threat comes from the power of the will. Your mind over some brute's muscles." He held Red's gaze, his eyes boring in; Red felt the man look into his soul. With force, the force of *his* will. "When you go all red mist on some poor dumb brute, horse or man, all you've got is dog-food. Learn this one thing. It's what turns men into masters."

"I'll sure think about it."

"All right, lesson's over. Now go out and use some of what I just said. Humiliate him, but just a little. Toss him around, but for Christ's sake, no killing. And keep the dog off him."

Red tried to look like he knew what Spatz was saying to him, but he felt kind of uneasy about that last bit about killing. Isn't that what power came down to? Big Dog eats Little Dog. End of story.

He went out onto the gravel drive, where a small circle of cowhands were eyeing a wary Page. Friskie was held back by one of the cowboys, but he was barking again, like he wanted a piece of the action. Red went over to the corral, got a loop of rope off a post. He tossed it to Slim. "Tie this little dogie up, boys." He went into the bunkhouse while they tried to throw Page face down in the dirt. He surprised them by breaking free. He immediately went for the nearest guy, a new hand named Brister, who got a solid right to the face. He went down gushing blood as Page turned towards another hand, caught him with a flurry of blows to the midsection. Page went down under a bull rush from the remaining cowboys. They held him down as Slim trussed his ankles and hands together, kneeling on Page's spine while grinding his face into the gravel.

Slim threw his hands out from the knot with a rodeo whoop, saw that Red had come out of the bunkhouse with a camera. It was a big thing. "Say cheese, asshole," Red said as he fired off a few shots.

Spatz came up to inspect Red's work. He idly took in the camera. "Nice rig. I had you as more of a Kodak man, Red."

"We'll have him on YouTube tonight."

"I like that. Now get this piece of shit out of here." The boys grabbed Page, dragged him over to the Dodge. They started to heave him in.

"Wait. Let's be traditional," Spatz said. He told Red what he wanted. Red went off to get the right stuff. Spatz looked in the bed of the Dodge, slid out the rifle in its scabbard. He unzipped it, pulled the big rifle out. He whistled appreciatively.

"Taking a man's gun—now *that* hurts." He tapped the tailgate of the Dodge with the rifle. "Let some air into this heap when you get on down the road. Off the property."

CHAPTER EIGHTEEN

Annie was in her office, blocking in some ideas on her computer. She had been retained to iron out the details on a new product called, tentatively, The Magic Ball. Job One was to deep six that name—even the designers knew it stank. (At least there weren't two balls in a handy pouch.) The basic concept came from the old style acrylic "magic" 8-Ball that told your fortune. Every kid Annie knew had tried one. About the size of a soft ball, it had a window that allowed you to see some message that swirled up from the dark interior as it was shaken. Most of the answers were middle-of-the-road blather, her favorite being "Signs are good." As helpful a life-message as any.

This iteration had been conceived as a software product, a virtual 8-Ball swirling across the screen, generating an infinite number of context-sensitive responses. Like the holographic ads in *Minority Report*, the program would tap into the user's web profile. Her part of the deal, after coming up with a better name, was to help develop the heuristic model, the decision tree that would tailor responses to match the end-user's biometrics. Just like Google or Amazon, the program would use a trail of "cookies" to create a map of the user's personality traits. A birthdate would yield a zodiacal sign. Sex — or sex interests — would help fill in character. The engineers felt all this wealth of data would make the prognostications "deeply personalized."

It was, on the face of it, a pretty trivial product, but the science behind it had always fascinated her. Semiotics, originally a European spin-off from linguistics, had been her commercial entrée into the world of marketing. Words and images, to her mind, twisted and turned through the ganglia of the brain. True, most cognition seemed to be made up of ready-made concepts, shortcuts that sped up — or short-circuited — the cognitive process. One of her clients had once told her that this was the key to political advertising, and that she had a genius for that work. He'd meant it as a compliment.

The effect with the Magic Ball, it was hoped, would be that the messages would ring true, like mind reading from the best gypsy seer on the planet. Better — and hopefully less venal — than *Futurama's* robot gypsy fortune-teller. The device would probably remain a virtual construct rather than an actual cue ball, although there was a prototype on her desk that had a USB port for downloads.

Ball of Fortune, Ball of the Future, Ball o' Fate. Basically, *Ball* was not going to cut it. She set that aside, went back to general thinking. Most of her problems were solved when she put them in the back of her mind. Unfortunately, her own personal problem, which was what had happened to Page, was already on that back burner.

It was late afternoon, and it had been warm enough that she had been able to keep her office windows swung open. There had been some tour buses in and out, disgorging the usual herds of amped-up kids crunching past on their way to see the wolf pens. The chopper had flown back in from its service, but that brief burst of noise had been hours ago. Now it was a pleasant background drone of bees pollinating, songbirds on the wing. Spring sounds.

The back burner kept coming to a boil—what to do about her own wayward heart. And about Page, and why he had gone. Just like that, with no warning. She picked up the proof-of-concept 8-Ball, its LED readout activated when she gave it a shake. "Relief is in sight," it read.

There was motor noise outside, tires crunching on gravel. It made her think of the Lucinda Williams album, *Tires on a Gravel Road*, and its fine, melancholic tone. Which was how she felt, despite the beautiful day. Car doors slammed. She looked out, saw Sheriff Manyhorse walking towards her front door with a thin black man, early fifties, in a blue nylon windbreaker. The guy from the Learjet. She got up, made it to the vestibule before the chime sounded. Annie opened the big door, nodded at the Sheriff. "Ben."

He stepped in, took off his big hat, smoothed back his dark hair. "Annie." He turned to his companion, who was taking off a baseball cap emblazoned, like his jacket, with "FBI." "This is Special Agent White."

White held out his hand; as she shook it she looked him over. He wasn't very tall, and with his delicate fingers and high cheekbones he looked a little bit like a burned-out Delta bluesman.

"I heard the FBI was in town. The missing kids, right?" Annie guessed.

He nodded. "There have been some developments, Miss Mann." He slurred the words together, like most people did: Mizman.

She smiled. "The Miss Mann thing always sounds doofie—call me Annie. Do you need some time with me?"

"A few minutes," Ben said.

"Then let's go in the kitchen." She guided them through the dining room. White looked around with the frank stare of an appraiser eye-balling a new listing. She offered them a spot in the breakfast nook. As they sat down, Annie went to the fridge, got out three bottles of beer. She popped the tops with an old Budweiser church key left over from her college days. She sat down next to Ben, distributing the sweaty-cold bottles. "To law enforcement, gentlemen." She took a swig, noticed White looking at the bottle. "Amstel. Euroswill." Annie laughed.

White took a swig. "Not bad. Nice finish. Ben?"

"Had worse."

"That's pretty much our comedy routine, um, Annie."

" On TV the cops always turn down the booze."

White smiled. "You must watch a different channel.

Besides, in Europe this is food." He took another swig, leaned back on the little cushion. "We'd like you to tell us about Page Deschamps."

"How did you know?" She seemed genuinely surprised.

"Know what?" White shot back.

"That he bugged out—he's not hurt, is he?" There was real panic in her voice.

White seemed to consider this for a moment. Ben's poker face was as still as the proverbial wooden Indian, she thought. Just a stereotype, but once in a while . . .

"Not as far as we know. We thought he was working here today. You know, undercover and all that." White looked at the Sheriff for a moment. "Could you give us your impressions? What kind of a man is he, that sort of thing."

"Well, you know the type—I mean, he's a lawman, like you." Both men just looked at her. "He's a man of few words. He knows tracking inside out and he seems to have an affinity for our wolves. He sat right out there and communed—there's no other word—with our White Wolf. That's what I meant when I said I was worried about him." Her voice trailed off.

White chewed that over for a moment. "You said 'bugged out.' That implies a hasty exit. Unplanned. Unexpected?"

"Yes. It was. I guess I got used to him working around the place. Honestly, I forgot he was a lawman. Although it was always clear that he was going to try to clean up the poaching in our valley. I have to say that was the one thing he was passionate about. I guess he's gone on to the next stage of the job. Only . . . I don't know why he took the Alpha." White looked puzzled.

"The White Wolf—the Alpha Male—is the one that was shot a few months ago," Ben told the FBI man.

"Gone, how?" White asked her.

"In the Power Wagon. He put the male in a cage and left before anyone was up."

"And you don't know where?"

Annie shook her head. She didn't, for some reason, tell him that the white male was carrying a new transceiver that was actually under the skin. All she had to do was put the gear in the chopper and they could at least find the Alpha Male. Of course, he was no longer an Alpha—the pack would have moved on to new leadership.

White thought for a moment. "Did he talk about his past?"

"As I said, he is a man of few words. I've met a few people who don't say much and are brilliant. I've met more who simply don't have anything to say. When it comes to the outdoors, to animals, tracking, weapons, I think—I know—he's probably a genius. But I never saw him read a book, listen to music. He never watched the tube, even the wildlife channels. He doesn't know a damned thing about modern culture, which is no knock, by the way. He's just a real quiet guy, but coiled up. A man of action, I guess." She took another sip of beer. "Is this any help?"

"We're kind of concerned about where he's gotten

to. Was he armed?"

Annie tensed visibly; these guys were rooting for something. "Enough, guys. What's going on here — you're fishing."

White rubbed his side reflexively. "OK, here's the story, straight up. He is *not* Page Deschamps." Annie looked stunned. She opened her mouth to speak, but nothing came out. White continued, "Sheriff?"

Ben pulled a folded sheet out of his jacket, handed it to her. She read it in disbelief. "Marion? His first name is Marion?" She laughed. It was one of embarrassment. "This is from a prison — he's a criminal? How did you find this out?"

"He and I had a little run-in last night. I managed to get some fingerprints off my spleen." Annie's eyes locked on him. "OK, a door knob. He did time for poaching about fifteen years ago. As far as we know, he paid his debt to society. So no, he's not a criminal."

"Then what the fuck is he?" She threw the paper on the table, got up, and went over to the kitchen's central island, bent over it and put her elbows down on the cold granite. She looked like she wanted to scream.

White came over to stand next to her. "What he is, is a suspect."

"For what?" She thought for a second. "Oh. Impersonating an officer, a game warden. A federal warden. That's bad, I guess."

"Yes, it's bad. The puzzler is where the hell is the real Page Deschamps? This Marion guy told me Page is dead, under the ice up in Alaska. That it was an accident. He got Page's badge—don't ask me how—saw the letter about the poaching. He acted like he was on some mission."

Annie looked completely flummoxed. White went on. "There may be some strange psychological twists here. Page Deschamps was nicknamed the Preacher. Like Jesus, he was a fisher of men; only the biblical one didn't hunt bad guys down with a gun. But when he got his man—and Page was the best man-hunter you ever saw—he set about reforming him. Made them, no, let me rephrase that, he *got* them to look into themselves. He felt poachers were economic victims, mostly good old boys with no education. Maybe crappy parents, a violent childhood. One guy had a speech impediment. Old Page converted a pretty fair number to his ecology thing. Then he sent them back out—set a hunter to catch a hunter."

There was a long silence in the room. Annie finally said, "I think Marion could be one of those guys."

Ben spoke up. "But he took the man's identity. That's not lawful. And we don't know what this Marion's priorities are. So you can see why we need to find him. To clear the whole thing up."

Annie tried to think, but her mind was whirling. "So, Agent White, you knew Deschamps? The real one?"

He nodded. "Mostly saw him now and then at conferences. He would rock the room—Page was that magnetic. Messianic, almost—except he made sense. But he had his failures, too, and he sent men to prison. He was humble, but hard underneath. Does that sound like your man?"

"Maybe a little. But he's no fiery speaker. Like I said, the opposite: a man of few words. As to his core beliefs, who knows?" She thought for a moment. "You said he read the letter I sent to Ben?"

Ben said, "When I got your letter I was already looking around. We were finding way too many animal parts during our other busts. I thought it warranted an official request to the Fish and Game people, and they bucked it on to Deschamps."

"And an ex-con named Marion got that request and is pretending to be a warden."

"That's about the size of it," said White. "He may have some save-the-world fixation—"

She interrupted him with a sneer. "As what? The Messiah, Junior? Sure, just some gun-crazy guy down here to snuff out . . . " She stopped, realizing she was rapidly making it worse. "If this Marion, this Page wannabe, is crazy, then so am I." She seemed to sag in on herself. "I've been around him for weeks, and he's been nothing but kind, just a quiet, handy guy. Likable."

"Annie, we have to tell you, he's no angel. He had a nickname: the Wolf Hunter. He's worked in Alaska for years culling the wolf packs. He collected bounty from the state. Basically, he's a hired gun." White finished his beer, looking at her as he put the empty down. He seemed to appraise her in the same way he had the house. Coldly.

She gave him a dark, smoking look. Anger seethed in her voice. She turned to the Sheriff. "I'll believe all this when he tells me. He's not dangerous, Ben. Anything else? Agent White?"

"Just the usual. If he shows up, if he calls you, any contact of any kind, you tell us." He pulled out his card, dropped it on the countertop. "This is not optional. You must contact us. I don't want you being an accessory."

"I'm sure you care."

Her vitriol rolled right off his back. "Now, we need the license number for the truck. And is he armed?"

"You bet your ass he's armed."

"Annie, that just makes it worse," Ben cautioned.

"I'll get you the fucking license number. Then you get off my property." She left them to get the truck ID from the office; the plates were twenty years out of date but there was a bill of sale somewhere. The two lawmen sat quietly. Neither man was much for small talk.

Agent White's cell phone finally broke the silence. He listened for a moment, hung up. He looked thoughtful for a beat, then cracked a tight smile. "Gruder got a hit on the computer," he said. "He called it a Grand Slam."

CHAPTER NINETEEN

Once, long ago, Special Agent Colby White had been required to take a defensive driving course, out at Virginia International Raceway. It was taught by a sadistic redneck named Jeb. "Rhymes with Reb" the guy had smirked. Jeb hurtled old Crown Vics around the track like the second coming of Richard Petty. Every smoky burnout, sideways drift, or wicked-fast J-turn was accompanied by a mouth that never quit its motoring; Jeb's goal in life appeared to be getting his passengers to bail. Or shoot him down like a dog.

Sheriff Manyhorse seemed to have the same knack for what Reb had called "car control." Mercifully, as a full-blooded Indian, he was a man of markedly fewer words. Ben was leaned up against the door, weight shifted away from his holster, one hand delicately sawing at the wheel. The Impala was strung out in second gear, the engine sounding tired and old. Rocks pinged off the undercarriage as they slalomed down a gravel road in the middle of nowhere.

White let his eye wander away from the road—there was nothing he could accomplish by looking for some nameless doom around the next curve. He took in the landscape he had come to love: the Big Sky Country, as

A.B. Guthrie put it. White had come here in 1996, after two events the previous year had seemed to flow together. One was the Oklahoma City bombing of April 20, 1995. A few days later the *New York Times* received a letter from a man who wanted his crazy-ass manifesto published in that august journal. The two events did not really connect, but nobody knew that at the time. White had been recruited from the backwaters of Savannah, Georgia to a new strike force focused on domestic terrorism in the Northeast. He was still unpacking when the letter was received.

The author was later identified as Ted Kaczynski, former Harvard genius turned madman, then living in a hand-built wood cabin near Lincoln, Montana. White and his team went straight to the big time, when they were tasked to analyze the letter and the mind behind it. The Bureau labeled the terrorist the "University and Airline Bomber", or in media-speak "the Unabomber."

The FBI working group convinced the higher-ups to accede to the letter's demand that the Unabomber's screed be published in full. The hope was that it would generate leads.

This it did, big time. Some of Ted's relatives recognized his twisted thinking, and dropped a dime on him. White's group went super nova when their strike team followed that lead to the ecology freak's funky log cabin. White, as a junior agent, was detailed to go in first. No one else seemed to want a heroic death. Colby never gave it a thought as he kicked the door down. The place was built like a log house of cards. And Mr.

Kaczynski turned out to be a putz.

After that, White was golden for a few days. In one of his finer bureaucratic moves, he asked for an assignment in the Northwest. His competitors on the team gladly shuffled him out of the limelight. White didn't care. The city boy from an East Coast ghetto had fallen in love with the land and the sky. It was so damned big. It also helped that the cultural landscape was fertile grounds for wingnuts like crazy old Ted. From Wyoming to Idaho, there were all the homegrown loons he could ever hope for, from eco terrorists like Mr. U-Bomb to Aryan skinheads and conspiracy flakes of every stripe. Add the more mainstream crimes as well, like the two missing Stanford kids, and he had a full plate. He had never regretted the move, although it meant his career would peak well below the highest echelons. Which bothered him not one whit.

Finally, Manyhorse lurched onto the main highway, even shifting up to third gear. The Chevy vibrated up to ninety or so, the rolling hills whipping by the window. A lovely part of the world, yet populated by kooks—he didn't quite understand the connection, how it had become something of a dumping ground for so many toxic personalities. They finally slowed down as they hit the city limits of Stanley, a relative oasis of what passed for civilization way out west.

Unfortunately, civilization and its discontents was milling in front of City Hall. A crowd had gathered, and where there were crowds in this day and age, there would be media—several TV vans had been parked near a sign-waving crowd. White wondered where all these media types came from; there wasn't a TV station in the whole county. "Sheriff . . ." White let his voice trail off.

"Ugh."

"Is that an Indian *Ugh?*" White tried to joke, but the wisecrack wasn't really in the big Indian's wheelhouse. The signs being held on the high ground—the steps up to the building—gave a hint: "Man 1, Wolves 0," "This is A White Man's Valley," and a personal favorite with FBI agents everywhere, "Remember Ruby Ridge."

There was a another, smaller crowd off to one side, separated from the steps by a flimsy trestle barricade that still wore a sign. A couple of Manyhorse's cops were behind the barriers, trying to look like a wall of steel. The whole event seemed somewhat home grown. These were agitators for sure, but neither side looked very polished. The banners and signs were poorly done, the messages not all that grabby. White had seen better. They lacked the creative spark of a Seattle or Portland riot.

The people down on the street looked more prosperous and younger than the wind-beaten types up on the steps. They also seemed to be pro-lupine: "Wolves Don't Kill Livestock," "F. The EPA." "Set Nature Free."

"What's this all about, Sheriff?"

"It's a big deal around here, ever since the EPA took wolves off the endangered species list. Oh, crap, look at that." Up on the steps someone was raising a rickety mock-up of a gallows. Something was hanging from a noose.

"Great, a dead dog. Classy," White said.

"That's not a dog." The hipper types down below surged forward, threatening to overrun the police. Ben reached for his microphone but reinforcements came around the corner, and the confrontation died down. But not the noise. The camera crews were clearly enthralled.

The Sheriff pointed out a man up on the steps trying to get a bullhorn to work. "See the tall guy in the straw Stetson?"

White nodded. "The homely white dude?"

"Harmon Taber. He's on the county board."

"As what—resident scarecrow?"

"Spokesperson."

"For?"

"Rednecks." Ben rolled down their windows, listened a moment. "Tea Party type—they packed the elections last year."

"He looks like a clod."

"Around here, that's not a negative."

Taber got the PA working, immediately rattled off a series of sound bites stunning only in their banality: big money hates the little guy, get off my property, who needs wildlife, God meant the white man to have the land, etc. The yuppies tried to drown him out, but they lacked electronic countermeasures. Ben assessed the scene a little more, then put the prowl car in gear, heading around to the back. "Doesn't this shit get to you, Sheriff?" White asked.

"Freedom of speech," Ben shrugged.

"Are you always the stoic Injun?"

"Are you always the Angry Black Man?"

White looked at him in some surprise. "Why, Sheriff, you're quick off the mark today."

Ben parked in back after seeing that there were no lurking reporters. Both men got out, Ben locking up their ride. They started up the steps, but Sheriff Manyhorse stopped for a moment. He looked at White. "Yes, it does get to me. So much anger."

"You don't show it."

"Not me. Angry white men." He paused. "The tea baggers might run him for my job in a few years."

"Christ," White groaned. "You drink, Sheriff?"

"Never alone."

That was cryptic, at least to White. He thought for a moment. "Never alone—what does that mean, exactly."

"Indians never drink alone."

"Because they're sociable? I'm not tracking you, Ben."

"If an Indian drinks alone, there's no one to stop him." He let it sink in for a moment. "Old Indian joke."

"Yeah, right. Anyway, what say we grab some ginger ales after work."

"Ugh."

The Sheriff's office was empty, and their boots creaked across the floor as they looked around. Even the radios were unattended, a complete no-no. It was the first time White had seen the Sheriff become angry. He started slamming doors, tromped into the break room, where Brenda leapt back from her very close inspection of Detective Gruder's grillwork. Apparently romance was in the air, which made Manyhorse even more visibly hot. "Who is on the radio?"

"Steeps, Chief," Brenda said. Preston Steeps was normally downstairs running the jail, but the cells were empty at the moment, which meant he should have been filling in upstairs. Steeps had an attitude problem, a barely suppressed racial animus that made him a thorn in the Sheriff's side.

"He's not there. Get hold of him. Now would be good."

"Right away, Sheriff." Brenda was halfway out of the room when Manyhorse asked her to wait up a moment. She skidded to a halt. "Did those people on the steps get a permit to assemble?"

"No, sir. It just happened."

"Who sent the reinforcements?"

She looked scared. "I did."

Manyhorse looked at her for a long moment, then nodded. "Good move. But get someone on the comms." She nodded, then shot out the door. Ben looked around.

Gruder said, "Uh, it's kind of my fault, Sheriff. Everyone went into the conference room to look at the photos."

"What photos?"

"Probably Lee's."

"Who's Lee—oh, right. The Stanford kid," said Ben.

"Are you sure they're his?" White asked.

"Pretty damn sure. It's from the same camera. Same type camera," he amended.

"So you found the what, Olympus?"

"No."

"Then why did you have my guys call me?" Agent White asked. "We thought it was the second coming."

"Actually, we're all set up in there. A picture's worth a thousand words —"

"I just got one when I came in the room." Ben said.

"Ah, yeah . . ."

"We're going to have a little talk, Detective." Ben pinned him down with a long moment of silence. "Soon. Now, show us what you've got."

The conference room was jam packed, the lights dimmed. Both Feds and locals were chattering away as they looked at a still image projected on a pull-down screen. It was a dim shot, black areas at both sides and at the top. It looked like a doorway, but off-kilter; the edges were rough and not quite at right angles. There was a man silhouetted by backlight. He was wearing a cowboy hat, and his shoulders were puffed out by what appeared to be an insulated vest. The figure had one hand raised; he was clearly holding a pistol. It appeared to be an old Colt, the Peacemaker type. The pistol and hat gave the image a Wild West look.

Agent White leaned over and spoke softly to the Sheriff, who was standing next to him. "This *is* shit hot." The room was quieter now that the brass, such as they were, had arrived. "Talk us through this, Detective," Ben said.

Gruder was at a laptop, which in turn was hooked up to a projector. "Unfortunately, this photo wasn't taken with a flash, so we can't make out the face."

"Why no flash? I thought all cameras had them," White said.

"This is a high-end camera," Gruder answered. "I looked it up on the internet when I was researching the chip thing. It has a clip-on flash unit. Not one that is built-in. If Lee were in a desperate situation, he would never have had the chance to put it on. He was doing outdoor photography up there, so he may not have been carrying it at all. We can bring out some shadow detail, but that would have to be done back in Palo Alto, or by you guys. The others are a different story."

"There's more?" From White's tone of voice, he clearly felt Christmas had arrived early.

"Oh yeah," Gruder smiled.

He started to show another one, but the Sheriff asked him to wait a moment. "Before we see anything else, tell us how you got this image. Images."

"They came in over the internet. They were sent to the young man's Flickr site he had set up with Stanford, so people could view them."

"I'll bet that was wildly popular," White said. "So how do we know this has anything to do with the two kids?"

"It's the same type of camera, same lens—all that info is embedded in the photo. What is called an exif file. We contacted the maker of the camera, and they can extract the serial number. We even know where this photo was snapped. As I said the other day, the memory chip records the GPS coordinates."

"And where was this taken?" Ben turned as he heard steps in the back of the room; the place was otherwise dead silent. He saw Brenda just inside the door.

"At the Stanford site. GPS can probably get us within yards of the crime scene."

"If this is the scene," Ben mused.

Gruder looked grim. "If this isn't a violent scene, I don't know what is. I think we're seeing what Lee saw just before . . . well, just before the end."

Everyone was silent for a moment, as the room seemed to realize, for the first time, what they were seeing. "At least it gets us a chance to find physical evidence," Agent White said. "And it gives us the date?"

"Yes. The same day they drove up there," Gruder responded.

There was another long beat as Sheriff Manyhorse worked things out. He again turned towards the door. "Brenda." She stood up straight. "We need to set things in motion up at the Stanford site. Full-court press— bring in the Staties. Cadaver dogs, too." She nodded. "Agent White, all your people now have wheels?"

"The vans are ready to roll. I'm going to request our mobile crime lab be flown in."

"Detective, you can go to the next picture now." Ben said. The next image was much brighter, almost achingly so. The clear light of day: a man was on the ground in front of a corral. Red was clearly visible kneeling on the man's back as he raised his gloved hands in a rodeo flourish. The guy on the ground, who had blood on his face, was trussed in barbed wire, like a little doggie at the county rodeo.

"When was this taken?" White asked Gruder.

"Today, actually," he replied.

"This case is something else!" White exclaimed. "I'm confused about one or two little things—why did the photos come through today?"

"The camera's card has to have a link to the Internet. Like a Wi-Fi hot spot. I think the camera was not around a link until today. And it has to be turned on."

"Explain that a little more," Ben said.

"Somebody thought it would be fun to take photos of this guy being wrapped up. They have Lee's camera. They obviously didn't toss it. So they turn on the Olympus to take a few snaps, there's an ethernet connection nearby. Bam, instant download."

"They must be idiots. Possession of the camera—I can get a warrant on that alone. Did we zero in on the IP the camera connected with?" White sounded hopeful.

"We sure did. The Rocking R Ranch."

White looked at Ben for information. "Wilhelm Spatz," observed the Sheriff. "Red there on screen—that's his foreman."

"Then I think we've got the fucks!" White's profanity brought a few laughs from the County side of the room; the Feebs had heard it all before.

"Do you recognize the cowboy wearing all that wire?" White asked Ben.

The Sheriff looked thoughtful. "Under the blood, I'm pretty sure that's Page Deschamps."

A ghoulish smile turned up the corners of the agent's mouth. "Do you think he's dead?"

Ben shrugged. "I don't think he looks too good."

"Well, if he's dead, we kind of kill two birds with one stone. If you know what I mean."

"Ah, Alaska. Yes, that would close *that* book."

CHAPTER TWENTY

Page woke up in a haze, his eyes glued almost shut by what he knew was blood. His brain refused for a time to go into gear. He could tell he was lying in the dirt, and that meant he was outside. He heard a breeze through some trees that he dimly saw in front of him. No, overhead. Just where they should be when you were flat on your back. Something was poking him, sharp and insistent. He didn't want to move, wasn't sure if he could move. But the pain was escalating. His arms were pinned to his torso, and damn they hurt too—a thousand tiny cuts, red-hot.

He rolled onto his stomach, planted his forehead on the ground, levered himself onto his knees. The pain in his back went down a notch. He got to his feet, almost went back down as the blood rushed out of his head. He regained his balance, finally worked open his gummed eyes. He looked down and saw he was wrapped in barbed wire from his chest to his waist. The wire was what had pinned his arms to his sides. This was serious; the boys had given him the classic barbed wire vest.

He tried to assess the situation, tried to see what he had to work with. About all he saw were some big cottonwood trees, which meant water was somewhere nearby. And he needed water. Needed it bad. But first, he had to unwrap himself. He staggered over to the tree, stared at it stupidly for a time. He suspected his bell had been rung, and he had the headache to prove it. Looking back, he seemed to remember Red working him over, first in the body, then . . .

Since he didn't remember it, he probably took a shot to the head. If they'd knocked his stupid brains out, he'd feel about like this. He looked himself over, located the loose end of the wire. He found a broken off branch growing out of a tree trunk. After a few tries he got the wire hooked into the little stub. He began slowly twirling out of the loops. As he got down to his skin, the pain was staggering; as each barb pulled out, it brought tears to his eyes.

But he was finally free, covered in a hundred little spots of blood. Not enough to kill him, but enough to make him feel faint. He staggered down a game trail, hoping it would lead him to water.

It did. He fell into a little stream, let the ice-cold water numb his skin. The water also loosened the fabric of his shirt so he could pull it away from his skin. Drinking the water, even if it was full of *giardia*, was pure ecstasy. Cleansed, numbed, he headed for high ground so he could get his bearings. This led him to a ridge, and on the far side was a little valley, dotted with cattle. He might be able to find a ranch—hopefully not the Rocking R, before dark. He didn't want to spend the night outdoors—he was in pretty rough shape.

By the time Page worked his way down the little

valley, it was turning cool. The earth, he knew, still hadn't built up the reservoir of latent heat he could expect in another month. But he had been in Alaska so long that he didn't have any real feel for the weather down here; maybe there would be ice on his corpse by morning. But the means of salvation was at hand, over there on that far slope: the Power Wagon stood all on its lonesome.

Up close he saw why the cowboys hadn't bothered to hide the Dodge; they had shot the living shit out of it. No glass, just shards all over the grass and in the cab. The radiator had bled out, every tire had been punctured, but the sidewalls were so tall and stiff that they would probably still roll. He looked in the bed, but there was no chance they'd left his rifle behind. The blankets and food were gone. Even the wolf cage had been tossed. He got the cap off the tank, smelled gas. That was good. But would it turn over?

He had to hot-wire the ignition, as the key was gone. He stripped the wires out from under the dash, pulled off the insulation with his teeth, twisted the strands together. The volt meter twitched, just. The Dodge used a separate push button for the starter. The solenoid clicked, but there wasn't enough juice to turn over the big Straight Six.

He fumbled around in the glove box, which had been nearly shot away, dug out an old screwdriver. He flipped back the rubber floor mat, sending glass fragments flying. He was so tired. Page knew he'd lost enough blood to make him seriously woozy. He used the screwdriver to take off the lid in the floor over the buried battery box. In it was the Glock he'd put in there back at the bar an eon ago. The sight of the 9mm somehow cheered him up. The battery was OK, although one terminal was loose; the whole truck had probably jumped around like crazy under the hail of bullets. He used the butt of his piece to hammer on the terminals as he wiggled them down.

It started right up. Apparently, the 1949 Dodge Power Wagon *was* bullet-proof. He put it in gear just long enough to point it back down to the stream. It was going to overheat pretty fast. He shut it down, leaving enough space to roll forward for a restart in case the electrics faded. He took the radiator cap off, saw lots of rust inside, but no coolant. It probably hadn't been serviced in this millennium. There were holes between the fins and a spray of small holes in the header tank. He rummaged around some more in the cab, found an old copy of a Burpee's seed catalog. He used the screwdriver to scrap up some of the mastic used to seal the sheet-metal seams of the floor. He chewed a chunk of paper into a wad, kneaded it together with the sealer, which was some sort of asphalt-based product. He formed it into plugs, rammed them in with the screwdriver.

He needed something to pour stream water into the rad, and also a way to carry it. If he left the cap off, the water wouldn't quite reach a boil, and he thought the sealer was as likely to melt as to hold. But it was all he had. He used the screwdriver to rip off a big square of vinyl upholstery, pulled wires from the seat to stitch together a water bag. He was set.

*****

Annie was hard at work in her office on an account that actually interested her. One of the bigger film production companies wanted her assessment of the new analytic software a mathematician had developed. It was used for predicting which elements in a script had the highest probability of scoring with the movie-going public. They wanted to know if it was better than using the hit-or-miss method of story development that had been the backbone of the industry from the days of the first talkies. Annie didn't know, so she was reviewing the whole situation here in her office. She had some quiet Vivaldi playing in the background, but she was suddenly aware of someone watching her. Wilhelm Spatz stood there in his big cowboy coat, hat in one hand and a piece of pie in the other.

"What are you doing in my home?" Annie couldn't help sounding incredulous. She mentally ran through a list of which staff were around. She had never been the kind to keep a gun in every drawer in the house, let alone lock her doors. She always felt that sort of fear eroded the very peace she wanted in her home. Now here was a man she had faced off against—the kind of action, she had learned, he just couldn't abide.

"I'm eating a piece of your Hispanic cook's pie. Don't deport her—it's really good."

"I didn't hear a car in the drive."

"I rode up on my horse. Just being thoughtful. I didn't want your werewolves waking up the kiddies. The ones you have left."

"No thanks to you." Josef should be in his room; she tried to casually push the intercom on his number.

"Calling your little Hasidic friend?"

"To throw your ass out."

"Why not get Marion to do it?" He saw her give a little start. She was such an open book. Annie obviously was tuned in on the dual identity thing. "He doing anything else for you?"

"You know the whole world isn't about sex."

"That was a big enough world for me. With you."

"Until you got sicko."

"You thought it was kinky, for a while. Dominance. You wanted it, way down deep."

"I wanted a strong man. I admit it. But you didn't know the meaning of the word no."

"It wouldn't be dominance if you said yes." He finished the slice of pie. "Can I sit down?"

She was surprised at his tone. He actually sounded calm. "You can leave."

"Just give me five minutes. Then I'll ride out, no harm, no foul."

"Are you going to talk about our sex life? Because that is long gone."

"I know." He was still quiet. She finally pointed to a chair. He was being careful not to radiate any menace, but she could feel the heaviness in the air even when he sat down, a coiled mass of energy. The sort of raw elemental force she had once been drawn to until she saw how close he skated to the edge.

"Five minutes."

He nodded. "You gave me a book once. *Le Morte d'Arthur.* Sir Thomas Malory. I found someone in there I identified with."

"It sure wasn't Arthur."

He laughed again, quietly. "Artie was a tool. Remember the Questing Beast?" She nodded. "I'm not great on literature, but I like to read. I dug the name: quests, questing. Looking for something. On a journey, maybe with some fate thrown in. Arthur was pulled every which way by everyone he knew. As I said, a tool."

"I didn't know you were so well read." She *was* literary, and she knew that for Malory, the Questing Beast represented violence, chaos.

"Bear with me. So we have a beast on a quest. Like a knight on some crazy-ass adventure. Tools for the job, Annie.

"Arturo was a tool for mean ol' Guinevere. Like her, I just wanted to get things done. Dominance, the sense of command—that's what I was all about. I never would have hurt you, but you had to bend to my will."

She gave it a moment's thought. "Your will. Jesus, how many women want to hear that?"

"More than a few. It's not all lesbian out there."

"How can I listen to you when you talk the same old idiot talk. Try this: maybe I'm a commander, too." She saw him start to smile, and held up her hand.

"Don't smirk—that's what got you in trouble." He nodded, surprising her yet again. This was turning into a crazy night. "But I only want to control myself. You want to control people—like Red is controlled. Talk about a kinky relationship. After that, rape the land, kill the animals. Rape. Kill. Not pleasant words. Your so-called *control* consumes, uses them up. I could never do that."

His eyes flashed, but he seemed to be controlling the inner anger she knew lay beneath his surface. "Annie, open your eyes. You manipulate, *you* control. You know where all the levers are when it comes to John Q. Public. Words, imagery. All that semiotics shit you used to tell me about. Who was that Nazi chick that made Hitler's propaganda flicks? Riefenstahl?"

"Don't you dare put me in that league!" He was still, amazingly, in his chair. "And your five minutes are up."

He shrugged his shoulders and got to his feet. "I try to look inward now and then. I'm no swami, but I try. And whatever I am, I don't fool myself."

"Good luck. The rest of us do. Now, leave."

"Your home is your castle, and I respect that." He gazed steadily at her, and there was, for the first time in years, no malice in his voice. "We can't call a truce?"

"Stop hunting wolves and we can talk."

"It's part of the life I've built. I'm a hunter, when you come right down to it. 'Once I was a hunter, I brought home fresh meat for you.' You turned me on to Tim Buckley, remember?'

"In the same song: 'Soon there'll be another, to tell

you I was just a lie.' "

"Christ, no wonder he iced himself. I guess we just aren't going to change, are we?"

"I'm not. You need to, or you'll kill everything on the planet. What will you do then?"

He looked at her for a long time. "Sometimes I miss your witty little thoughts. Thank the cook for the pie." He walked out of the room, leaving Annie to wonder how it had all gone so wrong; there really had been something between them at one time. It had died, and left a hole in her heart, one that had filled with dislike and then hate. The obverse of love, and with just as much power. And, she realized for the first time, maybe he had the same hole in his heart.

If so, what would fill it?

*****

She sat lost in thought for some time, until the phone interrupted her reverie. "Come and pick me up."

He sounded tired, far away in more than distance.

"Marion? Is it you or that Page guy?"

There was a long pause. "The Shell station at . . . Where am I?" he asked someone. "Guy says it's Barney's Bistro. There was another, longer pause. "If you get here, you can pick up both of them."

"That's a pretty clever line—" She realized he had hung up.

Annie had Josef drive; she didn't much like highways at night. And she didn't want to see Mr. Two

Face by herself. They found the Dodge easily enough. It's mangled condition made her think it had been shot up in the parking lot.

Josef had the same thought. "Stay in the car, Annie." He reached under the seat and pulled out a small machine pistol. He saw her look as he got out. "Old Israeli habit," he joked. He worked around the area in a cautious way, went into the gas station. She could see him talking to the attendant behind the counter; the kid didn't take his eyes off Josef's weapon, even when he put it away.

As she watched through the glass, Josef went into the back, then came out holding up Page. Even from forty feet away, she could tell the Wolf Hunter looked more like the hunted. He barely made it across the parking lot. Josef helped him into the back of the Range Rover, put the seatback into tilt so Page could loll back. "Hi," he croaked.

"I'm really pissed off with you," she said while Josef was coming around the front of the car.

"I'm pissed off with me, too."

Josef got in. "They rolled him up in barbed wire. Also beat the living crap out of him. He said his ribs hurt a little—they might be cracked."

"Let's get him to the E-room."

Josef put it in gear, but Page managed to sit up. "No. Just put me to bed."

"You need a doctor."

Page thought for a moment. "You have vets on call—let them work on me. It's important."

"You're going to have to explain," Annie protested.

"So I'll explain. fory-eight hours. Deal?"

"Why is it always forty-eight?" Annie groused.

"It's a movie thing," Josef said.

"He doesn't watch movies," she shot back. "But he looks like he's been living one. Take us home, Josef." He nodded, pulled out. Page was asleep in seconds.

*****

"I'm a big animal doctor, not a field medic," Dr. Aronson said. She was squinting under the harsh fluorescents in the barn's veterinary room at Annie's ranch. Rhona Aronson, a woman in her early fifties, was dressed in the surgical scrubs she used as pajamas; her tousled hair, iron gray and frizzy, was unbrushed. She had the sleepy, grouchy demeanor of someone who had been awakened from a deep sleep.

She looked at Page, stretched out on the stainless table more commonly used for wolf autopsies. He was on his back on a wool blanket that Josef had brought down from the apartments above. Under the artificial light, Page's wounds were pretty graphic, blood soaking his shirt in rust-red patches. "But I suppose we should at least take a look. While I risk my license. We have a hospital in town, you know."

"We need to keep this under wraps for a while," Annie said. "And you've worked on me before. Right?" Dr. Aronson ignored her for the moment, as she collected what she needed. "Josef, get me that spray bottle, fill it with distilled water. So I took a few splinters out of you. This man has either had a very bizarre accident with a combine harvester, or he's been assaulted."

"He said they wrapped him up in barbed wire," Annie said. She began unbuttoning Page's shirt. The doctor brushed her aside, as she switched into full-on doctor mode. "That's not a nice thing to do," Rhoda said. "We'll have to do a tetanus shot." She used the spray bottle to moisten Page's shirt, then carefully peeled it away inch by square inch.

Page moaned. "Can we give him some pain meds?" Josef asked.

"Not yet," the vet replied. "I need him to let me know if I'm hurting him."

Page gave a low chuckle, then groaned. They had thought he was out for the count. "It really does hurt when I laugh."

"So don't laugh," Dr. Aronson said. "What hurts the worst?"

"My short ribs—they kicked them in." She got his shirt completely peeled back. Underneath he looked like a crucified Christ in some hyper realistic Renaissance painting. Most of the punctures were peeling up at the edges, crusted in dry blood. Annie couldn't help audibly gasping.

"They did a number on him. Good." Aronson palpated his rib area, which was already a swath of black and blue flesh. Annie, in her cloistered world, had never seen the results of a beating. It wasn't anything like a TV show. It made her feel ill and angry, both at the same time. "How can that be good?" Annie asked angrily.

Dr. Aronson looked up from her work for a moment. "It covers my ass. Many a veterinarian has been pressed into service as an emergency medic. Besides, you've got some great lawyers. Am I right?"

The doctor completed her exam, then gave him a tetanus booster shot. She and Annie got a pint of plasma going into his arm. Josef cut away Page's pants while they made a point of looking the other way. They got him into some pale blue scrub PJ bottoms after Josef sponged down everything but his bloody torso. Dr. Aronson treated that area herself, cleaning where necessary. Finally satisfied, she said, "OK, Page. We're going to knock you out—I need to do some suturing."

"Go for it," he whispered. She put a syringe into the shunt, and in seconds his face relaxed in amazement and pleasure. In a moment, he was out, his breathing shallow and regular.

As she worked, the doctor asked where they were going to put the patient; getting him up the stairs was out of the question. Annie said the guesthouse was free. And there was an intercom that connected to the main house. Just across the small patio, she remembered, where they had first sat down together.

When he was done, wrapped in bandages like The Mummy, they dragged him on a gurney up the driveway. They put him to bed about 3 a.m. Annie was glad she'd ordered Swedish foam mattresses when they built the place. Maybe this was too plush for the hardy woodsman. Or for a two-faced hypocrite.

Well, she thought, you're stuck with it, buddy.

CHAPTER TWENTY-ONE

Agent White spent a few hours mapping out plans for the next morning, first with Sheriff Ben and his crew, then with his FBI grunts. He got back to his motel room in the dark hours of the night, alone as he usually was. He was a widower, not on good terms with his children. His few friends were also colleagues—too hard-bitten to be much use as a soul mate. He was anaesthetized to this, the quiet hours with no one to talk to. All signs, he knew, of a confirmed loner. He suspected the Sheriff was a similar sort of dude, two lawmen strapped into the harness that was their job. The big Indian was just about as talkative, too.

The motel was too backwoods to have a refrigerator full of drinks, and the only place open had been a gas station called Mom's. They only had beer, which he finally sat down to sip. He replayed the day back in his mind as he drank a Miller High Life. Things were starting to line up, especially at their high mountain crime scene.

He set his digital watch for an early wake-up but stayed in the room's one chair while he let his back unwind. It still hurt where the cowboy had hit him. Said cowboy now probably lying dead in some ditch on the backside of the Rocking R Ranch. What a bunch of boneheads those guys were, committing an assault on film—film that had a GPS coordinate yards from Spatz's front door. Well, not film exactly: digital images. That the cowboys were so tech-illiterate was going to put them—or at least some of them—in jail. But maybe not today; he and Big Ben would have to see how things played out. They needed to work the scene of that doorway photo up the mountain. If there was even a door up there. But if the scene of the crime led to the bodies, then they could move on the ranch in force. Boy, would the media love to be in on *that*.

White finished the beer, ripped off a belch or two as he shed his clothes on the way to the bathroom. He looked in the mirror, saw a guy who was getting old. He didn't really give a shit. He had survived well past his sell-by date. He had put his fair share of cruds under the soil, or at least locked them away for the rest of their miserable lives. A few had even sucked on the state's cyanide, an event he had once witnessed with no particular emotion. It was not elation when the nation put down a bad actor. The job satisfaction was just that: a sense that a mission had been finished. And after that, there would just be another one.

He got into the shower, his body finally relaxing under the steam; this was just another OK but not great motel room in a life full of them. But one thing you could say about America, it always had plenty of hot water. As he mellowed out, he thought about the television crews outside city hall. He had the lawman's usual dislike for them, the shallowness, their self-induced hysteria. But there had been times when they had proved useful. Maybe one of those moments was coming up. By the time he hit the sack, he'd made up his mind, left himself a mental note to place the call. Game on.

*****

This time the FBI didn't need to borrow Wolf Ranch's helicopter; two UH-I Hueys had flown in from Mountain Home Air Force Base to do the heavy lifting. The FBI's regional mobile lab was being trucked in for a late afternoon ETA. He'd also put in a call to Bob Dierdorff, asking him to bring in the special surveillance van from San Francisco. Agent White, despite the cold sunrise, felt at the top of his game. It was always this way when the Agency closed in for the kill, an excitement mirrored in his staff, most of whom were looking for that break-out moment in their careers.

The local cops, Ben's people, were also on a high state of alert, but they were a more ragtag looking force. To be fair, they didn't have the deep pockets of the Feds; their vehicles weren't too bad, late-model Suburbans and Tahoes, but their air arm was conspicuous by its non-existence. The SUVs had already wheeled out of the designated jumping-off point at the airport. Ben, who had been offered an airlift, was on the phone as they waited for the dogs. White theatrically shot a cuff to look at his old Casio. The

Sheriff hung up his clunky old satellite phone, bent down to yell over the jet blast from the nearest chopper. "They just hit town," he told White. The agent made a whirling motion over his head, and his people started boarding.

A minute or so later a big slab-sided van wheeled into the parking lot; "State Highway Patrol" was stenciled on its sides. A state trooper leapt out, went around to open the rear doors. A brace of dogs came down the steps, led by their handlers. White motioned them directly to the Hueys. Once the canines were settled in, White and Manyhorse boarded, the Sheriff slinging a khaki backpack down between his boots. As they lifted up and away, White looked down at the collection of ENG trucks and vans that had been parked outside the fence-lines of the airport's parking lot. The glass lenses of a full dozen news cameras lifted up to follow their flight. Through some unknown osmosis— or a leak from inside the law community—there were more units now than had been covering the Taber crowd yesterday.

The only action-dateline-news team missing was the one White had called several hours ago, a news crew he had reluctantly used before on another case. That reporter had proved just barely trustworthy. Which was saying a lot in the news business. That she was a double minority also didn't hurt: a café-au-lait hottie. The helicopter and crew had left Seattle in the dark, and would have to stop at Boise for fuel. He would then provide them with the co ordinates for today's operations. News Chopper 7 would be allowed to loiter once on station; he hadn't yet decided whether or not to let them land.

*****

There was no "Ride of the Valkyries" soundtrack as the two choppers whop-whopped into the Stanford property's confines, the air chillier than down in the flatlands. White had one foot out on the skids, showing off a little. He had noticed Ben Manyhorse was much more cautious, having belted himself in. The pilot flared in with the nose high, settled the skids onto the soft shale. They had used the GPS coordinates from the camera to guide them in; they were about fifty yards out from the exact spot, as they didn't want to disturb what promised to be a crime scene.

The Bell's single turbine spooled down, the rotors slowly whooshing their shadows across the ground. White let his people start unloading equipment as he signaled Ben to join him. The Sheriff hefted his pack up onto his broad shoulders, produced a portable Garmin from his jacket pocket. White knew this was a joint exercise, and since he didn't want to be the Federal bully kicking sand in the little guy's face, he motioned Ben to lead the way.

The two men went upslope towards a line of trees—mostly aspen with a few pines in the background. There was a fold in the earth that was hidden by the aspens; the two small ridges, no more than thirty feet high, made a little hidden gulch or gully that sloped up until they came together. It was like an open V, in which they now stood. "Did you guys ever search here?" Agent White asked.

The Sheriff gave him a long look, a blank one, even for the stoic Native American.

"That's not a criticism, Sheriff," White added.

"We did not." Ben looked around at the sky. "We wouldn't have seen it from the air."

"I see. It's got a sort of spooky vibe—you feel it?"

The Sheriff nodded in agreement. They went upslope towards the junction of the two ridgelines. Ben stopped, knelt down to look at the soil. He thought for a moment, then got down on his hands and knees, looking sideways at the loose accumulation of rocky soil and leaves that formed the floor of the ravine. The aspens, moving in the tendrils of wind, made a ghostly rustle. "Anything?" White asked. The back of his neck was crawling; this place definitely had a bad feel. Ben shrugged, got back to his feet. White heard voices behind, turned to see his crew standing back about thirty feet. He motioned for them to be still.

Ben and Colby took a few more steps and saw that the V was actually the letter A, with some sort of wall going from left to right. It had too many straight lines to be a natural feature. "Hey, there really is a door," White breathed. He realized his Glock had somehow gotten into his hand, which was silly. Any crime here had happened long ago.

But they took it the way movie cops did, guns

drawn, one man on each side. There was a Yale lock, incongruously shiny, on a metal hasp. The hinges looked flimsy, made out of straps of thick leather, which made White wonder why they had bothered with the lock. Any ten-year-old with a penknife could cut their way in, which is what they did. They peeled the door—which was nothing more than split logs—outwards, pointed their Mag-lites into the space.

It was about the most primitive man-cave Agent White had ever seen: parallel bunks running down the side walls, some shelves in the back. There was just enough open floor space for someone to walk sideways to the back wall. Two poles were set in parallel overhead; bits of rope or twine still hung from them. "Those poles—for drying things?" White asked.

Ben studied the floor, which was packed earth, leaned in to look, but took no steps inside. "No. Check out the floor."

White peered around the Sheriff's wide shoulders, realized this wasn't his area of expertise. "I got nothin'."

Ben gave him a little smile, his bad teeth making him look like someone out of a cave painting. "Feathers mixed in with the soil. Some bits of fur, dried blood."

"Human?"

"I'm not *that* good. I think animals were hung up on those poles—see the cords?" He stepped back. "And I think there was a fight in here."

"How do you . . . uh, see that?"

"The sleeping pallet on one side—the leg has been kicked in. There's blood on the wall—splash patterns you see in homicides. And I smell gunpowder.”

“You're the Native American Sherlock, you know that?”

“Maybe so.”

White thought the big guy was pulling his leg on that last one. “You're kidding about the gunpowder?”

“No.” Ben looked a little longer. “And there's something reflecting light under the back corner. Glass, I think. We should bring up your team.”

White stepped back out, signaled his crew to head on up. “Sheriff, this is your county, and I don't want to step on your feet. We can wait for your folks —”

“I'm not worried about that. Let your people do their magic. You and I should look for the bodies.”

“You think they're around here.”

“I do.” Ben said gravely. White didn't ask him how he knew. As they let the lab people by, White's satellite phone, clipped to his belt, buzzed. Oh yeah, he thought. News Chopper 7.

He gave the helicopter crew the final coordinates, with strict orders to orbit in a thousand-foot arc at an equal altitude above the site. He then had Ben use a PRC radio to order up the cadaver dogs. Unlike most people's images of search pooches, these were not bloodhounds, or even police dogs. They were tick hounds, specially bred in the Carolinas for treeing coons. Raccoons. They had found great popularity with law enforcement bureaus all over the country. The downside was that the demand and the training involved made them expensive to purchase; it was the rare county that had them. Thus, they were being handled by state troopers, which added another layer of bureaucracy that White didn't much care for. But this whole thing would probably go off the rails with leaks, infighting, and general hassles before too long. His calling in Tricia Helfer and her news crew was a pre-emptive strike on his part to at least control some of the information that this investigation would no doubt hemorrhage.

They worked the three dogs out from the buried hut, letting them run up the sides of the slopes as they sniffed their way back to the opening. White was opening up a bottle of ibuprofen—his kidneys still hurt from the poacher's fists—when someone yelled from behind the apex of the "A". Someone in a cowboy hat popped up from behind the "roof" of the structure, which in reality was a flat area covered with timber slash. This was in the opposite direction from the dogs and their handlers. Ben and Colby scrambled up one side, went to join a young fresh-faced deputy from the Sheriff's office. Ben identified him as Deputy Daniel Wesson, an easy name to remember: it was a brand of pistol. "I was, uh, gonna take a leak . . ."

"On top of a crime scene?" White asked incredulously. The deputy, who couldn't have been more than twenty-five years old, all but blushed. "No sir—I went up there quite a ways." He pointed back away from the gulch. " 'Bout fifty yards. Then I saw it."

"Saw what?" Ben asked.

"The leg, Chief."

CHAPTER TWENTY-TWO

Tricia Helfer normally didn't mind having tight, hard buns. It was what Pilates was all about. But she had been in a Bell Jet Ranger for over seven hours, and her ass was ablaze. True, she and the Chopper 7 crew had taken a break during the refuel in Boise, but this was way more seat time than she, at least, was used to. And she was wearing the wrong clothes.

They had crammed the cargo hold with ENG gear—cameras, lights, sound equipment. Which meant there had been no room for her street clothes. And no room in the cabin. In addition to the pilot, they had the chopper's camera operator in the back seat with Tricia's cameraman, Jens Van Zant. She had been outfitted back at the studio, which meant her producer had made the pick on wardrobe. It had been the wrong choice.

Every station kept foul weather gear, usually REI stuff, in the latest bright, camera-friendly colors. These in turn broke down into "Winter Storm" and "Summer Storm", which was today's pick: GORE-TEX in an unlined but hooded windbreaker with matching back-packer's overpants. Which would have been fine, except they tended to bag out on her tall, slender frame, so she'd had hers tailored. Their cut made them look great when she was standing in front of the camera, especially when shouting over a windstorm out on some wind-ravaged coast.

But that sexy cut had long since blocked her circulation, aided and abetted by the chopper's rock hard seats. Thus a severe case of what a motorcycling friend once called "monkey-butt, red as rhesus." From Agent White's tone over the satellite phone, she had a feeling they weren't going to get to land, so the end was not in sight.

Arnie, her pilot, cut back their speed as they came into the outer edges of the search area's co ordinates. He talked quietly into his mic, setting up their approach with Kwan, who ran the camera housed in its gimbaled pod under the aircraft's nose. Kwan's view was limited by a stack of monitors attached to the bulkhead that partitioned the cockpit front to back. With all the easy facility of a ten-year-old boy, he used a joystick to track the outboard camera. Tricia, who had worked with these guys for a long time, stayed quiet—they knew what to do. She did watch her portable monitor, which repeated Kwan's POV—his point of view. If Arnie wanted to see it, she would tilt it his way, but he was an old hand, and preferred keeping his eyes "outside the cockpit." She was all for that.

Tricia saw the vid image pull in on the vehicles parked near an open gate. Kwan gave her a countdown, and she began her voice-over as she watched his camera moves in her monitor. It was a basic set-piece she had done a million times, letting the viewers know this was a live broadcast, and explaining why they were here.

"This is Tricia Helfer, reporting from Chopper 7 for Eyewitness News, high above the Absaroka Range in southeast Montana. We are about forty miles from the peaceful town of Stanley, and below us is the Stanford Biological Preserve where Lee Chun and his fiancée, Lisa Betz, went missing more than six weeks ago.

"Now, through a series of breakthroughs—including the locating of Lee's missing Saab station wagon at the Boise Airport—investigators have what they call 'a new lead' on this desolate mountaintop. You can see the search vehicles from the Stanley police, led by Sheriff Ben Manyhorse. FBI officials are here under the command of Special Agent Colby White. I can also see the highly trained cadaver dogs from the State Highway Patrol."

She paused; this was where the broadcast team at home would go for their slice of the glory. "Tricia, Steve Raible here. Does the presence of cadaver dogs mean anything significant?"

You bet your ass it does, she thought. "Yes, Steve, my understanding from FBI Agent White is that they have enough information to warrant their deployment." Argh, 'deployment' was such a clinker, she realized. "As we zoom in you can see Agent White in the blue windbreaker." Kwan, following her lead, pulled in tighter on the men below. "The tall man next to him is Sheriff Ben Manyhorse. I—" She paused as Kwan spoke in her ear. He panned to the right, a little too fast, but Tricia knew he had spotted something on his monitors, which were much better than hers. Kwan also gave instructions to the pilot to move in closer. Arnie looked at Tricia questioningly. Go in, she gestured.

She heard Steve, back at the studio, fill in the dead air like a pro. "We may have a new development from Chopper 7, live and on scene. Tricia?"

The image on the screen was pretty clear and pretty gruesome. "Steve, I have some bad news for all our viewers. Horrific news."

*****

Page woke up feeling like he was on a cloud; he hoped it was the pain meds, because he didn't want to move. He felt like he had just been in an extended bar fight, after riding every bull in the rodeo, with a car crash thrown in for a chaser. Each a total beat-down. Yet the Cloud Nine thing persisted. He opened his eyes to the daylight, saw he was in some sort of log cabin, but very high-end. The logs had been squared off and finished with stain, or something that gave them a deep, warm honey glow. Same for the ceiling: big beams, bead-board, a hanging light that was a wrought iron imitation of a wagon wheel. The windows were framed in dark green wood trim bracketing closed chintz curtains. The room was dim, but not too dark. It was very, very peaceful. He wasn't used to that.

He rolled slowly on his side, groaning with the effort. He wanted to see what the heck was under him; it felt like cotton candy, soft and sticky. Page poked a finger in it, realized it was a material that instantly conformed to his pressure. Maybe some miracle stuff from a hospital, but he sure wasn't in one. More likely he was in the guesthouse across the patio from Annie's office.

He rolled over to the edge, felt light-headed before he was finally able to sit up. He needed to take a leak something fierce. He got to his feet, almost doubled over by the rib injury, found the bathroom. The tile floor felt cool under his feet. There was a toilet and also a sort of porcelain bowl with chrome nozzles at one end. Whatever it was, he didn't want a thing to do with it. He looked at the shower, amazed to see a good half-dozen showerheads. Though he yearned for some hot water, he was covered in bandages. After a spirit-reviving leak, he stared glumly into the bowl. He was not surprised to see he had some blood in his urine.

He found a door that led to a covered walkway that led to the house. He was in blue surgical scrubs, so he felt it would be OK to try to find something to drink. And some aspirin: a lot of it. The passageway led into a very big office, again done up in a sort of western look with hardwood floors, rag rugs, big hand-hewn furniture. There was a lot of high tech stuff in the room, very little of which he could recognize.

Beyond was the familiar foyer, then the dining room. He smelled coffee, followed his nose through to the kitchen. Annie was there, with the cook. Yolanda. They were baking some sort of rolls made out of thin sheets of dough. The scene surprised him a little. He didn't see Annie as the domestic type. "Morning," he said. Yolanda gave him a smile; Annie didn't. "I could use some aspirin," he added.

Yolanda quickly left the room. Annie gave him a long look. A pretty damned chilly one, he thought. She started to say something. He held up his hand, winced. "You gave me forty-eight hours."

"You just slept through twelve of them."

"That bed is something else."

"We could have put you on the floor—that's where you usually sleep, isn't it?"

"I feel lucky I was even indoors." Yolanda returned with several different bottles; she'd covered the spectrum of over-the-counter stuff. "You should take these with food," Yolanda said.

"I could use some coffee."

"And some apple pie." Yolanda didn't wait for an answer. As she got the pie out of the fridge, she asked if Annie wanted a slice. "Sure." Annie pointed at the little dining nook. "Sit your cowboy ass down, Page." She virtually hissed the last word. Gratefully, he settled into the cushions, used his elbows to hold up his lacerated torso.

"I'm not a damned cowboy," he said.

"Oh no? Really?"

"Look, knock the sarcastic shit off, would you?" Page responded. Yolanda set their food down, looking at him in some surprise. They were huge slices of apple pie, on thick colorful china. The coffee came next, big old Navy style mugs, cream, and sugar in brown cubes.

"Take a few minutes off, Yolanda," Annie said.

"Thank you," Page added.

"De nada." After she had left, they both sat staring at the table. "I feel like we're an old married couple—not a thing to say to each other." Annie said morosely.

"Do you always hold a grudge the morning after?"

"You don't know jack about me. Marion."

"I'm going to take a bite of pie. A sip of coffee. Twenty aspirin. If I could walk out of here, I would. Since I can't—what's the beef, really?"

"Lying would be the major one."

"Part of the job."

"You don't have a job. Unless you're here to kill wolves." She was bitter. Page was an iron head, but even he could figure out that her feelings had been hurt.

"I'm here to save them."

"To make up for your past?"

"There could be worse reasons." He took a handfull of aspirin, washed them down with coffee.

"Eat some pie or you'll burn out your stomach."

"Yes, Ma."

"Fuck you, Marion."

He gave her a long look. "If you hated who you were, you might change *your* name. Page was a good man, and it's a good name."

"Taking his name doesn't make you that man."

"I had to start somewhere." He groaned as he changed position.

"Hurting?"

"Don't rub it in, OK?"

"Come on, go back to bed."

"Man, they did a number on me." He got slowly to his feet, nearly keeled over. Reluctantly, she took his arm, helped steady him. "What were you doing out there, you big idiot?"

"Getting the shit beat outta me. And don't say 'good.'"

Despite herself she gave a little laugh. "Mind reader." She helped him to his feet and led him back to the guest cottage.

He almost fell back into the bed; there was a fine sheen of sweat on his forehead. Despite all her best instincts, she fussed around with his down comforter a bit. "Thanks," he sighed, settling in. "What is this stuff?" he asked, patting the mattress.

She gave him a long look. He really did seem more like a Page. "It's called memory foam."

"So this bed remembers everything?"

"Aren't you a little too beat-up to think dirty?"

He thought about it. "Ask me in, what, 36 hours? Are you going to let up on me?"

"Relief is in sight." Her life according to the Magic 8-Ball. He looked at her in puzzlement, then gave up and closed his eyes. Before she left the room, she looked at him for a long moment. She had a pretty good idea now why Spatz had darkened her door. He wanted to know what she knew about this guy. Annie knew she hadn't given anything away. Because she didn't know anything.

*****

The News 7 Chopper flared out about fifty yards from the ravine. By the time the skids hit, Tricia and her camera crew were jumping out of the cabin, tripping and sliding in the loose shale. Tricia had finished her onboard broadcast. Now they were into the news-gathering stage. She and her boys would also try to shoot as much camera B-roll as they could get away with. That footage would be edited down back in Seattle. She took a long, delicious stretch, trying to work her pants back in alignment without looking too obvious. She saw Agent White approaching like a low-flying storm cloud. "I didn't give you permission to land," he barked.

Tricia had her story ready. "We had some high temps showing in the EGR." She'd worked that out with Arnie as he brought them in for the landing.

"Tricia, you don't even know what EGR is."

"The pilot says land, we land."

White turned to look at the chopper. "I can see his concern all the way from here." Arnie was opening up a thermos of coffee. He held it up in a salute as he saw White glaring at him.

"You know, Tricia, I went out on a limb here, letting you guys past the gate. Now you bite me in the ass. And what about all those other boys and girls of the press — they'll ream me six ways to Sunday over this."

"They'd ream you anyway, Colby."

"Yeah." He slowly deflated. "I think it was why I was

put on this earth. How much did you see from the air?"

"A body. Body parts, actually. Spread out. By the killers?" She didn't think this was the moment to mention that the story had already gone live.

"Big predators, more likely. Is this going to go viral? 'Chunks-of-meat-are-missing-hikers' kind of crap?"

"You make us sound like the enemy." He looked at her for a long moment, then they both burst out laughing.

"You slay me, kid. So OK, here's what I'm prepared to say. And yes, on the record. The corpse is probably female, and that's about all we can tell. The skin is discolored—leave that part out, please—so we can't even be sure if this is a white girl. Betz, as you know, was Caucasian. That's about all we can say. Oh, a hiking boot on one foot, but no clothes."

"Is that a sign of rape?"

"Get your mind out of the gutter. Grizzlies don't eat shoes. I think."

"Not a much better image, is it, Colby."

"Ah, fuck it. I can never talk to you guys like a human being. We've got a body here, and the odds are overwhelming it's the Betz girl. Violence has been done. That's off the record, too."

"But that's your professional opinion?"

"Yeah." He thought for a moment. "We'll ID her through her DNA."

"COD?" She used the acronym for cause of death.

"At this point, impossible to say. We're bringing up the mobile lab, so we should get some preliminary data within a day."

"I know I piss you off, but can we film?"

He thought for a moment. "Yeah, why the hell not. But I've released this site to all the news organizations, so enjoy your ten-minute lead. In a few hours this place will look like they found gold."

"Colby, I love a good stampede."

She signaled Jens to get out the Betacam. Kwan would double as her sound man. In the next two hours, they got all the usual footage: the assembled personnel, the ravine, the entrance to the hut. She lobbied to get herself inside the probable kill zone, but they were working it as a crime scene. She did her most important piece with the door to the hut behind her. This was the money shot that would lead the evening broadcast. The house-of-death segment, she decided to call it. It wasn't gold. It was better.

They were done and loading up the chopper by the time her first competitors started arriving. Not one of them had a helicopter. Sometimes these crates paid for themselves, she thought, as they lifted away.

White had told her there would be a press conference in the city hall this evening. She would nail the best spot for her and her crew. Then out the door for a stand-up live as the 11 o'clock lead. Edited in with today's footage, she would hammer the competition into the ground like tent pegs. Too bad Nightline was on ABC, or she could steam all night. Suck on this, CNN, she thought to herself as the Bell lifted away from the riffraff reporters below. Even her butt felt better.

CHAPTER TWENTY-THREE

Page slept until sundown, awakening confused by the last rays of light. He couldn't recall ever having been this out of synch with the rise and fall of the sun. He had always been an outdoor man, his body's rhythms tied to those of the solar ecliptic. He was a hunter, had always been a hunter. And game disappeared with the night, at least for a man with a gun. True, he had set traplines, even fish weirs now and again. Netted a few birds in seething flyways. But even these passive hunts were best practiced in the light of day.

Yet here he was in this strange bed, with deep, soft pillows and a down comforter, in a sort of parody of the rough-life cabins he knew so well. He was aware of a tickling in his soul, one he wasn't sure he liked. He had always chosen a hard life, but one that was clean. As the outdoors world was clean and simple. His life experiences in the domain of men, including his time in prison, only reinforced his preference for the natural, the nonhuman. He liked the animal's neutral take on morality, the rough justice of a panther instead of some blindfolded dame holding a balance scale. So he had thought, until Page Deschamps came along.

Now what was he? He was among his own kind, the

humans he had avoided. He felt pressurized, like a man deep underwater. Not a good image. He remembered the face looking up at him from under the ice, the hands reaching for the sky just beyond his reach, beyond infinity.

Page turned his mind away from that vision. He tried to think about his present position. A few times, mostly when he was young, he had tried to fit in at school, in the military. Tried to fit in with a woman or two. But he had always felt like a guy with punctured eardrums: when you didn't know what you were hearing, you talked like you had a speech impediment. So you stopped talking. How could he speak, how could he make sense, when there were so many voices on every side of every goddamned issue, roaring like a glacial stream falling down the side of a mountain—a deep rushing noise, a thousand voices in some incomprehensible chorus.

He was aware of the hour by the lengthening shadows and a stillness outside as the day's breezes, no longer warmed by the sun, whispered away into night. He got slowly to his feet, stiff as a thick slab of saddle leather, went to open a window. The air had the high desert smell of sage and creosote, mixed with the piney smell of turpentine. There was even a hint of wolf from the direction of the pens.

Through another window, he gazed across the patio at the warm light from Annie's office. Apparently she worked late. He decided it was time to get The Talk over with. He looked around for his clothes, but all he had were these surgical scrub things and a big cotton robe hanging over the back of a chair. When he lifted it up, he saw slippers on the floor.

He went down the breezeway that connected the two buildings, saw the office door was open. He stuck his head in, heard some soft music. Classical, coming from some speakers he couldn't see. "Evening," he said. His voice was cracked—it came out as more of a croak.

She was at her desk, looking at columns of figures on one of her monitors. She had three of them, he noted, and they all seemed to be in use. "Got a frog in my throat," he added.

"Maybe it'll jump out." She gave him a glance, turned back to her screens. He noticed she was sitting on a giant inflatable ball instead of a chair. She was in loose clothes that looked like something judo guys might wear. She looked comfortable, at the center of the web that was her business life.

"I might just go on into the kitchen."

"We need to get some snacks out in your cabin." She seemed to give the problem about 1% of her mind. He felt like a toadstool growing next to the Queen's throne. He shuffled off towards the next room. "Wait. Seriously. Here, look at this." She picked up a black globe from her desk.

He looked at the Magic 8-Ball. "Give it a shake," she said. He did so.

"What's it say?" Annie asked.

He looked in the orb's window. "End of the Line."

She gave him a long look and a short smile. "It sees

all, knows all. Sit." Annie gave him a tight smile. "Please."

He dicked around with it for a few minutes while she finished her work. Some of the answers—he didn't bother to ask any questions—were amusing if vague: "Got Me," "Maybe," and his favorite "Your Guess is as Good as Mine." He tried to think up a few of his own, but the best he could do was "The Check is in the Mail." It didn't seem all that funny.

Annie finally finished her task. "Spreadsheets. For my taxes." She gave a tight smile. "Not a problem for the average mountain man, is it?" He nodded, started to put the 8-Ball down. "Did you ask it a question?"

"No. The answers are all pretty vague."

"Ah, but they seem to have more meaning when you have a specific question. Try it."

"Do I have to tell you what it is?"

"Not at all. Jut the answer, if you don't mind. Give it a good shake."

She got up, went over to a big walnut sideboard, opened a thick door to reveal a liquor cabinet. She poured some amber liquid into two small cut crystal glasses. She handed him one. "Amaretto." She pointed at the 8-Ball with the glass in her hand. "What did you get?"

He had asked if there was ever going to be anything between him and this woman from a different planet. He looked in the window. "Wait and See," he told Annie. She tapped his glass and raised hers to her lips. "Was that the answer you wanted?"

He took too big a taste; it was like fire in his mouth, liquid fire that slid down his gullet. About halfway down, the fire turned into something complex and sweetly hot. There were tears in his eyes as he tried to answer, "Close enough."

"Something to do with the future?" She looked at him as if she knew the question. He could only nod as the liqueur set him aglow. Then he realized part of the glow was this—something had just changed in the room. She was looking at him as if he was there.

She confirmed that a moment later. "I'm flying to San Francisco tomorrow. I would like you to come along. Do you know the city?"

He nodded.

"Do you like SF?"

He shrugged.

"I want you to see what I do for a living. I know it seems kind of nebulous. You can just be a fly on the wall. Later we can do the town, as much as your old war wounds allow. Josef will fly us. Deal?"

"I don't have a thing to wear."

She laughed. "I didn't know you made jokes!"

Neither did he. He just didn't know where his bloodstained shirt had gone. It had some sentimental value. It was also the only shirt he had.

CHAPTER TWENTY-FOUR

Tricia had been able to find both a good cup of takeout coffee and a brioche at the trying-too-hard cowboy café. What was it called? Oh yeah, the somewhat too fey "Range Rider." The bar section had looked more interesting, with plenty of hicks mixed in with the SUV crowd. Maybe it should have been called the Range Rover. She'd go back later for a meal.

For now she was ensconced in a front-row seat in what passed, in the courthouse, for a conference center. Folding chairs were the extent of the amenities, and she was sitting on the front edge of one, despite the protestations of her by now jet-lagged body. But she wanted to be front and center for the Q&A, so here she sat, quietly writhing. She hoped and prayed there was a hot bath at the end of the trail.

There was the usual buzz in the room, with other reporters talking over camera moves with their crews, all of whom had been consigned to the back by a reasonably attractive deputy named Brenda. Things quieted down on the dot of 9 p.m. as Special Agent Colby White stepped into the room. Very Special Agent White, she grinned to herself. The Sheriff followed, a good head taller; she thought most Native Americans were on the small side, and in Washington state they usually were. But this huge guy had the wide shoulders and narrow hips of an athlete. He was kind of impressive. Probably good for an interview. She wondered how he ever got elected in such a thoroughly white-bread state.

White did the talking. He ran through the usual background stuff, but it was camera-worthy enough. He knew how to talk to the media, as Tricia well knew from his frequent appearances back in Seattle. He reported on the body, which was female. There was still no cause of death, but they had a probable identification from the hiking boot found on the corpse. It matched a pair given to Lisa Betz by her parents, this confirmed from photos sent by Detective John Gruder of the Palo Alto PD. White nodded to acknowledge a very good-looking blonde guy over in the corner. Standing next to young Brenda. Aha, Tricia thought, they looked suspiciously like a couple. She filed that nugget away for possible later use.

Already the reporters were straining at the bit, trenchant, even pithy questions bubbling up in their minds. Each doubtlessly calculating how to ask that perfect question while getting their profiles around for the cameras. White added that the cadaver dogs had not been successful, as of yet, in locating Lee Chun's body. If, of course, he was dead. Tricia had a quick image of young Mr. Chun murdering his fiancée, for no known reason, then heading out for parts unknown. Boy, she thought, *that* seemed unlikely. But to play it safe, she would try to pump Colby on that angle somewhere on down the road. If the second corpse didn't show up.

Colby wrapped it up with the usual catch-phrases: ongoing, continuing investigation, every possible state and federal resource, yada yada. He turned to Sheriff Manyhorse—she needed to get some background on that name—and asked if the Sheriff had anything to add.

"No."

"Then I'll open it up . . ." Tricia leapt to her feet, but she wasn't the first. ". . . to questions." Colby looked around, as everyone shouted at once.

He paused a beat, pointed to Tricia. Bingo, her prep work had paid off; she was going to have to do something nice for the guy. Something extra special. "Agent White, we saw the state of the body from News Chopper 7—could you comment on the condition of the corpse?"

"The body appeared to have been partially buried in snow or possibly loose soil. It was still frozen."

More babbling voices, but he gave her one more shot on redirect. She got her good side around to the cameras as she dropped the kind of bomb that made a young reporter's bones. "It appeared to have been dismembered."

He looked at her for a long beat. Damn, he's playing to the camera, she realized. The Agent was so often by-the-book-White that it caught her by surprise. And his delivery was perfect. "It was." She had what she wanted: an image planted in the minds of the viewers. Reasonably gorgeous young grad student, dismembered out on some high peak, a lonely, horrible and violent death. It really was golden. Thank you, she breathed to herself.

The rest was the usual round of self-serving questions, each reporter trying to score some new revelation that would make them look good for the boss. She was honest enough to admit that she wasn't all that different. What counted in this business was face time. On-camera counted, deep research didn't. Which was how most of the people here operated — they were personalities, not frickin' detectives. As she had told her friends for years, the "story" was just a hook to get her on the tube, a vehicle for self-advancement. Because if you weren't seen, you didn't really exist, did you? You might as well be in the newspapers or on PBS. Which made you, like Ms. Betz, stone cold dead.

As the crews broke down their equipment, she gave herself a small pat on the back. True, she was first and last a TV personality, not a print reporter. But unlike the rest of this preening collection of egos, she knew that delving into the story would create more opportunities for Tricia Helfer. Because she wanted more than a local news slot, even though KIRO was a pretty good gig. She wanted to play on the national level, which meant digging through the backstory. And she could feel the undercurrents in this cow pony town. Something more was going on.

Out in the lobby, she got her producer on the phone, made her pitch. Today's ghastly footage had bought her some cred, so she got the OK. Jens and

Kwan were sitting on a bench with their high-impact camera cases next to them; they were also working their phones. "Jens, get hold of Arnie—where is he, anyway?"

"Drinking coffee over at the Cowpie Bar or whatever they call it," Van Zant said.

"So he can fly."

"You know he doesn't drink. He was born ready."

"He's told me that, once or twice." They all laughed.

"We blowin' this scene?" Kwan asked.

"You three go back tonight. They need the chopper on call tomorrow." Both men groaned. "I know. Seven more hours in the saddle. I did get the bean counters to agree to a layover in Boise. You'll have rooms at the Doubletree. Be back in Seattle by noon. I think you can still get fuel out at the airport." She thought for a minute. "We brought some of those little Panasonics? The C3s?"

"There are two back at the chopper. And the GoPros—but the audio sucks on those." Jens sounded like the equipment snob that he was.

"I'll just need one cam and a wireless mic set."

"And *we* need a ride back," Kwan noted. She started to think about that, saw Agent White come out of the conference room. "I think we just got one."

*****

After White dropped the KIRO crew off, he wheeled his van off the airport grounds. He pulled over in an unlit area, turned to look at her. "Where to, little lady?"

"I'm dying to get out of these stupid clothes. And a hot bath would be divine." He nodded, gunned it away into the night.

She schlepped the camera case into the motel lobby while White parked his Fed Sled. A quick conversation with the guy behind the counter left her with a room reserved—but unfortunately, not until tomorrow. She went back out, followed White to his door. "Ah, the ubiquitous motel room," she said. He held the door open for her, followed her in. He unloaded his pockets, his pistol thudding onto the desk next to an assortment of phones, keys, and a few coins. She dropped her camera case next to his pile.

"How's the bed?" she asked.

"Big enough." She stripped off her jacket, headed for the bathroom. He sat on the edge of the bed and unlaced his hiking boots. A wave of pure fatigue hit him. He could almost feel the years sanding away his resolve, which he had once regarded as rockhard. It was now more like the cheap laminate on these walls, peeling up at the edges.

He dropped back onto the pillows, heard the sounds a woman made when she took a shower: the running water, the curtain hooks sliding, the discreet toilet flush as Tricia waited for the water to warm up. Homey sounds. Worth the risk—the very small risk—to his reputation.

Later, in bed, she spooned up behind him, wearing one of his extra T-shirts. They had been this way for about three years. A few nights spent here and there, using each other, in secret to the world, but openly between themselves. It helped their careers, just a little. And it gave them someone to talk to when they needed to talk. Despite their pragmatic relationship, there was some comfort to be had. Neither of them seemed to require much of it, but it was there. And tonight it felt pretty damned good, especially to Colby.

She wondered what was on Colby's mind as his breathing slowly evened out. She would have been surprised to find he was thinking about drones.

CHAPTER TWENTY-FIVE

Josef had them at SFO by 9 a.m., the inner bay still half fogged in, the colors of the salt flats bleached out under the pale, clear light unique to the Bay Area. It was always a homecoming for Annie, with her childhood haunts of Mill Valley just a few miles from the north end of the Golden Gate. These days she kept a townhouse up on Nob Hill. It was a corporate write-off more than a home, but it was a much warmer environment than the Mark Hopkins next door. The Mark *was* good for conferencing, and there were plenty of good restaurants all over Nob Hill.

The Israeli had called ahead for a cab to meet them at the executive airport that shared the runways with SFO. She had the cabbie drop them off in Union Square, where she had the singular experience of walking into Macy's with a man in a bathrobe. No one gave them a glance; it was one of the reasons she loved the town.

Page put up a big fight about the cost of his new wardrobe, but she pointed out he had been as good as on her payroll during the last few weeks. And he couldn't have bought a thing if his life had depended on it — he didn't have a credit card, let alone a wallet to put it in. It was like shopping with a caveman, she thought, and not the bearded Geico kind. Just a troglodyte out of some nether world. She rather enjoyed it.

Most of the Macy's jeans were too "new," as Page put it, so she suggested some dark slacks, a plain white broadcloth shirt, and a light golf jacket. He really fussed over wearing regular shoes, but she had to point out that boots, even cowboy boots, just didn't mesh with his new look. He balked at tasseled loafers, so they compromised on some severe black oxfords. When they were done, he looked like a rather nicely tailored washer repairman. When she told him that he actually seemed to relax. He truly was blue-collar, she decided.

Before they left for brunch at Pagano's, she also treated him to a shave and a haircut, which cost a lot more than two bits. While he was being trimmed she went back to a specialty store and got him some western wear. They'd leave the new Levis out for the horses to trample, then he'd probably wear them.

By the time they walked to the restaurant, he was visibly tired. Annie had a pretty good idea that he was in some real pain from his wounds. When they sat down she noticed he took the gunfighter's seat, his eyes on the door. "Lookin' for trouble, Tex?"

He slumped back in his seat, looking glum. "I told you, ah, forget it."

She took a menu from their waiter and without looking up said, "So, what are you?"

"I'm tired. Cranky." He looked at the wine and beer list. "I don't recognize a single one of these beers."

"What kind do you like?"

"Cold. In a can."

She waved the waiter over. "We'd like two beers. In cans."

The waiter didn't even blink. "And appetizers?" he asked. Annie looked at Page, who shrugged. "I think we'll start with some scampi." The waiter glided away without a word.

Page looked around. "What kind of joint is this? "

"Basque." He looked puzzled. "Just think of goat's cheese and fish."

He made a face. "On the same plate?"

"My parents liked the place." She went on to tell him something about her life in SF, and that led to her Mill Valley days. She left plenty of space for him to talk because she wanted to draw him out. In her business, quiet listening was the essential ingredient in creating relationships. So while she was a good enough conversationalist, she was even better at quiescence, stillness, focus. Unfortunately, he had one of the great poker faces of all time, so she wound up doing most of the talking.

He seemed to be a good listener himself, or maybe just watchful, like the kind of man who watched doors. She had made it through her high school days by the time they'd had a couple of PBRs and a platter of fancied-up shrimp which he grudgingly ate.

He sat with his hands guarding his plate. She asked him why he did that. "It's an old jailbird thing. You guard what's yours."

"Was prison a hard place?"

"Being named Marion?" He snorted. "Yeah, kinda hard."

"Can I ask what you did?"

He looked surprised. "I thought they told you all about me."

"Not really." The waiter brought their main order—Annie hadn't consulted Page about the food. She put a small forkful of halibut in her mouth, poured herself a glass of a pale, dry Riesling. She didn't offer any to Page, assuming he wasn't a wine guy. The way he picked at his meal told her he wasn't much for fishy delights, either.

"I boosted a Trans-Am." He held up the wine bottle the steward had left. "May I?"

"My, what fine manners. Of course." She signaled for a wineglass, which was brought to them in seconds. "You know, *Page*, good ol' Page, they don't even put you in jail any more for stealing cars." She smiled. "Especially in Texas."

He looked at her suspiciously. "Pull the other one."

"Seriously, it was on CNN. Putting a million guys in jail for auto theft cost Texas more than the cars were worth, so now they get an immediate deal. They walk, you might say."

"What's CNN?" He gave it away by showing a little smile.

"You *can* do it!"

"It hurts my face, but yeah, I can."

"You haven't had much fun in life, have you?"

He tried the wine, made a face, but took a second

sip. "Not a whole lot."

"So let's change that. You up to a little running around?" She looked at him long and hard. "But I want to hear more about you. And your past. Deal?"

They ate a few more bites, Annie as always counting calories. Page just didn't act all that hungry. He finally put his napkin on the table. "I guess I can't put it off?"

"Until tonight." She put her Diner's card on the table. "You ride in limos very often?" She got out her phone and made a call.

*****

She kept the ancient Mercedes 600 in the parking garage of the condo. The *Grosser* Benz, as the Germans called it, was in a metallic green, with tan leather and matching curtains. She had always thought the interior looked like a miniature railroad car. It had once belonged to some South American general. Annie had the bulletproof glass taken out because the old V-8 was too damned weak to haul all that armor up the hills.

Josef picked them up at the curb outside the restaurant. The Israeli liked driving the Teutonic sled—a Jew driving one of the ultimate symbols of German overkill made him laugh.

He whisked them down to the ferry terminals, where she and Page caught one of the tour boats that ran out to Angel Island. She kept some jackets in the trunk, as well as lap blankets for cool San Francisco summers. But the sun was shining down, so they used them to sit on. She enjoyed the day, the two of them speaking now and then. But mostly they were both quiet.

She thought about quizzing him some more, but after a while she realized she could learn more just being next to him. He didn't like to reveal himself, that was true. But in his body language, in the way he looked at things, she began to confirm that he was no mute, stoic movie gunslinger. He had the equipoise of a watchful cat. A big cat. She had seen him in motion often enough back at the ranch, but in this enforced stillness of fatigue and wounds, she got a sense of where he got his mojo. She saw it in the watching eyes, in the patient stillness as his scan took in data—he undoubtedly saw things that she missed. She was an expert observer—but of human culture. He seemed to take in everything.

Sitting here with him, she realized he was that unique creature: a hunter. She liked the coiled-spring quality it gave him. He seemed to embody the inevitable pairing of the hunter's senses, alive and electric, with its goal, which was to bring death. It made her realize how out of his element he was in this urban landscape, where the subject of death was all but taboo. She shrank from it, but she suspected he didn't. Annie wondered how big a gap that would create between them. To him, her world must seem like some make-believe kingdom, full of crazy, complex values.

Which made her realize an amazing thing, and it wasn't often that she amazed herself. Annie realized she was thinking about him as a potential relationship. It wasn't one of those TV-land things: nice girl falls for bad boy. She looked over at him. He was looking up at the wind-whipped flag, judging the vectors of the air. The position of the sun, the direction of the waves, the smell of the bay. It all must course through him, she thought, hard-wired directly to his senses.

She thought those senses probably never rested. She touched his shoulder. "Page." He looked at her, asking a question without a word uttered. "I like you," Annie said.

He looked at her for a long time. "OK," he finally replied.

She gave his arm a little pat. "I won't call you Marion ever again." He nodded, looked her in the eyes for a long moment. She had been around wolves when they were calm, even affectionate. They had this same distant look even when they looked you in the eye. She always thought at those moments that the wolf was in two places at once. "I bet you want to get back to the ranch, don't you?"

This time he smiled.

"First thing tomorrow. I have a meeting early this evening—a grip and grin. Can I park you in the townhouse?"

"Then the big talk?"

She gripped his arm. "I changed my mind. A little. You talk if you want." He seemed OK with that.

*****

She got back to the condo just before midnight.

The place was quiet. The guest room's door was closed, but she could feel he was in there. There comes a moment, between a man and a woman, a hesitation to take the one critical, unalterable step into a new and strange future. You went over the edge—or not. The brain always fears and says: if I fail, I fall. It was the heart that supplied the courage. Either way, one step, and it would all change.

She thought about opening the door, she thought about going in, but she didn't.

CHAPTER TWENTY-SIX

Special Agent White was working with the Sheriff and Gruder when he got a text message: "look out your window." He picked up his coffee cup and detoured past the front window on the way to the coffee machine. A big white van was out front; some wag had put CNN on the side in big, peel-off letters. It wouldn't fool a child, he thought. He put the cup down. "Boys, could you meet me down in the parking garage? I've got a little surprise."

He waited until Ben and John left, then called the van. "Bob, this is White. Go around the south side of the building. There's an underground garage for city vehicles."

He listened. "Hell yes, it'll fit." He listened again, headed towards the stairs. "Because they keep the snow plow down there, that's why."

White went down to the lower level, part of which housed the cells. The entrance to the underground parking lot was at the far end. The big, bullet-headed jailer, Preston Steeps he recalled, was leaning back in a chair. A gun-buff magazine was folded face down on the table that held up his booted feet. Colby noticed a wad of chewing gum stuck on one heel. The cop was talking to an older guy in a big cowboy hat, his jacket made out of what might have once been horse blankets. White had to push past the citizen, who seemed to be somewhat deaf to his footsteps.

"Doing your homework?" White asked as he got around the human toll gate. Steeps barely looked up. "Yeah. I am." White, as he kept going, turned to see why the harness bull had an undeniable note of malice. He belatedly realized the other creepy looking guy was Harmon Taber, the blowhard who had been working up yesterday's crowd. White filed that datum away: two Montana white guys, a gun mag, what else could you expect?

The white van was cautiously pulling in as he pushed through the garage's fire door. The man driving, Bob Dierdorff, was a notorious little old lady when it came to taking care of his gear. On the upside, his gear always worked. The big antenna arrays on the roof were folded down in their transport mode, which gave at least three feet of clearance. Gruder stepped closer to look the rig over. "RPVs, or I miss my guess."

"You don't think it's a CNN remote broadcast truck?" White replied caustically.

"RPV?" Manyhorse asked.

"Remote pilotless vehicle." Gruder was lost in admiration of the technical wizardry on display. "Drones."

The Sheriff sounded interested. "Are we going to rain death down on our enemies?" White knew it was a joke, since Ben wasn't smiling.

"This isn't the Middle East, Chief," White observed. "Didn't you get the memo?"

"I'm just a podunk Sheriff. I got that message years ago."

"Touché. We need to keep an eye in the sky with those bad boys out at that ranch—what was it, the Lazy Eye?" Gruder laughed at White's joke, which made him the only one actually amused.

"I could just put a scout up on a ridge." Ben replied. He probably meant it. "On a Pinto pony." This time the Sheriff allowed himself a toothy smile. "Make much smoke."

White stopped for a moment to consider that all three of them seemed to be in a pretty good mood. Maybe it was the feeling that the case had broken, that they were starting to make progress. He wondered if that would survive Dierdorff, who could be something of a sour apple.

The driver got out of the van, a middle-aged man with a full beard and male-pattern baldness. He was wearing a maroon sweatshirt emblazoned with a USC logo. He stretched the kinks out of his back, nodded at the other three men.

"You made good time," White said. He made introductions, Gruder almost painfully eager to snoop inside. "So show off your toys, Bob."

"OK. But no touch." He used a remote keypad to unlock the back. "The whole roof jacks up, but not down here. You'll have to duck." The van was packed with work-stations, flat screen monitors, roll-out chairs neatly bungeed to the far wall. Ben stayed outside, but Gruder duck-waddled in to look at the joysticks, rollerballs, and handheld remotes that controlled the vehicles. "Where are the RPVs?" Gruder asked as he reemerged.

"Tucked under the chassis. We access them from the outside."

"Do you have blimpies?"

Bob looked a little surprised. "I haven't heard them called that. I'm surprised you know about aerostats."

"A couple of companies test them out at Moffett Field."

"Ahh . . ." Bob smiled. "In the old blimp hangers. Hence, blimpies."

"You guys can talk tech on the way out to the site," White broke into what threatened to become an extended TED Talk.

"What's the sitrep?" Bob asked. He shooed Gruder away from the van.

"Very rural," White told him. "Ranchland, got a ridgeline we can use about five miles out. I haven't been there yet but we have some sat photos."

Bob snorted derisively, "What you've got is Google Maps. Wind? Sky? Do I have line of sight?"

"Let's get there, then we can figure it all out."

"I gotta do one thing first, Boss."

White thought for a moment. "Bathroom's through that door, past the ogre, up the stairs. It's the executive can, so flush when you're through."

Bob nodded. "Who's the ogre?"

"Big guy, arms like tree trunks." White gave a small,

very bright smile. "He told me he hates intellectuals."
White pointed at the sweatshirt.

"Yeah, right. USC." He headed off.

"So he went to USC?" Gruder asked.

White laughed. "We took it off a dope dealer. You
remember *Pulp Fiction*? The sweatshirt on that college
kid? Brains all over the backseat?"

"That was UCSC," Gruder objected. "UC Santa
Cruz."

"The pusher we caught must have been dyslexic."
Detective Gruder gave him a long look. "I shit you not."
White added with a cheerful smile. Yes, he thought; he
was feeling pretty good.

*****

Sheriff Manyhorse led the way towards the Rocking
R Ranch in his piece-of-crap Impala, with Agent White
once again riding shotgun. Gruder was back in the van
as it followed the Sheriff's lead. Doubtless both techies
were exchanging arcane lore, which White didn't
especially want to hear. After a few miles on an
unimproved road, Manyhorse pulled over to the side,
waving the van up beside them. He rolled his window
down, Dierdorff doing the same. "You say you need a
ridge?" he asked.

"Yeah, I'd rather look down on the scene. Back
from the ridgeline, actually. I wouldn't want to . . ." He
belatedly realized he didn't have to tell some Native
American guy how not to be spotted.

"Can you do off-road?" Ben asked.

"I've got all-wheel drive. Not too rough, if possible—sensitive electronics."

"OK. Maybe two more miles." Ben pulled back onto the road, then took a left about a mile further on. White noticed that he drove on some hard-pan as he left the road; they wouldn't leave any tracks. They soon found some old cattle trails, again were careful not to flatten any cowpies. White had once been to a county fair where contestants flung the dung for big prizes. He thought that about summed up this part of the world.

They finally stopped, got out of their iron ponies. Ben led them up to a stand of Douglas fir, one of which was lightning-blasted. This turned out to be the edge of the ridge, which really was nothing more than a long slope down into a valley. Far in the distance—a good four miles—was a ranch: corrals, barn, a biggish house. Agent White got out his Polish-made PZO binoculars and took in the scene. Things looked pretty quiet down there: no horses in the corral, no picturesque cowpunchers spitting chew and whittling sticks. There was a small herd of big SUVs parked off to one side in two neat rows.

"Nobody home?" he asked Ben, handing the glasses towards him.

The Sheriff shook his head. "We checked. Out with clients on a hunt."

Gruder took the glasses from Colby. "How can you tell?" he asked.

"The Sheriff has the eyes of an eagle," White

observed.

"The pack animals are all gone. The SUVs are what the clients come in. And there's a note on the door," Ben said.

"I call bullshit." But Gruder tried to look at the door anyway. "I don't see anything—how do you know all that?"

Ben gave him a mildly amused look. "I phoned them before we left—there was a recorded message." Behind them, Bob sniggered. "They return tonight."

"OK. Big laughs all around." White looked at Dierdorff. "So, Bob, what have you got that's good?"

"Normally I'd tether an aerostat—that's like a balloon, Sheriff—to that tree over there. Look-down camera, sensor pack to detect movement. We're too far away for reliable audio. But I suspect we have some winds around here, right? So that limits how much load I can put on a leash. A drone would do the trick; it could loiter up there out of sight, but fuel would be an issue."

"Even for fuel cells?" Gruder asked.

"They're getting better range every year, but for more than a day, I'd go with something new. It's called an H-AS, Hovering Aerostat. Think of a little blimp, about two meters long, with carbon-fiber winglets, booms really, and it's got slow turning mylar props. Weighs less than five pounds, all-up. Loiters for three days, uses a fuel cell as well as some auxiliary solar panels."

"Can it be seen?" Manyhorse asked.

"It's fuselage is clear plastic film, the booms are just

sticks, and the payload is about twelve inches on a side. Three hundred feet up it's invisible. And noiseless," he added. "This little puppy station keeps—that is, it floats in an exact position via the GPS. Set and forget. When it needs to come down for more fuel, we put in some waypoints and fly it where it needs to go."

"So is this a good spot?" White swept his arm around.

"Not bad. I have to stay here in the truck, though." Bob sounded unhappy.

"What?" Agent White looked surprised. "What happened to set and forget?"

"It's the regs, Agent."

"FBI Regulations?"

"We got a few, it's true. You ought to read the operations manual for domestic use—that came from the White House, I believe. Plus, I get time-and-a-half that way."

"So you've just been jerkin' my chain."

"Mostly. But yeah, the book says we monitor the machines that monitor the bad guys. I know, I know."

Gruder cheerfully helped Dierdorff get the aerostat out of big fold-out bins tucked into the lower chassis of the van. They also jacked up the roof, and unshipped and oriented the antenna.

Bob cheered up a little when Gruder offered to stay with him. Manyhorse agreed to send a deputy out once a day with food and other supplies, including a shovel and toilet paper. Apparently the FBI hadn't thought of everything. Bob said they could get satellite TV so they wouldn't be too bored. Gruder also thought he could work out a link back to the Sheriff's computer so he could be contacted when the subjects came into sight. The sat phone would also be available.

The aerostat required delicate handling; it was not much more substantial than a kid's balsa wood glider. The propellers worked in concert with a miniature flight computer to keep the stresses and strains to a minimum. And since it could float on the wind rather than trying to push through air currents, the mylar envelope had adequate strength. The launch consisted of holding it up in one hand and letting it float away, rotors barely turning. As it lifted overhead, Bob guided it with a handheld remote. When it got further down range, he would program its aerial path from the van. As he had predicted, it was invisible within a few moments of take-off. Agent White thought it was a pretty slick piece of gear. The cowboys wouldn't have a chance, he thought, as he got back into Ben's heap. They didn't have a chance because he wasn't going to give them one.

*****

That night, as Spatz was sleeping in his own bed, he heard his dog Friskie barking outside the house. That was nothing new. He loved the big old mutt, but Frison Biches were noted for being overly zealous in guarding the property, something bred into them in their sheepherding days in the Pyrenees. He got up—the dog seemed to be right under his window. But the barking turned to low growls. By the time Spatz got out on the porch, he heard the yipping of his pet in hot pursuit of some critter, headed well away from the house. Spatz felt glad he had such a good guard animal, and went back to bed.

The next morning he took his coffee out onto the porch to take in the new day. He squinted as he saw something in the dust just a few feet away. He nearly lost his breakfast when he saw it was the head of a dog.

His dog.

CHAPTER TWENTY-SEVEN

Josef got the Citation back to the Stanley airport in the late afternoon. Surprisingly, it was warmer than San Francisco had been when they left—the banks of fog coming on over Golden Gate Park and the Avenues just a memory. Unfortunately, Annie thought, some of the cold seemed to have lodged in Page's bones. He looked tired and pale as they waited for her hot-shot pilot, who had showed up none the worse for wear, to bring the car out of a hanger. The Hughes was still out at Wolf Ranch, so they would go back in the Land Rover. They got Page in the back, and Annie turned on the rear's heated seats and reclined the backrest before she got in the front. The hunter noticed the warmth after a minute and let his shoulders relax. "You can control the heat with the switch, here." She pointed to the back of the console.

"I think I'll leave it up."

"You look like shit, cowboy." Josef said with the usual male kindness guys liked to share.

"I'm allergic to big cities," Page managed to reply.

"Or you may have an infection." Annie sounded worried. As she put in a call to the ranch, she noticed Tricia Helfer, the reporter, coming out of the tiny car rental shack just outside the airport. It mostly rented Subarus or SUVs to the skiers. This time of year it looked like the reporter would have plenty of vehicles to choose from. Annie vaguely wondered why Helfer was still here. Maybe something had broken on the missing grads story. She made a note to check on that. Annie called and left a message for her chief veterinarian to meet them when they arrived.

Page wound up in the same part of the barn as before, sitting on the stainless steel table while the same brusque Rhona Aronson prodded and pried. "Your ribs aren't broken, so that's good. When the marrow is exposed you can get some nasty bugs into your system. The cuts are healing pretty well . . . " The doc took his temperature with an electronic device in his ear; the last time Page had seen a thermometer there had been mercury in it. "OK big boy, you can put your shirt on."

"What's the verdict?" Annie asked as she handed Page what she thought of as his SF shirt.

"Lawyers give verdicts."

"For Pete's sake, the diagnosis."

"Flu." She thought for a moment. "Probably. If he were a wolf I could be more specific."

"Flu? Seriously?"

"Yeah, in a wolf I'd say maybe distemper. He's not a city guy, is he?" Dr. Aronson talked right through Page's back. With this kind of bedside manner, Annie had a pretty good idea why she was a big animal vet. Page was just a slightly more intelligent horse, apparently. "He's not been around the modern viruses and germs, bacteria even, that you find in that gateway to the orient. Need I say more?"

"So, plenty of rest, chicken soup, some TLC?"

"None of that hurts. Doesn't help, either."

"As I recall, you don't have any kids?"

"Some aspirin to knock back the fever. Keep him warm."

"I was going to sleep out on the ground," Page said.

"Sense of humor—they say that's good medicine. I wouldn't know. Now I'm going back to my trashy paperback. I do get some days off, you know. It's in my contract. Human patients, they're not. Look it up some time."

After the vet clomped out in her Doc Martens, Annie grabbed some fresh scrubs off a pile. "Let's get you to bed. No floors for you tonight." Annie had to steer him away from the barn stairs; she didn't want him up in that room all by himself. Probably lying on the pine with one thin blanket, like some kid in a Dickens novel. Having Josef next door would be like having nobody next door. She walked him towards the house. As she got closer, he veered towards the cottage. But that was not what she had in mind.

When Annie had built the house, after her heated break-up with Spatz, she had designed her upstairs as her refuge. There were no guest bedrooms, no guest amenities. Not even a maid had been upstairs. A pragmatist at heart, Annie had built this as her last home. On the assumption that she would someday be old and gray in this place, she had designed in a small lift for some far-off day when she couldn't handle stairs. So far, she had only used it for sending things like her big-ass speakers upstairs, piles of books and records, and the occasional fancy meal from Yolanda. Now it was useful for Page, who seemed out on his feet. As they lifted up, he looked around in puzzlement. "I thought we were at the ranch."

"It's my own personal elevator."

"You're kidding."

"And here's where I live." She led him into the sunken living room, let him collapse into the half ring of leather sofas. She put his feet up on the big oak table piled with music and books. He looked around, nodded at the far wall. "Nice fireplace," he said. "River rock."

"I'll get a fire going." The elevator had really paid off whenever it came time to bring up firewood. She used fire-sticks and a bed of dry pine for kindling, got the tinder snapping and crackling. Red oak, split in quarters, went on as the fire caught hold. A faint scent of burning wood filled the room before the draft caught and lifted the smoke away. The evening was coming on outside, but the hills were still visible out of her tall glass windows.

Page sighed, seemed to relax, letting his head go back. "I like the sound of a fire," he said. "Great view," he added.

"I wanted to feel like I was outside, but inside." She laughed. "All the good points of the outdoor life, but none of the bad."

"Sitting on a rotten log, trying to dry your socks by

the ol' campfire."

"Heatin' up a can o' beans, pickin' varmints outta your beard." They both laughed. "I think we should have a little drink—a treat." She got up, went out of the sofa pit to a small bar built into the bookshelves that defined one side of the room. She got out two tiny glasses, brought back a fat-bodied bottle made out of dark glass. She poured them both a small amount, handed one to him. "Don't ask what this is—at least until you try it." She held her glass up for a toast. "To Page Deschamps."

"Which one?"

"The one here in this room." He thought about it, finally touched his rim to hers. He took a sip, let it slide down his throat. He thought about it for a long moment, finally smiled. "Wow," he said. He stared into the distance for a long time, almost as if he had left the room.

He cleared his throat. Annie was very still. "Page Deschamps was called the Preacher. He could turn a bad man into a good one. He did it to me. But he died for it." He paused again, then told the story, but through the eyes of the original Page, almost as if he were reliving something out of his own life.

*****

A few weeks before, the real Page had been trudging through the deep snows of the Katmai, looking for Johansen and another guy called The Wolf Hunter, a sometime poacher who worked both sides of the law. He pushed through the shadowless wilderness of big conifers. On the far horizon, there was a crescent of sunset, its golden hues highlighting the indifference below. This world was silent except for the crunching of snow under his snowshoes. But he wasn't lost; his nose, rimed with breath frozen into a crust on his face, was following the scent of cooking bacon.

It led him to a cabin that looked like something out of Hansel and Gretel, a square of undressed logs, the pitched roof topped with a good two feet of sugary powder. The windows were small, lit by a warm yellow glow from kerosene lamps. A vague lumpy shape, buried in snow, was lit by the glow from a side window. There were urine stains in the trampled snow by the front door. The bacon smoke rose straight up, indicating a falling barometer. A big storm was near.

Page looked inside. There was only one man in the room, and it wasn't Johansen. He slipped out of his snowshoes, pushed the door open with the barrel of his rifle, let himself in. If he had surprised the other man, it didn't show. The warmth hit his face like a warm slap.

"Where's Johansen?" he asked. He cradled the rifle in the crook of his arm.

"Outside." He pointed with his spatula.

"Is he armed?"

"Not any more." Page stepped out, surveyed the lump. A frozen arm was sticking up.

He went back in. "So what happened to the Swede?"

"He thought 100% was better than 50. How you

want your eggs?" He was holding up an egg carton.

"That wasn't what I wanted, Marion."

Page put up his rifle. There was no feeling of threat in the air, and with the coming storm, they were stuck with each other for a good long while. He shucked out of his parka. "Over easy," he finally said.

The men ate in silence, Page taking in the place. It was piled with furs and animal parts, some hanging from hooks. It was dispiriting, and he resolved to clean the place up. Once he got some sleep. The heat was making him dozy. "Where do I crash?" Page asked.

"You can have the bunk—I sleep on the floor."

"The bunk would be good."

"Maybe." The Wolf Hunter almost smiled. "Johansen smelled."

*****

Annie was curled up on the couch as Page came to a stop. He was not a natural-born storyteller, but he had lived that moment, and not so long ago. "So he converted you?"

"He was really good. I was a victim, he said. I just needed to see where all the poaching would lead, he said. I kind of hated to hear it at first. Then I got sick of his voice. And then, after the storm went through, I dunno, a light sort of went on in my head."

"You saw Jesus." They both laughed. "So now you're a tree-hugger." She crawled up to him and gave him a big hug. "See, not so bad, is it?"

"You're no tree." They stayed that way for a time. But she knew she had to break the spell, because there was more to the story, something else that had happened in Alaska.

"So you know there's more, right?"

"What happened to Page 1.0?"

He went far away again. "When the storm broke we headed out. We left Johansen's collection behind. It made me sick—all those creatures taken for a few body parts. For money. They'd rot in the spring. Just like the Swede.

"We went down the Moose River because the snow was too deep. It was like a highway. Only there was some sort of current under the ice that weakened it. Page was in the lead. We couldn't have been twenty feet from shore when he went in. I grabbed his pack, but it came off in my hands. He got tangled up in the strap of his rifle. I couldn't hold him, Annie. I couldn't hold him. He was under the ice—I could see his face looking up at me, or the sky. Then he seemed to relax. His hand was still out. I grabbed for it." He stopped, emotion choking his voice. "I really got to like the guy. I never had someone care about me like that. I mattered."

She wanted to give him another hug, but he was screwing himself up for one last part of the story. "I reached, but he pushed *my* hand away. I was his last chance, but somehow he found the will to push me back!" There was moisture in Page's eyes. "And then he held that hand open and palm up, like he was letting something go free."

Annie was deeply moved by the portrait Page was creating of a man she had never known. "Like he was releasing his spirit?" she guessed.

"I don't know. At least not until I got to civilization. I still had his pack. I opened it up to dry things out, see if he had any next of kin. I don't think he did. His job was his whole world, he once told me. But I found the letter you had written to the Wildlife Service. I think Stanley was his next stop. And I knew what he had given me. 'Here is my work,' the hand said. 'Go forth and do it.'" Page gave a little laugh, dabbed at his eyes. "He was always kind of biblical." He exhaled heavily. "I haven't talked that much since those days in the cabin. Let's just sit real quiet, is that OK?"

She said it was.

They watched the fire for a while. She put on some music, Stan Getz doing jazz sambas from back in the day. Vaguely, she was aware she had picked a track titled "Insensetaz," sung by Astrud Gilberto. Insensitive, in Portugese. An interesting choice, she mused. She was feeling like the insensitive one, because her mind was out ahead of this moment. She had come to a decision, one of those fault lines in life.

She didn't think he was much of a jazz fan, but the music seemed to calm him. Here was his chance to find out something new about life. About her life. Her music, her work. Her taste in Napoleon brandy, she thought, as she poured him another one. It was time for him to find out, because she was going to let him into her world.

He was asleep now, looking more relaxed than she

had ever seen him. The coiled=steel quality, his essential tension, was slackened, for a time. But not for too long. She would see to that. She didn't want him to lose his core, because she hoped to use it. He was going to be part of her life, and part of her plans.

Insensetaz.

CHAPTER TWENTY-EIGHT

Shades of night are fallin'
As the wind begins to sigh;
And the world's silhouetted,
'gainst the sky.

The whole crew were sitting around the fire pit behind the bunkhouse. Slim was poking at the campfire as he sang the Bob Nolan part from the old Sons of the Pioneers chestnut, "Blue Shadows on the Trail." Spatz was packing some cherry-flavored tobacco into his pipe. The flames of the fire reflected on the faces around the pit. A horse somewhere out in the corral kicked at the ground with a hoof, as Red was tootling away on a harmonica. He didn't have a musical bone in his body, but the Ukrainians were eating it up. This was what they were paying for, a real wild wild west experience, guns all day, hokey cow pokey at night around the old campfire.

At times, Spatz felt like he was more in show biz than the ranching biz, but this paid more. He got his pipe going. He looked around for his dog, an instinct born of years of companionship. He felt a quick stab of sadness when he realized his dog was dead. He had never figured out what had killed him, but it would have taken a lot of coyotes—or wolves—to bring that big guy down. And wolves didn't drag trophies back to put in his front yard. No animal did.

Spatz heard a wolf cry in the near distance, outside the cone of light from the fire. Wolf calls were common enough out here, but this wolf seemed to be by himself—he wasn't getting any callbacks. Like any outdoorsman, Spatz could identify different wolf sounds, most of which were aimed towards other wolves. But whatever the bastard was putting into his call, it wasn't loneliness. It was more like a challenge: come and get a piece. Or maybe, Spatz thought, it didn't mean a goddamned thing.

He got himself out of the mood by trying to take in his surroundings, all part of the outdoor life that he loved. Things smelled better out here. The grub was better, life was better. This was, at its heart, a simple operation, running tourists out to fire big guns, bag a few otherwise useless critters, bring them home as trophies. Something to stick up on the wall back in some Uzbeki-bekistan backwater.

Blue shadows on the trail . . .
Blue moon shinin' through the trees

There was a moon coming up, but there wasn't any blue to be had—without poetic license everything was gray. Maybe a little silver if you were a romantic. Spatz puffed at his pipe, his stomach full of an antelope stew the boys had rustled up. It was a nice night, and he was reasonably happy.

It was a long time ago that he had begun the battle to get the ranch back on its feet. His father had been good with cattle, not so good with a ledger book. When Spatz came back from the rangeland management courses at Texas A&M, he'd tried to get Dad more up to speed on the financial aspects of the ranch. It had been too large for a family to handle, but too small to make a profit. They'd never had the cash to expand, and the decade long fight to survive had worn his father down.

With Mom long gone, the burden had fallen on the only son. And through a mixture of political wrangles, and this hunting thing, Spatz had finally achieved the critical mass that got the whole shebang into solid financial shape. Now, by God, he was one of the valley's success stories. He was glad his father had gotten to see the fruits of his son's labors.

But he was also glad that Dad was long gone, because it meant he could run things his own way. If he were brutally honest—and he was—the old man had been kind of a softie. If he were alive today he'd be a Prairie Democrat, and that was not what the times called for. The land was fallow, a neutral thing, until man took it and molded it. It was there for the man, the strong man, not some worn-out tribe of Indians or a feckless government that no longer supported the men with the courage, energy, and strength to work it. The measure of their success was money and power, and what was wrong with that? It was the world's metric. And his.

Sitting around this fire with his crew, catering to the fantasies of guys from yet one more screwed-up country, he felt just fine. A success. He puffed at his pipe, looked out at the starry sky, and felt on top of the world. Not lucky, but a winner by his very nature. He again heard the wolf call out on his ridge. The Ukrainians stopped gabbling among themselves, listened to the distant howl. Thank you, Annie, he thought. Her wolves were doing him some good, part of the lore these Slavic clowns would take home to the old country. Bagging a couple would be even better. He wondered if she knew how badly she had blown it with him. He could have given her a real life, instead of her pathetic Earth Mother shit. Who was she: Gaia? Annie Mann, Queen Goddess. He laughed quietly to himself. Fuck the bitch.

The wolf howled again, but this time Spatz ignored it, warmed by the glow of his growing hatred.

CHAPTER TWENTY-NINE

Annie let Page dream away on the couch, thinking about what to do next. Once upon a time, she had sat in on a meeting between one of her actor clients and his agent, a crusty old New Yorker. He'd not had much to say, other than one gem: "When does the hero ball the chick?"

The line had landed with a thud in the room, not least because a chick was in it. Most of the western world was hip to women making their own decisions re "balling." The agent seemed to be saying that sex —at least movie sex—was still a male-dominated thing, which she thought was a laugh.

Annie let the Getz album come to an end, futzed around the living room before making up her mind. She hadn't taken that step into Page's bedroom back in San Francisco. That had been her logical mind remembering the pain from her wrong choice with Wilhelm Spatz.

But her heart told her this was a different sort of man, and she was damned tired of listening to her own brain. James Joyce had once written: "The reasonable man achieves nothing."

Annie Mann decided not to be reasonable.

She sat down next to Page, nuzzled him under an

ear. "Come on big boy, time for bed." He gave a sigh, didn't open his eyes. "Page, let's go to my room . . ."

He yawned, opened one eye. "Say what?"

"My room. My bed."

He started to go back to sleep, but both eyes came open this time. "Man, that was some dream . . ."

"What were you dreaming?"

"Big leather couch, quiet music, drink in my hand." He looked at his empty hand. "Got *that* wrong."

"Then what?"

He smiled, stretched. "Then I was asleep."

"Probably the company you keep."

"Then I woke up, like there was something I needed to do."

"There was. Is."

"You sure?"

"Hell, no. No one ever is. Where will this lead? Am I making a fool out of myself? Who is this guy? Who am I?"

"Maybe we should answer that one question at a time." He got slowly to his feet.

She noticed his stiffness. "Maybe we could just cuddle, if you're too beat up?"

"Ha."

"OK. Let me just put on some different music."

"Do we need it?"

"I do. I'm nervous." She laughed. "It's been awhile."

"It's just like—" he broke off.

"Riding a bicycle?" They both laughed. She went to the record shelf, but skipped the LPs. She took out a thick cardboard tape box, read the note her dad had neatly written on the back: "To be opened in case of passion." He'd put a little heart in one corner with her mother's initials. It was corny and sweet, and Annie had never played it. She opened it and pulled out the 10" reel-to-reel tape. She put it on the Revox, got it spinning. As the music came up, she led him into her bedroom, where she had always slept alone. The music wafted down the hall, and she took him into her bed.

The tape was a wonderful blend of jazz and Asian music, with a lot of sensuous ragas, most notably Ravi Shankar's "Bhimplasi." Also, a killer version of "Concierto de Aranjuez," Charlie Byrd on guitar, Chet Baker and Paul Desmond on horns. She liked to think that Ravi's daughter, Norah Jones, was conceived under the influence of an evening raga, maybe out on a patio under a Lone Star sky. Her own parents might have listened to this very tape the night Annie was conceived; she'd never had the nerve to ask them. But the music made her feel closer to them and to the love that had always been there for her.

Whether in time she would feel love for this strangely simple man would have to be seen. But as they came together for the first time, the music swelling in her, then gliding down to a quieter place, as they moved together, moved apart, then back more strongly, she forgot to care. He was a sure-handed man, who knew when to go slow, even taking his cues from the music. She relaxed, felt herself cresting one wave—like some bad image from Hollywood—then coasting down for a time. In the end she found the timeless moment, found it with Page Deschamps, who was another man entirely.

*****

For the next two days Gruder and Bob Deirdorff worked out a rhythm, bringing in the RPV once a day for a recharge of its fuel cell, then sending it back up to its racetrack in the sky. The two shot the shit, exchanging war stories, comparing retirement plans, watching sports on the satellite feed pirated from ESPN. They looked forward to midday, when Brenda would bring out hot meals from town. She and Gruder would take a walk for an hour or so, getting to know each other a little better. Away from the Sheriff's office she seemed to have more confidence, he noticed. Brenda was from what she described as "the trailer park side of town," and she was proud to have what was, in Stanley, a pretty damned good job. She particular appreciated working for her boss.

"You like the Sheriff?" John asked as they headed back to the van.

"I do."

"How'd he get the name? Not many guys named Manyhorse in Palo Alto."

"He says his greatgrandfather was a notorious horse thief."

Gruder laughed. "Stealing from the white man? That's rich."

She gave his arm a squeeze. "From the Utes."

"I'd like to think he got a few horses from The Man, too."

"And now he *is* The Man."

"Really? I see him as having an independent streak. Think he'll win the next election?"

Brenda thought about it. "The county is changing. We have more people who are, well, like you." He laughed at that. "No, really," she continued. "Folks like Annie Mann. I guess what you would call progressives. Ben's got their votes. But we also have the old-timers: cattlemen and farmers."

"What we progressives call right-wing assholes."

"Not many of those in Palo Alto?"

He smiled. "We keep a few on display in the museum. So that Taber guy is going to run against Manyhorse?"

"That's the bet at the moment. He's got some pretty suspicious ties, but the Sheriff has to be careful about calling that out."

"How come?"

She looked for the right words. "You know we have our share of nuts out here. There's a real anti-government feeling in these parts. That's what attracts the white supremacy types, even neo-Nazis."

"And having an Indian sheriff might gin up the resistance." He stopped, lost in thought. "So there's a lot below the surface."

"And a lot above, too. You see it in town now and then, but it all seems to hide behind, I don't know, political talk. Code words like freedom of speech, or issues like that thing at the courthouse the other day."

"Taber and the anti-wolf crowd?" She nodded. "I can see where that would be a divisive issue. But I would worry more about the Aryan bullshit. When you get crazy around here, there's always a gun nearby, isn't there?"

"On both sides. Every side, I guess." She sighed. "Not like this in California, is it?"

"Just a different set of problems. Trouble is part of the human condition."

"Still, I'd like to see some other part of the world."

"My offer stands. Come visit me."

She took his arm. "I will."

*****

Page found it a little weird to walk around this big house in his bare feet. He was barely used to being in a house, he thought to himself as he headed for the kitchen. He opened the refrigerator, and that was weird too—there was food in it. Yolanda—not in at the moment—had taken to leaving cooked meals for him. Strangest of all was being in a household that had staff; it offended his innate sense of privacy. But it wasn't his place, and he wasn't going to make waves.

He thought a little wistfully of his room in the barn which had everything he wanted, including a window he could keep open at night. That and a blanket just about did it for him. Here, he was upstairs in a giant bed, or hanging out in the sofa pit. Of course it wasn't all bad—

he was liking Annie quite a bit. Although he couldn't see the slightest reason for her to show any interest in him: they were from different worlds.

He got an orange juice out of the fridge, started to go back upstairs. The door in the entrance hall opened, and he heard Annie rushing in. Amazingly, he had slept longer than she had. The last six days of R&R had brought him back to life. The great sex hadn't hurt, either.

Annie didn't see him, so he followed her into her office. She gave him a big smile when she saw him. "You're looking better, Page!" She gave him a hug and a kiss. "But I got up before you — getting soft?"

"Like a marshmallow. Been out?"

"Went into town to get something. Check the driveway." She gestured towards the row of windows. He looked out, saw the Dodge Power Wagon. "I brought it back from the shop," she added.

She took his arm and led him outside; he was still in his bare feet, but that didn't stop him from making a circuit of the truck, tippy-toeing through the gravel. It had a new windshield, and the radiator and grill looked redone, but the bodywork was still riddled with bullet holes. He stuck his finger in one, said, "Different."

"Gives it that East L.A. vibe." She patted a scarred fender. "The shop says it runs like new."

He nodded approval. "I might take it for a spin. Join me?"

"Not today, I'm already overbooked. Tomorrow, for sure."

"Deal." He looked at her with a pleased smile, which made Annie feel a sudden warmth. "I'll just give it a little shakedown cruise this afternoon."

CHAPTER THIRTY

Deirdorff was all but nodding off out in the sun when he heard the monitoring system set off its alarm. He got out of his lawn chair, looked around for Gruder, but he was already inside. "What we got?" the tech asked.

Gruder used the tracking ball to zoom in on the image. A big old pickup, emphasis on old, was pulling into the ranch, leaving a low trail of dust behind as it moved towards the main part of the complex. "Zoom in a little more," Bob said. "Now, capture a still."

"How . . ?" asked Gruder.

"Keyboard. Control L. OK, now let's look at the still frame." Deirdorff brought the image up on a much larger computer screen, which allowed him to do some fast image manipulation, including a window-in-window blowup of the license plate. He did some quick keyboard work. "Now, we send it to the database back in D.C."

"I'm not good on pickups."

"It looks out of the '50s, maybe even earlier. Really square, big-ass wheels."

"The ranchers like to jack them up . . ."

"But look at those fenders." A flag popped up on

the screen, and with a few mouse clicks he called up the data that had just come in. "Aha. 1949 Dodge Power Wagon. And look who owns it."

Page drove right up to the door of Spatz's big house. He had taken the precaution of phoning ahead, and the pre-recorded message made him reasonably sure no one was here. At least, he guessed, none of the crew that had messed him up. If one of them did pop up, he had the 9mm in his belt to calm them down. He wondered if he would have come out if they had been here. Page thought yes, but it would have been at night.

He got out of the Dodge, stood for a long moment taking in the scene. The place felt dead, cicadas whirring away in the background. The corrals were empty, and there were a lot of SUVs and late model pickups parked off to one side. Probably belonged to the clients, he guessed. Page went over, saw all but two had barcode stickers pasted onto their windows. He was pretty sure they were rentals.

He went onto the porch, tried the front door, felt that it was locked. He pulled out his piece, shot the lock away. The gun's big report boomed away towards the hills. He stayed outside for a good five minutes, but no heads popped up from behind the barn, or anywhere else that he could see. He went inside.

*****

Annie was having lunch on the patio when she heard the crunch of gravel on the other side of the cypress hedge. Tour groups had been in and out all day, as well as the usual visits from supply companies and official visitors involved in the study of lupine wild life. But whoever this was knocked on her door. She let Yolanda handle it, but that only bought her a few more seconds of time before her cook came to the door of the study. "You have a visitor," she said.

Annie slid her chair back, got to her feet as a tall, extremely good-looking black woman stepped onto the pavers. She held her hand out to Annie, and they shook. "Tricia Helfer, KIRO 7 News," she said. Her voice went with her look: deep, evenly spaced.

"I saw you at the airport getting a renter."

"That's cool." She got right to the point. "I'd like to get some background on what you folks do here."

Annie half expected to see a film crew. But Tricia seemed to be it, carrying a small camcorder down at her side. She invited the reporter to sit down, and they did a little small talk until after Yolanda brought out iced Nilgiri and some English tea biscuits. Annie Mann had met a few reporters in her day, but she had always talked on point to address some project she was working on. The relationships were always symbiotic, as each side wanted something from the other. In this case, Annie saw little advantage to any on-screen time, and said so. Left implicit was the quid pro quo Helfer could offer.

But surprisingly, she had none. "I really am looking for some background. I'll be honest—I'd never heard of you or your work until I came here."

Annie had to laugh. "At least you're no suck-up. Would you like to look around?"

"You bet." Tricia held up her camera. "Can I shoot some basic footage?"

"Sure. Just leave me out."

Annie led her out to the drive, pointed out the main buildings, the kids and tour buses, talked about the outreach programs and the educational components that she thought were critical for the future of wildlife in Montana. She ended up at the gate to the wolf pens, where she led the reporter inside. Some pups were chasing each other up in the rocks and didn't seem to notice the humans watching them. Tricia, like most people, seemed tense at first to be in the same general area as wolves, but she finally loosened up. A mother wolf, stretched out on the dirt, watched the two women for a moment, then put her head back down. "Wow," Tricia said. "This is really cool."

"In these wolves you see the archetype of all our family pooches. But these critters have that perfectly honed look. Like machines designed for hunting."

Tricia agreed. "You can see every muscle—and they're just pups. The adult—a female?" Annie nodded. "She's got that no-fat look, too," Tricia continued. "All killer, no filler."

Finally Tricia put her camera away. "Did you get what you needed?" Annie asked.

"Yes. I've got a little sense of the place, now."

"And a little sense of me?"

"I heard you were sharp. Yes."

"I've never seen a newscast that didn't have a human component. It just doesn't happen. I think I have a better sense of you, too."

"Guilty as charged. I would like an interview. I should have called your people, but that doesn't always work, does it?"

Annie gave her a frankly appraising look. "I think I'll give it to you. Here are my rules: no gotcha moments. No crew. Just you and your little camera. And we do it now before I change my mind. And there won't be any breaking news out of me—I'm pretty savvy in interviews."

"Fair enough."

They had Yolanda switch to some mimosas while they sat on the patio and talked. Tricia had gotten a little tripod out of the car, as well as a shotgun mic as big as the camera. She set them up to the side and just let it run.

Annie didn't mind talking about her work, and it was clear that she and Tricia spoke the same language when it came to marketing, branding, selling imagery and stories to the public. Tricia, in fact, was quite blunt about what she did: "Somebody said we're all whores to the public. You know, selling our souls to get a story, to get ahead."

"I might have heard that." Annie smiled.

"But sometimes the story really is there. Something complex. And my job, when I'm good, is to explain it."

"Does that get the ratings?"

"Sometimes it does. Sure, the public can be craven.

They eat up the blood and guts. It's elemental. That's probably what led me out here today. When I looked at those wolves just now, I can see them, and this is corny, as beings."

"Don't give them human characteristics."

"But do they have personalities?"

Annie thought about it. "Do you have a pet?"

"No."

"Well every pet owner, as far as I can tell, thinks of their own pooky-wooky as a being. But if you break down those personality traits, they are no more than the basic, atavistic characteristics of wild animals. I heard someone say that the family cat disappears the moment it goes out the door. They run on instincts, and those instincts are triggered by their environment."

"Yeah, but I have a feeling you love these guys."

"I love what they represent—wildness. The open spaces, their elegant design, how they fit into their world. And most of all, this invisible thing they have: social structure."

"Do they have a chance? I mean, they're trapped and shot."

"And poisoned, hit by cars. They are really pretty easy to kill. Believe it or not, wolves don't have an innate fear of humans."

"The dog in them?"

"Maybe. After all, they were the first animals men ever domesticated. Or maybe they domesticated us!"

Annie thought for a moment. "I think that's where all the passion comes in. On the side of the wolves are a lot of people who see the virtues of dogs: the loyalty and devotion. They are the only species in the animal world that seem to like us. Or at least find us worth hanging around."

"How about cats?"

"Cats are users; we're food and a warm lap. But they can live without us, or anyone. With dogs, it's always the pack. That's probably how Rover sees us. Not so much a pal as a packmate.

"We had a killing earlier this year—a wolf we had collared and released. We even gave her a name, Brindle, after her markings. Brindle carried all the pups that the pack was going to have this year."

"You're kidding. None of the others bred?"

"That's the way it works in the wolf universe. She was killed by hunters. Her mate, the Alpha Male, was also shot trying to protect her. That seems like a very human thing to do. Loyalty to your mate."

"You'd be lucky to find that in a human." They both laughed.

"We rescued the male, tended his wounds. He just sat right over there and looked out into the distance, and I swear he was remembering the whole thing."

"Remembering her?"

"We'll never know. But I think so."

Tricia thought for a moment. "I think I'd like to do his story. Did you name him?"

"We gave him a number, but he wound up being the White Wolf."

"That's perfect. Can I see him?"

"We just released him a week ago."

"Oh man, I wish I'd seen that—when he got his freedom back. That's a magic moment. How did he act?"

"I wasn't there."

"Could I interview whoever was? This angle would get a lot of people behind your efforts."

"I'll think about it. That would be up to Page. Page Deschamps."

"Tell me he's sexy."

Annie had to laugh. She pointed at the camera. Tricia reluctantly turned it off. "That is one shallow remark!"

"I know, I know. But a big-shouldered guy talkin' like some rider of the purple range, maybe in a cowboy hat—that would be cool."

"He's tall, and thin. No butt at all—you wonder how he keeps his pants up . . ."

"Ooh, Clint Eastwood! Even better."

"I'll tell you what we can do. The White Wolf has a transmitter under his skin. It's new for us—this way we don't have to fit him with a collar. We can find him whenever we want in the helicopter."

"You have your own chopper?"

"You bet."

"That is way cool. I live in those things. So I can bring my camera?"

"You can bring a camera. And I'll bring Page."

"So, one more thing."

"Off the record?"

"Absolutely. There's another part of this story that

fascinates me—you and this rancher guy, Spatz."

Annie finished her drink, but her face clearly gave her away. "Aha . . ." Tricia breathed. "So, there is—or *was*—something between you two."

"I asked you not to sandbag me."

"I want your side of the story, not what I heard when I was kicking around town."

"I hate gossip."

"Do you really? Most of the planet loves it."

"I especially hate it when I'm the subject."

"Then let me get your side of things. Spatz seems to have a hard-on where you're concerned. And not in a good way." Tricia smiled; Annie grimaced. "So dish out the dirt, girl."

Annie thought about it, then used the intercom built into the table to call Yolanda back out. "OK. But I need another drink. Or six. Thinking about that asshole makes me want to lush out."

"Honey, I know the feeling." Tricia sat back in her chair, and waited for the big scoop. Annie didn't disappoint her.

CHAPTER THIRTY-ONE

Deschamps was uncomfortable in Spatz's house. It felt like one of those home invasion things, but was it an invasion when the house was empty? Questions his old self never would have asked. He looked around uneasily, hardly noticing the day-to-day things people had in their homes: magazines on an end table, a pile of firewood next to the fireplace, some pretty good western art on the walls. But some things weren't mundane, like the brindled wolf pelt over the mantel. Not too many homes had one of those.

He didn't see what he had come for, so he went into the master bedroom, which occupied the back third of this floor of the house. There was a big California King bed, more artwork, some nice wrought iron and colored glass lamps. A masculine space, but free of the Great White Hunter vibe of the living room.

Except for the one trophy he was looking for. Up on the wall over a low dresser, resting on wooden pegs, was Page's rifle. As Page got the big Barrett off the wall, he brushed against a framed photo on the top of the dresser. When he straightened it back up, he saw it was a sepia-toned photo of Annie Mann. It was one of those touristy things where you stuck your head through some old-timey painting, in this case a girl in buckskins. It was signed,

"From Your Cowgirl in the Sand." Page didn't get that. But the "With Love" part, *that* he did.

Page looked at it for a long moment, wondering just why Spatz would keep a photo—or anything—from the woman he was supposed to hate. Something seemed to crawl over the skin at the back of his neck. It took Page a moment to realize that it was embarrassment. He felt like a voyeur, and he didn't like the feeling.

There was one more thing he needed to do. He pulled a small vial out from his vest pocket, opened it. He hesitated for a moment, wondering if this was going too far. He finally put a single drop on Spatz's pillow. He was probably going to regret the gesture, but this at least was personal, a little note from him to the Boss Man.

As Page got back in his truck, he put his rifle on the seat next to the gearshift. He looked around the property for a moment, wondering if he should burn the place down. The members of this ranch had beaten him, shot his truck, and stolen his gun. The last being a real good try at humiliating him. Now, like a game of capture-the-flag, he had reclaimed his standard, his symbol. Honor restored.

If this was a war. He didn't think he would go so far as to say so. After all, he had come uninvited onto their property and had shot them a line of bull-pucky that was, looking back on it, pretty insulting. So, he thought, the little reminder on Spatz's pillow was just about right—it would be between the two of them, unless the rancher made a big deal out of it. The important thing was to let Spatz have the option to save face with his boys; that way things could stop right here. Page would settle for a tie.

Yeah, it was a pretty fair balance.

He started up the Dodge, unaware that he was being monitored. He was also unaware of what was coming over the far ridge.

*****

"This could be kinda close," Bob said as he monitored the drone's feed. From its synchronous orbit the RPV saw every part of the valley: Page in his truck, which wasn't yet moving. Like the guy was sitting and waiting, or thinking, or rolling a handmade cigarette one-handed like Gary Cooper. And up on the ridgeline, about to come into view, the Rocking R's hunting party, a line of men and horses kicking up dust as they returned to their ranch HQ.

"Or kind of interesting. You noticed he came out with a rifle?" Gruder asked.

"Oh yeah. Here, you fly the RPV for a minute; I need to get on the horn with White."

Agent White was eating lunch at a hamburger joint down at the airport. He was reading the local rag, *The Stanley Reporter*, while chewing a pretty good BLT. He had the paper folded back to the local crime report section — those pesky raccoons were stealing kibble from old Mrs. Darnell's porch — when his satellite phone buzzed on his belt.

He listened for a moment. "Yeah, thanks." He listened some more. "I'll contact Sheriff Manyhorse. We'll go with the plan we worked out." After another beat, Colby added, "Well, he'd better get his ass off the ranch, is all.

What's Page doing there anyway? Let's avoid a shoot-out, for Christ's sake. I don't need 'Ruby Ridge II' inscribed on my headstone, Bob."

The waitress came by, and he ordered a slice of apple pie, warmed up, ice cream in a separate dish. He called the Sheriff's office, asked to have Manyhorse paged. He said he would be over to the Sheriff's office in fifteen minutes or so. Just enough time to get some sugar in his system. Then he'd be ready to rock 'n' roll.

CHAPTER THIRTY-TWO

Special Agent Colby White was online in the Sheriff's office as Bob Dierdorff, using the comm links that Gruder had set up, fed him the real-time images from high over the Rocking R Ranch. The whole operation was also being storeded to a hard drive array in the War Wagon as the wags had dubbed it. In addition to a full range of data streams, there was two-way audio. Since the electronic record was required by the warrants issued by the DOJ, White had to watch his language—and not just the saltier words. If the whole thing went down the way it was planned, all of these records could wind up in court.

In Agent White's opinion, the Department of Justice had long ago caved on the unfettered use of drones for security operations. Even simple flights, weapons-free, were zealously monitored by oversight panels. Hence the constant stream of warrants the AG's office had to run past some federal judge.

Sheriff Manyhorse came in and leaned over his shoulder to look at the imagery. "What do we have?" he asked.

"Hunting party coming back in over that far ridge. They don't have line of sight on the house yet," Bob said.

"Who is that in the pickup?"

"Page Deschamps."

"Is that what we're calling him today?"

"Until we change the story for the general public, yeah." Colby looked up to see Manyhorse shaking his head.

"Is he going to screw up the arrest?" the Sheriff asked.

"If he doesn't get out of there, yes, he will." But a few seconds later, the Power Wagon pulled away.

The two lawmen spent the next few hours monitoring the situation as they got their forces organized. From the orbiting drone they saw the hunting party return. There was a lot of milling around as the pack animals were unloaded. Some animal carcasses were tossed into the back of a white Ford pickup. After a lot of handshakes and the taking of pictures, the clients got back into their rentals and headed out, probably to someplace that had hot showers and restaurant food.

The pickup and its load followed after, driven by one of the ranch hands. From previous research White knew that it was going to the taxidermist in Stanley. He could only imagine what the rig would smell like by the time it got to town. He arranged to have one of the Sheriff's patrol cars intercept it on a phony traffic beef, just in case there was something interesting on board besides hides and heads.

Just before he left the Sheriff's office, White glanced back at the screen. A small gaggle of ranch hands was hustling across the gravel driveway towards the ranch house. The ones in the lead were already pounding up the steps. He waited to see what the hubbub was all about, but the focus of their panic was hidden by the eaves of the porch. He finally gave up trying to decipher the scene and left the room.

What had been hidden from his view was Red standing stiffly next to the door, his pistol raised over his head in a two-handed grip, like a cop about to go through a door. One that had been shot open.

*****

One of the tools of Annie's trade was the focus group. A sample of humanity, chosen by sophisticated demographic analysis, was put in a room and questioned. But in a variety of subtle ways. The questions, even the format, had been honed over the years as the science of marketing grew ever more precise. It was psychology bonded to metrics: the quantifiable, statistically verifiable data that made a product—or a face—a winner. Made it an object of desire, or of affection. Viewed with respect, made covetous by design. Where surface was all-important; it made the difference between a Lexus and a Camry. Same chassis, different vibe. It was Calvin Klein instead of Fruit of the Loom. Tiger Woods as a spokesman. Tiger Woods not as a spokesman. The focus group sought the positives because negatives didn't poll well.

Except, of course, in politics. The one area Annie had stayed away from, because she felt that the very thing itself had been destroyed by the atmosphere of utter cynicism. The vast wealth of the PACs had immolated the product in its own advertising excesses. What was left was a smoking crater.

Her office had been transformed into a conference room by the opening of a few wall panels. Hidden cameras and microphones allowed her to sit at her desk while observing, on the big screen, the consumers scattered around a table in a very blah room. The audience today was entirely female, nondescript, pretty much looking like they had been plucked out of Target. They were being shown a variety of products up on *their* screen. All were lotions, most in tubes.

Annie thought it was a sort of picture-in-picture viewscape: if you looked far enough into her screen, then their screen, she almost expected to see smaller and smaller images, shrinking all the way to the vanishing point, right out of the universe. Like the Incredible Shrinking Man. A girl could dream.

While she could hear them, her voice only went to Harve Cletes, the owner of Strategic Analysis, the company she had subcontracted to do the fieldwork. She had done enough of these in her day. She could still smell the slight body odor, hear the chairs creak as some matron, or a car guy, squirmed in their chair. Which she had made sure was uncomfortable—it helped them focus somewhere else. "What's the word, Harve?" she asked.

"Emollient, surfactant, body butter, and coming in last by five lengths: cheap skin cream."

"No, seriously. It's late in the day."

"Sorry, I get giddy from all this horseshit." There was a pause, the sound of papers being sorted. But Harve's mind was like a rolodex; he was just trying to sound like he was working hard.

"Harve . . ." she warned.

"'Caribbean' was the magic word, just like you predicted. Good imagery: they see sun and beach, dark skin—the kind all the white ladies want. But we found it needs some back-up. Help us out here."

"Remind me what this crap is, anyway."

"Lotions for m'lady."

"Face? Hands?"

"The whole shooting match," Harve laughed.

"You're in the bathroom, you've got wrinkles—"

"And baggy saggy skin. Dry, flaky, like leather."

Annie sounded exasperated. "Stay on point. So it's a cream for the body." She thought. "Pour le corps."

"So 'body cream for the corpse'." He deliberately mangled the French pronunciation.

"Make it 'crème' not cream. Accent grave."

"'Caribbean Crème. Caribbean Body Crème. Crème pour le corp." He said.

They both thought about it for a minute. Annie finally broke the silence. "How many more groups do you need to run?"

Cletes thought about it. She could almost hear the wheels grinding. "Say three more to really test out the name. I want to see if the French flavor is too exotic." They both knew it wasn't, but they were spending the client's money, not their own. "We also need to work out the colors, graphics for labels, packaging. The usual shit— we've all done this a million times."

Annie looked around as she heard tires on the

gravel. She saw Page get out of the Dodge; he was carrying a rifle. She felt a little electric shock run down her neck, like some danger signal. It seemed every time he showed up, there was some new angle. But it was not an unpleasant sensation. "All right, Harve. Let's button it up. Good job."

"I can't believe we get paid to do this," he laughed. But she was already out the door.

"Where you been, cowboy?" she said, trying not to sound too bouncy. She realized it felt good to be outside in a real world with a sage-laced breeze, a setting sun in her eyes, kids and parents wandering around, wolves in the pens stirring at some unseen signal. And this tall skinny galoot giving her that rarest of gifts, his smile of pleasure.

"I'm not a cowboy."

"That's too bad. I really like a fella handy with a rope." She tapped his rifle. "You got another gun?"

"Same one."

"I thought . . ."

"Yeah, he did. But now it's back with Daddy."

She looked impressed. "You went in his house?"

Page nodded. He was about to ask her about the cowgirl in the sand photo, but something made him stop.

"And?"

He shrugged. "Nice place." He guided her towards the front door. "But yours is a lot nicer." They went inside.

*****

Wilhelm Spatz was in a bad humor throughout the evening, but there hadn't been much he could do about it.

In his quiet fury, he sent Red and the boys out to scout the ranch, but other than the door, there didn't seem to be anything missing. He'd finally decided it was chickenshit vandals who didn't have the balls to actually rob the place.

When he went to bed that night, he almost missed the clue. He was getting out of his clothes, tossing his keys and coins on the dresser when he noticed the photo. Annie's photo. It was turned to the wall. He looked up, saw the rifle was gone.

Something seemed to break inside him, a dam that had held back some of the anger he felt for Annie Mann. It was a pain, a deep gut ache, the humiliating fact that he had missed her all this time. You could hate even when you still wanted.

As the emotions washed over him, he realized that, truly, hate was the obverse of love. Just as intense, just as primal. She had sent her agent, her new loverboy, into *his* home, right into this bedroom that had been both of theirs. Where they had made love and made plans. The signal couldn't be more clear.

He put on some sweats, went into the living room, reached for the intercom out to the bunkhouse. But he realized he couldn't let them know about the assault. Not just that it made him feel weak. But because it *was* weak.

And he didn't do soft. It took three stiff drinks before he was finally able to calm down enough to go to bed. But when his head hit the pillow, and he smelled the wolf piss that Page had left, the scent marking his new territory, that was the moment Wilhelm Spatz knew that he had to kill them both.

CHAPTER THIRTY-THREE

The Hostage Rescue Team—which often had nothing to do with hostages—set down at the Stanley airport around 0200, a squad of eight FBI operators in the back of the Westland twin turbine AW139. The ultra-quiet Westland, a special purchase from the Brits, was followed a few seconds later by a much noisier Bell Jet Ranger. The Westland did the heavy lifting, as each HRT operator, with full battle dress, added 300 lb to the payload. The Bell would stay above the scene, as its SAR—search and rescue—configuration included a swiveling nose ball that housed a spotlight as well as thermal imaging sensors. The TACO, Tactical Air Commander, would ride in the Bell. He, or in this case a she, would be tied into the communications net, directing traffic as well as linking imagery from the chopper, sending data to the troops on the ground as well as a live feed to the FBI operations center back in D.C.

Special Agent White was glad to see them arrive. He'd been in Stanley seventeen days and was running out of clean BVDs as well as patience. He had the warrants in his pocket, and his ground game would include a second tactical unit of Feds already out on the ridgeline with

Dierdorff's truck. They were, in fact, lined up on the ridge like Apaches looking down on an isolated ranch. But the Apaches never swung the way these guys and gals would swing.

The Sheriff also had a full complement either on the scene or headed there. The FBI would box in the ranch in a rough U-shape. White and Manyhorse would complete the box by driving a mix of Feds and locals up the main road as cleanup, once the main forces hit.

White had enjoyed working with the big Indian, and in fact admired the Sheriff's professionalism despite the cornball atmosphere of the county. White turned as the Sheriff pulled up in almost the last police vehicle left in town, an old, old Blazer eaten away by rust. Its rocker panels looked like lace doilies. Manyhorse had two riders with him. Tricia Helfer had somehow managed to find an all-black outfit that looked vaguely military; Gruder, on the other hand, was in his usual Levis and pullover fleece hoody. Both were kitted out in Kevlar vests, although the newsie wasn't going to be anywhere near flying bullets. On her it looked good, White thought. On Gruder, the frat boy, not so much.

Tricia took in the scene with her little camera perched on her shoulder like a beer can tipped on its side. The shotgun microphone was wrapped in one of those huge wooly wind socks. Having her along was a calculated risk on White's part; he was pretty clearly showing favoritism. In his defense, White *had* sent out a bulletin to the local news agencies about two hours ago. It wasn't his fault if they all were off in Boise, Salt Lake City, and other media markets. From the phone calls that immediately ensued, he knew they expected him to hold up operations until they could get resources on the scene.

Tricia, bless her heart, had a nose for news. She'd stayed around, talked to Annie, got the man-on-the-street interviews with her little Panasonic, kept the pot boiling back at KIRO. And the KIRO News 7 chopper was even now winging its way back. Her nostrils practically flared as she took it all in: the cyclic beat of rotors, the idling turbines, the big dark shapes doing a last weapons check as they stretched outside the choppers. The place smelled like night dew on sagebrush mixed with the reek of unburned JP4. White took her aside. "You're digging this."

"It makes me all wet."

They both laughed, which got a few looks. "You've been all wet for years, Trish."

"You know what I mean, big boy."

"Let's do it right here—blow my whole career."

"They teach you double entendres at Quantico?"

"French was for pansies. You ready to fly into the hellstorm of resistance?"

"A couple of snoring cowboys with their dicks in their hands?"

Gruder and Ben came over to join them. Gruder had an AR15; the Sheriff had unclipped a Mossberg 12-gauge from one of his patrol cars. "You're both smiling. Is that a good sign?" Gruder asked, adjusting his vest.

White noticed the Sheriff was protected only by a gabardine shirt; maybe his badge could just stop a BB. "You got a Kevlar T under there, Chief?"

"Just my rabbit's foot I got from my shaman." He looked at the dark figures over by the Westland. "They look pretty military."

"Let's hope they're not the Paraguayan militia. They flew in from Salt Lake—not my regular guys. Watch your language, by the way—one of 'em is a chick."

"Fuck you, White," Tricia said. They all laughed, feeling good now that they were getting it into gear. They followed White over to the AW139, grabbed seats in the back. They were given headsets and mics, as the chopper's flight mechanic plugged them into the onboard communications system. In seconds, they were lifting away, the big Westland surprisingly smooth as they rotated away to the east. White looked at his watch. *"Zero Dark Thirty."*

"I saw it. Hope *this* chopper doesn't crash," Gruder grinned. Tricia turned her shoulder cam towards them. "Look grim, boys." White flipped her off, belatedly realized they were now on the record.

"Don't worry, Special Agent Man—we'll fix it in post," Tricia said, her smile lost in the dark of the cabin. After that, their nerves kicked in, and they were silent, except for the quiet voices of the flight crew as they hurtled away into the dark.

*****

Red was locked deep in a dream—a big-assed freight train was bearing down on him out of the night, its headlight pinning him in a stalled car on the tracks. The tracks were wiggling like spaghetti sliding off a plate. He half woke up, the dream still in front of his eyes, as his mind came up enough to make him wonder if he'd had some bad Italian for dinner. But the last Wop meal he could remember was back at the joint, served on a metal tray with a hunk of oily French bread.

There was a huge roar over the roof accompanied by light shining through the curtains; it sounded like the mother of all windstorms. Then he heard the screams of sirens, men shouting, the door splintering in, with more screams—or shouts—mashing together into one big assault on his senses. Someone pulled him to his feet while they shined a super bright light in his eyes.

"Got one!" someone yelled as they whipped his hands behind his back. His guts went hollow as he realized what was going down. Whoever had his arms used them as a lever to drive him down to his knees. He tried to fight back, but the voice, so close to his ear he could feel hot breath, said "Go limp or I break it." He complied. At this point what was the use. His head was pulled back, and someone stuck something in his mouth, swabbing the inside of his cheek. "Chill," the voice said, and then the unseen man let him slump to the floor.

More boots were in the bunkhouse now as the other cowhands were marched out by men in dark khaki, faces hidden behind IR goggles. Someone had brought a full assault team, he realized. Despite the dire situation, he felt the dread ease back a notch. The worst had happened, now he had to suck it up.

Agent White, as On Scene Commander, stood out in the area between the corrals and the main house. Tricia was over by the bunkhouse, filming and talking to the camera as a frowzy looking bunch of cowhands were marched out.

The warrant that had authorized this raid was broken into sections. One stipulated arresting Red; he'd been caught on camera as he assaulted Page. No one else had made the cut with the judge. They would have to get the ramrod to turn in some of his buddies, or Spatz, if he was involved. Unless they found a smoking gun. With Red in the bag, the warrant authorized the immediate gathering of a DNA swab, hoping for a match between his sputum and the DNA found in the abandoned Saab. That was also now done.

Next on the warrant was finding the Olympus camera, any memory cards, computers and their files, and any cell phones or internet-enabled devices. Anything, in fact, that tied this bunch in with the murders of the two Stanford kids. This would allow Gruder and the FBI forensics team a chance to look for further electronic evidence.

And finally, they would be turning the place over for signs of the missing boy's body, although the odds were slim that it was anywhere nearby.

Spatz was led out of the house by one of the Sheriff's officers. While he was not named on the warrant, any resistance would get him bundled off to the jail for a night of bad sleep. He slipped on a jacket to fight the chill, then went over to one side of the front door to take in the scene, arms folded tight to his chest. He looked royally pissed, but cinching in his anger. White thought he was probably a pretty fair card player; there were no obvious tells of a guilty conscience. Of course, in three decades in law enforcement he had seen any number of guilty guys who had a poker face.

The Westland did one more circuit of the area before lifting off with Red on board, letting the dust swirls and rotor noise trail away. The FBI motorcade was disgorging G-Men armed with the usual gear, from fingerprint kits to klieg lights. Some of the agents were already set up in the house as White went up the steps. He stopped for a moment to look at Spatz. Neither man spoke.

White entered, to a scene he had taken in a thousand times. The place was rapidly being turned on its head as the troops tossed the house. The harsh lighting gave the room a real crime scene vibe. The colors of the throw rugs, the fabric curtains, were all washed out; the lack of shadows seemed to distort the dimensions of the room. The heads and pelts on the walls—that was downright macabre. White wondered what kind of person could sit with his pipe and slippers under those dead glassy stares. This was not the place for vegans.

Gruder came down the hallway, holding up a glassine evidence bag. He was smiling. "OM-D."

"That's the right model. Got a serial number?"

"It was peeled off the bottom. But each camera has its own metadata built in. I think the lens even has some hard data points."

"Data in a lens?"

"They have internal circuitry now that slaves into the computer in the camera body."

"And the chip?"

"I didn't want to handle the camera too much. We can look at it back at the Sheriff's office."

"Any computers we can tear into?"

"In the study, where I found this," Gruder said.

"Outstanding. Is Ben back there?"

"He's doing the bedroom."

White went into the master bedroom, which thankfully was trophy free. It was a nice room, with a king-sized bed and a mission style headboard and matching bureaus and dresser. White nodded to Ben, who was going through the drawers.

"Anything?" White asked. Ben pointed to a framed photograph on the dresser as he poked through Spatz's keys and wallet, which had been dumped in an Indian woven basket.

The FBI agent bent over to look, whistled softly to himself. "Why does he have her picture when he hates her guts?"

Brenda came out of the closet, holding her own small digital camera. She smiled at White. "Hold your enemies close and your friends closer?"

White looked at her in surprise. "You've read Sun Tzu?"

She looked puzzled. "Nah, it was in some weird movie with that British guy. Statham."

Gruder came into the room with a fresh supply of bags. "*Crank*?" he asked.

"No . . ." Brenda was trying to remember the name as she held a bag open for Sheriff Manyhorse. He dropped the wallet and keys in. "*Transporter?*" Ben asked. "That was a good one," he added.

"No, these two guys in prison . . . they framed him or something." Brenda shrugged her shoulders.

White recognized what they were doing: decompressing after the adrenaline jag of the raid. They had wanted to pull it off, and they had. Spectacularly well, in fact. Now they were harvesting the fruits of their efforts as they bagged and tagged. White found himself enjoying the company of this bunch.

Tricia came into the room, looking pretty flushed and excited herself. She had been forcibly held back when they landed, bantering away in the Westland with the flight crew until the takedown was complete. Since the all-clear, she had been literally running from one point to another, getting her breathless commentary down as she took it all in. Now she looked around, her little recorder still perched on her shoulder like a pet parrot.

"Nothin' to see here, lady. Move along. Did you find your Pulitzer moment?"

"Red looked pretty surprised. Spatz told me to get the fuck off his porch. The SWAT guys looked great. I feel like I'm embedded in the best goddamned unit in the annals of crime fighting!"

"Is that thing still on?" Gruder asked, laughing.

"Oh, yeah it is."

White smiled. "You want to go around saying nice things on air, do you?"

Tricia reached up and switched it off. She led Special Agent White out into the hall; she didn't want any witnesses. She looked around, pulled his head down and gave him a big, long kiss. "Thank you."

He gave her a quick hug. "You're full of shit, but thanks."

She flashed him a big, showbiz smile, then turned it, as if by magic, into a warm, genuinely affectionate one. White felt a little something blossom in his old, mostly cold, heart.

CHAPTER THIRTY-FOUR

Annie had stopped reading newspapers years ago when she became allergic to the ink—it raised blisters on her fingertips. And the ink, or maybe it was the paper itself, had a musty, stinky smell she disliked. So she had a half-dozen e-papers on her Google homepage, including several European ones. She also subscribed to the *Washington Post* and the *NY Times*. She had dropped *The Wall Street Journal* after one too many red state editorials.

As far as TV news, she would rather be boiled in virgin olive oil than have to watch any local news, anywhere. Just as with print journalism, she broke out in hives, at least metaphorically, when exposed to advertising. She didn't need the gastric relief on offer with the evening news, as neat a bit of symbiosis as was to be found in the media world.

She was therefore surprised to find out that Stanley was in the media mix, a headline banner popping up both at *The Huffington Post* and, amazingly, the *Guardian*. Truly, news was the new international opiate. After a quick read, she switched over to CNN with a pang of guilt; she had once worked with them on their marketing plan. She still felt a little responsible for

Larry King's demise. There was a big crowd in front of the Stanley courthouse in the "over-the-shoulder" graphic sharing the screen with the newsanchor.

CNN, of course, didn't shoot much of its own video unless the story was right under their window in Atlanta. The footage was from KIRO in Seattle. And only one KIRO employee, as far as Annie knew, was anywhere around here. Apparently Ms. Helfer was more than just a talking head, as witnessed by her grainy but serviceable video, which seemed to be a bunch of night-time shots of some raid. There was no SWAT team in these parts, but their origin was explained when she saw Special Agent Colby White directing traffic as his troops deployed.

Annie watched for a while, engrossed despite her usual distaste for such media hoo-ha. Her favorite shot was of Red, arms pinioned, being frog-marched out of what sure looked like the bunkhouse out at the Rocking R. He was dragged past some sleepy-looking ranch hands lit in chiaroscuro by the police high beams. Spatz didn't seem to figure in the story, which had her puzzled.

CNN then aired Tricia's live stand-up, the courthouse in the B.G. That background featured a real media circus in full swing at this very moment. From the camera work, it looked like she had a full ENG crew shooting the current footage. Annie watched a few more minutes until Anderson Cooper started to repeat himself. Annie used the intercom to give Josef a call, briefing him about the big doings at the courthouse.

She then went to find Page. He needed to get in on all the fun.

He was out with his favorite veterinarian, who was pulling out a few stitches. His new "western" shirt was off, his levis stiff and new. Page's bruises, especially the big ones around his ribs, were a sickening yellow-green. "How's the big animal?" Annie asked.

Rhona Aronson was looking a little less acerbic in the light of day. Annie thought maybe the older woman had finally gotten some sleep. "A week makes all the difference. He took a licking, that's for sure." She finished her snipping, carefully pulled out bits of suture. There was a light sheen of sweat on Page's forehead, but he wasn't groaning. Annie looked away; stuff like this made her a more than a little squeamish. "I ask one more time: do I need to file a report?" the doc said as she cleaned up the wound with some distilled water.

"What kind of report?" Annie asked. She handed Page his shirt.

"I could call this 'work-related stress,' unless he wants to sue your ass."

"How about: he fell down in the shower?" Annie teased.

"Then he sues your insurer's ass."

"It *was* kind of work-related," Page said. He mopped his brow with his shirt before he put it back on.

"Yeah, you kicked dumb old Red with your ribs."

The Doctor looked interested. "You never did tell me what happened," she said to Page.

"A horse's ass kicked him," Annie cut in.

"Whatever. You two lovebirds don't need me, I've got an abscess at noon." Page sat on the table while he put his shirt on. She shooed him off. "On this exact table."

"Come on Page. Let's go see Red." Page looked surprised. "He made it onto TV."

*****

While Josef prepped the Hughes, Annie ducked back into her office to download some of the news footage onto her tablet. Page joined her in the back of the chopper as the turbine spooled up. They lifted away, and once again Annie thought that there were a couple of things in life that money could buy: one was this kind of mobility. Even in a nice ride like her Land Rover, this would have taken forty minutes on a good day—much longer when snow covered the route.

And, as always, she thought about the tax write-offs, which in the end made her laugh at herself. She hoped she never became *that* mercenary.

Page studied the CNN footage as they flew low and fast over the terrain. It had only taken one flight before Page, who'd logged his share of rotary hours hunting wolves, had decided Josef was what pilots called a "hot stick." He just had a certain flair, never quite cutting past the edges of the performance envelope, but with a quick, sure touch that could make every ride a thrill. Personally, Page kind of enjoyed it, but it did make him a little air-sick to look at the iPad.

He gave that up and had Annie fill him in; by the time he was up to speed, they were approaching Stanley. "Where do I put down?" Josef asked over the intercom.

"I'd like to see what's happening in town. Around the courthouse."

"Low?" he asked.

"Let's show the flag a little, maybe two passes, so the film guys can catch our kick-ass wolf logos."

"Roger." The bottom dropped out as Josef headed down to 200 feet. He slowed as he came over the town's perimeter, booting the pedals so that they sailed over the crowd sideways.

Annie saw all the heads below snap up as they roared past. This was the sort of stunt that she couldn't pull in a more regulated area. But Stanley wasn't exactly on the FAA's map. Josef did his patented rising turn, burning off forward velocity by a quick sliding climb, followed by a dive back the way they had come. This time there were plenty of cameras on them as their shadow cut across the throng below. The Red Wolf on the side of the hull would probably make a great shot.

"Product placement in action! Now, on to the airport," Annie said. "Nice job," she added.

As they hovered down onto the tarmac, they parked near the KIRO 7 news chopper. Annie counted two other machines, one from Boise and the other from a station she didn't recognize. They got out of the back while the rotors were still slowing. Annie always instinctively ducked her head; Page, she noticed, stood straight up. Men were such show-offs, she told herself.

But she also liked that about him: if he had a fear of something, other than soft living, she hadn't seen it.

Tricia Helfer came out of the back of the KIRO chopper, slipping on a Channel 7 windbreaker. She was followed by the two members of her ENG crew. She came over and gave Annie a surprisingly warm smile. "Remember me?" she said in a nicely ironic tone.

"I think I've seen that face somewhere before." She shook Tricia's proffered hand.

"And is this our mystery man?" Tricia held her hand out to Page. He shook, but didn't say anything.

"Not one of my fans?" she asked Annie.

"He doesn't have a TV." She turned to Page. "Tricia Helfer—she talked to me a while ago about poaching."

He nodded. "Oh."

Tricia took Annie's arm and led her out of earshot of the others. "Tall dark and quiet. I didn't think there were any left."

"Yeah, he's two of a kind."

Tricia didn't get it, but she shrugged and got down to business. "I'd like to talk to him." She saw Annie tighten up, almost imperceptibly. "At his—or your—convenience. And I'd like to get a shot of you in front of your helicopter. I really want that wolf's head in the B.G."

"Be my guest. I'll talk to Page about the other thing. You're not hurting for stories—that stuff from last night was pretty impressive. How'd you get the jump on everyone?"

"I have my sources. Right, let's get you on TV."

"I don't want an interview."

Tricia looked at her. "It's time for you to tell your part of the story. This is Red State versus Blue State, Annie. Extermination against conservation. You've got pro-gun skinheads and gun-control longhairs fighting over wolves. And who has the guns? The bad guys.

"To people who love wolves, it's almost the family dog. Jerks like Red, those people kill them. They think they're vermin. And I think that's what got the two Stanford kids iced." Tricia came up for air. "Whew. I get excited over this stuff."

"Tricia, I also sense a certain excitement over the career ramifications."

"A lot of what I do is shallow. I know I'm a talking head. But I don't want to always be fluff. I've stayed here pounding the ground when no one else gave a flying fuck. I've done off- camera interviews with you and with others. For background. I've done my homework. If I'm doing it to advance my cute ass, then so what, if I do a good job. I—"

Annie held up a hand. "OK, OK, you've made your point. But let me think on it. I'll talk it over with Page. He is, at least in theory, still undercover."

"*That* sounds interesting right there."

"You'd be surprised. So let's get your shot, and I'll say a few words about the tensions in the valley. Then I'm going over to the courthouse. I want to see Red's ugly face behind bars."

*****

In the normal course of events Red would have been held in isolation for the twenty-four hours the law allowed. In reality, this was a small town with a very compact power structure. Wilhelm Spatz was part of that hierarchy, and that got him through the back door, which was opened by the county jailer.

"Mister Spatz." Preston Steeps looked out into the underground garage to make sure they were unobserved.

"Preston." Spatz pushed past the big man, strode down the hall. He looked the place over, the ancientfd barred doors that led back to the actual cells. He turned back to look at Steeps. "This place is a sardine can. Red could walk right out of here with one hand tied behind his back."

"No sir, he can't." Spatz's gaze made him feel a little tongue-tied.

"Why not?" He gave Steeps a tight smile. "Other than it would be illegal."

"The doors you see here in the hall may look old, but the cells themselves are locked and unlocked from the Sheriff's office."

Spatz looked up. "And I see they have cameras. Are they recording?"

"Just video. It's OK to talk."

"So they saw me come through that door just now?"

Steeps looked a little smug. He was tall enough to just reach up to where the hall camera was fixed. He pointed at the cord coming out the back. "It's been on the fritz for the last hour. Ever since Mister Taber said you wanted a private word with Red."

"That was good thinking." To himself, Spatz wondered how much thinking this lug could do. But you had to work with what you were given. "So which cell is Red's?" Steeps produced his keys, which unlocked the old-timey doors that divided up this part of the basement. Red's section, as advertised, was a row of four much newer steel units that looked like the fire doors in an office building. The windows were about eight inches square and thick enough to be bulletproof. There was a standard looking flip handle, but when Spatz tried it, there was no resistance.

"The door solenoids are operated from upstairs." Steeps indicated a card reader next to the jamb. "I swipe my card then wait for the office to buzz the lock."

"How do I talk to him?" Spatz rapped on the door, which barely resonated. He looked into a brightly lit cell with cinder block painted off-white. Linoleum floor, stainless steel toilet and sink combo. The concrete had been formed into a bedstead, and Red was sitting on the thin mattress. Wilhelm tapped again, but Red seemed lost in thought.

"Push the button, speak into the grille, sir." Steeps indicated a wire-meshed panel with a large button set in one corner.

"Red." Spatz had to take his lips away from the grille to look into the cell. It didn't seem very ergonomic. "Get off your cowboy ass, son." Red flipped him off.

Spatz looked at Steeps. "He doesn't recognize my voice."

"They're cheap-ass speakers in there. Anything good, somebody'd carve 'em up."

"Red, it's Spatz." He turned to Steeps. "How do I hear him?"

"The cells have microphones."

"We really do live in a police state."

"Down here, we sure do."

"And do they record this, too?"

"As far as I know, they don't. It would be illegal," he added.

Spatz grunted. "Thanks for the insight, Steeps. Now I'd like to speak to my foreman for a moment. Privately."

Steep thought about it, nodded. "I'll be just around the corner. Come out when you're through."

"Yeah, I kind of planned on that," Spatz said acidly.

CHAPTER THIRTY-FIVE

The Sheriff's office was crowded, and the energy level was high. Most of the FBI's task force had pulled out, including all of the SWAT team and their helicopters. White was the center of attention as he congratulated the people swirling in and out. He was particularly careful to praise all the members of the Sheriff's team, even those who only stood and served. It was not hard to make the gesture; White had gone from hero-to-zero more than once when the Big Dogs had stomped in.

That it would happen here went without saying. Even now, elements from the Hoover Building were doubtless jostling each other as they raced for the planes that would carry them west. White sat down on the edge of the desk in Sheriff Manyhorse's office, a styrofoam coffee cup in one slack hand. Truth be told, he was bone tired. Tired of living out of a suitcase and tired of this backwater. There was only one Starbucks, for Christ's sake.

He downed a last slug of acidic coffee and thought about walking over to get a mocha grande and one of those egg and sausage things. He tossed the cup in the trash, went to look out the window. If anything, the media circus was ramping up. He turned back his cuff to check the time on his wristwatch. They were obviously setting up for the six p.m. broadcasts for the mountain states. Tricia and her gang were not in evidence; her time would come an hour later. Truly, she was in hog heaven.

"Knock, knock." Detective Gruder stood in the doorway with Bob Dierdorff.

"Come on in, guys."

"Wasn't sure you wanted company," Gruder said.

"Man, I'm just tired. I haven't slept in thirty hours."

"I'm fresh as a daisy, Boss," Dierdorff said. In fact, he looked in pretty good shape. And Gruder—well, White had never seen him look anything less than West Coast glossy. It helped when you looked like a teenage surfer. "So I thought I'd head on out," Bob added.

"I can't think of any reason to keep you here. You must be tired of the inside of that van."

"One more slice of pizza and I'll throw up. I haven't seen a real bed in a week," Bob said.

"We've got fresh troops coming in from D.C., so you're good to go. Fine work, Mr. Dierdorff." The two men shook hands. Bob turned to Gruder, held out his hand. "Detective. It's been real. But I kind of want to see somebody else's face for the next few days." They shook, gave each other a nod.

After Dierdorff left, the two men headed back out into the main office. "Where's the Chief?" White asked.

"Out on the steps being interviewed."

White laughed. "I'll have to hear that. All three

words." Gruder saw Brenda working a computer, gave her a nod. She smiled back, but looked preoccupied. "Brenda working for you? White asked slyly.

"She's pretty efficient."

"That wasn't what I asked." They both grinned at each other. "Gruder, I'm going to break down and fraternize with the troops."

"They'll appreciate that, Colby."

"I mean you, you idiot. Uh oh." White saw Annie come into the Sheriff's office. Alone. "I wonder where Mr. Deschamps has gotten to," he said.

"Got me." White had not filled in Gruder on Page's dual identity. The Detective still thought Deschamps was the real deal. That was something White knew he was going to have to clear up.

He gave Annie a nod as he and Gruder came up to her. White made a point of looking around. "Grow up, Agent White," Annie said. Colby shrugged. "He's not here. For obvious reasons."

"So what brings you to this bustling metropolis, Miss Mann?"

"Once again, please just call me Annie. I wanted to go down and stare at Red for a minute. Can you do that for me?"

"We're not running a zoo here. He's off-limits until we charge him."

"And that will be . . ?"

"When the higher ups get here from the coast."

"To get their faces on TV." She grimaced. "Doesn't that gripe you?"

"Honestly? No. I'm a company man." He sighed. "And I'm so dead tired I've lost all interest in this case."

"I'm not sure I'm happy to hear that. Red wasn't acting by himself. You've just started to pry up the lid on this whole can of worms."

"Miz Mann. I have over three decades in this line of work. To continue your not very original metaphor, Red is just the first worm in that can."

"And worms can turn," Gruder said with a smile. Annie looked a little pissed for a moment; clearly she was being lectured. "Yeah, I asked for that. My apologies, Agent White." She turned to go.

"Don't go away mad, Annie," White said. She was amazed to see him give her a warm, almost shy smile.

She nodded. "More like a huff." She thought for a moment. "Oh, Page wanted me to give you a message."

"Ah-ha . . ."

"He'd like to talk to you. Tomorrow, if you're not too busy."

"I sort of wondered if he was going to be around."

"He is."

"Annie, we were going to get a beer. Celebrate the moment." Gruder said. "Join us?"

She smiled. "Being seen with you guys won't help my image with the locals. So yes, I'd like to stick them in the eye."

They got to the Range Rider and found half of the county was already there, a boisterous mix of locals and TV types from around the West. White, as the man of the hour, was spotted by the house manager and ushered into a booth near the bathrooms. The manager whisked a "reserved" placard off the table and personally offered them free beers. White tried to play the high-minded public servant, so Annie took up the offer for all of them.

"This place is a madhouse!" Gruder had to pitch his voice up half an octave to carry through the noise. Somewhere in the audio mix they could just make out the threads of some sort of music.

"You guys ever see a movie called *Aces High?*" Annie asked. They shrugged a no. "It's an old Billy Wilder flick. Guy trapped in a cave. Kirk Douglas is a newsman who brings the story out to the world via radio. People load up their families to drive to the site. They set up Coca-Cola stands. I think even a Ferris wheel."

"A media circus," White said.

"Literally," she replied.

"So how'd it end?"

"The guy died, down there in the ground. And the circus left town."

"Old hot dog wrappers blowing in the wind. Maybe some sad harmonica music. Is that about right?" White asked. The manager brought them a pitcher of beer and frosty mugs.

Annie poured, since it was theoretically her lager. "I kind of hate to see it happen to Stanley," she said.

They raised their mugs. "To crime," White proposed.

"To the media locusts," Gruder added. "They lay the ground bare, then move on."

Someone jostled Annie's elbow, spilling some of her beer.

She looked up to see Spatz looking down at her. Harmon Taber was right behind him. Annie and Wilhelm locked stares until she slowly turned her mug over, dousing his boots in beer. He didn't react, just held her in a cold, cold gaze before finally moving on to the adjacent poolroom. "Who was that with Spatz?" White asked.

Annie refilled her mug. "Harmon Taber."

"He looked at me like I was just off the slave boat."

"He's big with the second amendment crowd," she said. "Aryan nation type. They don't have the Klan here or he'd be Grand Vizier."

"Wizard, actually. Then he'd have even more reasons to hate me," White said with deceptive mildness.

Spatz wasn't interested in a game of pool, but he didn't want to be seen outside by any of White's or Big Chief Manyhorse's minions. In a loud, crowded place was where he wanted to be. So he picked a small round table in a far corner. He took some empty glasses off of it, put them on the floor. He absently wiped at the wet rings on the top as he sat down.

He and Taber waited until a waitress took their orders. The poolroom, through the vagaries of local law, was a smoking zone. Spatz lit a cheroot, offered one to his companion. Taber lit an old meerschaum pipe. With his white beard and bald, pink pate, he looked like an old Dutchman. He certainly had the limited worldview of one; Taber was a blockhead.

"So, you talked to your man?" Taber asked.

"I did."

"And he is innocent, no?"

"No. He's guilty as hell."

Taber raised one eyebrow. "He said this in the jail? That is asking for trouble. Unless you . . ."

"I didn't know he wasted those two Stanford weenies until a half-hour ago."

"Then you are not implicated."

"They've got this thing they call 'accessory after the fact.'"

"They have a law for everything. It is why — "

Spatz cut off the other man. He was in no mood for a harangue about the unalloyed rights of man. "It means I can swing for something my guys did."

"But would he implicate you?"

"There were two of them in on it with Red. Slim, and that Indian of mine, Chester. Right now they just have the goods on Red. He can hang pretty tough, but this White guy is sharp."

"For a coon."

"For anybody."

"And you talked about this in a cell? How do you know — "

"I'm not an idiot." Spatz pulled a wad of file cards from out of his pocket. "I slid cards under the door. Read this one."

Taber pulled out some Ben Franklin reading glasses. His lips moved as he read. When he finished, he

handed the cards back. Spatz tore them in strips, put
them in an ashtray and lit the fragments one by one,
careful not to set off the smoke detectors.

"He came back to our little hideout." Spatz looked
into the distance as he pictured the scene. "They'd
killed a bear; Slim and the half-breed stayed behind to
pull the teeth and claws. Red goes on up to the camp we
had hidden in a gulch. The door is open. He sneaks up,
his gun in his hand. He sees movement inside, and
Red—you know his impulse control isn't so good—he
fires away. He drops the Chinese kid—the boy. After
that . . . Well, after the first one, the second one's free.
So he does her."

"The Jew girl."

Spatz looked at his companion for a long time. He
didn't consider himself anything like a New Age guy,
but he also didn't have Taber's casual dismissal of
someone just because of an accident of birth. For
Wilhelm, hate had to enter into the equation. But hate
was a personal thing. It came out of something done to
you. Like Annie, and the way she'd ridden his ass for
years. And, to be honest, he'd done it to her, too. Hate
was war, not like this clown's knee-jerk reactions. But
he needed this same clown's help, and he needed it
tonight. "Yeah, the Jew."

They sat for a minute, sipping their beers like any
two old farts. Taber seemed to be waiting for more. "So,
Harmon, that's the picture. Red can fuck me up, sure.
But if the law gets to one of his two sidekicks, who are
dumb as shit, I'm cooked."

"And all of this because of this camera I hear about?"

"Red kept the damned thing. Like a trophy. Then he uses it right in front of me. And I have to admit, it never occurred to any of us that it could send pictures out into the world."

"You were bitten by the technology."

"I'll tell you what else. I hear they used drones on us. Eyes in the sky."

Taber's brow lowered. "This makes me angry. We have no right to even the air any more. They look down, they spy. Big Brother. We need to stop this."

"Exactly. Which is why I need your help. And I need it tonight."

"Perhaps. Do you have a plan?"

Spatz did. He had put part of it in motion years ago when he had built a cache up in the mountains, hidden away. Like those for the old fur trappers, it was a supply of guns, food, all the things needed to live off the land, should trouble come. All they had to do was get to it. Slim and Cecil the Indian were already headed up there with the horses—Spatz had sent them out earlier today. They should make it without being observed—as far as he could tell, the FBI and the Sheriff had pulled their resources away from the ranch.

"Yeah, Harmon. I've got a plan. And here's how you can help me." He smiled. "And strike a blow for liberty." He looked at Harmon Taber for a long beat, reached into his jacket pocket to pull out a fat manila envelope. "What I've got in mind will make you the next sheriff."

He pushed the envelope across the table. "A few bucks for your campaign." Spatz then told him, in detail, what he wanted. They both agreed it would make a hell of a night.

After Taber left to set things up, Spatz sat alone, nursing his drink. He felt calm inside, which was a little surprising considering how the next few hours might go. He thought about his life, the things he'd done or not done. He had always tried to live it with some guts— Hemingway's grace under pressure. Now, like the aging writer—and at nearly the same age—he was going to roll the dice. There would be no gun-cleaning accident like Papa Hemingway had in Idaho; how much guts did that take? But he had been feeling the first hints of autumn in his life, from reading glasses to stiff knees. Maybe even a fall-off in his mental acuity. Just a half-step, a first hint. Life was still vivid to him, but it had to be said that much of it was also repetitious. Not unpleasant, but sort of grooved. The same.

He sipped his beer. The last cold one for a while. He felt a tingle of adrenaline, of danger. He was going off the charts, into the unknown and, by God, it made him feel more alive than he had in some time. Maybe he should thank Red for going off the rails last month, maybe even thank Special Agent Whitey for arranging the raid last night.

But not Annie Mann. Chances were he was not going to be able to do anything about her for a long, long, time. He had to admit he'd never worked out a plan, and now he was playing things by ear. That day was on hold until he pulled off this present caper.

Revenge might have to wait, but he knew her day would come. He knocked back the rest of his beer, looked at his watch. A few more hours. He went over his mental checklists. Spatz had a money belt wrapped around his middle—he'd cleaned the safe out at home. The rest of his liquid assets had piled up over the years in the Caymans. He liked to think it was nestled up next to Mitt's. The ranch had been unencumbered for a long time now, and the title had been with his lawyer for years.

The cache was in place, the horses were on their way, and the boys had packed plenty of weapons. He had a satellite phone, battery out just in case somebody was tracking it. He'd ditch any other electronics before they could zone in on them. The truck was gassed and in position. He assumed they had ways to track it, so they would switch to horseback about fifty miles out.

Once up in the Absarokas they would disappear. No federal high-tech bullshit could track men on horses in that immense wilderness. Fuck the satellites, if they even flew over Montana. And fuck the drones, and all the electronic snooping. The truck would be at the bottom of the river, so the posse wouldn't even know where to start. It was a pretty good plan, for spur-of-the-moment.

He was feeling the adrenaline for sure now. He went out the back to burn off steam. He didn't want to walk past Annie. He might spoil it all by belting her right where she sat.

CHAPTER THIRTY-SIX

The action began about three in the morning. Agent White, alone in his motel bed, was vaguely aware of the smell of smoke. Was it a dream? Light flickered on the other side of his lids. He awoke to the sound of doors slamming on either side. The rooms that still housed the last of his crew. He sat up, his body stiff and cranky.

He got to the window, looked out to see both of the Agency's remaining vehicles on fire, dark smoke roiling out of their heat-shattered windows. The gas tanks hadn't lit off, but they were going to. Basically a tidy man, he always parked his shoes in the closet under his neatly hung clothes. He pulled on his sweats, grabbed his shoulder rig and pistol, and a walkie-talkie he used for short-range communications. He was just opening the door when the first gas tank went up, the characteristic yellowy orange of the blast driving him back into the room, which was now full of flying glass. The detonation hit his eardrums like the back-blast from a bazooka.

Colby retreated to the bathroom, which had a high, small window, divided into two panes, one of which slid. He got it open, saw he would never fit. He went back into the room where the curtains were starting to smoke, grabbed a chair, went back to beat out the aluminum frame—this was his only way out. He knocked away the glass, cleared out the metal divider and dove through, head first, ending in a shoulder roll. He found himself sprawled in a blessedly cool alley. He thought he might have some flash burns on his face and hands. It was lucky he'd gotten his clothes on.

As he went down the alley he drew his Glock, chambered in a round. He came around to the front of the motel, checked to see if everyone had gotten out. It looked OK—all the doors were open, and he saw most of his people standing well clear. In the distance he heard a siren, but only one. Stanley probably didn't rate two fire engines. It took a moment to realize the siren was headed away from the motel.

The fire truck had been routed towards the residential area. The unit rounded the corner and pulled up to the house of Sheriff Manyhorse. He was standing on his porch wearing his robe while he looked at what was burning on his lawn. He held his service revolver down at his side as he took it all in. He almost felt like he was a Negro back in the civil rights movement of the '60s, right down to having a cross burned on his lawn. This, he thought, must be a first for an Indian.

In the distance, back towards town, he heard the single boom of some sort of explosion over towards the airport. He stood one more second, surveyed his street, where the only people in sight were his neighbors standing around in their nightclothes. The firemen started to get out of the pumper, then got back in and roared off.

Things must be worse somewhere else, he thought as he went back into the house to get in uniform.

*****

Spatz felt he had a pretty good plan, if Steeps came through. The big man went up the front steps to the courthouse, banged on the locked front door. Steeps was supposed to be on the other side. Spatz would use his gun to "threaten" the jailer, who would be forced to let Red out. He had to get past the electronic lock downstairs, but he had that all worked out. He stood. He waited. No Steeps. He banged again.

Steeps was in the lobby, as planned. He could just make out the rancher's form through the pebbled glass of the doors. But he was having second, even third, thoughts. He hoped Spatz would just go away. It had seemed like a good idea at the time, strike a blow for the free men of the world, his white brothers in this wimpy liberal world. But now the reality was something else.

He started to head back down to the basement when he heard footsteps coming down the stairs. The building was supposed to be empty. The lights came on: it was Brenda, from the Sheriff's crew. What the fuck was she doing here? Then he noticed her blouse was hanging loose, and the only thing holding up her pants was a button. She wasn't geared up.

Brenda went to the door. "Who is it?" she asked.

There was a long pause. She repeated the question.

The glass exploded as Spatz shot it away. Steeps nearly jumped out of his skin—he had always thought it was bulletproof. Brenda leaped back. Steeps noticed she was barefoot. She rolled away from the glass holding her face, which was streaked with blood. This was getting out of hand. Steeps stepped out of hiding, instinctively going to the aide of a woman, then realized Spatz had knocked away enough glass to fit through. Spatz got all the way in, aimed at Brenda on the floor.

"No!" Steeps shouted. "She's down." Spatz had no intention of wasting the young woman; he was just making sure she wasn't heeled. She was leaking blood from a wound in her thigh, gritting her teeth as she tried not to moan. He veered the pistol around to put the jailer in his sights. Steeps hoped he was doing it to make it look good. Outside he could hear a siren headed towards town. "Jailer!" Spatz boomed. "I want Red."

Steeps relaxed. Spatz was playing his part. "I don't have the key," he said. All part of today's briefing.

"Up the stairs, asshole." The deal was that Steeps, under duress, would let Red out. He couldn't be in the two places needed to unlock the downstairs, but Spatz had given him a little trick to use. The two men headed up to the Sheriff's office. Once they were on the second floor, Wilhelm lowered his pistol. The jailer noticed it was a fine old 1914 Colt, a museum piece with a real .45 kick. "What was she doing here—I thought everybody went home," Spatz asked, clearly pissed off. "And why didn't you get the goddamned door?"

"She could have seen me letting you in. I'm glad I

was late."

"Lucky you. Show me the door switches."

The Sheriff's office was never locked. The jail used a two-control system, with one upstairs that had to be enabled at the same time as the jailer swiped a card in the downstairs door lock. They headed for the radio and comms area, since the staff normally would have to use the intercom to coordinate unlocking a cell downstairs.

Brenda had been here for a reason: a cot in a side room that was occasionally used for an off-duty officer waiting to go on shift. It also, now and then, had been used for more interesting things, which is what she had been up to with Detective Gruder.

When he heard the shot downstairs, Gruder immediately put his shirt back on and picked up his weapon. He was headed towards the comms center to call in a shots-fired warning when he saw two men come into the room. One was Steeps, the other Wilhelm Spatz with a big automatic in his fist. Curiously, he wasn't pointing it at the guard.

Gruder moved carefully into the room, looking for anyone else, especially Brenda. He was getting worried, fast. "Freeze!" he shouted. He felt a little like a TV cop; he had never actually had someone in his sights.

Spatz was really fast. His gun was up and firing instantly. It was a real cannon, spewing smoke as each cartridge went off. Steeps wisely dived to the floor. Gruder also dropped down behind a desk as the shots sailed over his head. He knew the stats: a pistol was not much good beyond forty feet. Unfortunately, Spatz was one hell of a lot closer.

The young Californian stuck his head out to return fire, and was pulling the trigger when the bullet hit him in the chest. Without a Kevlar vest he had no chance; the impact knocked him back. He saw the ceiling, so far above, through a veil of gunsmoke which began to wisp away as his sight failed. A great numbness came over him, his hands fading away, all feeling gone from his body. He began to wish for something, but he never figured out what it was.

"Great," Steeps said, looking down at the dead Californian.

"*Sic temper tyrannus,* dude." He looked angrily at Steeps. "What's a surfer doing in this place?"

"He's the detective from California. He wasn't supposed to be here," Steeps lamely added.

Spatz was angry with himself; he hadn't planned on a cop killing. Now they would crank up the pursuit another whole notch. "Well, no shit. You did your card downstairs the way I told you?"

"Yeah. Man, this is one bad scene." Steeps had used Spatz's simple trick: a folded wad of paper was wedging his jailer's code card in the slot next to Red's door. It was ridiculously simple.

Steeps went over to the control panel, pushed the numbered button for Red's cell. "So what now, Mr. Spatz? You gonna do me, too?"

"Relax, we're on the same side. But I need to give you a little love tap." Before Steeps could react, Spatz butt-stroked him across the side of the head, opening a gaudy red flow of blood. He dropped like a poleaxed steer. "Stay on the floor, Steeps."

He took the key ring off the fallen jailer. He went downstairs, used the keys to open the first tier of cowboy era jail doors. Red was already standing there with a big grin on his face. "You the man!" he bellowed as Spatz gave him a high five.

They went out through the garage to their waiting truck. On the way they set fire to every vehicle in the place. People would remember this night for a while, Spatz thought as they drove away. This was how legends were made.

Across town, Sheriff Manyhorse was just getting in his car when he heard gunfire and more explosions out at the airport. He hit the lights and siren, skidding around corners, headed towards what were clearly multiple fires. The flight line was littered with wreckage as every airplane—and the KIRO 7 chopper—was fully engulfed in flames. It was something straight out of a movie, he thought. Down the runway, he could see the retreating taillights of pickups, or maybe SUVs, escaping into the night. He looked up where the security cameras were supposed to be and wasn't surprised to see they had been shot away.

He didn't think it could get much worse if Cuban paratroopers dropped out of the sky. But then his radio crackled. He recognized Brenda's voice. Even over the airwaves he could tell she was in tears. "Officer down. Officer down." He made a hard U-turn and headed back to town. His town, on fire.

CHAPTER THIRTY-SEVEN

In the dawn's early light, the town of Stanley looked like it had been bombed, smoke still curling up over at the airport. Agent Colby White stood in front of the motel taking in the burned-out hulks of the Agency's vans. Fortunately, Dierdorff and his rig were long gone, or the cost to the Agency would have been in the millions. The Chevy panels were down on their metal rims, the tires and interior plastics having melted onto — or into — the liquified pavement, which had congealed into shiny lakes of black goo under each vehicle.

The motel had survived, but the front was scorched, the remaining windows blackened with soot. His people had all gotten out; White wasn't the only one who had used the rear egress. He was still in his sweats, his clothes in the room rendered toxic by the smoke that had billowed in through the smashed front door. At least he had the Agency credit card in his pocket, along with his wallet. He'd treat anyone who wanted a cowboy outfit — on the FBI's dime.

He also needed some wheels. Sheriff Manyhorse had stopped on the way over to the hospital to clue him in: the Sheriff's office was down to two vehicles, Ben's old Impala and one other prowl car that had been out on patrol on Highway 89 when all hell had broken loose. White thought about Detective Gruder, who had died in the line of duty. Brenda had been in bad enough shape from her wounds before she found out what had happened to John. But she had been able to identify Spatz as the shooter. The jailer guy, Steeps, was also in intensive care with a nasty head wound.

Red was long gone, of course. Steeps's lock card was still wedged in the reader for the electronic lock for Red's cell. It was a low-tech breakout, the 21st century equivalent of pulling the bars out of a window with a horse and rope. But Spatz was not really of this century, was he?

White's taxi arrived. He was headed over to the airport to rent whatever he could find from Enterprise. He sat in back for the short trip, lost in thought. Spatz might be low-tech, but that didn't mean he didn't know what he was doing. Obviously with some help: he couldn't have been in three parts of town at once. He had effectively carried out his plan, had survived the unexpected. No one had known Brenda and Gruder were getting some up in the office. Steeps, that was a different story. There was something there, White felt, that wasn't quite right.

Otherwise, Spatz had made sure the pursuit was delayed by destroying every law enforcement vehicle in the area. As well as anything else that could get airborne. As White pulled into the airport, this was abundantly clear: every last airplane or helicopter was wrecked, most burned. The KIRO helicopter was still smoldering, little more than two rotors attached to the power plant. There were a couple of aircraft left in hangars, but they were all in for repair.

There was just one lead: Manyhorse had radioed White that two guys in a Ford F-350 had taken some shots at the last remaining patrol car out on Highway 89. The deputy, who was flat-out headed back to town, had lost them right away.

White paid the driver and went in to find his choices were all Subarus left over from the ski season. He'd hoped for something bigger, although new FBI units were already headed this way. White signed the papers; the kid behind the counter made it a point to tell him the Subies, while all-wheel drive, were not to be taken offroad. The young guy probably had visions of White in hot pursuit up into the mountains. Pounding over hill and dale.

The question now was how to locate the bad guys. Recon Satellite assets were non-existent in this part of the world, and while Dierdorff was now heading back to Stanley, his drones would all be pretty damned slow. And contrary to popular belief, their lenses were not super wide-angle—they took time to cover big areas. They were by no means the best tool for the job.

Old-style photo-recon from aircraft would be more effective, which would be the Air Force's bailiwick. He had already put in the call, but that would probably have to be greased from the Hoover Building.

The DMV had revealed that Spatz had a white F-Series pickup—which matched the shooters out on

Highway 89. But even with an R4C bird, finding the official Montana state truck would be a daunting task.

He gathered up the keys and paperwork to take back to his people. As he got in his car the same taxi came back with Tricia and her crew. He'd forgotten they were also on foot. They got out, looked forlornly at their Bell's ashes. Her guys unloaded their cameras from the trunk—it made sense they had kept their gear at the motel. He waited until she came over, leaned down to give him a grim smile. "Colby." Tricia said.

"Some night, huh?" She and her crew's rooms had been at the far end of the motel. It was probably as well that she hadn't run bare-assed out of his room.

She looked towards the wreckage of their helicopter. "One very weird night. You figure they wanted to keep all the planes out of the sky?"

"Jesus, Trish. Ask me a hard one."

She laughed. "And a burning cross on a Native American's lawn?"

"This is a weird town. What can I say?"

"How's the female officer?"

"I'm going over to find out. Any other questions?" He started up the motor.

"Join me for lunch?"

He thought about it. "If I can."

"Don't want to be seen with me? You hesitated."

"No. I don't care anymore. I just don't know when the Agency will get another helicopter in here. Supposed to arrive midday."

"Any chance we can get a ride?"

"To where? We don't know where those two even went. You might recall Montana is pretty fucking big."

"I'll take that as a maybe."

"Like lunch, let's wait and see."

"Fair enough." She started to pull away, but leaned back down. "I'm really sorry about Detective Gruder. I think you liked him."

"Yeah. I did." He put it in gear and drove away without another word. She watched him go. Such a tightly coiled man, she thought for the millionth time.

*****

Far from the world of man, from civilization, three men on horseback rode towards the headwater of the Boulder River, some ten miles above the state park at Monument Bridge. They were angling for the one-lane span over the river where the forest service road looped around to the base of Mt. Douglas. Once they made their rendezvous with Spatz and Red, they would leave the road for a game trail into the high valleys of Custer National Forest. It was a route to nowhere, but that was all part of the Boss's plan. Slim, Brister, and Chester, with their pack animals in tow, would soon meet up with Red and Spatz. With the packs full of supplies, as well as the equipment laid away in the cache, they would go to ground.

Spatz had explained it all to them before they left yesterday. He had given them the option to strike out on their own, after explaining the legal facts of life to them.

All they had really understood was that Red's murders were theirs, too. They would all swing together, or they would swing separately. If they stuck together and did what Spatz told them to do, they'd get out of this.

The plan was simple enough. Most people would head for the nearest border, in this case Canada, 400 miles to the north. Spatz had explained that wouldn't do them any good: Canada would just send them right back. But if they went to ground, disappeared off the map for months, the search would dry up. By then, they could just get some more wheels and drive on down to a new life in Mexico or other points south.

That was the plan, and it depended on their getting off the ranch as quickly as possible, and they had. The boys were old hands; in all their years of poaching, they'd never been trailed, never been caught. Chester, true to his Indian blood, was a master at this. Spatz had told him once it must be in his blood. And Chester *was* good. No human had trailed them.

But they weren't good enough to lose a superior tracker, the one who had been watching the ranch ever since being released by Page. The White Wolf was patient; time meant nothing to him. He would wait and watch, and somewhere he would do what nature had designed him to do. No human could really know what was in the heart—or mind—of an animal, but Annie would have said they had at least a vestige of emotions. Fear, joy, confusion. They could even show, she felt, a clarity of purpose.

And she might also have said they could hate.

CHAPTER THIRTY-EIGHT

Annie had given herself a 24 hour hiatus from electronic news. The weather was too nice for talking heads, bloviators, or political hit men and women. She had her horse, Page had a horse. They also had a great day to enjoy, full of sun and warmth. The birds were on the wing back north, honking geese making Vs high in the cut-glass sky. It was a sunglasses kind of day, their down vests stuffed in their saddlebags.

But they were doing a little work, too, mixing it in with enjoying each other's company. They were rapidly approaching the border regions of an official relationship, although they certainly weren't about to pick out their silverware pattern, she thought to herself. Annie knew from bitter experience that the first infatuation of sexual chemistry was bound to fade. And then what?

Page, of course, was only barely aware of this. His had been a life of one-night — or at most one week — stands. He still hadn't wrapped his head around this whole deal. He was one of the rare people who had no illusions about himself: if Annie was a thoroughbred, he was a plug horse. But up here in this nice saddle, with a good horse under him, and a fine woman smiling at him, life was pretty good. His darker side wondered how it would all end. Probably not well. And he wondered what was beneath the surface of this new life. Page figured he would only find that out when it hit him in the face.

"Hold up, Page. The elk were just over that ridge, yesterday." She got her iPhone out of her pocket and consulted the wolf map. This was loaded, Page had learned, with a custom map of the region, overlaid with data from the various electronic aids used by Wolf Ranch. Josef had been up in the Hughes yesterday, downloading information from remote sensors that had been set up throughout the area. Some even fed video feeds up to satellites, then back to Wolf Ranch and its staff.

Others were very low power, broadcasting in short microbursts triggered by the helicopter's own electronics as it passed over. The 500C could then serve as a relay to the same satellites that Annie had contracted for her other data services. Most of this went right over his head, but Deschamps knew the results worked. Almost every time they had gone out they had found what they were looking for.

This time a stationary camera had reported that a herd of elk had come down from the high country to forage and mate. And where there were elk, there were wolves. Sure enough, they found the elk over the next ridge, down in a small valley that their maps listed as BLM land. It was unfenced, so there wouldn't be any cattle. They sat down on the ridge, let their horses graze as they studied the terrain below with big 7x35 binoculars. They were by far the best optics he had ever had: image-stabilized, the field-of-view rock steady. A far cry from the old Barskas he normally used. Sometimes, rich *was* good.

They spent a companionable hour looking for wolves, but none showed up. The elk grazed and courted without more than an occasional raised head as some old bull scanned the far horizon. Annie and Page had a snack — Yolanda had made steak sandwiches. Annie took just one bite of hers and had a sip of his cold beer. Page wondered, yet again, how Annie could stay nourished on her diet, which seemed to be primarily composed of lettuce with a big heaping helping of fresh clean air. It was one of life's little mysteries, along with their relationship. Page didn't know much, but he knew that "mystery" was the right word for what was happening between them.

After failing to locate any predators, they had a leisurely ride back to the ranch, breaking into a canter as the buildings came into view. The horses headed for the barn and the feedbag, requiring some force on the reins to bring them down to a walk. They handed the sweating horses off to one of the ubiquitous interns, then headed to the Visitors Center to talk with some of the researchers. The place was part museum, part offices, divided by a fairly large theater that was normally used for documentaries for visitors, including some animated shorts Annie had commissioned for the kids. In the evenings, the staff had been using it to watch movies or just to hang around and bullshit. There was even a full-sized popcorn machine salvaged from an old theater.

Annie talked to the kid who was entering the data at the map table. It was a large flat horizontal display panel, at present showing an area covering the southern part of Montana and over the border into northern Wyoming. Yellowstone National Park formed the lower edge of the map. Various colored dots represented wolves that were wearing collars, or like the White Wolf, the newer implanted transmitters.

Page had been checking it out every day to see where the white Alpha Male was ranging, but so far the signal hadn't been picked up. Until now.

"Hey," Annie said, "There's your guy. I think Josef flew over there the other day—we just updated the data this morning. " She pointed at a red point of light. "He's over in the Absarokas. By the Boulder River. He might be heading for Yellowstone."

"Finally." Page said, bending over to look at the map. "I was wondering . . ."

"You want to go see your wolfie?" Annie smiled.

He looked up, thought a moment. "I guess I would. I'd like all of you to see he's doing OK." There had been more than a few pissed-off researchers after Page had freed the wolf. So Annie could understand why Page would care, at least a little, about proving his point. Or maybe he was just hoping the wolf had found another pack. It would be worth a trip out there to see if any wolves were in his area. Annie went to a wall phone, called Josef's cell. "Crank up the bird," she said, and hung up.

Her pilot had standing orders to keep the chopper ready at all times, so all they had to do was walk over to the helipad behind the barn. They went out, crunching through the gravel and past a couple of tour buses. There was a school outing scheduled, and there were kids lined up at the fences staring at the wolves. The wolves were too bored to stare back, but the kids were mesmerized, as they always were.

A familiar Subaru hatchback came into the parking lot, hot and fast. Tricia Helfer piled out, looking harried for a change. "Tricia, what's up?" Annie asked.

"Haven't you heard?"

"No, what?" Annie saw Tricia was clearly upset. "You look like you have bad news." She didn't think it necessary to add that bad news was Tricia's business.

"The town has been shot up. Red was sprung from prison. Detective Gruder is dead. The airport looks like Baghdad."

Annie almost rocked back on her heels at the machine-gun delivery. It took a second to sink in. "Red broke out?"

"No, Spatz shot his way in, got Red out of his cell. That was when Gruder was hit—there was a gun battle right in the Sheriff's office. There were diversions all across town. They burned a cross on Sheriff Manyhorse's lawn. And every last airplane, including my helicopter, was shot up or burned out at the airport."

Page looked grim. "How did they escape?"

"They were in a pickup. Oh, and Brenda, one of the Sheriff's people, was wounded. She identified Spatz as the shooter."

Annie tried to think it through. "Gruder. I can't believe it. He was such a nice guy. So Golden State . . ."

"How do they know they were in a pickup?" Page asked.

"They blew by a patrol car on the way in, took some shots at the deputy. They got away."

"Probably booking it for Canada," Annie said.

"No, they were headed south on 89."

"Towards Wyoming? That's strange," Annie said.

"Does the wolf map have roads on it?" Page asked.

"What's a wolf map?" Tricia sounded puzzled.

"It was something I was going to show you sometime. I thought you might use it in a broadcast." She saw that Tricia's mind was elsewhere. "Anyway, let's go look."

They went back to the map room. The topographic template was easily reconfigured to include roads. "Here's Highway 89. It's the main road leading down to Yellowstone." Annie pinched in to expand the scale.

"Can you get all the minor routes like fire or access roads used by the BLM guys?" Page asked.

As Annie made the specific area smaller, more obscure roads began to appear. "They've got plenty to choose from." Page finally said.

"Plenty of roads?" Tricia asked.

As Page looked up he noticed she was aiming her camcorder down at the map. He thought she carried it around like some women carried a purse. "Yeah."

She looked up but kept her camera pointed away from him. "Do you mind if I record you while I ask a few questions?"

"I mind," he said.

Tricia didn't seem put off. She switched off her DV cam. "Fair enough. But why do lots of roads matter?"

Page looked at Annie. She shrugged. "Just tell her your instincts." Annie gave him a little nudge. "Whatever they are."

"Well, a run for Canada would never work out. Not in a vehicle. They'd have to cross over using a road— Homeland Security would be all over that. And if you get to Canada, so what. They'd send your ass right back."

"So they're headed south for Mexico? Don't they extradite, too?" Annie asked.

"I don't know," Tricia said. "But it's got to be over a thousand miles, across multiple states. That's mighty risky."

"Is Spatz any kind of a planner?" Page asked Annie.

"He's a devious, scheming asshole."

"But I got the impression he's pretty smart?" Page persisted.

"Yeah," Annie reluctantly agreed.

"Well, I think he has a plan. You said there were diversions in town, so he had help. That's planning. He broke into the jail. Planning."

"You make it sound like a pattern." Tricia could smell another great story brewing here, and it got her juices flowing.

"This all started when those Stanford kids found the cache," he pointed out.

"What's a 'cache' mean around here?" Tricia asked.

"Old beaver trappers would put stuff in a hole in the ground, or maybe up a tree. Emergency supplies, dry powder for their guns, pelts." Page replied.

"So they're headed south, maybe to hole up?" Tricia thought out loud.

"Until the heat is off. Maybe for months." Annie completed the thought that was in all of their heads.

"So . . . instead of gunpowder, they might have an arsenal. Food, shelter—maybe a six-string guitar and video games. A hide-out." The word rolled off Tricia's tongue. "So here's the deal, kids. I came out here to try to borrow your helicopter. It's the only one around. Do some tracking from the air. Sound like fun?"

"It's a big state, Tricia," Annie said.

"Well, let's go fly around some of these back roads. Look for the white pickup. Then on into town, if you don't mind?"

"With your camera running the whole way."

Tricia shrugged; after all, it was true—it would be exciting. Visual. Punchy.

Josef came in to report that the Hughes was ready to go, with enough fuel for about four hours. Annie asked him to put one of the dart rifles in the luggage compartment, just in case they needed to tranquilize any wolves they came across.

"Why would you do that?" Tricia asked.

"Some of our wolves need their batteries replaced on their collars," Annie said.

"And put my Nosler in there, too." Annie looked at Page. "Just in case," he added. Josef went back out.

The two women headed for the door, turned to see Page still staring down at the map. Annie went back. "More thoughts?" she asked.

He touched the gleaming red light on the display. "It's kind of funny. The White Wolf is in that area." He looked up at her. "Maybe that's where everyone goes to hide."

Annie gave his arm a squeeze. "This is probably a wild goose chase. So we'll make it a wild wolf chase, too." He gave her a little smile. He was often a hard man to read, but she thought it meant appreciation.

CHAPTER THIRTY-NINE

By two o'clock, Colby White was well on his way to
losing control of the case. A Gulfstream 12 had just
whispered in from Los Angeles with a Deputy Director
named Emily Crispin. Her presence puzzled him a little.
She was known as a rising star, which usually meant, to
Colby, an ass-covering political animal. Crispin was
certainly political—she lived for the fight—but she was
also laying her butt on the line by dropping herself into
this present situation. After all, the whole thing had
been going sideways since early this morning. Spatz and
his crew were calling the shots, as the FBI and the local
gendarmes were struggling to get back on their feet. But
here she was, breathing down his neck.

Some resources were starting to come online: he
had an order in for an Air Force helicopter, a search
and rescue Blackhawk from Nellis AFB. It was
unfortunately not equipped with a FLIR nose turret. Its
Forward Looking Infrared was designed to locate warm
bodies at night.

In the meantime, the Air Force had a
reconnaissance jet that could do photometric surveys of
considerable swaths of wilderness. It was slated for
daybreak, which meant the FBI, or somebody, had to

give them a starting point. White only had the Highway 89 report from the inbound deputy to go on, and that had been six hours ago.

White stood on the tarmac as the Gulfstream dropped its built-in ramp. Deputy Director Crispin was first out, looking sharp in a charcoal power suit; both the outfit and its wearer looked uncreased by travel. I'd look that good if I flew in a Gulfstream, White thought. But he kept his observations to himself as she strode up, full of purpose. She barely came up to his chin, but she didn't seem to care. "Special Agent," she said, hand out.

"Deputy Director."

She looked over at the piles of burned aircraft. "What's the technical word for this scene?"

"I'm favoring 'cluster fuck' at the moment."

"So how do we get a handle on this thing?"

"By flying in a high-ranking political operative?"

She gave him a long look. "I heard you were getting along towards retirement."

"You heard right."

"Do you want to go out on a roll, or dead on your shield?"

"I don't much care at this point. I do want to bring these assholes to justice."

"Then how about you can the attitude."

He thought about it. "I could do that."

"Good. Fill me in."

White gave her the rundown as he took her over to his rental. She looked at the Subaru in surprise. "You brought your own car?" He explained about the sudden shortage of law enforcement units that had occurred in the wee hours of the morning. He told her more vehicles were on their way, including the Blackhawk and more FBI UH-1s. He also informed her that Dierdorff, having made a U-turn near Spokane, would be here within an hour. His van and any drones, along with the inbound Blackhawk, would represent the sum total of the assets they would have by sunset.

They had barely started to talk before they were pulling up to the courthouse. "This certainly seems to be small town America." She saw that there were close to a dozen film crews and their vans parked in front of the building. "Can you take me around to the back—I'm not playing to the crowds today."

White was glad to hear that. Gruder was dead, and he didn't want some big city orator standing on the kid's grave while she played to the crowd. "There's an underground garage, but it's off-limits until they clear the wreckage away. It's full of toxic fumes from the fire."

"Fire?"

"Spatz and his asshole buddy torched all the vehicles on their way out."

"I didn't know that. I'm surprised the place didn't burn down."

"They retrofitted it a few years ago for fire. Spatz even burned the city snow plow."

"Boy, that's cold." She adjusted her shoulders. "Then let's do the walk." He led her up the steps as cameras and reporters closed in for the kill. He admired her sangfroid as she ignored everyone; she did stop to inspect the shattered glass front doors before stepping inside. She gazed at the dried blood that still showed drag marks leading to a wall phone. She looked at White. "The female deputy, Brenda, took some glass to the side of the head and a bullet in the thigh." White explained. "She got to the phone, called in the shooting."

"What's her last name?"

White thought for a moment. "To tell you the truth—"

"Get her name for me when you have a chance. She's going to pull through, is that right?"

"She's a tough kid." They went upstairs. The office was still in ruins, with chalk circles on the floor marking spent cartridges. There were strands of colored twine illustrating the vectors of bullets that had punched holes in the walls and furniture of the room. White's forensics team was just finishing up. There was more blood behind the desk. "Detective Gruder," White said as he stood next to the stains.

Director Crispin stood for a long moment looking down. White was impressed with what he saw: a quiet pain. "It never gets easier, does it?" she said. He decided they were maybe going to get along after all.

A very tired looking Ben Manyhorse came out of his office with a clipboard in one hand. White made the introductions. "My condolences, Sheriff. This is a tough one for all of us," she said.

"Thank you ma'am," he replied.

"Do we have any further leads?" Crispin asked the Sheriff.

"Nothing solid." He turned to White. "Have you told the Director about our man?"

"No. Why don't you go ahead?"

"Would you like some coffee, ma'am?" Ben asked.

She gave him a little look. "Quit calling me 'ma'am.' And no, thank you."

Ben took them back into his office to fill them in on a new development: a police investigation by a deputy had determined there were no longer any ranch hands at the Rocking R Ranch. And not a single pack animal was left.

After the Sheriff finished his summation, the Deputy Director proposed just how they would launch one of the biggest manhunts since the ill-fated Ruby Ridge shootout. Crispin's specific mention of one of the FBI's greatest fiascos emphasized how important this search was to the prestige of the organization. Which certainly explained to White the presence of a very senior member of the FBI leadership.

What surprised the agent was Crispin informing him that he was going to continue to lead the task force. He briefly wondered if she was trying to further his career or put a bullet in it. He found that he didn't much care, as long as Gruder's killers were brought to justice. He owed the detective that much. And damn it, he thought: he *had* liked the guy.

*****

The F-350 was a problem. When Spatz blew out of the ranch, he'd given the boys directions to the fire road they were now on. It was a continuation of the road that branched off Highway 89. The paved section led to the state park at Monument Valley; past the park, the forest service road became gravel. It went another six miles down to the one-lane plank bridge that crossed the Boulder River. The road then went along the river valley—little more than a narrow gorge—before petering out at the base of the Absaroka Range.

They sat in the Ford by the rushing waters as they waited for the horses to appear. The road had been closed off by a locked gate, which they had forced. They'd also swiped away at the tracks they left in the dust; if someone found their trail, it would be days from now. By then, they would be at the cache deep on the far side of Granite Peak, the highest mountain in the state. They would have an open view down the slopes, an area without any appeal to hikers and where hunting was banned. So someone would have to step right on their heads to find them. And that would be the last thing they would do, because Spatz's merry men were bringing up the heavy artillery from the ranch, including assault rifles and his personal Barrett .50-caliber long gun that fired slugs the size of lawn darts.

Spatz passed the almost empty bottle of Jim Beam to Red as they lounged in the cab of the truck. Red was antsy, but that was his way, Spatz thought to himself. But personally, he was feeling OK. Last night had been a watershed in his life: all the things he had done to build up the ranch were gone now. He would never go back. He was surprised that he didn't feel more regret.

Truth be told, he'd been in a rut. Being chased had an invigorating effect on him, like chains falling away. It would be a simple life for the next few months. With the supplies they had and with fresh meat everywhere they looked, they'd be comfortable enough. Then, when the heat was off, Mexico or points south. Maybe even Brazil. He had enough money socked away overseas to give him a comfortable retirement. Red and the boys, too—he'd look after them the way he always had. The loyalty cut both ways.

"I see horses." Red was sitting up in the seat. They killed the bottle, got out and stretched. It was the rest of the crew, Slim and Chester with one other rider that Spatz couldn't make out. "Who's the third guy?" he asked.

Red got some binoculars out from behind the seat, took a look. "Brister."

"That blockhead. Who invited him?" Spatz didn't seem particularly pleased with the news. "One more mouth to feed."

"But one more gun."

"I don't think we're headed for a shootout, Red."

Spatz got back in the Ford, started it up. This part of the plan was a little more freeform: the goal was to get the truck into and under the river. There was no use leaving signposts behind, and a truck sitting in the middle of nowhere was not cool. The Boulder was running deep and fast, swollen by snowmelt. There was a ten-foot drop off the verge into the water below. Hopefully, the truck would turn turtle; he didn't want the white roof and hood visible from any aerial snooping.

He put it in gear, slid off the seat as the pickup lurched forward. The windows were down, so there wouldn't be any air to hold it up. It banged over the edge, caught some air as it plunged. The nose hit on the rocks with a satisfying crash, then the tail came up and over. It began to sink as the current rode it down under the bridge. It popped out the other side, rotated as it sank, right side up. The cab roof, a big white square, stood just out of the foam. Oh well, he thought.

Chester pulled up next to him, leading Old Thunder by the reins. It was his favorite horse, named by some client's idiot kid years ago. But the name had stuck, mostly because you had to call a horse something. It was just a fact of ranching life, you couldn't go around saying "get me the bay gelding." It took too long. The horse nuzzled Spatz as he stroked its head. "Hey, Chester," Spatz said to the Indian.

Spatz gave a nod to the other guys, looking at Brister for an extra moment. He was a big, meaty guy with a craters-of-the-moon complexion and not much of a brain. He hoped he wasn't going to be a liability. "You don't have a dog in this hunt, Brister," Spatz said. "You can head on back if you want." Brister just shrugged.

"Where we headed?" Slim asked around his chaw.

"The cache up by Mystic Lake. Chester knows the way from here, don't you, Redskin?"

Chester gave a wheeze, which meant he was laughing. "Up in the Forest."

"And which forest is that?" Spatz prodded him to finish the thought.

"Custer."

Spatz looked at his crew, who were no better than they had to be. Loyal, good outdoorsmen, and not a brain among them. "That's right, you lunks. Custer National Forest." He paused for dramatic effect. "Where we make our last stand."

Slim looked a little worried. "I thought we was goin' to Mexico."

"I'm making a joke, meathead. We hide out for a few months, then we blow south. Fair enough?" They seemed to agree. He got up in the saddle, led them on down the road. They had to make another six miles, then up through a narrow pass that was little more than a big game trail. It was fine for horses, and even better for men on the run.

An hour or two later, as they worked their way up slope, they heard a helicopter.

The White Wolf, who had trailed the three cowboys since they left the ranch, rotated his ears but kept his gaze on the line of horses he had been following. The chopper meant little to him, since he had heard it so many times at Wolf Ranch. That was a place he had all but forgotten.

For he was in the here and now—where he would trail, watch, and wait.

CHAPTER FORTY

From a mile high, the terrain below looked like folded green cloth, with water features set in as silvery inlays. The sky was clear and free of turbulence, so they were comfortable in the cockpit. Page and Josef had worked out roughly where the Sheriff's deputy had taken fire from the escaping duo. They had then used that as the center of the spiral search pattern, but had modified it as they decided the forested area to the east was not navigable by any vehicle.

So they concentrated on fire roads for a time, occasionally dropping down to investigate a patch of white or some object that looked at least vaguely man-made. After two hours, they decided there was far too large an area to cover so they went on to a different mission: following up on any wolves they might find. The electronic suite of the Hughes had some very sophisticated tracking gear, and it wasn't long before they locked in on a signal from the White Wolf.

Annie could monitor this from a fold-down screen in the back. She told Page, who was next to her, to take a look. "There's your boy," she said, indicating a cursor on the screen.

"Give me a vector," Josef said over the intercom.

Annie gave him the coordinates and he made one of his gut-churning turns to the new heading. Up front, Tricia cranked up her cam as they dropped down. She knew that the terrain streaking under the chopper's nose bubble would give the viewers a kick. She was not used to flying with a show-off like the little Israeli, and she was enjoying it, her usual caution overridden by the thrill of the hunt. To her, this was more like a mission than a news feature. If they were lucky—really lucky— they could break this thing right open.

Josef got them a few hundred feet above a river. Annie reported the wolf was only two or three miles ahead, up on a ridgeline on the right. The river was flanked by a road on both sides, joined by a small bridge. They flashed over the bridge and Page, looking out the side, saw something in the water below, a square of white making a large V of water. "I spotted something," Page said. But the chopper was already rapidly slowing as Josef replied, "I saw it, too."

He came to a hover as they looked down, the helicopter slowly turning so they all could take it in.

"What are the odds of a white pickup being here in a stream?" Tricia asked.

"Can you see anybody in the cab?" Annie joined in.

"I think they dumped the truck in to hide it—see where it went over the edge?" Josef observed as he backed up to the bridge.

"If they're not in it, where are they?" Annie asked.

"They might have changed vehicles," Tricia said as she filmed away.

"That makes no sense. They could have just driven on to wherever this goes." Annie sounded puzzled. Page asked her to put the map overlay up on her screen. "The fire road goes a few more miles then ends at the base of Mt. Douglas," she told everyone. "I wouldn't want to hike over that."

"We should contact the Feds with this location," Tricia said, excitement tingeing her voice.

"We can't radio from down here—the gorge blocks all the signals. Satellite phone would work," Josef observed.

"Let's go down this road a little, first," Annie suggested. "They can't have gotten that far." All thought of the wolf had left her mind.

"I don't think they're on foot." They all listened, waiting for Page to say more. Annie finally nudged him in the ribs and he continued, "Tricia, Ben told you the Rocking R Ranch was empty? They might have brought up some horses. Pack animals with supplies, maybe."

"So we follow the road?" Josef asked. The chopper began to slide forward, picking up speed.

"Look for a pass over the ridgeline. On the right. Maybe a game trail."

Annie looked at the map, widening it out to the east. "The Custer National Forest is just over that ridge to the right. In those trees, they could wind up anywhere."

Tricia laughed. She had always felt more alive when on a story, and this was more than that—it was a hunt. And she was the huntress, her vision almost unnaturally

sharp, palms moist, mouth dry. Pure uncut adrenaline,
like you felt on a fast ski run or on a motorcycle hurtling
down a high desert road.

Something that sounded like hail rattled on the skin
of the Hughes. Tricia saw lights winking at her from off
to the right. Belatedly, she realized there were horses
standing right out in the open. And men.

"Holy shit!" Josef yelled as the helicopter did a
multi-g lift that made them sink into the floor. Parts of
the right side of the chopper's canopy shattered, the
wind shrill through what were clearly bullet holes.

"They're shooting at us—Annie, get on the horn.
Tell—"

They all felt a harder series of impacts from the rear
and the Hughes began to gyrate, just short of a full spin.
"They dinged the tail section!" Josef was an experienced
aviator, and had fought with the Israeli Defense Forces.
He knew what was happening, and he knew what to do.
The tail rotor, which countered the lifting rotors'
torque, was damaged—he could feel it in the foot
pedals. The more he kept the throttle up, the more the
engine's power would spin them like a falling maple
leaf. He had to reduce engine thrust to slow down the
spin. But now, he was losing lift; he had to trade one for
the other.

A helicopter without power does not necessarily fall
out of the sky. The 500C' rotors would auto-rotate as
long as he maintained some forward speed, again
spending altitude for lift. It was a delicate ballet, and he
played it for all he was worth. He also had to find a

relatively level place to land, and it wasn't going to be in the direction of the guns. He applied some throttle, bought some up-force at the price of a head-banging half spin. Out of the corner of his eye, he saw Tricia trying to aim her camera. His mind was in hyper-drive as he wondered if she was filming her own death. He'd seen cameramen do it before, hiding behind the eyepiece as they waited to see how it all came out. The thought flashed and was gone as his body, all instincts and reflexes, kicked it up yet another notch.

He bought them a couple of miles before something audibly snapped in the tail boom, and they went completely out of control as they did several quick 360s. He chopped the throttle at the last moment; the Hughes had enough forward momentum to go in nose first, instantly flipping on its side as the big rotors lashed into the earth, burrowing into dirt and shale before snapping apart. The stubs of the rotors, wobbling on what was left of their bearings, bit into the top of the cabin in a hail of shearing aluminum and shards of Plexiglas. Annie had her head between her knees, Page's hand pushing her down into the cushion. The sound was like an explosion in a corrugated aluminum factory, the blades hammering shock waves through the disintegrating structure. She smelled hot oil just as the 500C gave a gigantic thrash that levered it around one last time. The impact knocked her into a gray, confused daze.

*****

"Yee-ha!" Red gave a victory whoop as he lowered the AR-15 that was smoking in his hand. They had all taken part. The distant sound of rotors had given them just enough time to unship the weapons the boys had brought from the ranch. Spatz had a big grin on his face and a vintage AK-47 hanging by his side. It had been re-chambered for a .45 round that packed a tremendous amount of kinetic energy. It was wildly inaccurate, and he wouldn't know if he'd made any hits until he saw the wreckage. But it sure as fuck felt good, he exulted. He'd been wanting this for years.

"That smoked the bitch!" Red continued his yelling. The wolf blazoned on the side of the Hughes was all the evidence they needed to know whom they had wasted.

"You know what else is a bitch, besides that one?" Spatz snarled. He high-fived his foreman. "Payback." He knew that somehow the stars had aligned: he had his revenge, hot and sudden. He liked the taste of it.

*****

Page's head was ringing as he tried to figure out what the hell had happened. One thing he knew, he smelled burning plastic, probably wire insulation. The cabin of the Hughes was on its side with his door on top. He forced it open, got out of his seatbelt by standing on the edge of the front seat. He saw Annie below him, struggling in her harness. She moved in a dazed, confused way. Her door, which was now the floor, was crinkled like foil. She stood on it, wobbling, her hair matted with dirt and transmission oil from the shattered gearbox. He gave her a hand, lifted her up and out of the rear cockpit. They both used the skid to get down to the ground. Somewhere Page could hear the crackling sound of parts burning in the engine compartment.

He held her head up to look her over. "You all right?" he asked. He couldn't hide the fear in his voice. He felt a surge of emotion; he really did care about her. Not just a little, a lot.

She hugged him. "Check up front." She was crying. "I can't stand to look."

Her fears were warranted; the front of the helicopter had been pretty much beaten apart by the impact with the ground and by the flailing rotors. Josef's door had been peeled back. He got up on the skid and looked in.

Page had been around a lot of death in his time on earth. He had killed a man, Johansen. But he knew and liked the Israeli pilot, and it was a hard thing to see. The rotor had gone through the top of the canopy like a hot wire through cheese. The top of Josef's head had been sheared off. Page was looking directly into the brain. Josef was slumped forward, his broken legs splayed out in a way that made Page feel even sicker.

Tricia was a lot worse. The rotor's arc had cut right through her torso. She was bent forward at the waist, and her body ended at her shoulders. There just wasn't anything left of her above that point. He surprised himself as he reached in and tugged out her KIRO parka, which had been tied around her waist. It was a cold-blooded thing to do, but he knew the odds were poor of them getting out of this mess alive. Any edge he could get might make the difference, because there were men coming to kill them. And it might well be in the cold of night. He felt this in his bones.

He brushed against Josef as he was getting out, and -the pilot's hand came up and reached for Page's arm. Deschamps gave a half shout and nearly fell off the skid. "What is it?" he heard Annie cry out below him. Page got himself together, reached in to feel for a pulse. There was a thready one, the beats irregular, and on some level Josef was still alive. But he was never coming back from that kind of head injury. It had to be his autonomic system keeping the heart going. Josef, and all the things that made him, was gone. Page felt a great sadness as he got out his knife and did what he would do for any wounded animal.

Annie attributed his white face to what he had seen inside. "They're dead, aren't they?" she asked.

He nodded. "We need to get out of here." He handed her Tricia's jacket.

She took it automatically, still looking dazed. "Why? The rescuers will be here."

"How do they know where we are?"

"There's a beacon on board." She bent over, put her hands on her knees. "Josef briefed me on it, once. The crash will set it off."

He was about to ask her more when she jumped back, and he felt heat on the back of his neck. He turned to see a red blossom of flame in the engine compartment. They only had a few seconds. "Annie! Get my rifle out of the compartment." She clambered up to open the cargo hatch and he was glad to see that she was still functional enough to comply. They were both going to have to be sharp in the next few minutes.

He got up on the skid next to her and reached into the forward cockpit for something he'd just remembered: the little orange SAR rifle. It was still clipped to the heavily distorted doorframe. He also grabbed the rescue kit below it.

They both dropped down, ran away from the rapidly propagating flames. They turned as the fuel tank ignited and the dark smoke began to billow. A perfect marker as to where they had come down. Which was just fine, he thought. They could hide up in the rocks, and he could pick them off with his Nosler.

He turned to Annie, intending to take his gun from her. But it wasn't his; she'd grabbed the wrong gun case. He started back to the chopper but it was fully engulfed. Page led her away. In the background he could hear his bullets back in the compartment cook off in the heat and flames. The sound emphasized how much trouble they were in, but he couldn't blame her for the mistake. She'd just been in a plane crash, and people she had known had died.

As they dragged themselves away, he wondered how well his own brain was working, although he felt as if he hadn't even been scratched. But that could just be the adrenaline rush. Like an escaping animal, he was aware of the price they might pay for any mistakes. His rifle had been one. He should have gone for it over the little SAR rifle, but he hadn't. Strike one. Now they were leaving a trail away from the burning pyre. If he'd had more time to think, he could have used more guile. With a little attention to where they stepped, the killers wouldn't have known there were any survivors. He doubted they had counted heads in the few seconds they had been in view. But a five-year-old could follow the trail they were now leaving. That was strike two, he thought, as he helped Annie go upslope to the first of a series of escarpments leading towards a nearby ridge.

Once over that ridgeline, he felt he could make up for things by taking advantage of whatever natural features they found, using them to evade and escape. He scanned some of the helicopter debris that had been strewn around from the crash site, looking for anything useful, but most of it was too big.

Annie bent to pick something up: Tricia Helfer's camcorder. "It's still running," Annie said in wonder, turning it over in her hands.

"Keep it." He thought for a moment. "There might be evidence on it," he added. Before she switched it off, she turned to take a shot of the burning wreckage, a last testament to the young reporter.

CHAPTER FORTY-ONE

Bob Dierdorff was rubbing his lower back as he tried to unkink his stiff body. He'd been in the saddle almost twenty hours after his U-turn, which included a quick side trip to the regional Bureau of Land Management headquarters in Missoula. He had gone to the airport where the BLM kept their aerial firefighting equipment in the off-season. They had something he needed to pick up.

But Dierdorff was more than just tired. He was pissed. The news of Gruder's death had hit him like a heavy fist in the gut. His work was at the clean end of the sword most times, not the point where things got messy. He had never lost a co-worker, especially not to violence. Despite his fatigue he was ready to pull a lot more hours to see this thing through. He was out at the airport where Agent White had directed him; they were trying to avoid prying media eyes. Dierdorff opened up the back doors to show White and Director Crispin the twenty foot long tube that was tied down in the central aisle. "The General Atomics GR-20. We call it the Cowhawk."

Crispin tapped on the fiberglass container. "Wasn't General Atomics in some Isaac Asimov story?"

"The boys and girls at General have a sense of humor. Cowhawk is a nickname: spots the heat signature of cattle on BLM lands, soars like a hawk. It's loaded with IR sensors. Instead of rangeland management, we're going to use it here to find horses or mules." Dierdorff sounded a little dubious.

"You don't have any faith in it?" Crispin picked up on his doubt.

"Never been used for this type of mission."

"And was this your bright idea?" she asked.

Dierdorff, who had no qualms about poking a stick in management's eye, was about to speak when White interrupted him. "I made the call," he said, looking directly at her.

She looked him right back. "You seem to have a wide-ranging mind, Special Agent."

"I read about it in a BLM post."

She gave him a nod. "Well, I think it's worth a shot. When can you get it in the air, Bob?"

"I can launch from here. It unfolds right out of the tube, runs on avgas. I can control it from the van. Maybe park it behind a hanger, keep a low profile."

"Range? Loiter time?"

"It's got a Rotax engine—pretty efficient. Good for eight to ten hours depending on air density. It's also fairly fast, maybe seventy knots. So, a two hundred mile radius with a little fudge factor built in."

"We'd be better off with a vector from one of the reconnaissance jets, but we don't have any hits yet," White said.

Crispin thought for a moment. "Maybe we should go out on that highway—89? Work out from there?"

White thought about it. He got out his iPhone and called up some maps. "That was about fifty air miles from here."

"It's kind of a puzzle, eh?" Crispin asked. "How about this: we can land it on a road, right? So we fly it down-range, orbit out from the last-known sighting. Do a box search. We refuel on the highway."

White liked the way she thought on her feet. But he had to add, "Can we do guidance while the van is on the road?"

Dierdorff shook his head. "That fouls up the satellite link." He gave a small grin. "Fortunately, it has an autonomous mode, so I can get it from here to there. It uplinks to our satellite net, so any info gets stored. I can land it down to Highway 89 when it needs to refuel. And I can modify the search area when I'm on station."

"But the satellite people can't fly it?" Crispin asked.

"Not *that* sophisticated. The BLM guys gave me the freqs and I can ride it around from my console. Maybe next generation will be better. We still have too many different platforms, and a lot of them can't talk to each other."

"So, do we have a plan?" Crispin asked. Both men nodded. "Then let's go nail these creeps."

*****

Spatz and his men were on their way, heading

towards the spot where the Hughes had staggered over a line of hills that transected the river. But once they saw the smoke they knew exactly where to go. Both Spatz and Red were still on a high, the other three men a little stunned by what they had done.

Unlike the Boss and his foreman, they were farther removed from murder. Slim and Chester, in fact, had conveniently all but forgotten the two Stanford grad students. And Brister didn't have the slightest idea what had gone down a few months back, let alone the killing last night. But he was in too far now to back out, he belatedly realized.

The sun was nearly behind the western ridgeline of the little valley by the time they reached the wreckage. It had settled down to a smoky pile of hot ash, the turbine and gearbox the only major parts still recognizable. They all crowded around the forward cockpit, staring in at the two charred figures melted into their seats. The fire had reduced the bodies to shriveled, charcoal caricatures of the human form. It was impossible to tell if the right hand seat held the remains of a man or a woman. Brister, who had never actually killed anyone in his life, felt sick to his stomach. He looked away.

"Don't punk out on us, Brister," Red said, grabbing him by the arm. "You're in this up to your neck, bro."

"Yeah, I can see that," Brister said, pulling his arm free.

Spatz jumped down from the half-melted skid after looking in the back. He began walking around the wreckage, spiraling out as he looked at the broken rocks and gravel. "Chester," he said to the Indian. "You see what I see?"

Chester got down on one knee and used a low angle to sight along the ground. "Yeah, I see."

"What we got, Boss?" Red asked.

"Somebody survived. Looks like hiking boots going away from the wreck."

"Two sets," Chester said. Spatz looked up to see Slim hawking some chaw onto the ground.

"Pick that up!" Spatz barked. Slim looked puzzled. "Your ball of spit, you idiot." The cowboy looked uncomprehending. "We don't leave any more evidence than we have to. That's got your DNA all over it." Slim complied, as if he gave a shit.

Spatz calmed down, asked Chester "Where did they go?"

The Indian pointed up the hill. "See that trail?" Spatz didn't, but he took Chester at his word.

*****

The Cowhawk lifted off into the sunset. Colby thought its engine sounded like a really virile chainsaw. Dierdorff closed up the van as White and Crispin got in the Subaru. Colby looked at his watch before moving off. The plan was to settle the deputy director back at the Sheriff's office. Then White would head to the airport to wair for the Air Force Blackhawk.

"When did you last sleep, Colby?" Crispin asked. He noticed she was now on a first-name basis, but he wasn't about to call her honey. She was sharp, though, and he must have given some faint "tell," because she added, "When we're alone, call me Emily."

"Are we buds now?"

She smiled. "No."

"In that case, I'll buy you a drink." He didn't bother to answer her question. They both sat quietly, lost in their own thoughts, as they made the two minute drive to his home away from home. She looked at the neon logos as they got out. "The Range Rider. Cowboy coffee, dried buffalo jerky?"

"They have a fine Beaujolais. I think you'll be amused by its pretension."

They sat at the bar, which was full of reporters padding their expense accounts. He tried to look around in a subtle way, but Crispin had eyes like a hawk. Or maybe a married woman, he decided. "Looking for Ms. Helfer?" she asked.

Uh-oh, White thought.

"I'm a deputy director for a reason," she said drily.

"Meaning . . ."

"Meaning I keep track of things—especially in our own shop. You two have had a desultory relationship for some time."

"I wouldn't call it that."

"Then give me a word."

"Haphazard. Catch-as-catch-can."

She almost smiled. The man was either pretty brazen, she thought, or he just didn't care anymore. She found the second one more worrisome. "Are you feeding her information?"

"Ah, that's a complex question."

"A simple yes or no would cover it, either way."

"I don't tell her anything I don't tell any other reporter."

The bartender came to take their order. Crispin ordered a white wine. "Hemlock," White said glumly. The bartender had obviously been to college. "One Socrates, coming up." They both looked at the kid in surprise.

He shrugged. "Philosophy major. What can I say?" White ordered a tap beer. "From any tap," he added.

"'I don't tell her anything I don't tell any other reporter.' That's your whole defense?" Crispin sounded incredulous.

"Hey, since we're on a first name basis here, fuck off. I've never sold an investigation down the river. Never."

Their drinks came while they sat in silence, each trying to figure out the other. They didn't get anywhere.

CHAPTER FORTY-TWO

By dusk, Page and Annie had gotten over the first ridge, the crash site several miles behind and below them. Annie was bent over, her hands on her knees, as she tried to heave her guts. She was racked by nausea and a banging headache. Page gently lifted her head up, examining her eyes. Her pupils were not quite the same size, and he thought she might have a mild concussion. He opened up the aid kit, spreading the contents out on a big flat rock next to the path they had been using. There was basic first-aid stuff in sealed packages: bandages, antibiotic ointment, sunscreen. There was a package of Tylenol, which he split open. "Take these," he said, handing them over.

"I can't swallow them dry," Annie weakly protested. They had already found there wasn't any water in the kit, a pretty serious omission, to his way of thinking. He put the tablets in his shirt pocket. He looked around, but the sun was down, and the shadows were deep up here. They had been using some sort of game trail, which wasn't the greatest idea ever. But they needed to put some distance between themselves and the wreck before dark. Page had no doubt that they were being pursued—it made sense Spatz would see their tracks going away from the wreck. And it seemed unlikely he was about to leave behind any witnesses.

Above them, Page saw a series of low ridges, and beyond—about six miles at a guess—should be the dark carpet of the forest they had seen from the air. There would be water there. As they had flown in, which seemed eons ago, he had automatically taken in the terrain. It was what hunters did, and he was glad he had some sort of mental picture of where they were headed.

He used the failing light to do an inventory of their survival gear because the next few hours were going to be critical. He also was assessing the situation as he cataloged what they had. The tactical picture had been on the back burner of his mind as they had slogged away from the wreck. The cold, hard fact was that their pursuers had horses. They would be slowed a bit by the way he had been breaking trail, using every bit of his experience to avoid leaving any signs. But Annie was having trouble with her walking, and in the end he was pretty sure they were not even pulling away, let alone losing, their pursuers. The men below them were hunters, and they knew the tricks of the trade, too. And they sure as hell would know how to read spoor.

"What have we got for goodies?" Annie asked.

"The little Ruger from the Hughes and the dart rifle. That's it for weapons. Energy bars, some fishing gear—line, hooks. I've got a Leatherman."

"And I've got a lousy video recorder." She sounded small, almost broken.

He tried to cheer her up—she had been kicking

herself off and on for the last few hours about not grabbing Page's long gun. "Keep it. It's got a battery we might be able to use. We're in pretty good shape, really. Once we get to the forest, I think we'll shake them for good. And we can get water there." He pulled Tricia's jacket up a little higher over her neck, gave her shoulder a pat. He noticed there were spots of blood and some white specks of gristle on the nylon, but it was the reporter's, not hers. He casually brushed off what he could.

"I'm miserable, Page. I feel responsible for Josef and—"

He cut her off. "We need to keep our heads on straight. Be here and now. You want to kick yourself around, do it when we get back to civilization."

She tried to smile. "You sound like some sort of New Age guru."

"I'm just a guy who feels at home out here. Which is why we're getting out of this. We've got some resources." He indicated the little pile of gear. "And we're doing OK physically. Right?" She groaned but got to her feet to help him repack their meager goods.

He stopped as he suddenly thought of something. He hadn't actually looked in the dart gun's scabbard. "Annie, does the dart gun have a scope?" She said she didn't know. He unzipped the nylon carry case, saw that it did. He unscrewed the optic from the barrel of the rifle, put it in his vest pocket. He opened up the breech, sighted down the dart gun's bore. He estimated it had a diameter close to a shotgun's. He got out the dart pack, counted six. They were banded in a range of colors, presumably for different body weights. There were also six separate cartridges that would punch the darts down the barrel. He wished he knew which dose was which. When he asked Annie, she said she didn't know; she'd never used the gun herself.

"At least they don't have dogs to track us," she said.

"Haven't heard any. All you saw were horses?" Annie nodded. She already had filled him in on the brief glimpse she had caught out her side window just before the bullets began to hit.

He zipped the rifle back into its scabbard, went over to a ledge of rock. He laid down, scooted up to the edge to look down the way they had come. He got out the scope, put it to his eye, sighting back down the slope. It was a decent optic from Sweden, and it let in a pretty fair amount of light. He easily spotted them, less than two miles away. He and Annie were losing ground rapidly. The horses were just plain faster, and the guy kneeling on the ground sure looked like an Indian. Great, Page thought to himself—the bad guys had brought Tonto.

The odds were that he and Annie were not going to make it to the trees in time. Certainly not in the dark. And if they stayed on this trail, they might survive tonight, but they were sure to be ridden down in the morning. He didn't tell her this, but instead got her moving, while he let his mind think a few steps ahead. Annie started down the trail, instinctively taking the easiest path. "Let's go up that granite slope."

"Head for the high ground?" she asked.

"We'll bed down up there. It'll be safe."

"I never slept on rock before."

He didn't answer. It was time for some new moves. He began to deliberately scuff his heels now and then over the rock, dislodging some lichen here, chipping off a sliver of granite there. He began to work out a few things in his mind as they headed upslope. Despite the closeness of the pursuers, he felt a little thrill of excitement. Game on.

*****

Down below, there was some grousing in the ranks. None of the crew had slept or eaten a hot meal in the last day. Spatz, who actually had read Melville, knew how Captain Ahab felt as he tried to get his own crew to stick to the task at hand. He even knew they might have a point, should they mention that Annie might just be his White Whale. "She tasks me," they might have quoted, had they been literate.

But he hadn't picked them for their mastery of World Lit. In fact, he was pretty damned sure at least two of them couldn't read the back of a cereal box. They were never going to start a Thursday night book club. They were hired guns, mule drivers, cowpunchers down on their luck. Hard cases. Just good enough for his purposes, and no better.

He decided to throw them a bone. He got down off his horse, stretching out his back as he told them to take a ten minute break. "We're running out of daylight anyway. One more hour, maybe two, then we'll bed down. Been a wild couple of days, eh boys?" He got a few grunts.

After their break, they continued up the narrow path. Like all the trails up here, it had been made long ago by animals traversing the ridge to access the trees and high meadows on the far side. Forty minutes later, despite the failing light, they saw a change in the little clues left by their quarry. Annie and Page had left the easy path to go up onto the slope of solid granite that loomed above. Chester had almost missed it, but a little backtracking had revealed some scuff marks, probably from a boot heel.

Spatz lit a cigar as he looked up towards what was left of the skyline. The last light was all but gone. "What do you think, Chester?" he asked.

The Indian chewed his lower lip as he ruminated. "They know we are behind them."

"Because they're taking the harder route?" Spatz laughed. "Big deal. They would have hung around the wreck if they thought we weren't chasing them. Try again."

"We are gaining. One of them — the girl — may have a bad leg."

"Can we catch them tonight? It's going to be a half-moon."

Red came up to join in the conference. "We didn't bring any IR gear."

"That was a mistake," Spatz groused.

Red shrugged. "The boys were in a hurry."

"Yeah." Spatz puffed away on his stogie for a spell. "Here's how we play it. Brister, Red, come over here."

The younger cowboy was sipping from a canteen as he came over. "Boss Man."

"Brister, I want you to take the horses on up the trail. Keep going in the dark—the horses will find the way." Spatz got a map out of his breast pocket, spread it out on the ground. "We're here." He pointed with his cigar. "Trail curls around to the north. Maybe two miles. You'll be on the edge of the forest if the map is right. I think our two survivors are up there on this tor."

He saw their blank looks. "Hilltop. They think they can hide up there until daybreak. Take Slim with you. Come sunrise, you have your big guns out. Right? Try to pick them off. We'll be going right up the slope after them, either push them your way or drop them when they pop over the ridge. They're boxed in."

"But they've got the high ground. They could pick us off." Brister said.

Spatz looked at him like he was an idiot. "You hear any bullets whizzing past your jug ears? These people were in a helicopter crash. All they've got is the clothes on their backs. No water, no food, no shelter. They may be injured. Sound all that dangerous to you?" Spatz sneered.

Brister shrugged. "I guess not."

"Then let's go finish them off." Spatz made a pistol out of his fingers. "Bang."

CHAPTER FORTY-THREE

Colby White was talking to Sheriff Manyhorse and Director Crispin in the Sheriff's office when one of the Sheriff's office staff came into the room. "You have a radio transmission from Helo 1," he said, not sure if he should be telling White or Crispin. He split the difference as he talked between the two Feds. White was all but out the door—he was supposed to rendezvous with Dierdorff out on Highway 89. He gave Crispin a lifted eyebrow, in case she wanted to take it.

"It's your show," she said. They followed the young man down the hall to the communications center. The call had come in on the command channel that Dierdorff had set up when he had first arrived. White had slipped up and never closed it down, but he wasn't about to tell that to Crispin. He needed all the brownie points he could get, after that bit about tipping off Tricia.

The call was from a Lt. Janet Guthrie, who was in command of the Blackhawk. "Go ahead, Lieutenant," White keyed the mic he'd been given.

"We have a report from the SARSAT communications center in San Francisco." SARSAT was the search and rescue satellite system that monitored downed aircraft, sinking boats, or even lost hikers who were carrying personal rescue beacons. "A helicopter is down in your area."

"One of ours?" White asked. He realized belatedly that all his aerial resources were out on the flight line, shot to shit.

"No. Civilian."

"Then it's not our business."

There was a beat before the lieutenant came back on. "Helo 1 is SARS-rated."

"I know. You are the exact kind of asset we requested to search for some very dangerous men."

"We've been asked by the state police to join in the rescue attempt." The lieutenant was being maddeningly persistent.

White let a little of his impatience come through. "I want you here ASAP."

Guthrie came back, an edge to her voice. "They asked Helo 1 for help because all of their choppers are being reassigned to *your* manhunt."

White started to say something, but Crispin held up a finger. "Wait one," White said and clicked off the microphone.

"This is a bit sticky, Colby." Crispin dropped her eyes as she thought something out. "We actually are soaking up everything that can fly. Even the Air National Guard is coming in on the search for Spatz and his merry band. It's an important mission. But I don't want to be roasted after the fact if we are seen blocking a rescue attempt."

"I need Helo 1."

"I see that. But maybe we can do both at once. Does Lt. Guthrie have coordinates?"

White reconnected with the Blackhawk, which sent out the data. Manyhorse joined them at the computer as they entered the waypoints on the digital map they had been using for the search. "That's interesting," the Sheriff said. He didn't have to explain why: the crash site was nearly in the search box that they had been using, based upon the last sighting that morning on Highway 89. "Not twenty air miles from where my deputy took fire. That's kind of eerie."

"Lt. Guthrie," White asked. "Did they say who owns the downed helicopter?"

They could hear, over the doo-wop of rotors, Guthrie asking the question over the radio. "Private owner. Annie Mann."

White felt a bead of sweat run down his temple. The coincidences were starting to pile up. "We're going to discuss this while you continue on in. How far out are you?"

"Fifteen minutes."

"We'll meet you at the airport. We are planning to refuel you right away," White said. Helo 1 signed off. The FBI agent turned to Manyhorse. "Sheriff, could you call out to Wolf Ranch. Find out when they took off, where they were going, how many souls on board."

White went into the Sheriff's office to refresh his coffee, even though he didn't really want it. It gave him something to do. He definitely had a bad feeling, the kind you got when someone you knew, someone like Annie Mann, was suddenly in a world of hurt.

Manyhorse came into the room, and from his look, even more stoic than usual, White knew something bad was coming. Bad on top of bad. "Four people on board. Annie Mann, her pilot, Page Deschamps, and the reporter, Tricia Helfer." The last name hit him in the stomach like a giant fist. He visibly flinched, and the big Indian put his hand on the agent's shoulder. It looked like the Sheriff, too, had known all along about their relationship.

White could hardly trust himself to speak. "What time did they lift off?" he finally managed to ask.

"I talked to the vet there. She said they took off about 4 p.m. The signal was sent at 5:40."

Crispin looked at the wall clock. "That was over two hours ago! What happened?"

"I don't know," the Sheriff said. They went back to the communications center.

White asked the radio operator if they could directly contact the SARSAT people. He flipped through a directory and found a phone number. They were put through right away and were told that the helicopter's ELT had given one quick burst and then had gone off-air. That usually meant the crash had been severe, they were told. The digital signal had been corrupted, and it had taken most of those missing hours to reconstruct the data that had been received. The SARSAT team took the opportunity to directly ask for any assets that could be released from the manhunt. Crispin told them they would have an answer once Helo 1 was on the ground.

"A word, Agent White." Crispin led him aside. Despite his pain, Colby noticed they were back on formal terms. "I only have an inkling of how you must be feeling. But we have a horn of decision here: find the bad guys, or find the survivors."

"Yeah," was all Colby could get out. He knew what *he* would do.

"So, I'll make the call. We get Helo 1 down. That's only minutes away. They hot refuel. The bird is configured for SAR missions, although I don't know if it has FLIR. Then we go to the crash site." He looked at her with something like relief. "We survey the scene, then we see if there is any reason we can't continue with the manhunt. You hear what I'm saying, don't you?"

"I hear."

"Then let's get to the airstrip."

*****

There was still heat in the rocks as Annie and Page huddled together under a ridge of granite. Page knew it wouldn't last. Thank Christ, he'd gotten the jacket for Annie. His own vest would do the job, until the moon came up and he moved out. Moving would heat him up. They were not going to make it to the forest anytime soon, and Annie needed water. Page knew he was going to have to be, what was the word? Proactive.

She spooned up behind him, her hands sunk in his

vest pockets. Annie had never felt lower in her life. There was too much death in this day and probably more in the next. She was all too aware that the situation had come out of her own stubbornness and the years of warfare between Wilhelm Spatz and herself. A war she had dragged others into—the deaths of Josef and Tricia weighed on her heart and she hugged Page even closer. She felt his strength, not just in his body but in his quiet spirit, the one she had come to count on. And yet she had all but deliberately used him, taken him into her bed. For what—to get a hired gun, a powerful man to counterbalance her powerful enemy? That seemed so low, so beneath the high opinion she'd always had of herself. It made her wonder where all her self-confidence had gone; when had she lost it?

Annie found herself softly crooning some song, seeking a little comfort for her mind. Page couldn't place it. "Ring of Fire" was about all he had on his personal playlist. "What's the song?" he asked.

"I played it for you when we first, uh, did it. You remember?"

"That we did it?"

She squeezed him in the ribs, which made him groan.

"Page! I'm sorry. Are you sore from the crash?"

In truth, he hadn't gotten a scratch. "I'm still feeling the thrashing those boys gave me. I guess I do remember. Jazz. You gave me some of the doc's wolf tranks, or something. There on the couch."

"My big, dreamy couch."

"Not digging the granite tonight?"

"No. 'Insensetaz,' that was the song. Portuguese for 'insensitive.'"

He laughed. "You got that right."

"I got that wrong. You turned out to be really very sensitive. Gentle. Even kind. *Sensetaz*." She couldn't help it; she started to cry.

He started to make a joke, but he felt the first tears land on his neck. She was shaking now, racked with sobs. He started to roll over to give her a hug.

"Don't move for a minute. I can't look you in the face."

"Why not?"

"I picked that song because I was an asshole. I figured you wouldn't appreciate the finer things in life. Like Annie Mann."

"So why pick me at all?"

There was a long pause. "I guess I was hoping to use you."

"You did," Page chuckled.

"For the whole thing with Spatz. I've loathed him for a long time. He's a powerful man, and I felt I needed some backing. From my own guy. My own paladin."

Page lay there and thought about her words, about the things you learn when facing death. "That wasn't very honest, was it?" he finally said.

"No." Her voice was very small.

She started to roll away, but he put his hand over hers, kept her close. "You could have just asked."

"I've been independent my whole adult life. Spatz

wanted to take that away. In some ways we were good for each other; inside our little world, we made our own heat. There was a flame there. We both liked that.

"But he wanted to control me, like he controls Red. The way he wanted to control nature. He has a strange dark streak. I liked it at first. I thought he was a guy who liked to win, and to my eternal shame, I liked winners back in those days. I was one, too; we were masters of the universe. But I made more money, I moved into the world of start-ups and showbiz, and he started trying to whittle me down.

"He would belittle me, at first just little things, like his wisecracks and jokes. He got darker in the bedroom, and I hate to say this, but I found that kinky, for a little while. But then he really got into the domination thing, and I mean physical.

"And then I was out of there. I wanted to hit him where it hurt, so I bought the land he coveted. Got into the whole wolf thing just to hit back. I think I went too far; I didn't know when to let up. If I sent him over the edge then it means I've caused all these deaths." She was sobbing again, all the day's terror working its way to the surface. She felt the hurt right down into her soul.

He waited a while before speaking. "I never fit in with anyone. I was just a gun that killed things. What the real Page did was strip me down. They try to do that in the service, but I was too stiff-necked for their shit. It never took. I decided I wouldn't want anything from anyone. The animals I killed and sold, that was just enough dollars to buy more shells, some boots. I never wanted a home or a car or a television. Live off the land, I thought. Kill to eat. Nothing more. Page said I was an economic outcast. I thought that was an insult. But he said that in my own way, I was trying to be free. My gun didn't bother him. It was the way I used it. I was a one-man wrecking crew. Plowing through species, he called it."

She gave him another, more careful, hug. "I was ready for him, Annie. That old preacher man. That's why I'm calling myself 'Page' even in my own head. Like the old me is dead. I wish I could be half the man he was." He told her about that open hand rising out of the water. The image that still haunted him.

"What do you think it really meant, Page?" She had cut back on the tears, but her nose was running. She pulled her hand out of his vest, wiped her nose on her sleeve.

"It was him handing something off to me. Like a mission or pointing out a direction. But you know what got me the most?"

"No." But she had an idea.

His voice was choked as he said, "The man's last moments on earth, he's in pain. And he thinks about *me*. Points the way ahead. Gives me a purpose."

She stroked his hair. "He offered you a lot more than I did. All I could see was a tool. When I played that song. A dumb guy who wouldn't even catch my oh-so-clever musical selection. What a jerk." She sighed.

"But there's nothing wrong with the tool itself, is there? When it's crying out to be used in the right way?"

"I was wrong."

"I don't mean you. Deschamps. He saw me as a tool. A hand holds a tool. His hand reached for one at the end."

"Page, I wish more of us could think that way. I guess I'm like a lot of people my age — or occupation. We want to be the driver, not the vehicle."

"So here we are, Annie. You needed a hired gun. It all works out."

They were slowly freezing to death on a slab of cold rock with the hounds of hell figuratively baying at their heels. Their compatriots had died violently, the town of Stanley had been shot up big time, the next sunrise might well be their last, and this man she was hanging onto for dear life sounded downright upbeat.

Like his whole life had been leading up to this point. And who could say it hadn't. Thank you Page Deschamps, she thought. The old Page, the one under the ice who was also here with them both. And thank you Marion, she added, then retired that name forever.

CHAPTER FORTY-FOUR

The Blackhawk sat squat and dark in its Air Force livery as its twin turbines gently idled, sounding like a giant vacuum cleaner. The crew chief, who looked to be about eighteen, was arguing with the driver of the fuel truck, who was trying to get them to shut off the engines. White and Crispin were getting a briefing from the pilot, Lt. Guthrie, who had turned out to be a willowy young woman with her hair pulled back in a ponytail. She looked barely old enough to drink, with a spray of freckles that made her look like a tomboy. But she was all business, one of the young professionals that White was seeing more and more regularly in the service of their country. It made White feel old, but maybe it was just the whole sad evening that was draining his last dregs of energy. He had rarely been prone to hopelessness, but when it hit it was like waking up and finding out you were beyond middle-aged.

Crispin was doing all the talking. "You say you don't have FLIR?"

"We don't have much use for that in the Air Force, ma'am."

Guthrie had a clear, somewhat deep voice with a touch of the South in her vowels. "We usually know where our people are on the ground. GPS, the combat net, radios. When we fly at night, we wear night-vision goggles. That's how we train."

"But I've seen those turret things under the nose of choppers . . ." Crispin said.

"That's on gunships, if you are Army. The Coast Guard has a few, but those are smaller air-frames. Bell Jet Rangers, or Sikorsky's S-92. But we're good. And we have a vector right to the crash site."

"I'm thinking more about tracking criminals."

"Again, we're the best you have. At least until tomorrow. And I respectfully suggest every moment here on the ground may be a life-or-death delay." She looked over to the fuel truck. The driver was finally unrolling his hose, instinctively ducking as he dragged it under the rotors.

By the time the fuel was in, Sheriff Manyhorse had arrived with two deputies. They had, at Crispin's request, put on Kevlar vests, and carried an assortment of firearms. The Air Force crew also had assault rifles, and White had delegated two FBI teammates to bring along an assortment of weapons, as well as stun and gas grenades, which probably would be useless out in the open.

Crispin took the Subaru and headed back to the Sheriff's office to monitor communications from that end. She would also be waiting for the more heavily armed SWAT team due in at sunrise with some Hueys. As White got on board, he belatedly realized Dierdorff was by now parked out on Highway 89. As they lifted, he checked in with the drone pilot and clued him in on the new developments. Dierdorff didn't mind the change from one mission to another, although he wasn't sure how much aid the Cowhawk could provide. It was, as he put it, "too damned slow." White thought about it, then asked Bob to keep it out of that airspace until Helo 1 was on the ground. All they needed at this point was a midair collision.

The flight took about twenty minutes. The whole way, White sat on the edge of the door, one foot down on the skids, just like a real FBI stud. He thought about unclicking his safety harness, letting the fates roll dice for his soul. But some tatter of his professional life remained, and it kept him from tumbling out into the cool evening, to float away from it all.

Maybe Tricia had survived. Maybe they were all hunky-dory. Only, the transmission had been cut off so quickly. By fire, or impact. He looked up at the rotors over his head. There were arcs of St. Elmo's fire describing circles of green phosphorescence as the rotors chopped the air into ions of light. Back in the days of sail, the masts and rigging of the old schooners had glowed the same way at night. The sailors had considered it bad luck. He was pretty sure they were right.

*****

Spatz chewed slowly on a short rope of buffalo jerky as he thought about his next move. He catalogued his advantages: he had maps of the terrain and had even been through here once, years ago. So he knew the lay of the land. He had weapons and men and horses. Whoever was up there in the rocks—and he had a pretty good idea it was Ms. Mann and her lover-boy—they didn't have shit. Maybe they could lob a few pinecones. The thought that it was not Page Deschamps had crossed his mind, since they hadn't actually put eyeballs on the pair of them. But Page and Annie had been attached at the hip ever since the clown had come out to the Rocking R—his personal turf—to beard the lion in his den. To mess with the picture in his bedroom, a randy male scent-marking new territory. Well, they'd picked the wrong hombre to hassle.

He washed the jerky down with some water. All their real equipment was over the pass, maybe two miles away, with Brister, Slim, and the horses. Brister was a bit of an unknown quantity, but Slim could babysit him well enough. He got to his feet, unkinked his knees, looked up for the moon, which was just on the rise. There was enough light for the next part of the hunt. In military terms, from time immemorial, it was called hammer and anvil. He and Red—and Chester, for what he was worth—would be the hammer. Slim and Brister would be the anvil for the hunted.

*****

Farther up the tor, Page was getting ready for his next move. He was going to leave the SAR rifle with

Annie. She would have two full clips, eleven rounds plus one in the chamber. It would only do single shots, but was otherwise easy to use. As a last resort.

"I hate to leave you, but I need to scout on ahead." Page patted her on the shoulder. "Don't let the moon get behind you. Stay low. No silhouette."

"I've got it." She looked at the rifle in her hand. "I've never held one of these in my life."

"You look like you want to throw it away."

"I guess I hate what it stands for."

"Let's not go there tonight. If you need to pull the trigger you will. It's your life or theirs."

"You make it sound so simple."

"We're down to the basics here, Annie."

"It seems so . . . raw."

He smiled in the dark; he wasn't sure if she could see it. "But don't you feel it?" he asked.

"What?"

"Being alive. Like kids being chased."

She gave a little sigh. "I had a sheltered childhood."

"Well, I'll be back in an hour. You remember the call sign?"

"'Don't shoot?'" They both laughed, but quietly. He patted her on the butt, then he was gone.

Page had a pretty good idea of the threat below them, to the west. The bad guys would probably play it like a tiger hunt, the guns in one direction, nets and beaters closing in from the other. The question was, where were the hunters lying in wait? He was hoping the hunters were predictable, with the pressure from below pushing the hunted up over the rim, then down the other side towards the perceived sanctuary of the forest to the east. If they had split their force, someone would lie between here and the forest. That's how he would do it.

But he needed to be sure before he and Annie committed to another, safer direction. North and south were no good. That would keep them on the hard spine of the mountain, without food, shelter, or water. The longer they put off their breakout, the weaker they would become. So now was the time. Time, probably, for some sort of end run.

There was plenty of light from the moon, enough to highlight the way down the east slope of their little hilltop. He could just see the slight glow on the sandy trail he was following. But he lost it around a turn and nearly stepped off into space. It was only the extra-deep darkness, as well as a slight breeze coming *up*, that kept him from taking that last step over the edge. He felt his heart hammering in his chest as he squatted down on his heels. He felt around, found a good sized rock. He dropped it over the side. The stone landed pretty quickly; he guessed it was a good thirty feet down to the bottom.

He moved to one side cautiously, brushed against some low junipers that had found thin pockets of soil in the rocks. He filed the location away in the map he was building in his head. Page returned to the path and immediately saw a flash of white ahead of him on the trail. He froze. The white moved over to a large boulder, lost in the shadows before reappearing as a dark outline on top. It was clearly a wolf. He thought it was white.

Page was frankly stunned by this apparition. For a moment, he wondered if it was a dog, somehow lost up here. But the shape was unmistakably deep in the chest, the tail sweeping down and back with easily discernable "feathers." It looked towards Page, clearly aware of him. Then it subtly changed its position as it looked away and down. Page knew something of the body language of wolves. The big guy was saying: here's the prey. The wolf was practically pointing with one paw.

Page had never once heard of a wolf doing this sort of thing with, or for, a human. A dog, sure, but this was just off-the-charts weird. But maybe there was something in it. The wolf disappeared, and Page went over to the boulder. He knelt in the same spot and looked down below. About a half-mile away, he could see a flicker of light. A campfire.

CHAPTER FORTY-FIVE

They didn't need night vision goggles to survey the wreckage below. Hovering at fifty feet, Helo 1's lights cast the field of debris in a harsh, actinic light that hurt Colby's eyes. The Hughes, which had once been teardrop shaped, had been sheared through the canopy like a soft-boiled egg cut by a knife.

Then it had burned. His mouth was as dry as the ashes blowing out from their rotor blast. "We're going to set down just ahead of the debris field," Lt. Guthrie said over the helicopter's intercom.

"Did anybody see any tracks around the crash site?"

"I don't think anyone walked away from this one. You saw how far away the tail boom is. She broke up in flight." White didn't question the observation. Guthrie had probably seen one or two of these in her short life. They set down, the nose of the Blackhawk pointing its lights towards the crushed hull of the 500C. The combined force fanned out, with Ben Manyhorse in the lead. White was a step behind, partly because the Native American was a natural athlete. And partly because he didn't want to see what was up ahead.

The Sheriff gave the upper skid a tug, rocking the wreckage slightly. White came up next to him, started to step up. Ben put his hand on his arm and held him back. "You don't have to see this," he said.

But he did. "I'm lighter." White got up on the skid, noticed the door had been blown open. The interior of the helicopter was a well of darkness, with a few deep shadows highlighted by the Blackhawk's lights glaring through the shattered, smoke-blackened canopy. White shone his Maglite, saw the two shapes, lumps of charcoal shrunk down to the size of a ten-year-old child. It was impossible to tell the sex of either corpse, let alone their identities. The rear door was also open. The FBI agent looked in the back.

He spent a moment in thought, then jumped down. "We only have two bodies in there," he said. He saw Lt. Guthrie walking away to the rear of the crash, her eyes down on the trail of debris that led out into the darkness. White asked Manyhorse to join him as he walked after the pilot. "Lieutenant," White called out.

"Bring your light over here, Agent White."

"Where does the pilot usually sit in a Hughes?" he asked.

"Left hand seat—that's where the collective is. Like the throttle." She took the light from him, shone it on a long tube of aluminum. A small propeller, the tail rotor, was dangling from the structure.

"Then the pilot is one of the two corpses," Manyhorse observed.

"Two?" Guthrie didn't look up. "There were four souls on board." She turned the tail section over, illuminating it.

"It looks like two people got out," White said.

"Or their bodies were thrown clear," Ben pointed out.

"If they're alive, they may be in big trouble," Guthrie said.

"From their injuries?"

"From bullets. Look at the aluminum. Those holes." The aluminum had clearly been punched through. "I think they shot away the driveshaft that powers the tail rotor," the lieutenant added.

"They?" Ben asked.

"Who's running around out here with guns?" White asked, not expecting an answer.

"Wow." Guthrie put down the tail. "It's like all the pieces come together out here. What are the odds?"

They headed back toward the lights of the Blackhawk. Manyhorse stopped, kneeled down to sight along the ground.

"We blew up a lot of dust coming in," Guthrie said. "That might have been a mistake."

"See anything, Chief?" White heard a slight note of hope in his voice. Maybe this could play out, if Tricia had been in the back. Which meant she might be with the guy calling himself Page. Maybe he was a head case, maybe not. But if you dropped two people into some God-forsaken wilderness, you'd want one of them to be Page Deschamps. The Wolf Hunter, in his natural environment.

"I can't tell too much in this light. But I know horses were here."

"You have great eyes, sir," Guthrie said in admiration.

Ben stood up, lifted one heel to show her his boot in the beam of his flashlight. "No, but my nose is pretty good. I stepped in horseshit, and it's fresh."

*****

Page squatted on his heels just outside the circle of light from the flickering fire down below him. A small stone circle held a pile of coals with a few larger pieces of tree limb flaming up now and then. There were two sleeping forms under blankets, their saddles used as pillows, hats over their heads to keep out the cool night air. Standard cowboy sleep hygiene, he thought. But not much on securing their position. He wondered for a moment if these were two innocent backwoods travelers. But he decided he couldn't take the chance.

He had already loaded the dart gun. It fired with a much louder report than he had expected. The dart hit right on target. The sleeping man didn't flinch. Page reloaded with a second dart that he thought was the same color—it was impossible to tell under the moon's silvery beams. Again, no reaction from the second target.

Page heard a little alarm bell go off in his head. The darts, of a necessity, had long, barbed points. No way they wouldn't at least cause a flinch. He tossed himself backwards. His conscious mind's conclusion came at the same moment as a fusillade of shots sprayed across the spot where he had just been. The "sleepers" were rigged up, blankets over old clothes or saddle packs. The shooters—and there were clearly two of them, had been lying outside the circle of light waiting for him to make a move. The hunters were here, not back behind him.

By the time he reached that conclusion, he was already taking a roundabout way to get behind the shooter on the right. They were both potting away, which allowed him to move quickly, ignoring the scuff of his boots. As he went, he reloaded, taking whatever dart was next. He saw one skinny guy, now highlighted by the fire, as the man yelled out: "Brister? You nail him?"

Page was no more than twenty yards away when he put the dart into the back of the guy's neck. He yelped and turned, firing off what seemed to be a small machine pistol in a loud angry buzz of expended ordnance. He missed, by a mile. The gun, which looked like an Uzi or maybe a Mac-10, was hardly noted for accuracy—no wonder he had missed with his first rounds.

"Slim?" The other guy called out from the darkness. He went down on his knees, the gun dropping from his hands as he pitched forward.

"Slim just left town." Page yelled. He heard a muffled "Oh shit," followed by a few more rounds from what sounded like a conventional rifle.

Page duck-walked over to the writhing figure. He looked reasonably like the Slim who had helped beat him up back at the ranch, but in this light he couldn't be completely sure. The cowhand lay on his side, his tongue lolling out of his mouth. Page thought about stuffing it down his throat, maybe pushing some dirt up his nostrils to finish him off.

But he didn't. He found a rock, put it under the man's thumb, broke it with the butt of the dart gun. Slim bucked once, then twice, as Page broke the other one. He pulled Slim's belt off, tied up his ankles. With broken thumbs, it would take hours to work the belt loose. He took the gun, an Uzi, saw that the clip was empty. He searched Slim's pockets, found a small flask and a folding knife, but no extra ammo. He took the weapon anyway, went to hunt down Brister.

From the sound of his voice, the second shooter did not seem very keen on a faceoff. That became obvious when Page heard the clopping of hooves, at first quiet, then deepening as the horses—a lot of them—disappeared into the night. Page swore to himself; he sure could have used the animals and their equipment.

On the other side of the ridge, Spatz heard the gunfire, which he considered a good sign. Especially since he recognized the staccato burp of an Uzi. Apparently, Slim and Bristow had spotted the quarry. "Let's go, boys. Up the hill," he said. They locked and loaded and began to work their way up the rock slope to the tor.

They were less than five minutes into the climb when they heard, far behind them, the faint beat of rotor blades.

*****

As the Blackhawk lifted, White got on the horn with Dierdorff. He wanted the Cowhawk rerouted from out by the highway to this side of the ridgeline. Maybe, just maybe, he hoped, it could pick up the heat signatures of both the survivors and the bad guys. In the meantime, he'd asked Lt. Guthrie to fly a spiral out from the crash site in hopes of stirring up some signs. The crew and passengers were on high alert, all but hanging out of the open hatches as their eyes strained over the terrain below. They had to stay low enough to spot any suspicious shapes before they resolved into shooters firing up at them. It made the hunt seem more real, knowing that these guys had taken down one helicopter already.

The news from Dierdorff wasn't good. The RPV unfortunately didn't have the sort of flight instrumentation that precisely measured its exact distance from the ground. It had been following the highway when it had gotten too low and pancaked in. The machine had been designed for fairly rough landings, and when Bob got to it, pitched nose-down in a ditch, it looked almost unmarked. The propeller, unfortunately, had been spinning when it hit, and one of the carbon fiber prop blades had delaminated and split at the tip. The nearest parts were back in the depot in Idaho. Bob said he might be able to shorten both blades, but getting them to balance would be a crapshoot.

White asked him to do his best, then signed off. He placed a quick call to Crispin to touch bases. He told her about the possibility of two survivors and that there were no positive IDs on the two fatalities. The deputy director gave him the ETA for the SWAT teams, which was still going to be just after sunrise. He suggested she relay the crash site coordinates as a jumping-off place once they had refueled at the Stanley airport. They both agreed it would give White and his lone helicopter time to refine the search.

Crispin cautioned him to avoid taking gunfire; she had been genuinely upset to hear that a civilian helicopter had been shot down. Truly, both agreed, things were devolving into a royal clusterfuck. Part II.

CHAPTER FORTY-SIX

Spatz, Red, and Chester had a short, whispered conference. Chester was the most worried by the sound of the helicopter. He said the horses had left a pretty good trail, and they needed those horses to stay undiscovered if they were to keep to the plan, the one where they got out of Dodge with their scalps still under their hats. Red was all for that, but he also had some of Spatz's bloodlust going down. He said the way to the horses led through Annie and Page, who might have already been shot by their cronies. They agreed to keep going up the hill.

Annie, too, had heard the helicopter. She wished she had some way to signal or better yet, a walkie-talkie. But she realized this was magical thinking and that she needed to stay with Page's program. So she huddled with the gun in her lap, cold and feeling very alone. Even though she wasn't. "Don't shoot," she heard out in the dark.

Annie jumped, but said, "I won't." Page slid in next to her, gave her a kiss. "I heard the gunfire!" she whispered. "Are you OK?"

"Never better." He laughed. "I made a joke, Annie."

"I was scared shitless. What happened?"

"Some of the boys were laying for us on the other side. They had the horses, but they got away. I got this," he showed her the gun. "Empty, unfortunately. And this." He passed her the flask. "It's probably not water. Slim was more the whiskey type."

She took a sip, gagged. "Bad whiskey. Was that Slim, as in the past tense?"

"I thought about icing him, but the dart knocked him out. The other dude ran away with their horses."

"Doesn't sound like their A-Team."

"Nah. I was looking for the hitters, but now I've thought about it, they were more like the backstop." He pointed down the slope. "I think Spatz is coming up towards us."

"Did you hear the rotors? There's a helicopter out there. To the west—back towards the crash, maybe. A big one, I think."

"Didn't hear it."

"Maybe twenty minutes ago."

He thought for a moment. "But *they* must have. You know, they were trying to drive us to the east. Now, with the helicopter behind them, they have to come east, too. And pronto." He looked around their little campsite, found the rescue kit. "I saw some fishing gear in here."

"No fish up here, friend."

He ignored her remark. "And that camcorder. Does it still have a charge?"

She got it out of her jacket, switched it on. "Looks like."

"Find that interview you told me about. If it's still

there." She switched it to playback, ran it back. It was.

He had her stop at that point. He took the Panasonic and disappeared up the last bit of rock they hadn't yet climbed. He came back a couple of minutes later. "There's a cliff we're going to use. And some stunted little junipers. Let's move out."

"Are they going to let us push them over?" Instinctively she could tell this was the last part of the game, the end of the hunt. She really didn't know who had the upper hand here. Spatz and his crew had guns, food, and water; she and Page were tired, and beaten up in a major plane crash. She had a splitting headache, was beyond thirsty, and neither one of them had eaten today. But on their side of the ledger, they had the SAR rifle and a couple of knives, a first aid kit, and some rescue items including the fishing tackle.

Page had an answer for her. "No, they'll do it themselves." He paused for a long beat. "I hope." He looked at the moon, which was heading down towards the horizon. "We need them to follow before sunrise lights us up."

*****

Spatz and his team worked their way upslope. Moving cautiously, Spatz was aware that he was taking more precautions than was probably warranted. But it was the word "probably" that, as always, had kept him out of trouble. That Page, let alone Annie, posed any sort of lethal threat seemed kind of farfetched. But he had acquired over the course of many a hunt a cautious streak that he noticed had been passed on to the two men with him. Chester, as expected, moved quietly. And Red was doing himself proud, moving almost gracefully, with an economy of movement that reminded Spatz of a big terrier on point. This dog could hunt.

The moon was starting to fade now, as the first hint of dawn washed it out. But the light was good for the business at hand. The hard rock seemed to level out, and a faint breeze picked up in their face, coming out of the east. They were on top of the tor. They held in place, breathing through their mouths as their ears strained for some telltale sign. Chester held up a hand and pointed ahead, where a slight downslope faded into the black of the landmass a few miles away. He moved the extended hand next to his ear, cupping it. He had heard something.

Spatz carefully moved up next to him; he could feel his adrenaline kicking in. "Voices," Chester said. Spatz listened, caught a low murmur below them: a woman, talking. He couldn't make out the words, or who it was, but he knew. Annie and her big mouth had made a big mistake. Typical.

Spatz thought for a moment, then whispered his instructions in Chester's ear. The Indian moved ahead and down a modest slope of smooth granite. Spatz signaled Red to come closer. He whispered to the foreman: "I can hear her talking. Chester is going to flush out the dude."

"What's my play?" Red whispered back.

"Keep down. Look for a shape against the sky. Chester's going to stay low. You got your headlight ready?"

"Yeah." They had both put on the little LED lamps that strapped around their hats. When the big moment came, they could light up the night. And light up Annie and Deschamps, too.

Page was waiting in the last shadows for them. He had a round in the dart gun, and the last two darts in his pocket. He'd left Annie with the SAR rifle after showing her how to put in the next clip after she emptied the first. Annie wasn't sure she would even fire once, let alone reload, but Page refused to take it from her.

Page was also mouth breathing, trying to keep his nose as sharp as possible, despite a major case of cottonmouth. He was worried about Annie; if he went down and the other guys didn't, she was not going to survive. If it hadn't been for Annie, the old Marion would have almost enjoyed this—the last moments of life, he had always felt, would be the sweetest, all the senses amped up.

And it had turned out to be so. He waited for the moment to break, Annie's soft voice just out in the deepest dark. She was talking about wolves. To Tricia Helfer.

Chester didn't know Tricia was dead. He didn't even know who she was. So he made an error in judgment, not differentiating between the two voices coming out of the camcorder, which Page had hung over the edge of the cliff with a length of fishing line. That was not in itself enough to induce a fatal plunge, but Page had run the rest of the thin nylon filament between two juniper stumps.

Chester caught on at the last moment, probably when he saw the darkness at the base of the cliff. But he got tangled in the filament for a fraction of a second, which gave Page the chance to butt-stroke him in the skull with the dart gun. The Indian plunged over the side, too surprised to even yell. Thirty feet was enough to do the job.

Spatz heard a sound like a falling sack of wet meat hitting pavement. He half stood up as he realized in a flash he had somehow been tricked. He dropped as a loud phutt came out of the dark and something slammed into his thick vest. It was too soft to be a bullet. The noise gave Spatz a rough idea where the noise had come from. He still had the AK-47 from the shoot-down; he closed his eyes against the muzzle flash, knelt and cut loose. He reveled in the hard kick in his hands, and despite himself, he had to look. The backblast strobed the landscape. He was firing low to counteract the tendency of the weapon to climb, chips of rock streaking out like fireflies.

Red dove down next to him. "Which way, Boss?"

"Spread out!" Spatz snarled, elbowing Red out of the way. The foreman rolled off to the left. Spatz finished off the clip. He didn't bother to reload. He wanted a pistol for the close-in work, anyway.

But those few seconds did not go his way. Someone—Page—yelled, "Annie! Now!"

A bullet ripped out of a stand of junipers, bits of wood and needles flying up into the first hints of sunrise. From its sharp crack, Spatz thought it was some sort of small round. Whatever it was, it was a nasty surprise. But he didn't care at this point. He rolled onto his side, reaching for the 1914 Colt automatic he had in his holster. Someone slammed into him, a whole body thing. Page was all over him, punching him in both sides of the head. Which burned way too much.

Spatz felt a moment of panic. Was Page coming after him with knives? But the fucker rolled off right away, leaving the stinging in his skull on both sides. He got the gun in his hand, fired a few rounds into the shadows.

"Watch it!" Red yelled. "I'm over here."

Give yourself away, you dumb cluck, Spatz thought. His head was spinning. He touched one temple—there was something sticking in it. He pulled it out, almost yelled; it had barbs. Another flopped around below his ear.

Page was already headed for Red. The darts he had hand-delivered to Spatz should knock the big man out in a few seconds, which meant it was just him and the foreman. Red, still crouched, was coming up as Page rammed into him, Slim's foldout knife in his left hand. He slashed down on Red's gun hand, hoping to cut a tendon. He missed anything vital, but the blade buried itself in Red's hand as the foreman's big old Navy Colt banged away just past his ear. He grabbed the barrel with his free hand, used its leverage to twist Red's wrist.

He tried to break the joint, but Red was just plain bigger. The knife flew away.

Page realized it had all come to this, a moment rooted, it seemed like ages ago, when he'd first met Red pulling down that silly little puppet show. Two guys who had that instinctive dislike that didn't make any sense on a civilized level. Because, when it came down to it, they weren't civilized.

Annie yelled, much closer than he had expected. "Page, get back!" Red was winning the battle, bending Page's arm down to his waist. "Suck on this," Red hissed, and head-butted Page, who felt himself going down. The gun was coming around, and all he could sense was Red's gusts of breath, the sweaty heat of his iron grip, the moon swirling above his head as Red twirled him like a big doll.

Page tried every move he'd ever learned in a bar fight, raking his opponent in the shins, stomping at his toes, dropping like dead weight then arching back up. Red was laughing now. The moon seemed to shrink as Page ran out of air; he was in a last moments of a cop-style chokehold. There was a flash of light, a loud bang in his ears.

Red yelled in pain and rage. He tried to toss Page aside, who got in one gulp of pure air. Page knew how this had to end, and he had to end it the best way he could. He twisted, but not in the direction Red expected. Not away from the cliff but towards it.

For the very last time ever, Page looked at Annie, who was staring wide-eyed at them both as she tried to squeeze off another shot. Her lovely face was just visible in the half-light, and he was glad, because he wanted her to see what was in his eyes.

"Annie," he said, and he knew she heard him even as he left his feet, his hands locked in the other man's clothes. He launched into the air, off the cliff and down into the dark. Unlike Chester, Red did scream.

Annie stood, the rifle dropping from her hand. There was nothing but silence. "Page?" she moaned. No answer. The scream, she was sure, had been Red. She had shot at him; Red had to be dead. Someone staggered towards her. She ran towards the dim figure. "Oh, Page!"

"Oh yeah, baby. Oh yeah." She couldn't help it; she cried out at Spatz's slurred, half-drugged voice. He staggered towards her, arms held out. She had her back to the cliff, and she hesitated before she tried to move.

"Die, bitch." Wilhelm Spatz snarled.

He was almost on her when a white streak launched itself at him, knocking the big man back on his ass. The snarling, angry wolf came at him again. Spatz reflexively put up his arm, but the White Wolf, the true Alpha in this world, ignored the blocking move. He went for the throat. Spatz would have screamed, but his trachea and jugular were both ripped open in one quick snap of the jaws, a twist of the wolf's great head. The animal stood, front legs on the dying man's chest, watching as the human who had killed his mate drowned in his own blood.

Then the wolf was gone.

*****

Bob Dierdorff had pulled off a miracle, hacksawing the prop on the Cowhawk. It had launched before the full sunrise, and eventually its sensors had located at least one warm body. He used the data points to vector in Helo 1.

White and the rest of the crew found the scene at first light, hovering over a man's body spread-eagled in a tremendous pool of blood. It still looked wet in the crimson glow of the rising sun.

A small figure sat on a rock some distance away, looking out at the forest to the east, staring at the first soft contours of a new day. White, looking down, felt his heart leap as he saw that the hunched, sad-looking woman was wearing Tricia's KIRO jacket.

Next to him, Manyhorse scanned the scene below, silently taking it in, as was his way.

But as the Blackhawk spiraled in, White recognized the auburn hair of Annie Mann. He felt Ben's hand on his shoulder, but there was no comfort. In his heart the last hope died.

THE END

ACKNOWLEDGEMENTS

No writer is an island, even if he lives on one. And so he would like to thank the following for their support, guidance, and criticisms. Every last one of which was justified.

Liz Brenneman — for everything
Priscilla Atwood — proof-reader extraordinaire
Colby Atwood, who kept me going
Cdr. Claude F. Giles, USN (retired)
Bryan and Sandy Giles
Colin and Carol Giles
Kevin and Jenny McMurdo
Laura Robb
Mary Tuel, a fine editor

And Robert Heinlein, who gave a college kid a job and some great advice. Thanks, Bob.

giles5440@gmail.com

noirwest.com

www.ingramcontent.com/pod-product-compliance
Lightning Source LLC
Chambersburg PA
CBHW071223250626

47163CB00001B/78